The Way Life Used To Be

Sandra Gutierrez

Prelude

I was raised in a house full of love and security. My parents have been married for close to nineteen years. They are still as close and loving as the day they met.

I idolized my older brother Mark almost as much as my dad. They have been my protectors as long as I can remember.

Who knew my childhood would end on the floor of my favorite store? My brother saved me, and for that I will be forever grateful.

My life changed after that night. Maybe for the better, maybe for worse. Who knows? All 1 know is, my life is forever altered, starting with a stranger, and a knife.

The Way Life Used To Be

Copyright © 2019 by Sandra Gutierrez

ISBN 978-0-5785486-0-9

All rights reserved. No part of this publication may be reproduced, distributed, or transmitted in any form or by any means, including photocopying, recording, or other electronic or mechanical methods, without the prior written permission of the publisher, except in the case of brief quotations embodied in critical reviews, and certain other noncommercial uses permitted by copyright law. For permission requests, write to the publisher, addressed "Attention: Permissions Coordinator," at the address below.

ORIGINS PRESS
904 W Riverside #877
Spokane, Washington 99201
www.akkadianmediagroup.com/origins-press

Printed in the United States of America

Sandra Gutierrez
The Way Life Used To Be
ISBN 978-0-5785486-0-9

First Edition

10 9 8 7 6 5 4 3 2 1

Sandra Gutierrez

This is a work of fiction. Names, characters, business, events, and incidents are the products of the author's imagination. Any resemblance to actual persons, living or dead, or actual events is purely coincidental.

This novel's story, and characters are fictitious. Certain long-standing institutions, agencies, and public offices are mentioned, but the story is a product of the author's imagination.

The Way Life Used To Be

Chapter 1

August 1996
Fort Worth, Texas

This August night is sultry and humid, without a cloud in sight to lower the temperature, even by a notch. It's only the start of the month. The rest of the month seems endless.

I had so many plans to go to the river, ride bikes, and plain get some exercise while enjoying the fresh air. Little did I know there wouldn't be much rain to offer relief. There are many thunderstorms to enjoy for most of July, but it's August and school was about to begin for the year. It's one hot day after another.

I thought once I'm done with the ninth grade, I would be queen of something important. I would eventually have a big head, and attitude from hell, and be the envy of everyone around me. Middle school is fun in a lot of ways, and I made lots of friends during those three years, but I would never want to repeat any of it.

My best friend in the entire world, Carla Fleming promised me we would spend every day at the river, getting tanned, and fit from all the swimming we will do, but so far there has only been three trips. Carla started seeing her fourth boyfriend in the ninth grade alone, and so far, they seemed to be the perfect couple.

I had two classes with Taylor Johnson, he's a nice guy. Tall with blond hair, and not a single freckle anywhere. I am jealous of that fact since I had a ton of them, but as my mom always said, freckles are kisses from angels, so I must be adored.

Sandra Gutierrez

Carla is not too particular with boys, and each boyfriend is full of "I love you" in her diary. When they would break up, the diary gets thrown in her fireplace, and a new one begins. I tried to convince her this was a dumb idea, and to cherish any memories, but she only cried a few tears of self-pity, and she'd move on to a new guy within weeks.

Eventually she will get a bad reputation, but with Taylor, she seems different. More mature, and able to handle a relationship. I give my full support on this one. Boyfriend number three was Bobby Jankins, and he was handsome no doubt, but I would have to admit, he is also a player. As much of a player you can be at thirteen. He likes to look at girls, and when they would return his glance, he would start to flirt.

Carla ignored it for a while, but during a dance, he was brazened enough to fondle Jane Adams on her behind, she called it quits. Jane was a nice girl, and Carla is grown up enough not to hold any grudges or call her names because of it, so I have even more hopes for her, and Taylor.

Taylor comes from a broken family. He lives with his mom, and younger brother. His dad took off when he was five or six and hasn't been seen since. His mom works two or three jobs when needed as Taylor wants to go to college, and she doesn't have near enough money in savings to send him.

Also not having any child support doesn't help things much, but she was a determined lady. Taylor is hoping for a scholarship to pay for most of his tuition. That will be his only opportunity to attend.

I stood in the open doorway of our two-story Victorian house my parents bought eleven years ago when I had turned four. Now that was a fun year. I had a party at Chuck E. Cheese, and my picture taken with the big mouse. My birthday is on May 13th. Right smack in the middle of spring I love to say.

I still have that picture on my dresser with me wearing a pink dress that barely reached my knees, and black strapless sandals that flopped whenever I took a step. I threw those away as they were too uncomfortable. I gave the dress to my little sister who never wore it herself. To this day I don't know what she did with it. Doesn't matter though, I will never forget that party.

Our house is a deep gold color with midnight blue trim. Dad, and Mark did most of the painting. Mom has a small flower garden that surrounded the base, she proved to have a natural knack with it.

Now that I'm a blossoming fifteen-year-old, and a more mature young adult, I stared at the black night resenting the fact that the night

The Way Life Used To Be

is so hot, sweat poured down my face, and into my nightgown. The gown was flannel, which was a poor choice, but it's one of my favorites. It has both my favorite colors pink, and purple with tiny hearts.

It's a short sleeve at least, but it still clings to my skin. I attempted to pick the gown away from my chest, but as soon as my hand left, the gown clung like a burr refusing to let go.

My dark brown hair that is full of curl, and something I'm proud of most of the time was now frizzy from the heat. I tossed it to one side where it hung dampening my right shoulder, but I left it there. What was the point? It hangs halfway down my back. I thought so many times of cutting it, but always end up changing my mind. somehow, I can't go through with it, so I suffer, but it's not anybody's fault, but my own.

I'm resenting school starting next month because I'm supposed to be enjoying the summer, I'm also looking forward to it. This year I will be in the tenth grade. High School for us is ninth through twelfth. Freshman, and Sophomores are typically treated like shit, and I have heard many horror stories from my older brother Mark, of boys, and even some girls being shoved in their lockers like old garbage.

Carla, and I are both hoping it will never happen to either of us, so far it hasn't. We have each other's back on everything. I stared out the doorway and stepped out to wonder outside for a while. I looked down the block and smiled as I remembered our restaurant.

My parents own and operate Starlights Restaurant. It's a soup, and sandwich place, but mom has dreams of one day expanding to include breakfast sandwiches, but for now we're open for lunch and dinner. They open the place at ten each day until six. Mom bakes homemade pies each morning that they sell and spends most of her day in the kitchen making the soups.

My parents are Zeni, and Keith Harris. Dad is responsible for the dining area, and their system works out well so far. Mom has always been my idol, and someone I will always admire as she is the hardest worker I have ever met. I hope to be like her when I become an adult. She wears her dark blond hair short, and wavy. It frames her beautiful face and makes her look ten years younger than she is.

Dad has jet-black hair, which may account for my dark brown. I have never understood chemistry or genes or whatever that trait falls under. I'm jealous of them, and happy at the same time.

My dad is equally important to me, but I'm a mama's girl at heart. I never had it in my heart to tell my dad that. When they first opened

Sandra Gutierrez

Starlights, mom's intention was to have a full-service restaurant, and dad wanted a bakery. They settled in the middle as serving so many varieties of food would have overwhelmed both of them at some point.

Efficient, and order are Keith's famous words. My parents bought the building twelve years ago when it was an old garage. They got it for a song as it stood empty for five whole years before Zeni bought it using funds from her grandmother's inheritance. It's her one big splurge, and she has never regretted it.

They spent most their savings rebuilding until they turned it from a dumpy place to a dazzling restaurant that is now the bright spot of the neighborhood. Both friends, and strangers stopped each day filling the house until Keith had to turn away customers. Something they both hate to do as the customers pay their bills, and without them the restaurant will fail.

I love the restaurant, I try work there whenever I have a free moment, but I have no desire to work there the rest of my life. My favorite part is gossiping with the customers. I have learned a lot through the grapevine and being fifteen I sometimes let my tongue slip.

Speaking of customers reminds me of last week when I got my first job at Hankins Grocery. It's a large, locally owned store right outside town, and only four blocks from our house. Close enough to walk to, and even quicker on my bike. Today is Saturday, and my first day is on Monday

I'm scared, nervous, and excited at the same time. It's about time I earn my own money. The paper route I took over from Mark two years ago was decent enough money, but I have never felt I had the right clothes or makeup or anything my rich and spoiled friends had.

I remembered going on that first interview. I showed up in slacks, and a long sleeve blouse that turned out to be a mistake. The interview itself, was held in Mr. Hankins office that has no air conditioning. Before the first hour is over, my armpits are full of sweat, and I'm sure the front of my blouse was dripping with sweat. That was the most embarrassing moment of my life.

Mr. Hankins was too nice to either notice or didn't care as he hired me on the spot. I'm almost too excited to thank him. I ended up running back to the house and tore off my blouse on the way up the stairs, leaping onto the bed, and yelling hooray at the ceiling. Thank God nobody was home.

The Way Life Used To Be

It's going on midnight, and still no relief from the heat. All I'm doing is trying to cool off, and besides there is no set curfew for teenagers. In downtown Fort Worth, the curfew was set at ten in the evening during the summer, and nine during the school year. Since we are on the outskirts, it's up to the individual neighborhood. Ours was quiet so nobody cares much if someone is out late.

Rarely does someone's house get broken into. I remembered Karly Simons house got burglarized eight months ago or so. It was right after Christmas, and she is a single mother who lives two blocks away. Carla used to babysit her daughter Clarissa, who was four, and a little hellion. She isn't supposed to answer the door even if she recognized the voice on the other side, but she did think it was one of her uncles who is saying the usual ho, ho, ho as a greeting. The door swung opened, two masked men barged in knocking Clarissa to a wall, before dragging her to the bedroom when she started screaming.

Karly was in the backyard, and heard nothing as she had her headphones in, jamming to rock music. She never even realized what happened until she stepped in her house to find her stereo, TV, and toaster gone. Whoever the robbers are, they have not been caught, and nobody could figure out why in hell a toaster was stolen.

Nothing happened since, at least in our area, so we remain grateful, but still cautious. Mom, and dad also have strict rules to keep our own doors locked. Sitting outside in the moonlight was a stupid idea, but I love the quiet.

Clarissa has since calmed down, and Carla now enjoys babysitting her. both her, and Karly come in Starlights regularly. Mom always charges her less than our regular customers since she has a small income and can't afford to eat out too often.

Around one o'clock, I gave up trying to cool down as the outside was as hot as indoors. I shut the door as quiet as possible. I am too wound up to go upstairs, and to bed. The thought of my job is enough to keep me awake for a week. I only hope I will do a good enough job to make the owners happy. Nothing would be worse than being fired from my first job. I have no back-up plan, but it would suck, anyway.

The main duties will be to help stock the shelves. I'm not near old enough to man a cash register yet. You have to be sixteen to do that, but in a year, I will be able to. I don't know if it's legal to hire someone as young as me, but when I saw the ad in last Sunday's paper; I followed instinct, and since Mr. Hankins didn't question it, and knows damn well how old I am since we have been shopping there for years, I accepted it without question.

That would be so cool if I made it to cashier level to handle checks, and cash all the time. I'd be so friendly, and efficient that the customers would insist on coming through my line and ignore the other cashiers. I would be the fastest one as well so my customers would only spend a few minutes in line and would never complain. They would be thankful for the speediness.

That was just a dream. A very nice one, but still, a fantasy. That has always been my problem though. Daydreaming, but I can't help it. My imagination sometimes run's overtime, and I can't help myself. Unlike my younger sister whom I adore, but she is moodier than a houseful of teenagers.

Elizabeth was only twelve when she had gotten her first period a few months ago. She had to make a big to do over it and spent four days in bed howling at the pain and having mama fuss over her. I'm grateful she didn't want me around.

Mama was so proud that all her kids are growing up. Mark also has no intention of working at Starlights forever, but for now he is earning a decent wage bussing tables. It's hard work for someone at only seventeen, but he is strong. Also, it doesn't hurt he is as handsome as our father, standing at six feet, two inches tall.

He is my protector. He never thought it was beneath him, to walk us to, and from school. The neighborhood is nice, but Mark would take no chances with our safety. Bessie would always walk a few paces ahead of us, claiming that she was old enough to walk by herself. I loved those days.

They will end this year because Mark has classes starting at eight, and my first class don't start till nine. When we walk together, Mark seems to open up more, and would talk about each crush he had. Beginning with Denise Anderson, who he was convinced he would marry by the end of their senior year.

That lasted only two weeks though when she decided she liked Bryan Bates better, and they ended up going to junior prom together, and he never gave her another thought.

Next came Betsy Robins. She was a bubbly talkative tiny thing that never shut up. She idolized Mark and lasted over a month when he had enough of the constant chattering and called it quits.

The Way Life Used To Be

By June of his junior year he had his third crush, but never acted on it. Sara Bevins who was also a shy junior. I didn't know her very well, but Mark could not stop talking about her. It's because she didn't return his glances. She waited until he passed her in the halls before she allowed her eyes to look up, and follow his backside as he walked away, and her face would fall.

I saw the looks she would give him and wanted to let him know but kept quiet. Once my job started, I would see her at Hankins, so they would start up a relationship there. I would love to play match maker with those two.

Surely once school starts Bessie, and I would walk together, and become closer. Bessie is a good girl, but sometimes tries to act older than she was. Our dad came up with the nickname Bessie. He named her Elizabeth Sue after his grandmother but had to have nicknames for everyone.

Mark was the only one he called Mark. Guess it's hard to nickname that. He called me Reesa since I was born. I'm not named after anyone important, but Teresa is a neat name, I guess. He loved pet names and has a thousand of them for mom.

The clock struck two, and I decided enough daydreaming. At least for now. The spotless living room is to the left of the entry way. I, along with most of the family had helped mom decorate it two years ago from a grotesque Halloween orange to a soft peach and cream. The couch was huge, comfortable, and is decorated with peach and ice-blue lilies covers.

Mom also had the carpets changed on the entire lower floor including the stairway leading to the bedrooms, and bathroom. It was a thick ice-blue, and so comfortable none of us wears shoes when we are inside.

The kitchen was at the rear of the house and reflects the same pattern. There are window treatments in the two windows overlooking the park, and you could almost see Hankins if you strain your neck and look between the trees.

We placed an oak dining table at the far end of the kitchen with six upholstered chairs with heart motifs in the backs. Zeni sat in one chair, clad in a bathrobe, and slippers. "Mom?" I questioned as I entered the kitchen. "What are you still doing up?" "Having something to drink." Zeni picked up a mug. "Want a cup?" "What is it?" "Hot chocolate" "On a night like this?" I smiled and sat down in a chair opposite her.

Sandra Gutierrez

"Habit, I could not sleep. What are you still doing up?" "I could not sleep either. I'm so excited about starting work soon, and it was so hot upstairs. I've been thinking about how I want my job to go." "You sound inspirational. I would suggest you take it slow, pay close attention, and do your best. You will make mistakes that you may or may not be able to fix." Zeni took a drink from her cup.

"That I had already planned on. I keep picturing myself being the head cashier, and everyone's favorite." I got up to get a glass of Diet Pepsi. Plopping back down I opened the tab and poured it into the glass. "I'm dreaming, but I can't wait to get started. What mistakes did you mean?"

"Not any specific come to mind. I guess for example let's say you are putting spaghetti jars on the shelf, and you ignore how close the jars are to the edge. Your elbow brushes against one jar, and smashes on the floor, spilling sauce all over the floor. A customer comes along at that same moment, and slips. A lawsuit could come of it, and there would be nothing you could do except for apologize, and most likely lose your job over it. It's one of those preventable incidents that is not."

I nodded in agreement. "I see what you're saying about moving too fast without thinking ahead. Zeni smiled. I love giving useful advice." She glanced at the clock over the stove. "You should get some sleep."

"I would sleep if I could." I finished the drink, but continued sitting at the table, running three fingers along the side of the now warm can. It's quiet this time of night, and I didn't feel like moving. "I know what you mean. A cold shower might help you relax."

"I might do that. Do you think I'll do a good job at Hankins?" "If you try, it took dad, and I, a solid four years of busting our ass day, and night to make a decent living. The first year was touch and go. We sometimes thought we would starve in the meantime but look at us now." She raised her hands around the room. "You could not expect much better than this."

"You're such a wise person." I smiled at her and dumped the empty soda can in the recycler. "Good night mom." I kissed her on the forehead. The stairway leading to the bedrooms was on the opposite side of the kitchen, and the stairs themselves rounded two corners before you reached the upper level where the bedrooms, and bathrooms are located.

I climbed the steps and felt the temperature rise a few degrees with each stair. Even with the heat, I love the feel of the carpeting on my bare

The Way Life Used To Be

feet. It's thick, and comfortable, and my feet seemed to sink in every time I took a step. I reached the top of the stairs, and turned left down a long hallway, past Mark's, and Bessie's rooms. Their doors are shut tight. I reached my room across from the bathroom that all three of us kids shared.

I get jealous sometimes that our parents have the biggest bedroom, and an attached bathroom. How spoiled can one be? The jealously faded as I realized how good we have it. More than a roof over our heads, our house is special due to mom, but I like to think we all played a big part in it.

My room was decorated in hot pink, and purple. An odd combination, but I have always loved those two colors, and instead of having to choose between the two I combined them. After all it's not fair to leave either color out. Might get their feelings hurt.

I cover the queen size bed with a homemade quilt mom had made when she was pregnant with me. She said it helped pass away the time, and she loved sewing. I tossed the quilt aside and climbed under the pink sheet still covered with sweat and giving up on relief anytime soon. There will be no shower this time of night. I would suffer through the night.

The moon glowed in the single window that was open and letting in the heat. The curtains didn't move as there was no breeze. I fell asleep a little before three and woke up to the sun shining as bright as the moon did, right on my face. Only six thirty, and I moaned as I tried to block out the light. Once my eyes stayed opened for longer than a few seconds, I sat up, and cursed the morning.

It's time to rearrange the furniture and stop the brightness from ruining every morning. I dragged my sorry self out of bed with reluctance and could smell breakfast cooking even way up here. Never again would I stay up so late. It's not worth the lag I'm feeling now.

I threw on faded green shorts, and a white T-shirt, and flip flops. After breakfast, I have full intentions of spending the day on the river. After all, there is only one more day of freedom before I will officially become a working girl.

As soon as breakfast was over, I would be out the door, and before either of my parents could volunteer me for kitchen duty. I bounced down the stairs with my hair tied in a loose ponytail and skipped into the kitchen where I found mom at the stove stirring bacon in a skillet. Dad is reading the morning newspaper, and Mark, and Bessie arguing.

Sandra Gutierrez

"Good morning!" I greeted and hoped nobody would notice the circles under my eyes or the yawn I tried to stifle. Zeni looked up from the pan where she is frying eggs for breakfast. The bacon was already on a plate on the counter. "Mornin' baby, Sleep well?"

Her hair was freshly washed, and she looks so refreshed. Unlike me who she could tell was exhausted. We decided by unspoken agreement to keep our conversation last night quiet. "I guess it's so hot it's hard to sleep sometimes." Keith looked up from the newspaper with a smile, "well not much you can do about the weather. Just grin and bear it Reesa."

Mark looks almost like dad, but Keith has a full mustache, and over six feet tall. His jet-black hair is beginning to thin, but Zeni always says it makes him look more distinguished, and mature. Bessie, and I both take after mom, and her own hair hasn't even shown signs of graying. It's rich, thick, and she wears it short reaching her shoulders.

Bessie stopped her griping to swing her head at dad, and frown. "Dad, you always say that, It's so lame." Lame was the current hit word, and everyone is saying it. It wears on everyone's nerves, but to make a scene over it would only fuse the fire.

Keith glanced over at his youngest child and fought the urge to lecture her. Sometimes having a twelve-year-old was too much to handle. "Thank you, Bessie, eat your breakfast." he nodded to the plate of eggs, and bacon that Zeni had placed before her.

"Yuck. I wanted scrambled eggs. I hate yolks." she complained, and moved the food around with her fork, and scowling. "Scrambled eggs have yolks too, just eat it." Keith repeated. "Or you can get your happy butt up and make your own. A thank you to your mother wouldn't hurt either."

Bessie glanced up at his face and looked over to where mom was sitting down with her own plate. She smiled quickly, and said, "Sorry, thank you", then looked back down at her plate without another word. Bessie shoved a bite of bacon in her mouth and looked down as she ate. She fought the tears that seemed to come all the time for no reason at all.

I'm silent for the first part of this. I normally don't interrupt them, but I know my sister. I piped up. "Come on Bessie. After we eat, let's go to the river. Taylor, and Carla are coming." "I don't want to go. I'm having cramps again." She rubbed her stomach and made me laugh. "No, you don't. You had cramps last week when you had a reason to.

The Way Life Used To Be

It's physically, mentally, and emotionally impossible to have cramps every week. Come on." I offered again.

"Come with us. It will get your mind off your issues." "You don't have to make fun of me Reesa." Bessie started crying, and I felt sorry, and forced my smile to go away. "I'm sorry, and I didn't mean to make fun of you. I want to spend the day with you."

Apologizing was something that happens a lot with her, especially lately, but we do it without complaint even though it doesn't help the situation, or Bessie's attitude. "Go, kiddo." Mark piped in amused by this. He speared bacon on his fork, smothered in egg yolk, and popped them into his mouth.

Bessie threw down her fork. "All right, I'll go." She left half the food on her plate, and left both the plate, and her glass on the table. She wondered upstairs to her room to change her clothes. Appearing fifteen minutes later wearing a tank top, and jean shorts with strings hanging down, she announced. "I'm ready."

Truth was, she is looking forward to getting out of the house. She doesn't know why she was so snappy all the time but can't help it. We left the house together arm in arm, and Bessie's laughter ringing through the house as she slammed the front door.

Once we were gone, Keith put down his newspaper, and sighed. "Well here's to a peaceful afternoon. I give it until two before they come storming back with Bessie leading the tears." Zeni laughed as she put their plates in the sink and ran water over them. "You are terrible. I understand being a woman how hard it is being an almost teenager. You have mood swings like a teeter totter and can't help it." She gathered up the butter dish and milk from the table, and Keith playfully slapped her butt.

"I know, I know. It's taking all my patience dealing with her. At least Reesa seems to be over the emotional roller coaster. Hopefully this won't last too much longer." He got up, and joined her at the sink, and kissed her on the neck. She smiled back at him as he started putting dishes in the dishwasher.

"Only a few years if we're lucky. Reesa was never this bad though. She's always been the rational, calm one. Anyway, I need to get dressed for the day. We are opening in less than an hour, and I still have two more pies to bake."

Mark left the house shortly before them and opened the restaurant relishing the quiet even though it would be short lived. While our parents got ready for another day doing what they love best, we are walking towards Carla's house. She lives on the next block, and we took our time reaching it.

While enjoying the morning coolness I turned to her. She is showing no signs of a recent cry. She was laughing, and her eyes sparkled. "Feeling better?" "Much, thank you for asking me along, and I'm sorry I have been so moody. I don't know why I get this way."

She tucked her hands into her shorts and looked down as she was embarrassed. "I do, and believe it or not, I understand. But enough of the serious talk. Look there's Carla." I pointed a finger at the doorway of a wooden one-story house at the end of the block.

"Hey you two." Carla called as she bounced down the cement steps holding a bag filled with her towel, and a Gatorade. Carla was always giddy, and today it shows as she reached us. Her hair tied in a ponytail, but the curls still exploded around her face. She has longer hair than mine, and freckles sprinkling her arms, and face. She loved coloring her hair, but right now it's her natural coal black. I always thought she looks best that way.

"Hey back." I greeted. "Taylor called He can't make it. He has to go in early for work, but he said, hello., and speaking of hello, hey Bessie. Are you coming too?" I answered for her. "Yeah, we will enjoy a day of fun before I have to start my job." Carla reached the end of her driveway, and we continued walking towards the river.

"Where are you working again?" Carla asked, swinging the bag back, and forth with one arm. "Hankins, I start on Monday." "Oh, that might be a bad idea. Did you hear there was a robbery there last month? The guy who robbed the place is still hiding like a wuss."

I shook my head trying to remember, but I came up with a blank. "No, I didn't hear that. Was anyone hurt?" "Not that I know of. The people who work there are shaken up. A few of them had some counseling, but I guess it's old news now."

Bessie asked. "Are you sure it's okay to work there?" She was getting uneasy about this news. Even though she doesn't always show it, she loves her older sister, and worried about this news. I shrugged my shoulders. "Sure, I'm not worried. I'm sure whoever the guy is, he's gone, like Carla said, nobody with half a brain sticks around the scene of the crime."

"I hope so." She was still uneasy about this, but Reesa was very mature for her age, and has always been responsible. Unlike herself at

The Way Life Used To Be

least most of the time. That is the fun part of being twelve. "I'm sure of it." I'm sure I sound a lot more confident than I feel inside. "Carla, do you know the guy that robbed the store?"

"Greg Oakes, I don't know him, he attended to high school while we were still in middle school. Dropped out before he graduated though. He's still at large, so take extra care." She advised. "Was he caught on camera at least? I asked. He was, didn't even have the brains to wear a mask. His face was caught as he pulled out a gun on one of the cashiers.

We reached the river, it's smooth as silk, and cold, but we don't care. It's so hot already at eleven and only going to get hotter. The robbery is forgotten as we looked forward to a refreshing swim. We threw our shorts in a pile on the sand and waded in trying to avoid the rocks. "Burr!" I shivered as I wrapped my arms around my chest trying to keep warm. I'm only up to my ankles.

"You said, it." Carla answered as she dived in. "Get in already." "You're crazy." Both Bessie, and I laughed as we got splashed by Carla who was already heading to the middle of the river. We edged our way in carefully, and by the time the water reached our chins, Carla had reached the other side, and standing on the shore waving at us.

"Hurry slowpokes." she laughed. We laughed as well, and dove in. The water is ice cold, it hasn't warmed up from the sun. It's fun anyway as we spent the next hour going back, and forth from shore to shore, exhausting ourselves. When we had enough swimming, we lay down on the s, and enjoying the sun, and the fact that we had this awesome way to relax that didn't cost a single dime.

It's only when the sun started lowering, we realized it will be dinner time soon. We dried off and began the long walk back into town. Once we reached Carla's block, Bessie pointed to a brick one-story house close to Carla's. "He is so hot." She observed referring to Trey. He was bent over with his back to us showing off tanned muscles as he carried crates from his truck to the porch.

"Go for it." I teased and earned a punch in the shoulder. I laughed at Bessie, amused at her. She was already blushing. "It's okay to have a crush on him. Most everyone around here does." "You don't." Bessie answered.

"I'm alone." "If you like him, do something about it. Can't hurt to try." "Oh, it can't be like getting my butt burned. Either they'll do it or worse, dad. Can you picture it, me, and the farmer?" She started laughing realizing how ridiculous she was being.

I however looked shocked at her. True Trey is a farmer, but he was the nicest person besides my family, and maybe Taylor around. Bessie's not usually this judgmental, but I kept quiet on the subject. We reached Carla's house which was only three blocks away from our own. "See you next week. Call me and let me know how your first day goes." Carla said, waving goodbye from her gate. She disappeared into the house.

"I will." I answered to her door, and Bessie, and I walked the few remaining blocks until we reached Starlights. It's still open, and Bessie said, she would wait at the house. I walked in the back doors through the kitchen and saw Mark cleaning off a table in the dining area. He looks busy to even notice me, so I helped. "Hey thanks." Mark said, smiling down at me. "No problem. I enjoy helping." Getting some plates, and glasses I turned to take them to the kitchen.

He followed me. "So." He glanced down at my shorts which are almost dry. "Have a good time?" "I sure did. I will miss going to the river once I start my job." "Nobody said, you can't have any fun. What time do you get off at night, anyway?" "Eight starting when school begins. For the rest of August and most of September, I will get off by six."

"Well that is late enough by that time. I will walk you home." He didn't wait for an answer but turned towards the kitchen carrying the tub filled with dirty dishes. I trailed after him already angry but waited until we are through the swinging doors before answering. "That's stupid, look outside, it's not even sunset, and it's after seven now. There is plenty of sunlight, and I'm not a little girl anymore." This is met with a scowl. "Mark, that is not..."

"Yes, it's necessary." He finished for me. I hate when he did that. Finished our sentences with his own opinion. "What are you two arguing about?" Keith asked. He had entered the kitchen and is surprised by the tension. He expected it from Bessie, and her daily issues, but not with these two. "I'm telling Reesa that it would be best since she doesn't get off till late that I will walk her home. Better safe than sorry." he said, as I opened my mouth to protest again.

Keith nodded. "Baby, he is right. If Mark didn't offer, I would be the one to do it. Think of the shame being walked home by good old daddy. You are getting a good deal here." He teased. He said, "You are not to walk home by yourself under any circumstances. Especially with that robbery a few weeks ago or if I catch you doing so, you will find yourself out of a job so fast, your ass will spin."

The Way Life Used To Be

He frowned in my direction, and I shut my mouth when I was about to protest, against my better judgment. Dad never swears so I can tell he means it. "I would prefer you find a different job. Any chance of that?" Keith asked. I glanced up, and stared at both, of them.

I shook my head even though I'm shooting daggers through my eyes at them. They did nothing, but smirk at me. Obviously, this is a losing battle. "Yes daddy. I hear you, and no I can't find another job right now. The daily Dallas News has already found a replacement for my old route, and this will be good for me. Besides, Bessie, Carla, and I were talking about that earlier, and we think Greg is long gone now."

"He is still hiding so I would not place any bets on that. I sure hope so for everyone's sake that he is gone for good." He forced a deep breath. "Okay. How is your day?" as he kissed the top of my head.

"Good, Carla went swimming with us, it was a lot of fun." I hopped up on a stool and began to put clean silverware away in a wooden drawer. "I'm glad. Mom, and I will be done in half an hour. Can you start the hamburger for dinner?" "Sure, what are we having?" "Spaghetti." "Yummy." I answered, rubbing my stomach. It's already growling reminding me I skipped lunch. It's too late now to eat anything that wouldn't ruin my appetite for dinner, so I waited.

"Get Bessie to help if you can." "I'm sure she will." I finished putting the silverware away, and hopped down, gave dad a kiss on the cheek, and escaped out the back door. Reaching the house a few minutes later, I called to Bessie, but received no answer. I shrugged my shoulders and smiled. She is listening to her music or something.

I got the hamburger from the refrigerator and helped myself to a sprite. There is not anything else to drink that looks appetizing. While the meat cooked, I started the noodles too. As I reached under the cupboard for a pan to boil the water, Bessie stuck her head around the corner. "What are you doing." "Making spaghetti. Want to help?" "Sure. why not." She pushed herself off the wall with four fingers, and got an onion, and garlic.

The smell of the garlic filled the air as Bessie chopped the clove into tiny pieces and added them to a pan. "How long has Carla, and Taylor been dating?" she asked as she started on the onion. "A few months, I guess. They seem happy together." Bessie nodded. "Yeah, they do. Do you have your eye on a guy yet?" "No, besides, we are not allowed to date until we are sixteen. Seems pointless to have a crush on someone who I can't even see for a year."

"Yeah. I guess you're right." She had her eye on Joseph Marlow. A boy in her seventh period math class. He is so dreamy, and she wished she could see boys. "Doesn't hurt to flirt though. That is innocent." "Forget about Trey already?" I teased. "No, I don't think so. Trey is nice to look at with all that manliness oozing out of him, but he is too good for me. Joseph is more in my line of fire." Bessie said,

"I guess he is, flirting can be fun, I guess. I have never done it myself, so I have no leg to stand on that subject. I'm always afraid that it will get out of hand, and I will get into a situation I can't get out of. That is my biggest fear,", I confessed as I stirred the sauce. It's boiling when the front door slammed, and Mark, Keith and Zeni entered the house talking at once.

"I'm going out for track this year." Mark is saying as he threw his jacket on a peg near the front door. "You should concentrate on your grades instead; you only have one more year." Keith responded as he, and Zeni walked arm in arm towards the kitchen.

"Yeah, but I might get a scholarship through a sports program. That should help ease the burden, right?" "True, it might. It's up to you if you want to try out, but I would not worry about college. Mom, and I have that covered."

"I'm not sure what I want to do yet, I'm thinking about it." "Let me know." "Well what is this?" Zeni smiled at her daughters working side by side and whispering. It was definitely a switch, from this morning, but she is grateful for every second of peace. "Dinner is served." I stated as I placed the sauce, and noodles on the table, and we sat down to enjoy dinner together.

Once everyone's plates are empty, I did the dishes. Bessie disappeared as soon as she was done eating, and I thought for sure she would want to hang out with me. We could watch a movie or something, but that isn't likely going to happen tonight. I shrugged my shoulders like I don't care, but I'm not fooling anybody especially myself. After a day of deliberately making her part of my plans, I thought she would start changing, and want us to get closer.

I strolled upstairs intending to organize my clothes, but once I stepped inside, I changed my mind. Today is busy enough, and I didn't want to do anything but lay down to relax. I put a movie in the DVD player and settled against my pillows.

I will miss that when I start my job. I love these times together, and since I would not be off until way past dinner time, most likely would

The Way Life Used To Be

have to eat the leftovers or find something from the store's deli. I fell asleep with a full stomach and should be happy, but I'm depressed at the same time.

Sandra Gutierrez

Chapter 2

The next morning, I woke up early with the sun beaming through the windows with a glare that made me throw a pillow at the curtains in anger. It's high time to rearrange. I did it before I start my job, and no time for such necessary chores.

Only one more day, and I will make my own money. First thing on the agenda is to buy a cell phone. Everyone who is anyone has one. Even our friends have one, and spent so much time texting each other, and having the damn things glued to their ears. It's not a requirement, but I want one, anyway. Something small, but classy.

It would be a cool hot pink or midnight blue. That would be a pretty color too. Getting more excited than angry now, I threw the covers aside, and grabbed a pair of shorts, and headed to the bathroom to take a shower.

I plan on helping in the restaurant later on and want to look decent. Shower done, and my hair hanging in damp ringlets, I bounced down the stairs only to find the kitchen empty, and even Bessie is not in the house.

I like the quiet as I made myself a bowl of cereal and ate it quietly at the kitchen table with a good housekeeping magazine for company. Flipping through the pages, not caring what is on them I ate my cereal, and dumped the bowl, and spoon in the sink.

Something caught my eye. I saw the note on the refrigerator in mom's handwriting, large, and graceful.

The Way Life Used To Be

Reesa,

Sorry to leave without saying goodbye. Dad, and I are at Starlights. Come on by later on this morning if you don't have any other plans. We'd love to have your help.

Mama

That made me smile. That is just like mom to ask for my help when I love to volunteer, anyway. It's nice being in Starlights, and visiting with the customers who came in gossipy, and hungry. May as well get started on the room while it's still cool, and the quiet gives me time to think how I want to rearrange. I made a floor plan first.

I'm always surprised to find more clothes scattered on the floor than on the hangers. Guess that is what I get for being lazy. I turned on my television set, and found nothing on, but the local news. Oh well, it's better than listening to silence. I kept half an ear on the reporters and got to work.

I'm hoping to hear Greg is arrested, so I would not have to worry, but he wasn't mentioned. I racked my memory for a picture of him in my head, but I couldn't come up with anything. I even thumbed through my brother's old year books and saw his unsmiling picture from the tenth grade. He is ordinary looking.

Probably someone nobody noticed even if they are concentrating. His dirty blond hair is on the long side covering his ears, and neck, and something about his whole demeanor spelled dangerous. I could not put my finger on why, but it did, anyway. I folded the book back and placed it back on the bookshelf.

Starlights is quiet as Zeni, and Keith still had several hours before they opened. Zeni had the homemade biscuits with the soups she served cooling on a rack when the back door flung opened, and she whipped her head around to see Jacob Matthews come in arms laden with crates of vegetables, and berries.

His son Trayson trailed behind him, and she smiled. He is so polite, and hard working. Not a bad combination, and so rare for someone of his age to be. He had turned seventeen, and like Mark he will be a senior himself this year.

"Good morning Jacob, bright, and early as always." The Matthews have been delivering their produce for four years, and they are always pleasant to be around. They are neighbors a few blocks down and arrived early in the morning before it got too busy. They have a lot of customers to deliver to, so most days are packed.

"How are you doing Trey?" She turned her attention to the tall dark-haired boy who stood behind his father carrying raspberries, and strawberries. He always went by Trey. A nickname given by his mother, and she only called him Trayson Daniel when he is in trouble, which for him is very rare.

He is a handsome young man who is always nice to everyone he came across. You never know who might become a potential customer. "No complaints, at least not yet. However, it's early so who knows if that will change." He smiled and strode out to get more crates piled up in the back of their pickup.

He reentered the restaurant to find the kitchen empty, and set the remaining crates on the counter, and walked through the swinging doors to find his father sitting at a table with a steaming mug of coffee before him and waiting.

"Hey Pop." He smiled and sat down across from him with a Coke in one hand. He hates coffee. Zeni always offered them coffee in the morning, and Jacob is more than happy to accept. Trey had never developed a taste for the stuff, but a soda first thing in the morning hit the spot. Besides, he liked it when the place is quiet, and gave him a chance to talk with his father before things got too busy.

"I realized we have a few minutes before our next stop, and the smell of coffee is too much for me to refuse." Jacob smiled as he took a sip. He is not a handsome man, but Trey is. He never had trouble finding girls to date, but he kept quiet about it. Jacob is not the type to kiss and tell. Jacob wished he is a lady's man, especially when he is young, but now, he has the love of his life, and he would not trade her for anything.

"Coffee is always hard for you to refuse." Trey teased him. That is pretty much his only addiction. Thank God he never drank or is a mean spiteful person. He would not be as close to him if he were. Probably would not have any respect either. "Pop I'm thinking." He began and stopped to take a drink.

"Never a good thing." Jacob teased. "Let's expand the farm. We could use more customers." He took another drink of his soda. ", and we have that space next to the corn. It's all ours, and it's acres of property that is not being used for anything except for growing weeds."

"Because we have so much to do, anyway. If we add chickens for eggs, and poultry, I'm afraid we would get in more than we can handle." "I don't think so. If we build that barn you have been talking about forever, we can make it happen."

"Think of how happy it would make mom not having to worry about every penny. You know as well as I do how much she worries about everything." Trey is careful not to disagree too much, but his father always valued his opinion. "I know this would be a good move."

"You might be. I'm drained at the end of each day, and we never have days off. At least during the Spring, and Summer. But you're right about mom. I would do anything to take the wrinkles out of her forehead."

"That will go away." Trey teased smiling. "You're probably right about that too. The joys of getting older. However, I would do everything possible to make her happy. I hate her worrying about every damn penny, and I also hate working you to death. You should be living the high life."

"If that was important to me, I would. I only have one more year of school left, and I'm not going to college. That is never something that appealed to me, and so you will soon have me to help all the time." Trey offered finishing his Coke. "We will see, I'm sorry we can't even afford to send you to a trade school or anything else that would help you in the long run. I would hate to see you be content with only a high school diploma."

"I'm not though. Being a farmer suits me fine." "With that being said, we should get going." They however ended up talking a few minutes more while enjoying their morning. They reluctantly got up and left a dollar on the table for a tip and left the restaurant still talking. I came in the back door as the front door closed behind them. I looked around the kitchen and found it empty which is fine with me. Rarely did I see anyone, but mom, and dad this time of day.

"Mama." I said, as she pushed through the swinging doors. I rushed into her arms, and she gave me a kiss on my cheek. "Hello my baby. Come to say hello to your favorite mother? What brings such a smile to your beautiful face?" "You bet, I finished my room, and it looks so much better now. My uniform laundered and ironed to make a good first impression. I smile because you're the beautiful one."

Sandra Gutierrez

"Why thank you, and you made that point with your interview. I'm glad however your taking pride in your appearance. It makes for good habits later on in life." Zeni advised, and finished chopping the tomatoes, and grabbed a handful of carrots from the huge refrigerator.

"I know that, I want to do well there. If I work hard, I can work my way up to a cashier, then assistant manager in a few years." Zeni laughed. "That is a positive outlook. Make sure it doesn't interfere with your grades." "Never. Hi dad."

Keith had entered the kitchen from the back door I had come through a few minutes before. He had finished emptying the garbage. "Hi Baby. Helping mom?" he glanced at the counter. "Yeah. I had some free time before my job starts, and I could not stand still."

"I know what you mean. Zeni you need any help with that soup?" He nodded at the stove. "Nope, got it all ready." Zeni smiled. She added beef barley, and chunks of meat to the pot. Today's special is hot beef sandwiches, and stew. The kitchen smells delicious already with the soup simmering. It's a hot day to offer those foods, but whatever the weather customers came., and they ordered.

An hour later we opened the front doors, and customers started walking in. It promised to be another full but fulfilling day. I waited tables instead of going back home. It's boring there with no one to talk to. I grabbed a soda first and kept it on the counter by the register so I could get a drink now, and then.

I filled two orders of roast beef sandwiches, home fries, and fruit cups, and hurried to the next table. It's filled with loud kids banging forks, and knives against the table making me wince, but I introduced myself with a smile, and took their orders as quickly as I could escape before one fork found its way close to my apron.

Back in the kitchen I hung up the orders on the post and yelled "Orders ready." I slapped the bell. I hurried out to take more orders. It's close to two before I realized how long I have been doing this, and the afternoon waitresses arrived, so I decided enough helping for today. I tossed my apron on a hook and waved goodbye. Mom stopped me at the front door and asked me to make whatever I want for dinner. I nodded and headed outside to freedom.

Once I'm outside I realized I have nowhere else to go. I will have to go grocery shopping most likely, but other than that I have nothing planned. Bessie is sure in one of her moods again, so I wondered down

The Way Life Used To Be

the block not paying much attention and found myself at Hankins. I decided grocery shopping is on my agenda.

Trey, and his dad are on their way home to get another bushel of corn, and peas. They already had made several stops, and Jacob parked at a local Subway to get sandwiches to eat in the truck. The late afternoon sun is beaming down on them from the windshield and made their foreheads sweat along with everything else.

"Dad, I'm serious about expanding our farm. Lord knows we have the room, and like I said, earlier we have the room. Back behind the shed alone there's at least half an acre we can build the barn, and fence. I'd love to raise cattle, and chickens or even pigs." He could already see it.

Jacob intently listened to his son try to convince him this is a good move. Deep down he agreed. He also is aware how much time the fruits, and vegetables took to grow, maintain, and deliver to their customers on time.

Adding on more stress to their lifestyle doesn't seem worth it both he, and Cynthia are forty-three, and they are not as quick on their feet or anywhere else to take on any more than they are now. He could also picture the barn, and all those animals, and it made him smile.

"Trey..." He began. "Dad, I know what you will say, and I'm right about this. Believe me it will give us more money too." "I will think about it." He promised glancing at his son and grinned wider. "I will. I promise. Do you know how persuading you have become, for a young man, barely seventeen?"

"Thanks dad. You will see it my way." They reached their brick one-story house, and Jacob parked the truck in the street by the steps. They would be a minute to grab the corn, and peas already by the curb. Cynthia had it ready for them to help cut some time off.

Trey jumped out of the truck to grab a barrel and glanced up to see Carla waving at him. He lifted a hand in acknowledgement, and grabbed the barrel with both gloved hands, and placed it in the back of the truck. He followed it by three more barrels full to the brim with corn still in their husks, and somehow, they smell wonderful. He loves that about his life. The fruits are especially hard to resist.

Jacob added two crates of pea pods, and placed them by the barrels, and they took off. They repeated that routine two more times before calling it a night. Exhausted, and dirty as hell Jacob parked the truck for the night and locked it. They hurried up the steps, and into the house where dinner waited.

"Hey Ma." Trey smiled at his mom who is still in the kitchen finishing up dinner. "Hi. You guys done?" She asked. Mom is a small woman topping five two, but she never let her lack of height restrict her. She lifted crates of vegetables every day without complaint. Mom wore her chestnut colored hair in a ponytail or bun as it's always too hot to wear it down. She has an infectious smile, and a kind word for everyone.

Jacob answered. "Yup. Had a full day. Thanks for having the vegetables ready for us. It saved us an hour." "No problem." She said, "Dinner is ready. I need to get the drinks ready. Wash your hands." "I will shower first." Trey said, "There is so much dust today, it's like it's inside me." He bounded up the stairs without waiting for an answer, and stripped off his dirty clothes, and shoved them into the hamper next to the bathroom door.

They sat down minutes later to homemade cheeseburgers, tossed green salad, and blueberry muffins. Once they started eating Cynthia asked, "so what did you think of Trey's idea?" Trey had talked to his mom the night before, and she agreed.

Jacob took a drink of ice-water before answering. "Trey." Cynthia interrupted. "Now Jacob. Admit what Trey suggested is a good idea. That extra money would put a new roof on the house and add on to the living room like I have waited to do for years now."

The living room is square, and plain. It has a brown plaid couch a wooden coffee table, and a TV stand that is missing one wheel, and has two books in its place to keep it level. Cynthia always hated that room, but there is never enough money to do more. They had enough to pay the mortgage, their bills, and a little extra for a movie now, and then.

Jacob knew what a sore spot that is. He also knew that the whole house needed major repairs. "Cindy, I don't want to bite off more than we can chew. To lose this would be devastating for all of us." "Maybe." She shrugged her shoulders. "But on the positive side it could mean everything."

Jacob laughed. As always, he could count on his beautiful woman to see the plus side of everything. "I can see you both are in complete agreement on this. Trey, I promise you, and my darling Cindy, I will think about this. I have a feeling I'm going to say yes and regret it every day." "No, you won't." Cindy chastised as she began clearing the table.

It's close to seven when Keith and Zeni closed the restaurant for the night. I said, goodbye hours ago after putting in close to four hours

The Way Life Used To Be

helping. I wanted to be up at six to get ready for my first day. Instead, I didn't go back once I found something to make for dinner.

There is training for four hours before I take a one-hour lunch. I would spend the afternoon learning the ropes. I'm getting more, and more excited, at the same time extremely nervous. Mark had played basketball when Starlights closed with friends from school and headed to the park. Keith and Zeni trusted him she never worried about a curfew. He is home well before midnight every night, anyway.

I had made chicken sandwiches with French fries and again had the table set when my parents walked in. Dad had his hand on mom's shoulder. Bessie is in her room pouting again., and again, there is no reason for it, but she had her records playing as she sat on her bed crying.

"Hello baby." Mom greeted me, and gave me a hug, and kiss as a thanks for getting dinner ready, and also for helping without complaint. "Mama sit down. I have dinner all ready." "Ok. Thanks." Zeni sat down with a grateful sigh and took a drink of her ice-water.

"I will miss having dinner ready once you start your job." "Me too." I smiled as I sat down myself. "I'm not looking forward to deli dinners." Zeni placed the ketchup on the table and called upstairs. "Bessie. Chow time."

Keith washed his hands in the kitchen sink and headed to the head of the table where he always sat. "I will miss this too. I'm spoiled having supper ready every night when we get home. You ought to talk with Mr. Hankins about letting you off by six instead of eight once school starts." He smiled as he ate a fry.

I giggled. "That would be nice. I'm not keen on getting home after dark. However, I still have the whole month of August and almost all of September when I'm off by six, so the later shift won't start for a while."

"I mean it when I said, Mark is to walk you home every night. I want you to stay inside the store until he arrives. Clear?" "Crystal." I said, as I'm resenting this again. "Mark has the freedom to play basketball, and do whatever damn thing he feels like doing, but I have to have my hand held each night,"

"Teresa Ann." Zeni interrupted. "Speak respectfully to your father. You know damn well we only have your best interests at heart." "Yes ma'am." I said, quieter, and held back my true feelings. "I'm aware of that, but it will not even be sunset. I can run straight here." When my mother says my full name, she meant business although I hated being

25

reminded of it, looking at my father for support. "No," Keith said, "Not another argument."

He took a bite of his sandwich before bellowing "Bessie. Where the hell are you. Supper is almost done." My father is the only one who used the word supper instead of dinner. I said, "She is in her room. Been there with the door shut tight since I got home, and who knows how long before that. She is having another moment." I'm hoping that she will stay there. I didn't need her sour puss attitude ruining my evening. It would be wonderful to have a night without being graced in her presence.

"Then I would rather eat my meal in peace." Zeni smiled agreeing with me. "Lord knows we've had enough moments." Once we had finished eating without the grace of Bessie's presence I offered to clean up, and Zeni, and Keith both said, they will enjoy the evening news before getting ready for bed.

Alone in the kitchen I glanced up at the window overlooking the sink and saw the sun make a last bright light before lowering. See, I said, to myself. It's going on eight, and there is plenty of light to see me home from the store. My parents are being overprotective. Well that is fine for a few weeks, but I have every intention of seeing myself home after that.

If I threw a couple of Bessie moments, I would have my way for once. Not likely. All that would accomplish is they will think I'm too young to hold a job and make me quit before I have a chance to prove myself. I finished stacking the dishes in the dishwasher and ran lemon scented soap in it.

Once the gentle hum of the machine started, I folded a towel over the oven handle, and headed upstairs to get ready for the morning. My slacks, and blouse are hanging on the back of the desk chair pressed, and clean. I shut the bedroom door and flopped on the bed to watch a movie on the TV before bedtime. I wanted a little relaxation time. It reminds me of last night.

I kept the volume on low, and snuggled against the pillows closing my eyes, and half listening to the movie, and wondering about tomorrow. The clock struck eleven before I'm tired enough to shut down the TV and go to sleep. I will regret that in the morning.

I didn't even wake until the alarm rang in my ear and slapped the snooze button. There is still plenty of time to get ready as it's only six thirty. I ended up using the snooze button four more times before dragging myself out of bed sorry now that I accepted that job.

The Way Life Used To Be

It would be so nice to stay in bed, and forget about working for another year, but I'm determined to make my own money. One can't do that sitting on their butt waiting for the bills to fall into their hands. I shut my bedroom door and headed to the bathroom. I showered, and once I'm dressed, and my hair in a neat ponytail.

I made my way downstairs where my parents are already up and reading the newspaper. Bessie's door is still shut tight, she never made an appearance the night before. I'm not sure if she is even in the house or spent the night at one of her depressing friends complaining about everything, and anything.

I skipped down the stairway now awake. The shower did wonders at waking me up. "Good morning" I greeted entering the kitchen. Dad took a sip of coffee before smiling at me. "Well, morning Baby. Sleep well?" The previous argument seemed to have been forgotten. He ate a bite of his eggs.

"Okay, I guess. I'm nervous about starting today." "That is understandable. Make sure you listen to your boss and treat the customers with nothing but respect." He advised. "Trust me that's why they'll keep coming back."

"I will, I learned from the best." I said, while pouring a bowl of cereal for my breakfast. I carried the bowl, and a glass of orange juice, sat at the table, and started eating. Keith put down the newspaper. "You get off at six, right?" I shook my head. "No, five. I forgot until I looked at my schedule last night. Today is training and starting tomorrow I have to go in at ten, and I'm off at six. I get an hour lunch break in between. It's not till the end of September when I get off work at eight."

"Okay, Mark will meet you outside., and Reesa once you get comfortable, and mom, and I get comfortable as well you can go home on your own." "Okay." I said, and nothing more. At least my parents will give me a little breathing room once I proved myself. I have full intentions on doing that immediately.

"Well you have a good first day. We will see you tonight. Don't forget to give me all the details." Mom kissed my forehead. "Keith, it's time to go." "Yes boss." He smiled as he rinsed out his coffee cup, and they left shortly after. Once the house is quiet again, I finished my cereal, and headed back upstairs to get dressed in my work uniform.

At nine thirty I'm ready to leave. I knocked on Bessie's door once in a half-hearted attempt to talk to her, but there is no answer. Shrugging my shoulders, I left the house, and rushed down the block. I turned right for three more before the store appeared. It's huge, and brightly lit. Several cars are already in the parking lot. I held back a minute to get my heart beating. This is silly, but I can't help it. I'm so nervous.

I entered through the back as instructed. The employees lounge is to the right with the men's, and women's restaurants on my left with a sink for drinking water hooked to the wall between them. the bathrooms are next to each other, and are kept clean, and orderly which impressed me.

I walked a little further down the small hall and turned left into the owner's office. Mr. Hankins is at his desk, which is covered with junk, and old coffee cups. He has a huge smile on his face as he saw who had entered.

"Well good morning Reesa." He greeted. "Ready to get started?" He is balding, and overweight, but all his employees love him for his big heart and giving attitude. he loves donating the local charities when he had the funds available.

"Yes. Mr. Hankins. I wanted to thank you for giving me this opportunity. I won't let you down." He gestured to a seat opposite his desk, and I sat down. I held my back straight and looked him straight in the eyes like Mama had taught me. She said, that is the best way to make a good first impression, and it seems to work.

Jake Hankins laughed. "I bet you won't., and Reesa don't worry. You will do fine." Jake stood up, and his full height of six feet seems gigantic to me. I'm barely over five feet. His eyes are twinkling giving away his natural happiness, but he is still very handsome at thirty-five, even if he is losing his hair.

His wife of twelve years Aimee is the day manager of the deli, and the front-end cashiers. She is friendly, and almost as tall as Jake, and had very red hair, and a face full of freckles. She also has the cutest dimples that showed when she smiles, and she smiles a lot. They are a happy couple who had no kids, but they seem fine with it. The employees are too polite to ask why, although the questions hung in the air.

It's no wonder the employees love it there. There is very little turnaround, and most of the employees have been there for years. "Well the grocery section is where you will spend most your day. Boxes of food, and staples are in the back past the frozen food area."

"There is a sliding door that leads to the storage area. I will take you there in a minute so you can familiarize yourself with where the boxes are located. It can take a few weeks to learn everything so don't

The Way Life Used To Be

feel bad about asking." I have learned the layout of the store as we have been shopping here for years. We used to spend whole summers earning coins so we could come here and spend them all at once. Made for very poor savings, but we didn't care.

Those bins are long gone now as the penny candy phase dissipated much like a lot of other things. Plus, the store didn't make a large profit off of them. Still, I can't help, but smile at those bygone days. Life is a lot simpler since we only had to do a few chores to earn those lovely nickels, and dimes. To us it's like gold. I realized I'm daydreaming as Mr. Hankins, and I are already in the frozen food section. I have to stop doing that as I will learn nothing this way.

"Top four shelves are for the canned goods. They are easy to reach, but there is a step ladder if you need it. Make sure you use a back brace as it can be torture on the muscles if you don't." He pointed with his left hand. "These two shelves are for the frozen foods. Easiest to reach at ground level, and since they need to be distributed as soon as the trucks come in."

"That would be your first job before stocking the shelves. I decided not to have a separate freezer as this works so much better." He smiled as we left the storage unit. I'm more relaxed as I have a better idea of how my day will go.

I nodded while Mr. Hankins explained. It makes sense as I hate grocery shopping where the foods are all mixed haphazardly. It makes for a long, and dreadful experience. I like the arrangement of the aisles, and why each item is placed where it is.

I'm introduced to the other stockers who smiled and greeted me. We moved on to the deli, and bakery. It smells delicious with the doughnuts fresh out of the grease. They're made first thing in the mornings, and ready by six when the doors opened for the day. This must have been the second batch.

We moved on to greet the cashiers. Two of them had customers, and they worked at break-neck speed while maintaining eye contact, and a steady stream of conversation at the same time. One can't help but admire them, and I wanted to learn things that much quicker so I could be one of them as soon as I turned sixteen.

We made our way back to Jake's office where he has the new employee forms ready to sign. Once I filled out the forms, he showed me where the employees sign in, and out each day. Everyone had their own slip with their name, and employee number on it. It was located it right outside his office.

Next came the training. I'm paired up with Zack Zeller who is the manager of the dry goods area and had been with the store for five years. He is short, stocky, and friendly at the same time. He held a notebook filled with items that had to be checked off at the time they left the storage area and are stocked on the floor shelves.

According to the book, I learned what time to go to the storage area to locate the boxes to refill the shelves, and how to arrange the cans, and boxes, so the labels faced front, and lined up. Jack also pointed out where the brooms, and mops are stored.

The floors need to be swept down and mopped each night. That task would not be completed until the last customer left the store, and we lock the front doors. I would not be doing that job for a while because of my schedule, but he wants me to know where everything is stored in case.

I glanced at the clock over the deli counter and am shocked to realize it's almost one o'clock. Time flew, and I'm happy about that. Nothing is more boring to have a job that drags, and you would count the minutes that seem endless until you could escape and go home. Jack left me alone after that with three boxes on the floor to empty.

I love this. Much better, and more satisfying than the paper route. Several customers had approached me and asked where to find things. I'm confident enough to answer them with a smile, and head right back to my unpacking.

Each thank you is like a shower raining over me. My smile is huge, and it shows how much I enjoy my new job. At least I hoped it does. Once my lunch hour started, I headed to the employees lounge to find my purse. I had left it hanging on the knob with my sweatshirt in the lounge when I first got there.

I headed to the deli to find something to eat. Once I turned the corner Carla is there bouncing up, and down. "Hey there, working girl," she said, and ran her hand down my blouse sleeve. "You done?" "Nope, getting some lunch." I opened my purse and found a five-dollar bill from tips I earned yesterday bussing tables with Mark. "Hey let's eat together." She offered, and slipped her arm through mine, and we walked to the deli together.

We ate outside where the sun is shining bright, and hot. We sat on a bench near the park. "So, tell me how's your first day going so far?"

The Way Life Used To Be

She asked taking a bite of her turkey sandwich. "Good so far. I'm hoping this all works out because this is what I need." I took a bite of my ham wrap. "Has the robber been back?" Carla asked. It's obvious she is worried, so I didn't take offense like I would with anyone else. I shook my head and found I enjoyed eating outdoors. I decided I'd do it from now on as long as the nice weather held.

I finished my lunch and leaned my head back to enjoy the sun. The bench is warm even if I'm not comfortable. "What classes do you have for this year?" She asked taking a drink of her bottled water. I shook my head keeping my eyes closed.

"I have not even looked to see if any paperwork got mailed yet. I will find out soon enough. I hope I don't have Mr. Kennedy for US History. Mark had him for his sophomore year, and hard as he tried, he couldn't get more than a C for his grade. He even did a lot of extra credit, but it didn't do any good. I want Ms. Turnbell."

"She is nice. I hope I get her too. This may be our hardest year yet." "It doesn't sound like a piece of cake or anything. I promised my parents I'd do my best. That's all they've ever asked of us." I said, squinting my eyes to look at my watch. "Is it time to go already?" "In a few minutes, I guess. I'm enjoying the quiet." "You're my inspiration." Carla laughed and dumped the empty bottle in a trash can. "Why is that?" I crumpled my paper and threw it in the trash.

"Getting a job, and good grades. I wish I didn't have to put forth so much effort for the things I do." She sounds resentful suddenly. This is a new behavior for her. I have never seen her down before, and I studied her face. It's grim and determined.

"Think I would be okay working too? Make my own money for a change. Taylor never minds giving me money for things, but I hate having to ask. Like it doesn't belong to me which it doesn't." She has pocket change from babysitting, but it's not like having an actual job.

"You can do anything you put your mind to." I smiled at her. I said, "as far as asking for things. I have done my share. Getting a job at our age may not be the answer for everyone. It so happens to be mine. At least for now. Who knows what will happen once school starts? Maybe I will get so burned out I will quit and become a beggar or something."

"Keith and Zeni would not allow that. Why don't you work at Starlights more and ditch this place? You could make awesome tips waitressing." "I do every few days when I have nothing else to do. I want to venture on my own for once."

"Independence, right?" Carla grabbed her purse from the bench. "You bet your ass." I laughed and got my own things together. I needed to be heading back for the afternoon. "Well I guess you better get back to the grind." Carla smiled. "I'm so proud of you." She kissed my cheek making me laugh out loud. "Thank you." I kissed her back. "I love you." "Love you more. I have to be going now. so many things to do, and so little time." She stated brushing a hand across her forehead. "Ta, Ta."

I waved goodbye and headed back inside. I still had close to fifteen minutes left, so I headed to the back to sip my iced tea and relax a little more. The quietness is comforting. There is a small TV showing a 24-hour news station that needs very little attention.

There is a small window that overlooked Mission Park, but all I could see from the seat is a bunch of trees that swayed gently in the breeze. The lounge is air conditioned and feels so good. I wish I was outside though. A quick glance at the clock reminded me once again how time flew. I threw the empty bottle in the trash and headed out to find Jack.

Jack watched me for a while and left after a few minutes. He smiled to himself as he decided all is okay.
He headed to the storage area to grab toilet paper, and napkins from one bin. This late in the afternoon, the frozen goods are long put away, and these are on the bottom of the list.

I opened a box with the box cutter, and started arranging soup cans, not noticing Jack had disappeared. I looked up after a while and found myself alone. This means he is already trusting me. I crushed the box and started on another.

It's going on four when Mark entered the store. He needed corn, and rice for tonight's dinner. Keith scooted him along saying he, and Zeni would be happy to close, if he will start dinner.

He is more than happy to get away from Starlights as it is approaching the dinner hour, and tables are filling. Zeni had it covered though. He rushed out the doors before she could change her mind. Even with the front doors opened to welcome the breeze, it's stuffy.

He felt a rush of ice-cold air from the air conditioner and would have been content to just stand there for hours. However, with more customers arriving he would just be in the way, so he hurried away from the entrance way in search of Ressa.

The Way Life Used To Be

He is still concerned about her with the robbery only a few weeks ago and didn't want to make a fuss. He made his way to the fresh meat section realizing they are out of meat. The freezer is getting pretty empty.

He thumbed through the meat and found one with little fat. He turned at the sound of his name. "Hey Mark. How's it goin' "He glanced to his right. "Oh, hi Trey. All done for the day?" "Yep, mom needed some hamburger for dinner. Dad, and I got off early for a change, so we are all having dinner together. That doesn't happen too often." He replied reaching for a pound of meat.

Mark smiled. He had always liked Trey, and his family. They are friendly, and efficient. They both attended the same school but had a different circle of friends. Except for each other, and Jim Stevens. Jim is friendly with just about anybody so it's no surprise he befriended them too.

"That sounds nice. What are you guys making?" "Lasagna. I have never made it before so it should be interesting." Mark smiled again. "You can always cheat and have Stouffer's instead." Trey laughed. "I don't

think she will buy that. She is never one for store bought stuff if she can make it herself." He put the hamburger in his basket and waved a hand in farewell. "It's nice seeing you. Sorry to rush, but mom's waiting for me. See you around. Say hi to your family for me."

"Will do. See you and have a good night." Trey left to pay for the meat, and Mark headed to the next aisle for some corn. He didn't see Reesa anywhere, but it appears quiet, so it looks like all is well so far. Trey grabbed a bag of corn and headed to the front. He wanted to see Sara, one of the cashiers.

He had a crush on her for the better part of two years. All he wanted is to get to know her better. She seems on the shy side though so it's sometimes hard to approach her, and just start talking. Would she just ignore him or respond?

Reesa working here might just be the answer. She has a way of bringing people around even when they didn't realize it or want to, except for Bessie. Sometimes no matter how hard you tried; she is who she is. He got in her line even though there are two people already ahead of him. There are two other open lanes, but he didn't care. He waved aside their offers to help and waited until the woman ahead of him paid for her groceries. He then put the chicken, and corn on the counter.

Sandra Gutierrez

Sara looked up at him and smiled. She has been hoping since April when she herself was hired that he would make it through again. She wanted him to talk to her. The one, and only time he came through her line was about a month ago and didn't say much at all. She didn't realize until just now that Reesa is his little sister.

"Hey Mark. How are you?" She greeted. May as well take the bull by the horns. What is the worst thing that could happen? She would use the friendly, and courteous excuse all cashiers used if he said, nothing. Mark however smiled. So much for the shyness factor. "Fine, just getting some things for dinner. How has your summer been?"

"Busy so far. How's it goin' for you?" "Busy at Starlights at least." He answered getting out his wallet. He could not remember how long she has been working here. She watched him, admiring his muscles as he reached behind him.

He didn't appear to notice her staring at him. She focused her attention on the task at hand, and scanned the chicken package, and corn, and placed them in a plastic bag. She kept her eyes on his while she did this. His eyes were absolutely, gorgeous with a deep brown color.

"Listen, Reesa's been looking forward to working here for a while now, but now that she is here, I'm nervous what with the robbery, and all. Have you seen her?" Sara shook her head. "Not for a while. They gave her the tour earlier this morning. I saw her stocking shelves a little while ago but have not seen her since. She looked happy when I saw her."

Mark glanced at the clock. It's four thirty, and she would get off soon. He wanted to be out of there before he is spotted. There is still plenty of daylight out, and he knows she will be okay to walk home alone despite his resolution he made last night.

"Oh, here she is." Sara said, as I approached the front of the store. "Mark?" I questioned with a confusing look on my face. He is not due for another few minutes. "What are you doing here?" I'm full of energy, and a wide smile on my face I could not get rid of. I'm so excited it's hard to stand still.

Mark pointed to his bag dangling in his right hand. "Getting dinner." "Oh well, if you want to wait a second, I'm off now, and I can walk with you?" I'm happy to see him. I'm also happy to see the look that passed between him, and Sara. The thoughts of resentment I am sure I would have never entered my mind once I saw both their faces.

The Way Life Used To Be

"Ok, I will just wait outside." He offered, and I headed to the employees lounge to get my purse. Once I left, Sara turned her attention back to Mark who is still looking in my direction. "Well." She said, and nothing more.

Mark came to the rescue. He turned his head back to Sara, liking the fact that she didn't move him out of line. There are not any customers behind him. Usually cashiers like to check out their customers and move them along so they could attend to the next one. Sara however seems in no hurry to get rid of him. She rested her elbows on the counter.

"She looks happy." He whispered. "Will you do me a favor and look out for her at least for the next few weeks? That robbery a few weeks back still has the hairs up on my arms." "I have heard nothing new about that. I was not working that day, but I would be happy to keep an eye out for you." She replied with a smile. It's nice that he worries about his family.

From the few times she went into Starlights, she saw both his parents, and Mark working side by side. They were always kidding around with each other. Not like in her own house where fighting and hitting were the only forms of communication. She heard about the robbery for a week straight, but gossip had died down since.

Mark placed a hand on her arm. It felt good, and warm. "Thank you, Sara." He glanced over his shoulder. "You have customers now." A middle age man, and a woman holding hands had approached the counter. Sara moved away from him to move behind the counter.

"Your welcome Mark. I hope to see you soon." This followed by a shy smile, and a wink as she turned to her customers. Mark left the store and waited as promised outside on the same bench Carla, and I had lunch and sweltered in the heat regretting his promise.

About five minutes later I approached him still wearing my uniform and smiling. "Hey. I'm done now. Ready to leave?" "Absolutely, it's torture being out here dying. Thought you were not off until five though. It's only ten minutes till."

I laughed. "There were not any more items to stock. Jack who was my trainer, let me go a few minutes early. I even got a compliment from him, and everyone there said, a good word from him is scarce." I pointed to his armpits which were already soaked. "I'm sure you were just fine sitting out here waiting for me, Sara was checking you out when you left. She was smiling too. She was looking right at your butt."

Sandra Gutierrez

Mark blushed, "Thank you for the observation. She is just a friend from school." We started walking down the block. Even though it's approaching the heat of the day, we are in no hurry. This is the time of day I like best. Mark always seems more open without the rest of the family around especially Bessie. She has a way of making someone clam-up because of her sour attitude.

"If I were you, I would make her more than a friend. She is nice and seems to like you. Especially your backside." I laughed and poked him in the chest. "I will take that under advisement. How is your first day besides the long-awaited compliment?"

"Wonderful, I spent the first part of the morning learning the ropes. After lunch I was left on my own. I didn't make any mistakes, and I love this job. Even some customers thanked me."

Mark smiled down at me and placed a kiss on the top of my head. "I'm glad, this job is just what you need. I'm sorry that I showed up on your first day right there inside the store. I am not trying to be nosy. I thought you would like to help me with dinner. Mom asked me to pick up some stuff for it."

I agreed. "I would like that., and I didn't think you were checking up on me. I never mind that even when I act like I do." "Good to hear. It's just one of the many responsibilities an older brother has." We reached the house and opened the front door. It's much cooler than outside, and much more comfortable.

It's quiet as usual as mom, and dad are not expected for at least half an hour. "Give me a second. I want to get out of these clothes, and into something cooler." Mark is wearing shorts, and a T-shirt, so he is already feeling better. "Sure. See you in a few." He headed straight back to the kitchen and got out a frying pan out of the cupboard.

While the pan is heating, I rushed up the stairs to find Bessie's door is opened. I poked my head in smiling. "Hey Bessie, how was your day?" I wandered in further when she glanced up. No tears, so that is a good sign. Bessie is sitting on the bed folding socks. She has more clothes scattered on the bed. She smiled at me. "Pretty boring. I'm looking forward to school starting soon. There is not much to do in the summer." She tossed the clothes near her closet to put away.

"I hear you. Want to go back to the river tomorrow? I do have to work the day after, but I have the day free. Sound fun?" "Yeah. Thanks. Are you asking Carla, and Taylor too?" "Or we can just make it us.

The Way Life Used To Be

Whatever you want." I offered. I'm just happy Bessie is not having another mood swing, and the river sounds perfect.

"Just us." Bessie answered. She is already looking forward to it. Going to the river by herself is boring, and she enjoys being with her sister. Much more than she let on. "Okay, it's a date. Dinner should be ready soon." I jumped off the bed, and left her room, and skipped down the stairs to help Mark.

I entered the kitchen to find Mark at the stove stirring something that smells just short of wonderful. Already my mouth is watering, and I'm already ready to eat. "What can I do to help?" Mark turned from the stove. "Hmmm. I'm almost done. Why don't you nuke the corn real fast?"

The chicken was placed on a plate waiting for the rest. There is an onion, and garlic chopped up on the cutting board. The rice is almost finished, while the corn heated to temperature, Zeni, and Keith appeared, and two minutes later we all sat down.

"Oh Reesa." Bessie said and clapped her hands. "I can't go with you tomorrow. Jennie called while you were making dinner and wants to go to the mall tomorrow. Are you mad?" She asked scrunching up her face. I shook my head not wanting to upset her. "No, it's fine, I will find something to do. Have fun." Bessie sighed and started eating.

Thank heaven for the small things. My phone rang while I was changing for bed. "Hello?" "Hello back working girl." It's Carla. Just hearing her voice brought a smile to my face. "I had the best first day." I said, digging through my closet for a T-shirt. So much for my rearranging. Most of my clothes are shoved in here for lack of space.

"Sounds like. What are your plans for tomorrow?" "I was going to the river with Bess, but she dumped me for her best friend. Now I'm plan-less." I doubted plan-less is a true word, but I like it anyway. Carla giggled. "I'm plan-less too. Taylor has plans. Want to do something?"

"Sure" I answered without hesitating. "Want to meet me at Starlights?" "Okay, eleven sound good?" "Yeah, that'll give me time to get ready." I hung up the phone. I found a T-shirt near the bottom of the pile and pulled it over my head. By the time I went to bed my tummy is full, and I'm already looking forward to the next time I worked.

Sandra Gutierrez

Chapter 3

The sun woke me at six, and I groaned out loud. I forgot yesterday when I was cleaning, to move the bed. It's still facing the window, and the glare is overpowering as always. I threw a pillow just for effect.

It's hours before Carla is supposed to meet me, and I want to sleep in, but that will not happen. I'm already wide awake so I took a shower. I got dressed in a jean skirt, and a red T-shirt I found on a hanger in the closet that didn't have any wrinkles.

My hair is still frizzy from all the dry heat, so I brushed it the best I could, and tied it in a ponytail. I didn't bother with makeup this morning. It's hot enough without having to worry about makeup making my face itch.

I didn't bother with breakfast, but instead headed over to Starlights early. I could always use a heart to heart with mom. Bessie is already gone when I left the house and started walking down the block.

Mom was alone in the kitchen when I walked in. "Hey Baby, what's new?" She asked and started wiping down the counters. "I have plans with Carla later on, but I don't want to be at the house right now." I got a soda from the fountain, and hopped on a stool to talk, and relax.

"Any particular reason?" I shrugged my shoulders. The kitchen is cool this time of day and felt good on my skin. "No, I just don't want to be there." "Sometimes you don't need a reason." She leaned over and kissed my forehead. "I always love your company." I smiled. Sometimes it's nice to be understood without having to say anything. The back door opened, startling me for a minute. I turned around and smiled as I saw who is there. "Hey."

Trey stood in the doorway with two crates filling his arms. Jim is next to him with a crate of his own. "You hired an assistant?" Trey

The Way Life Used To Be

smiled. "Nope, Jim is too lazy to bother helping, but he is looking for a job. Thought it would be good to have volunteer work on his resume." Jim laughed. "I'm girl prowling." "Yeah. That'd be the day." I teased, and Jim leaned closer to my side. "I have found the someone to make all my dreams come true."

"She real or a blow up?" "Now, now, don't be jealous Reecie." Jim shook a finger in my face. "She is real and going to be a junior." "Has she just moved here?" I asked taking another drink. "Yes. A few weeks ago. Moved in down the street from us. She doesn't know me yet, but that will change soon." "Hence why you're prowling?" "Hence." He laughed again. "Zeni how's it going?" Zeni appeared through the swinging doors. She had just finished putting together an order moments ago.

"Good as always. Trey, how much this week?" She brushed loose hair out of her eyes. Trey got out the tally sheet and gave the total. She wrote a check and handed it to him with a smile. "See you next week." She is off again. "Well we should go too. Reesa, it's nice to see you. Take care." Trey smiled over his shoulder as they took off.

Once it's quiet again, I headed to the dining area to wait for Carla. It's almost ten thirty, and she would be here soon. Dad is at the serving counter when I walked up and squeezed his waist as a hello. "Hey baby, why don't you make yourself useful?" He handed me two plates. "Table seven."

I delivered the food and received a warm thank you in response. I then found my seat close to a window so I could see Carla when she came in. There is not anybody around me since it's still early. She bounced in ten minutes later all smiles, and ready to hit the road. "Want a sandwich first?" I offered. "Let's take it to go. The parks empty right now. We can have a picnic." She replied taking out her purse to pay for our food.

I waved goodbye, and we headed out. It's hotter than this morning, and the coolness of the kitchen is long forgotten as we walked. I carried the bag containing our sandwiches, and my other hand was holding another soda. "So how is your first day?" Carla asked hoping that Greg had not made a return visit. "Good like I said, before. I even got a decent workout carrying all those boxes."

I glanced at my shoulders. "They are already stronger." "So sexy, why do you get tanned just by looking outside, and some of us including poor me has to suffer with tanning salons that don't do a damn thing, but make us sweat, and burn?" Her arms were burned as she rubbed them making it worse.

"Just naturally lucky I guess." I shrugged my shoulders. "Or maybe I'm blessed." I laughed making her laugh too. "Oh, here is the park. I am right. See, almost empty." She hopped up, and down with excitement, and we found a place to have our lunch facing the river, but up the bank, and sat under a tree.

I stretched my legs out. "It's times like this I wish I was not so gung-ho about working. I love this." I closed my eyes and sighed. "So, who says you have to. I bet Mr. Hankins would understand if this is just too much for you this soon. This way you could enjoy being a teenager like the rest of us." Carla proceeded to take a bite of her turkey melt. "This is cold already." She frowned and shook her head. She took another bite. "I'm hungry so I will just ignore it."

"Why did you get a hot sandwich?" I can't help but ask, when it's as hot as it is. "Not thinking, I guess. Plus, I am craving turkey, and this just stood out for me. Though if you want to quit, I will go with you. I will provide the moral support."

She held out a hand and rubbed my arm. "I will think about it. I enjoyed yesterday, so much and this pays so much better than the paper route. I love having spending money." Shaking my coin purse for effect. I will not see a paycheck for a week.

"There is that benefit, I guess. That would be hard to give up cash." Carla took a drink of her water. We continued eating and enjoying the shade. I thought about taking a quick detour to the river. Then decided against it. My next day off would be soon enough. I took a long drink of my soda, and a bite of my sandwich.

We finished eating and headed back. Carla wanted to meet Taylor before it got too late. I headed upstairs to check on Bessie, but she is still gone. I headed to the kitchen and pulled out a package of bacon to make BLTs for dinner.

Bessie entered the house moments later and stuck her head in the kitchen when the bacon is cooking. The aroma is enough to make anyone's mouth water. The bacon made a sizzling sound when I turned them. "Can I help?" She asked. "Want to wash the lettuce? That is about all there is left to do." I smiled over my shoulder.

"Sure." She answered and grabbed the lettuce. she washed it under the kitchen sink and began breaking it apart to place it on a paper towel. "You sure you're not mad about earlier? I'm sorry I broke a promise,

The Way Life Used To Be

but I was not thinking." Bessie apologized. "Don't worry about it. Besides, I had a good time myself. Carla, and I had lunch at the park. It's nice too. You have fun shopping?" I asked.

Bessie nodded and popped a slice to tomato in her mouth. "I'm jealous, that sounds more fun than shopping at the mall. Are you looking forward to working tomorrow?" "Yes. I'm looking forward even more to getting my first paycheck. I may even frame it." "When I get a little older, I can work there too. Might be fun." "Definitely." I nodded while popping a tomato in my mouth. I put some bread in the toaster. "Are you ready for school to get started? This will be your last year of junior high."

Bessie nodded. "Yes, I sure am. I'm making a lot more friends this year than last." "Oh yeah." The toast is ready. I began spread mayonnaise. "That is because they are growing up a little. I remember even just a few years ago how petty, and jealous my classmates were, and suddenly it's like they grew up overnight. I think Carla will remain my best friend though. At least I hope so."

At this point I don't know what I would do if we traveled our separate ways. She is as close to me as a real sister. I popped more bread in the toaster. At that the front door opened again, and Keith and Zeni found dinner ready as always. Two days later I found myself too busy for words as it's approaching the noon hour, and I had already been at work for several hours with no time for a break, much less a lunch.

For the first time since I started working, I am looking forward to getting off my feet, and relaxing. Mark had agreed to make dinner that night, and I for one is thankful not to be the one doing it. I heard my name and turned around. I came face to face with my first-grade teacher Ms. Mason.

"Reesa?" She questions looking hard at me. I smiled up into the tall gray-haired woman with a broad smile. "Hello Ms. Mason. How are you?" I'm surprised she even remembered me from that long ago. I recalled she is one of my favorite teachers who gave out suckers on Fridays for good behavior, and I loved the cherry ones the best.

I also remembered my first time in her class, when I giggled out loud with Carla who sat next to me. She was whispering about kissing another student. I can't recall his name, but she is blushing, and Ms. Mason heard us all the way in the back. She made Carla stand up and tell her what the big secret is.

That caused the other students to starting laughing, but I'm sure they didn't understand why. Then she continued the punishment by making us stand in two corners. One is by the coat closet, and the other by her desk.

We had to stand with our hands behind our back. We were so humiliated! We both vowed that day never to do anything like that again. So far it worked, and that also got me thinking that is when we became friends.

Mutual trouble. That is us and look at us now! Nine years later, and we are just as close. Sheila Mason patted me on the shoulders in a friendly hello. "Well my goodness you're all grown up. How have you been?" "Very well. I just started here a few days ago."

"One would never guess. You look like a natural. How's your mama, and daddy doing? Still managing Starlights?" "I don't think they'll ever quit. Mom likes it just a little too much. You should come by and get a sandwich soon."

Sheila nodded. "I surely will. I haven't been there for years, I guess. I'm always too busy. You must know how that is." I glanced over my teachers shoulders to find more, and more customers had entered the store. All of them seemed intent, and on a mission. No nonsense attitude, and all business like.

Sheila followed my gaze. "Oh, forgive me dear. You have customers. It's nice seeing you. I'll be on my way and let you get back to work. I'm so proud you're being so responsible having a job, and all. I hope to see you again soon." "I do too. I'm sorry if I seem rude, but it's an absolute mad house in here. It's so nice to see you too." I smiled at her, and she again patted my shoulder, and wondered off.

Left alone for a few seconds, I smiled. I rarely think about my elementary school days, but I remembered Carla did kiss the boy she giggled about. She told me all about it during our very first sleepover. It was at her house, and we were nine years old. I'm so happy my parents told me yes when I asked them. I packed my snoopy suitcase full of snacks, and a pair of shorts to sleep in. Then I walked over there all by myself.

It's still broad daylight when we were supposed to be tucked in bed, she whispered about that first kiss. I didn't even realize it until just now, I'd never had a first kiss. It might have been because neither Bessie, nor me could date just yet. Bessie also confessed to having a kiss back when she is eleven.

The Way Life Used To Be

I had to promise to never tell, and so far, I have kept my promise. I just want something too. Something I will never forget. I realized just then I am daydreaming again and turned towards the soups to finish arranging cans. I came face to face with a man who looked to be in his twenties. He seemed familiar, but no name came
to my mind. He is not smiling, and clean shaven.

He is tall, close to six feet with long scraggly blond hair that looked desperately in need of cutting. His blue jeans are torn in the knees, and thighs, and his shoes had holes in both heels. He looked homeless, and like a bum.

I smiled a quick, and polite hello, and turned towards the cans still spread on the floor. He walked past me. I got an instant uneasy feeling in the back of my neck. My heart started beating fast, and I resisted the urge to turn around. If I just appeared busy, he would leave.

Thankfully another customer approached me. She is a young woman with a long French braid and asked me where the spaghetti jars were located. I jumped up pleased with the interruption, and again I avoided looking behind me. I am convinced he is still staring.

Once the customer had located the sauce, she said, thank you, and disappeared down another aisle. When I returned to the cans, he was gone. Thank God. I finished putting the cans back on the shelf straight and looking nice. Once the clock struck the noon hour, I headed towards the back office to clock out, and sat down ten minutes later to a salad, and a tall glass of ice-water.

It felt so good to get off my feet as I sipped water and ate. I glimpsed the river from outside a window and smiled. It's time for another swim. The employee's door opened, and Sara entered carrying a sandwich and a Coke. "Hey there. How's it going?" She asked. "Not too bad, but it's so busy out there." Should I tell her about the strange looking man? Sara knew about such things and could ease my mind.

"It's always like that about this time. I swear anybody, and everybody can only shop at noon." "That is believable, since this is the first time I have sat down all morning," I explained seeing the look on Sara's face. "I love it here and appreciate Mr. Hankins giving me this chance. I don't want to blow it."

"I don't doubt that. You seem like a hard worker. I love this time of day. Only time I have for myself." So, she understands. I stuck a carrot on the fork and ate it. "I want to make a good impression. Hopefully with some time. I will be a cashier like you."

"That would be nice. Sometimes, in the afternoons it gets so busy I'd like to tell the impatient customers to just leave and come back later. Most of them think nothing of being short, and disrespectful. Then they think out loud, and tell you how slow you are, and that they have better things to do than stand there wasting time." Sara said, taking a bite of her sandwich.

"You ever say anything?" "No, we are supposed to apologize for the long lines, and everything, but even that isn't enough sometimes. Mr. Hankins understands. I had one customer who is an elderly lady, and very impatient. She kept tapping her fingers on the counter slowly. She only had three things, but I can't remember what they were. Anyway..." Sara waved a hand. "She spoke up, and said, could I be any slower?" I looked up from scanning her things, and said, "As a matter of fact I could, but she took it the wrong way." I laughed, and Sara continued. "She stamped one foot, and said, how dare I be so rude. My face got red, and I didn't say another word. I was hoping she would just leave, and if she ever came back, she wouldn't go through my line again."

"She demanded to speak to the supervisor in charge, is how she put it. Mr. Hankins is standing right next to her. I tell you my heart leaped to my face, and I am sure my customer service job is about to come to a screeching halt. Mr. Hankins raised his hand, and said, I'm the owner. She started yelling at him about how dare he hire such incompetent employees and tried to shove a hand on my chest. I stepped back and slapped her hand away at the same time."

"Mr. Hankins got red with anger and whispered. Leave my store now and never come back. You are mother fucking lucky if I don't file charges for assault. He turned away from her, and towards me. He smiled and told me to attend to my next customer. It's your brother Mark, and he started laughing. He heard the whole thing. That is the best day."

"Kicking her out or seeing Mark?" I teased, and Sara blushed. "Both I guess. I don't know if you're aware, but high school hasn't been a bed of roses. I thought I would be one of the popular ones that everyone is jealous of and envied. That hasn't happened, and I will be a senior this year. I can't wait to be done and forget all about high school. It sucks."

"Kicking that bitch out of the store is a brief highlight of my life, and one I will never forget. Mark's another story. Is he seeing anybody?" She held her breath. I studied the look on her face. She is so pretty with

The Way Life Used To Be

her dark blond hair that hung just below her shoulder blades. She doesn't have any curl to it. It's silky, and straight. She has deep brown eyes. I could not figure out why boys are not all over her, but the more I talked to her I realized she has a lot more confidence, and heart than people gave her credit for.

I shook my head. "Mark has always been the popular one. I guess I have lots of friends too, but he wants only you. He has a soft spot where you're concerned. If I were you, I would act on that subtle, but deliberate comment." I smiled at her as I ate a tomato. I finished my salad, and grabbed the plastic fork from the table, along with my empty water bottle, and dumped everything in the trash.

"I will think about it. I have had a crush on him for too long now not to. Now I have to get back to the grind. Let me know if you need anything." She smiled and waved goodbye. The clock struck twelve thirty, and I got back to my aching feet, none too eager to get back to work. It felt too good to sit and enjoy myself. I also remembered the feeling from earlier.

It's just nerves or something, but I never want to see him again. Somehow, I just knew he wasn't there to shop. I didn't see him again when I reentered the store and started on the frozen vegetables. The truck had just arrived five minutes ago, so the bags needed to be placed in the freezer bins right away. The crowd from an hour earlier was gone, and the store was almost empty.

I breathed easier now, and it's almost four when I realized how quickly the afternoon gone by. Only two more hours, and I will be off. I convinced myself during lunch when I was talking with Sara. that it's just nerves, and I am overreacting. I am in the far north aisle which is hardly used because there were boxes of spare items stored against the wall, and any only a few customers wondered around in that area.

I put some cans of tuna on the shelf, and reached down for another box for the macaroni, and cheese. It's close to four thirty by now, and I'm feeling normal again. I looked up when someone reached for a bag of frozen peas in the freezer bin across from where I was squatting. I stood up thinking I'm in the way and came eye to eye with him again.

His smile grew, and his eyes bore into mine. Instead of being flattered, I wanted to bolt. I opened my mouth to yell to Mr. Hankins and found I couldn't speak. I whipped my head around and found we are the only two people in the area. The front registers are completely gone from my view.

Sandra Gutierrez

This is absurd. Why would someone wait four hours for nothing? Or maybe he left and came back. Something told me in the back of my mind that he had stayed this whole time, and the focus was on me. I thought of just a few days ago when Bessie, and I were making dinner, and how simple everything seemed. I wanted nothing more than to return to the comfort of our house.

"Someone help", I yelled to myself. I could hear the words wanting to come out, but my mouth flapped. How am I going to get out of this? I started sweating, and he licked his lips. My hands were still shaking along with everything else. I could feel the panic rise from my stomach to my chest and keep rising.

I am surprised to find I was still standing. If I could stand, I could run, but my legs would not move. I'm frozen! "Mark!" I yelled again in my head. I need you now. I could not see the clock, but I wish he would come before six, and save me.

I turned my head back towards the dry good section and found it empty. No customers browsed by the frozen area, and I prayed with all my might that some good willed stranger would find the need to mosey back here.

I'm in the last aisle closest to the north wall, and just a few steps over, and to the right I would have been outside. He is on the other side of the bins and blocked my exit. If I made a run for it, he would beat me. He is still a good two feet away from me, but he is inching closer. He smiled showing two very crooked front teeth, and that look bore down on me with a vengeance.

While I'm thinking this, Mark is glancing at the clock in the restaurant, and found it was only five fifteen. he is so looking forward to picking up Reesa so he could see Sara. They spent the last three hours last night talking on the phone and talking about nothing. They are enjoying getting to know each other better.

Zeni interrupted his thoughts. "Order up." "Coming Ma." He reached across the counter, and grabbed two plates full of meatball subs, and potato salad. He carried the plates, and two glasses of lemonade to a small table near the window. He greeted the couple who were waiting for their dinner.

It's early for eating, but neither of them had lunch and were starving by this time. "Here's your meal Mr., and Mrs. Oakes" he greeted. Gerald Oakes glanced up and recognized Mark from school last year. His son

The Way Life Used To Be

Gregory is a year ahead, but both played junior varsity football last year before Greg dropped out.

After that Greg moved out saying it is time he got out on his own. He claimed to have a good job to support himself. He didn't say where or what he is doing. They have not heard from him in close to two months, and it seemed like he is gone from their lives.

They were sad, but relieved, Greg is not the easiest teenager to handle, so they are relived at his absence. They also felt bad that he robbed a store. As much as they love him, they would turn him in, in a heartbeat if they ever saw him again. It would be for the better.

Mark knew all this and refrained from mentioning it. They look a lot happier than a few weeks before even though their smiles don't quite reach their eyes. "Thank you, Mark." Lisa Oakes greeted. She is a plump woman who has short brown frizzy hair, and a big smile.

"Your welcome. It's good to see both of you. I hope you enjoy your meal." he smiled a goodbye and turned to the next table to clear the dishes. He started thinking about Greg as he stacked the plates, and glasses in a plastic bin.

He is tall for his age and very shy. At least that is what it looked like to his classmates. He had a few friends, but mostly kept to himself. Never hung out with anyone after school, either. Mark could not imagine just leaving home like he did and not saying boo to your parents for months. he cares about his family way too much for that. he tried to understand feeling like there is no other option than to force someone to give you money. There had to be an explanation for it.

At five thirty Zeni stuck her head out of the kitchen. "Mark?" "Yeah, Ma", he finished cleaning up the silverware, and headed towards the kitchen, and folding doors to the prep area. Zeni is at the counter stirring minestrone soup. "Hi. I forgot you are cooking tonight. We need some green onions for the stew."

"Oh, thanks, I'll get some when I pick up Reesa." "Can you go now?" Zeni stopped stirring to put together a turkey, and sprout sandwich. "It's dead here, and the stew needs to simmer for a few hours." Mark tore off his apron with a huge smile. "You don't have to ask me twice." This meant he could see Sara for a little while. "I will go now,", Zeni laughed. "I guess you have your priorities."

Mark left by the back door in the kitchen and ran the three blocks to the store where the front doors are wide open, and he saw only three customers in the aisles. It's dead here too. He grabbed three onions from the produce section and didn't see Reesa anywhere. Mark assumed she is still hard at work, and sure seems to love it here.

He strolled through Sara's line. She is waiting with a wide smile on her face. "Hey you," he greeted. "How are you? It has been quiet here for a while now. You should have been here at noon. It was wall to wall for almost an hour." She is happy to see Mark. Happy to have a break even if it's only for a few minutes.

She is thinking about their talk last night, and with Reesa earlier. It didn't occur to ask if he already has someone special. In three hours of talking about everything under the sun, that subject never came up. She also thought about Reesa's comment, and as much as she wanted to, now is not the time to ask.

Mark paid for the onions. "Oh yeah? It's busy at Starlights too. At least the lunch crowd seemed to be. Ma sent me here early to get the stuff for the stew I will make as soon as I get home." "Your cooking for your family?" She is already impressed.

"Yep, we all take turns. Now that Reesa is working, we have to work a little harder, and pitch in more. I have to admit we have become used to her handling the dinner portion for us." They continued chatting for a while. He glanced up at the clock several minutes later and realized it's almost six. Reesa would get off shortly, and it didn't make much sense to go all the way home just to come back in an hour.

He said goodbye with a smile, and a promised to call her that evening, and left in search of Reesa still smiling. She is not in any of the aisles putting away food. He even knocked on the employee's lounge door, but she is not there either. Maybe she got off early and decided to just walk home alone.

It ended when Mark rounded a corner and found me on the floor. I have my hands tied behind my back, and there is a man kneeling almost in front of me but facing away from Mark. Mark can see I'm trapped. My eyes are dry, and full of terror as Mark realized the man has a knife to my throat.

I turned my head at the movement to my left, and I realized Mark is standing right there. His eyes had turned from their brilliant green to nothing, but red-hot anger. The man beside me had no clue as his attention is so focused on me. His eyes got wide, and he screamed out loud as Mark grabbed the back of his hair with one hand and pulled him up. The knife had fallen to the floor, and skid under a shelf.

The Way Life Used To Be

"What the fuck?" He yelled as he scrambled to his feet and turned around as best he could. Mark still had his hand fisted in that knotted hair. He realized we were not alone any longer, and he has no way out of this. Mark is standing there with his feet planted wide apart.

Mark plowed his free fist between his eyes knocking him to the floor. I had scooted further to the right avoiding his weight. My hands were still tied behind me, and I looked right at my brother unable to say anything even though I'm still screaming inside.

"Rees?" Mark whispered. The anger is gone just like that. His eyes were now tearing up. "What happened?" He asked while rubbing my cheek. He tore off the rope that is binding my hands, but I can't move them even though they are now free. He slipped them to my sides.

I'm frozen with fear and can't talk. I can't do anything but continue to lie there. My mouth is wide opened, but no sound emerged. I started shaking, but my arms stayed still. Why the hell couldn't I move? He paralyzed me. That would be why I can't talk.

Mark turned my hands over and found burn marks on my wrists from feeble attempts to free them. "Rees?" he said, again. No response, oh hell. I'm in shock, my eyes turned to glaze right before him, and I closed them falling limp in his lap. It turned black for me, and I welcomed it.

He lifted me up in his arms like I weighed no more than a feather. Mark ran out the front doors oblivious to the questions the customers, and employees were yelling at him. He didn't stop until he reached his car in the parking lot and placed me in the back seat.

Mark jumped in the driver's seat, and tore up the hill towards downtown, and to the hospital. He didn't even notice he forgot his onions which had fallen to the floor near Greg Oakes, who is still passed out cold. Mark reached the hospital in five minutes flat speeding the entire way. Tears ran down his cheeks, and onto his blue shirt which bore huge wet spots on either side of his chest. He didn't bother wiping them away.

He didn't realize he ran every light, and it's a miracle he didn't hit anyone. All he could think of is getting Reesa to the hospital before it's too late. He can't think straight. Can't remember where the emergency room is and honked his horn at one entrance. He is greeted by four paramedics who rushed to his aid with a
stretcher.

Sandra Gutierrez

"What happened?" One of them asked as he reached into the backseat to take my vitals. I lay in the seat. My eyes are still dry, and vacant. The paramedic opened them gently to shine a small light at my pupils. I felt like I'm spinning out of control and heading down a dark well. I can't seem to crawl out of the dark, no matter how hard I'm trying to climb.

"She is not responding." The young man said, and two of them reached inside to lift me up, and onto the stretcher as quickly as they could. "What's her name? Are you kin?" He asked to Mark who looked almost as frozen as the young lady on the stretcher. His eyes are full of tears, and he looks as if he cares a great deal about her.

Mark answered, drying his face with the back of one hand. "Her name is Teresa, I'm her older brother. Can you help her?" He asked. They told him to wait nearby until the situation is under control. "Pupils dilated heart rate is way too high and irregular for someone of her age. Let's get her into emergency now, she's in shock!"

They headed towards the emergency entrance. The two paramedics disappeared from Mark's view as they forced him to stay behind to answer some questions. I felt myself moving, and tried in vain to focus, but my eyelids kept fluttering. I sank back into my hole. It made them feel better that I'm trying to respond.

The oldest paramedic who is balding, and short led Mark into the reception area, and asked him to fill out the paperwork. "You over eighteen?" Mark shook his head, "No Sir, seventeen. I'm her older brother, I'm the one who found her." He calmed down only as he faced the paramedic who had remained behind. The one who asked the initial questions had remained inside.

"Can you call your parents?" "Yes Sir. right away." He hurried to a payphone not believing he didn't think of that himself. Reesa must not be the only one in shock. He dialed with shaky fingers, and Zeni answered the phone. "Starlights. Can I help you?"

Oh, dear god. How could he tell them what happened? After all the excitement Reesa had shown at her first job, he had to be the one to squash her dream. He cleared his throat, and said, in the shakiest voice he had. "Ma, It's Mark."

Zeni interrupted, "Hi Honey. have you started dinner already?" She had no clue what happened in the last hour and sounds so happy. "No, I have not ma. I don't know how to tell you this, but Reesa..." He could

The Way Life Used To Be

not go on. Fresh tears started falling, and he tried to clear his throat again, but couldn't. He just stood there holding the phone.

"Reesa what?" Zeni demanded. "Where is she?" "She is in the hospital Ma. I need you..." She shouted, "Hospital? Which one?" "General Mercy," Mark answered, and Zeni flung off her apron shouting. "Keith, we need to go now!" She hung up the phone without a goodbye.

That may have been humorous in normal circumstances, but this is no norm. She still has no clue what happened, but it doesn't matter. Her baby needs her. She slapped the dishrag she was using on the counter with more force that was needed, but she didn't care. She grabbed her car keys out of her purse.

Keith is at the stove taking out a meatball sub. "Zeni, what is the shouting for? Who's at the hospital?" He too doesn't understand what just happened and assumed it's a stranger who has horrible news. Zeni is already reaching for the door. "Reesa, something happened, and we need to go now." She is shaking, and Keith grabbed the keys out of her hand. Her voice is not its usual sunny, and upbeat one. She is breathing so fast and wants to cry before she even knew what happened, it's bad.

That much she knows without asking. "I will be driving," he whispered, though he feels like yelling or punching someone. Keith still doesn't understand what happened to their daughter. He left hasty instructions to their wait staff Peter, and Lisa Higgins who has been working there for several years now. They said, they will be happy to mind the store.

Keith ran out of the restaurant, and jumped into their red Ford Taurus, and he broke the same speed limits that Mark did half an hour ago. They reached the hospital, jumped out of the car, and ran inside without bothering to lock the car first.

"Mark?" They shouted together as they ran inside the automatic doors and found him in the waiting area. He had his head between his hands and is still crying. He shot his head up at the sound of their voices, and they plopped into empty seats beside him.

"Ma, dad, thanks for coming." He had calmed down somewhat during the ten minutes since phoning them. "Reesa's in the emergency room." He glanced at his hands realizing for the first time there is blood on them. "She was attacked at work today."

Zeni again interrupted, "Attacked? By whom? What the hell is going on?" She fired one question after another. She began crying before she even knew the answer. "Where's my baby?" She whispered. She drew her hands in front of her face, covering her mouth. The words came out muffled.

"Ma. Please listen." Zeni nodded and shut her mouth determined to hear him through. "When you asked me to pick up the onions, I was happy to do it because I got to talk to Sara. You remember her? She is the girl I was talking to last night?" Zeni nodded.

"When I got there, she was at her register. We said, hello, and started talking for a few minutes when I realized how late it's getting, and I decided to just stick around, and wait for Reesa to get off instead of going straight home." He stopped talking long enough to take a drink of the water that one of the nurse aides handed him when she told him to wait.

"Anyway. I was looking for Reesa, and by the time I found her, she was on the floor with her hand's tied, and she looked so terrified. I didn't even think. Remember Greg Oakes?" They nodded realized he had made a return visit.

"He is the one who attacked her. Greg had a knife to her throat, and I don't know or even want to know what would have happened if I had not shown up. I reacted first and grabbed him by the hair and punched him out cold. I didn't even call 911 or answer any of the questions the customers, and coworkers were asking me."

"I just grabbed her, and drove as fast as I could get here, and then called you." Mark realized at that moment he didn't know if Greg is still alive. He might have killed him when he hit him. Keith didn't feel bad about it. Greg deserved it. he deserves anything that happened to him now.

"I was just talking with his parents at lunch. I asked how they were doing, and it didn't occur to me until now, it was their son who did this. I don't want to be the one to tell them." Keith then spoke up with a voice not his own. "Is she hurt?" "I'm not sure. I picked her up and ran towards the car. She is not responding to me yelling, and..."

"It's okay." Keith could not hear any more. "And about Greg's parents. I sat with them after you left and brought them coffee. We talked for a few minutes about the weather, and other chitchat. I never asked how they were doing either. It didn't even occur to me to ask. I just gave them a smile when I left the table and went on about my day."

"Mr., and Mrs. Harris?" They were interrupted by a short forty-year-old man with brown hair. He was dressed in a dark blue smock, and

The Way Life Used To Be

a white coat. He is looking very serious. "Yes?" They stood up together on shaky legs but determined to find out the truth.

"I'm Dr. Gustafson." He shook both of their hands. "They have assigned me as your daughter's main physician. I'm sorry for what happened, but she is doing fine." Zeni, and Keith were both so relieved to hear him say that they sighed and waited for him to continue. "From what I understand she was attacked earlier today?"

Mark had stood up by then, and stood next to his mother, draping an arm over her shoulders. He is also feeling a little better. "I'm Mark, her brother. I'm the one who found her, is she okay?" he asked.

"Mostly, she is stable, and has a stab wound on her left shoulder. It wasn't life threatening, but she required 18 stitches. She will be in pain for quite some time. I will need you to fill out some paperwork, but that can wait." "A stab wound?" Zeni whispered and started crying all over again. "He hurt my little girl?"

Gary Gustafson nodded, "I'm afraid so. It has already been bandaged up, and hopefully it will not leave a scar. If it does, it will be minimal. She has been asking for both of you." He nodded at Keith than at Zeni. "Follow me."

He gestured, and led them upstairs, and down two corridors before they entered the recovery area. I lay on a bed covered up to my chin, and I had my eyes closed. There was not any pain yet. Even with the stitches, I felt nothing, but numbness. That might have been a good thing. I remember every second what happened. No temporary amnesia to ease any of the trauma or pain.

I also remembered to keep my eyes opened so I would remember every detail of the man who had hurt me. Opened to see my savior, Mark. I never realized until that moment just how much my brother loves me. True, he shows it in endless ways, but to see the way he grabbed at that guy and heaved him back like he is only a rock that had to be demolished. The look in his eyes will stay with me forever. The way they turned red in an instant.

I also realized any career as a cashier would be even more short lived than I had ever imagined. Never in my wildest dreams did I think this would happen. Even after the warnings, I didn't believe it. Why me? What the hell did I do that would provoke such a violent attack?

A movement to my left started my heart beating again, and I breathed with relief seeing my parents, and Mark standing by the open doorway. They approached my bed. My eyes are still dry when dad kissed my cheek, and when Mark held my hand rubbing softly.

Mom leaned over to smooth my hair back from my forehead, and the second I felt her soft touch, I started crying. Cried like I never had before. Mom wrapped her arms around me and buried her face in my hair as I joined her tears. She can't speak. All she can handle is holding her baby girl and comforting her.

"My baby." She whispered unable to say anything else. "Mom," I choked, and lifted my good arm to hold her. It feels so good to be loved. "We came as soon as we heard. Are you okay?" She glanced at the bandage but can't see anything. She has a slight smile I know is for my benefit. She can't hide the look in her eyes. She is scared for me. Even more than I am, and it hurts my heart to see her like that.

I nodded my head. It's all I can manage. I took a deep breath and continued. "I think I got a shot and had some stitches. It doesn't hurt right now. The doctor said, it will hurt a lot once the stuff they gave me wears off. I can't remember what it's called."

"Don't worry about it. We will stay right here for as long as you need us." Zeni waved a hand in dismissal. She sat by my side until my eyes started closing. I'm falling asleep again. Mom smoothed my hair back, and I kept a small smile on my lips. Yes. It feels so good to be loved.

After a while she lifted her face, streaked with tears as she kissed my forehead. "Baby, we have to go now. I'm so sorry you got hurt, and we'll do everything possible to make sure it doesn't happen again. You need to rest, and we'll be here first thing in the morning to come and take you home."

She touched the bandage and turned away so I would not see the worry in her eyes. Too late. I saw the anger, hurt, and sorrow all at once. It's the same as I was feeling. I'm no longer tired. "Can you stay here with me tonight?" I asked in a voice that is not mine.

Zeni glanced at the doctor who remained in the doorway to give the family a little privacy. "Teresa. I'm sorry, but it's almost past visiting hours. We have a uniformed guard outside to keep watch till morning just as a precaution. Your injury is not life threatening. However, due to your injury, the shock you were in, plus you are still too pale for me to release you tonight, I want to keep you here overnight, but the rest of your family will have to leave soon. Visiting hours end in half an hour."

The Way Life Used To Be

He smiled to take the sting out of his words. "If all goes well, I don't see any reason you can't be released first thing in the morning." It's heart wrenching to see the disappointment on my face. Mom patted my arm. I want to be rude, and snatch it away, but don't want to hurt her any more than she already is. "Honey, you will be fine. The guard will make sure nothing happens. Dad, and I will be here first thing to take you home."

I watched mom, dad, and Mark leave. Once the room is silent again, I wanted them back. The silence is too much. What if that man came back? What if I am worse off than the doctor said? What if…? I can't think anymore.

I glanced out at the single curtain less window and saw the night approach. The sun went down, and the full moon glared back. There are so many stars. It's almost pretty. If I was in my own house, it would have been. We would have a barbeque with dad's famous hamburgers, and Mom's homemade potato salad. It made my mouth water, and hunger for my house in a way I never had before. I never missed anything before.

Just thinking of food brought a night nurse to the doorway. "Are you up for some dinner?" She asked smiling at me. Her name tag said, Sheila, and she is plump, and cute with frizzled brown hair. She moved further into my room. I nodded. "A little."

"Here. Let me set up your tray." The nurse offered with a polite smile. She left a few minutes later, and I'm once again left in silence. The aroma from the tray started filling up my nostrils. I lifted the cover to find meatloaf, mashed potatoes, gravy, and some French style green beans. It's no barbeque by any stretch of the imagination, but it still looks edible. I took a bite of the meatloaf. Swallowing, I drank ice-water to wash down the food. It's not half bad as I took another bite.

Once the food is gone, I left the tray on the nightstand to get ready for bed. There is a cotton hospital gown on a hanger that looks just is it seems. Stark, and clean, but not my own. I pulled up the thin blanket and willed myself to settle down. It's cold, and lonely, and I hate being there. So much I cried all over again. Huge tears slid down my cheeks as I lay on my side with one arm folded above my head, and tissues in the other.

Take me home. I closed my eyes and fell into a fitful sleep. I woke up a dozen times all before nine o'clock at night. I am usually settling down with a movie in my room by this time of day. Back at home, Zeni, and Keith entered the house arm in arm, and found Bessie at the foot of the stairs, wearing a hurt expression, and had her arms crossed in front of her chest.

She glared at them, they forgot about her. She had been home for hours by herself, and it's getting so late. It didn't even occur to any of them to call her and explain. "Where in blazes have you been. Dinner's been ready for hours. At least it's ready." She accused crossing her arms. The front door is wide open, and they can smell the food. It reminds all of them about the stew.

"Bessie come here. We need to talk to you." They each put an arm around their younger daughter and led her into the living room to explain. Bessie started crying once she heard. "I just knew something would happen. I tried to warn her, but..." She dropped her arms and held them out for her mother.

Zeni interrupted. "We all did; however, nobody could have predicted this. We thought the robbery was over and done with." She hugged Bessie close and kissed her forehead. "Greg will never be free again." Mark piped up. "The police will take over from here."

"That is right." Keith pointed a finger at Mark. "That bastard will never walk the streets again." He is still so angry, but the anger is now directed at the person responsible for all this. He intends to do everything, and anything possible to make sure of that.

"You sure?" Bessie asked. "Positive. This is the third strike. That means automatic ten to life. I'm hoping for life, and then some." "Third?" "That is right. Two years ago, when he dropped out of school there was a break in at the school. He took a computer, and a register from the office. Not much is done as they chalked it up to immaturity, and all. I don't think he even had to pay for anything. After the robbery at Hankins, now this."

"I bet this doesn't get chocked up to anything, but assault at the very least." Bessie stated. "I bet too." Zeni whispered. She sighed and smacked her hands on her knees. "Well enough wallowing. Anybody hungry?" She is determined to be strong. They will get through this like they do everything. Together, and as one.

"A little." Bessie mumbled. "I could make sandwiches. I made cheeseburgers earlier, but then threw them out. They were burned anyway." She shrugged her shoulders. "Nah, we have enough sandwiches at Starlights. Let's go out for once." Keith offered.

The Way Life Used To Be

"No, Let's order a pizza, and have a family movie." Zeni stated and pushed herself out of her favorite peach rocker to grab the phone book. "I just feel like staying home." "Sounds great." Keith feigned happiness and got out the phone book for her.

Thirty minutes later they settled down in the living room with only one floor lamp for light. The four of them snuggled together on the couch with Bessie's head in her father's lap. He stroked the brown curls and had the most difficulty eating just one slice.

He forced it down with a Coke and put the rest of the pizza on the floor. It was only half gone with each of them not in the least bit hungry, and thinking about nothing, but Reesa all alone in the hospital. They all went to bed getting very little sleep.

Early the next morning, past seven, Keith and Zeni drove alone to pick me up to take me home. I was sitting up in bed with a big smile on my face, and sadness in my eyes. "I'm ready." I announced. "Not yet." A male voice sounded from the doorway.

It's a police officer who had arrived to take a statement. He looks about thirty, and on the short side. Barely five foot eight. He has short jet-black hair, and clean shaven. He wore a smile to cover the tension that filled the room. Keith towered over him.

"I'm glad you're awake. You must be in a lot of pain. I need to write your version of the events from yesterday. Do you want to wait awhile or get it over with? I can meet you at your house if that would make you more comfortable?"

I shook my head. "No, I want to get it done now." I hope I look determined. "What do you want to know? I remember a lot." Mom looked at me to stop me. This time I interrupted. "No, it's okay." Keith asked. "How did all this happen? I figured along with a lot of other people that he is long gone by now."

"Nobody can answer that except Gregory. I would trust nothing he said, Teresa, are you ready?" "Yes. I will tell you everything. I sighed and began a half hour monologue with Ted writing everything verbatim. He didn't interrupt. Nobody did. This time my eyes remained dry. Only Zeni can see how it is the night before. There is hiding nothing from her, much as I want to sometimes.

When I finished, he lay a hand on my good shoulder, and squeezed gently. "Thank you. I'm very proud of you. Mr., and Mrs. Harris, you have a very brave daughter." He stood up to shake both their hands. "Call us Keith and Zeni." Keith offered. He has a good feeling about this man. "Thank you for making this as easy as possible. If it was up to me, that bastard would be lying six feet under by now."

"Perfectly understandable. I wouldn't blame you in the least, but..." Ted smiled. Keith interrupted. "You don't have to say it. I know what I'm supposed to do. It just breaks my heart that one of my children got hurt."

"You sound like a good man, and father. Let that carry you through this. There are some good counselors I can connect you with if you're interested." Keith nodded saying nothing further. "Now that is my advice for the day, and I have got to get going." He waved a quick goodbye, and Dr. Gustafson came into the room just as he is leaving.

"You look much better this morning. Let's do a quick exam, and then you can go home." He said, with a smile. He did a quick checkup, and it's just shy of nine when he gave the okay to get discharged. I have the bandage still on my shoulder, and you can't see any of the stitches. He gave strict instructions to keep the area dry for the next three days and make a return visit when he would cut the stitches.

I opted to walk out of the hospital. Wheelchairs were for invalids. Once the hot sunshine hit my face, I closed my eyes, and smiled up at the sky. "Now this feels better." Mom gave me a quick squeeze trying to smile for my benefit. "Sure does. You ready to go home or is there any place special you would like to go?" I thought of somewhere to go, but nothing came to mind. "Home, I can't wait to sleep in my own bed."

We got in the car, and dad drove slowly having a hard time keeping his eyes on the road, and not on me. I am sitting in the back seat too straight to be comfortable. We reached the house to find both Bessie, and Mark on the front steps waiting for us.

"Reesa?" Bessie asked hesitantly as I exited the car. "You okay?" I smiled. "I'm fine Bess," as I'm favoring my shoulder, and even though it's covered, I looked up to find Bessie's gaze had focused on that spot. She has a question in her eyes.

"Here, let me help you." Bessie rushed forward to take my arm. "Are you okay?" She repeated. "Thanks. I guess I'm still a little shaky." Bessie walked with me up to my room and settled me on the bed. She rushed the other side.

"I'm sorry" she whispered, not knowing what else to say. "Don't be, it's my fault. I should have known something is wrong, and I said, nothing, I just froze. I was so scared inside, but I could not say a word.

The Way Life Used To Be

I still remember the feeling of being paralyzed. I doubt it would ever go away. I don't even want to think about it."

"And you don't have to now. We will just sit awhile, and it's not your fault. Don't say that again." "What is this? I'm supposed to be the older sister, and here you are taking care of me." I attempted a half smile. "This is me taking care of you. Want to watch TV?" "Sure."

We lay on the bed with pillows stacked behind us and watched a movie not paying the least bit of attention. We love it anyway. As much as we can love anything under these circumstances. We even ate dinner in bed. Something our parents never allowed, but we did it, anyway. My appetite is still not very big, and I only at half the burger, and didn't touch the fries. Bessie carried our plates downstairs and rushed right back up.

When she settled herself back on my bed, she exhaled. "Remember just a short time ago how our lives were so simple. Very few complications." "I do, and I wish it were that way again." I agreed, "So do I. I want to look back someday and say this happened for a reason. I might feel better if that were the case." Bessie nodded at her statement, and we continued watching the movie.

When the sun lowered, and my eyes could no longer stay open, Bessie helped me undress, and tucked me into bed. While I slept, Bessie sat in the rocker watching over me. I woke up screaming in the middle of the night. Bessie is there to hold me in her arms. We both cried. Bessie didn't know it, but she is my first counselor. she talked me through the nightmare and held my hand the rest of the night.

Chapter 4

Two weeks later, I got the stitches removed. It didn't hurt at all. Dad took me to get an ice cream cone afterwards just like he did when we were kids and had to have shots. If we were good, and didn't cry, we got a double scoop. If one tear fell, the scoop is diminished to one.

That is until we reached the parlor, and dad melted each time giving both himself, and the child whose arms were stuck double scoops. It didn't matter in the end, if we cried. He is naïve enough to believe we didn't know any better.

"Feel okay?" He asked as he took a lick of his chocolate chunk ice cream. "Yep, I love this part of getting hurt. Ice cream takes away all your troubles." I took a lick around the lemon sherbet. "Mom found a counselor for you." I shook my head. "Only if you want. She comes highly recommended from the hospital, but only if you're ready."

"Dad, I don't want to talk to a stranger." Keith took a bite of his cone. "How about a friend then? We can find someone who knows you. Through the school if that would be easier." "I will think about it." I lied and finished the ice cream. "Want me to pay? I got my first and only paycheck." Keith reached for his own wallet. "No way. This has always been and will always be my treat. Let's go cash your check, and you can have some fun." I waved my check in front of him and made him smile.

I stopped at Hankins the day before to say goodbye to Mr. Hankins and thank him for letting me work there. It's sad, but I will never work in that store ever again. It would never be the same after this. I avoided the frozen food section, heading straight to his office instead.

Once I got my check, I gave him a friendly hug. I also hugged two of the cashiers who are manning the registers. One of them was Sara. "Reesa, I'm so sorry. I didn't even know that piece of shit was in the

The Way Life Used To Be

store." I laughed. That is all I could manage. "I didn't either. Not until it was too late. Now the piece of shit awaits trial." "I hope the piece of shit rots in hell."

"I heard Mark is the one who found you. Is he here with you?" She asked bringing her hands to her face and squeezed her cheeks. The light came into my eyes. "No, Sorry, but I came alone. I wanted to say goodbye and thank all of you for helping me. Mr. Hankins gave me my only check. I hope the piece of shit dies." I'm sure I sound grim, but under the circumstances, one can't blame me.

"You sure you will not give it another chance? A lot of my regular customers were talking about you, and how helpful you are. I would sure like it if you came back." "It wouldn't be a good idea. I will come back often to shop though. That is all I can do for now."

Sara hugged me long, and hard. "I understand, I do. Make sure when you shop, you make it a point to say hello to me. I would like to keep in touch with you." And Mark she didn't say, but the look is in her eyes. I can tell.

I said, goodbye. If I don't get out of there soon, the tears would start again. I'd cried enough to last a lifetime. "Ready daddy?" I asked finishing my cone and throwing a napkin in the trash. "You bet," he stepped down too, and we left to cash my check.

It's two hours later when we drove home, laden with bags. Only the sound of the radio kept us company. Both of us are far too exhausted for much else. I lay my head against the headrest and closed my eyes. I am enjoying the music. "Reesa?" Zeni called from the kitchen when she heard the front door open. "Keith. You guys just get home?"

"It's us mama, come see what I bought." I dangled the bags as I met her in the middle of the foyer. Zeni clapped her hands. "Well open up." She pointed to a bag and walked back into the kitchen. I followed her. We sat at the kitchen table while mom oohed at the new jeans, shirts, and necklace I found. "I'm almost broke, but we had the best time."

"I'm glad, now go put your things away. I need to talk to your father, and before you get that look, it's not a big deal." I already have that look, and I know damn well the subject will be about me. I left anyway, and put the new clothes away while Zeni, and Keith sat together.

"What is wrong?" He asked. "I heard from the prosecutor while you two were gone. I just didn't want to spoil Reesa's day." "What did he want?" "The prosecutor assigned to their case is Samuel Presauret.

He has been with the courts for ten years now, and has the reputation for being a hard ass, and doing everything humanly, and inhumanly possible to win each of his cases. He wanted to let us know the first sentencing will be in two days. At one. This will be a non-guilty plea as all defendants plead not guilty. Then in two weeks, we go to trial. That means Reesa will have to testify." Keith shook his head, "No, she has been through enough. Why can't they just plead it out?"

"Because even though he said, he did it, this is the proper channels. They don't want any chance of him walking the streets again ever. Samuel is going for life even though that is a long shot." Keith stood up to get a root-beer. "Want one?" Zeni nodded, and he returned moments later with two tall glasses full of ice, and brown bubbly liquid.

Zeni took a drink before speaking again. "Samuel said, this first sentencing would only take a few minutes, and we don't have to be there. Only for the trial." "I would rather not be there at all. I guess we will do what we have to. The sooner this is behind us the better."

I stayed in my room sulking. I could hear just a little of their conversation. They told me to stay out of it so I have no choice, but to stay put, and pout. My new clothes are put away, and all my earlier excitement is gone now. I ended up going to bed without a good night to either of them, but they are so wrapped in their so-called important talk, they didn't even notice.

Mom, and dad skipped the first part since it's just a formal plea, and on Monday, we received the summons to appear for the first phase of the trial. The entire process took over a week to select the jury, and when I faced Greg for the first time since the attack, I held back my misgivings, and doubts, and held my head high focusing instead on Samuel.

He didn't even let the defense intimidate me. Both Keith and Zeni had never been so proud as they sat day after day behind the podium lending their support. It took three days to argue their points. The jury is finally dismissed and are instructed to meet tomorrow morning at ten for final arguments.

The judge pounded the gavel and announced to everyone in the gallery we would also adjourn the following morning at ten, and we stood up. We all left the courthouse sober faced and looking more than a little tired. We are however glad the ball is rolling.

"Wow. I never expected this would last so long." Zeni said, as she tossed her hair back from eyes. "Me either. I still think the best way to

The Way Life Used To Be

handle Greg is to bury him." Keith is only half-way joking. He wants that bastard dead.

"I agree. Now enough of all this negativity. Let's go home and enjoy our evening." Once we reached home, I raced up the stairs to change into sweats, and a T-shirt. I'm already tired of wearing skirts. I grabbed a pair of black sweats, and a gray T-shirt, and headed for the shower to wash the grime out of my hair. The courtroom is stuffy, and I for one can't wait for it to be over.

While the water heated, I glanced at my arm, and found the scar just beginning to form. It will not be huge, but it still bothers me. Much more than I let on. The rest of my family didn't hear my heart-beat when I saw Greg for the first time. How he leered at me right under his lawyers' nose and smiled that disgusting smile that made my skin crawl. I wanted to jump over and punch him in the face for what he did.

They didn't see me the night I spent in the hospital all by myself. I kept the lamp on, and looked over, and over at the doorway shut tight. The guard is right outside, but I didn't feel safe, not in the least bit. They didn't see that I still don't sleep at night. The terrible night sweats that soaked my nightgowns. In the mornings I'm the first to do laundry so nobody had a clue.

They only see my silence. The mask I wear to hide my true feelings. I stepped into the shower and feel instant relief at the steaming water that fell. I'm so tired that I could barely keep my eyes opened but forced myself to stay awake. I washed my hair, and the frizz fled under the lavish conditioner.

I stepped out a few minutes later, got dressed, and headed downstairs where my parents are still talking. They stopped when I appeared in the doorway. "Feel better?" Zeni asked smiling. "Why are you talking about me?" I sound defensive but I always hate when any of us are talked about behind our backs. We are never allowed to do it so why should they?

"We were just talking about the trial. Reesa this is not about you. We are discussing the sentencing, and how to handle tomorrows hearing." "I can handle it." I stated firmly and sat down in my chair. I have a firm but determined look on my face. "Want a root-beer too?" Dad asked. I nodded. "Then we will tell you everything." He promised. He had a hard time not smirking at the look on my face.

I thanked him, and they repeated everything, careful not to leave anything out. Neither of them notices this is a repeat from yesterday.

They are even drinking root-beers again. "Reesa we would never leave you out of any important conversations. However, some discussions are private, and need to stay between your Dad, and myself. You need to trust us when we say we know what is best for you, and for this family." Zeni said, refilling her glass.

"I know that mama. I know when to leave my nose out of your business." Zeni smiled. "Good. That is settled then. You hungry?" "I little I guess." I shrugged my shoulders and attempted a smile. "Good. How about some Chinese?" "Sounds yummy."

I offered to go with her to the Chinese Garden who offers the best and freshest meals around. Part of it is I just wanted to get out of the house for a while. The rest is I just loved getting takeout. Arriving home thirty minutes later laden with Lo Mein, fried rice, sweet, and sour pork, and shrimp, and beef, and broccoli, and egg rolls. It looks and smells so good we had a hard time not digging into it in the car.

Tonight, I slept almost through the night. Just when I thought I am making headway, about four in the morning I had my first full blown nightmare. The scene is the same. I am on the floor of the store, and Greg is on top of me. He is naked and stroked my hair while kissing my cheek.

I wanted to throw up each time his lips pressed against my skin. I wanted to crawl away while he whispered how much he loved me, and would fuck me over, and over. He knew deep down how much I loved him back as he undid my blouse button by button until it's completely undone, and off my shoulders. He used the knife to cut through the bra in the center until it popped open, and my breasts were exposed.

I had my arms at my sides so I could have punched him or raked his eyes out with my fingernails, but I did nothing, I kept my arms pressed to me, and squeezed my lips shut. I did nothing. He pressed his lips to my nipples sucking roughly while I finally screamed for him to get the hell off me. I screamed it repeatedly, but nobody heard me. There were customers all around, and nobody paid the least bit of attention.

Men, and women swarmed all around me, laughing at each other, and some stepped right over me not seeing anything. When Mark finally showed up, Greg saw him first and jumped up still naked, and shoved his knife at Mark missing him.

I threw my arms up to Mark to help him and woke up with a start when my hands brushed the blanket that had bunched around my waist. I quickly sat up and listened around the darkened room to see if the

The Way Life Used To Be

screams were real, and when nobody came running, I concluded it's all in my head.

I got out of bed and wondered to the window to look out at the night. It's very dark, even the moon is hidden. Somehow, I know Greg is standing out there waiting. All is quiet though and nobody is there lurking. I even stretched my neck so I could see down both sides of the block. Nothing, but the warm wind, and stars. It reminds me of the hospital, and how I wished I was anyplace, but here.

My house, my bedroom, my safe place. Would any place be safe again? Going downstairs I again have such a sense of Deja vu. Last month right before I started working, I couldn't sleep because I was so nervous. How much simpler life was just a short time ago? I would wake up to go to the river with Carla, and Bessie, and enjoy life again.

The house is silent. I made it to the kitchen and helped myself to a root-beer from the fridge. No Diet Pepsi to quench my thirst, but a root-beer is not a bad second choice. Once the can is empty, I threw it in the recyclable bin, and wandered back upstairs. I contemplated watching a late-night movie until my eyes could not stay open anymore. What if I continue the nightmare? I just want plain sleep. Is that too much to ask for?

It took two hours of trying to fall back to sleep. I nodded off right before the sun rose, and the company of the radio I kept on. I had the volume on low so it wouldn't disturb anyone. I didn't tell anybody about my dream when I dressed for the day in a skirt, and button-down sweater. Today is the deliberation, and I'm anxious for this to all come to an end. It only took an hour though before they had a verdict.

Guilty on all three counts. Assault in the third degree with intent to cause bodily harm. Theft in the third degree as he had a candy bar in his back pocket he never paid for. The last charge is the hardest to prove. The prosecutor used it to his advantage anyway to strengthen their case. Greg's lawyer kept pushing for that charge to be dropped since Greg never left the store. The fact that he had it in his possession, and it was hidden made for a stronger case on the prosecution side.

He is led to his new home and never apologized for his actions. I didn't care. He is gone, and now I could move on with my life. It's a month of hell, but so worth it. Sam Presauret came over to shake Keith and Zeni's hand before we left the chambers. "It's a pleasure representing you. I'm glad it turned out in our favor." He smiled at us.

"I'm glad too. Thank you for all your hard work." Keith complimented as he shook his hand hard. "Let me know if you need any help in the future. You all take care now." We came home with all of us in a much calmer mood than this morning or even for the last month. Greg is gone, and now I can look forward to the future.

Once I entered the house, I noticed the message button on the machine blinking. Three missed calls while we were in court. The first is Aunt Sylvia on mom's side. She wanted to wish us luck, and for Zeni to call her once the verdict came in. The second is a hang up, probably a wrong number. Third is Carla wanting me to come over and visit with her. That brought a smile to my face.

I quickly dialed and am relieved when Carla picked up on the second ring. "Reesa." She said, she recognized my number on the caller id. "Hey you. It's finally over, what is his sentence?" "Twelve years. He will be eligible for parole after ten years, but only if he shows good, and promising behavior. Even then, he could get denied. We are all crossing our fingers he gets denied." "I will join you. Let's hope he never walks free again. Speaking of free, can you come over for dinner?" "I would love to Carla. Do I need to bring anything?" I'm already looking forward to going.

"Not that I can think of. Taylor won't be here so it will just be us. My parents are going to a movie tonight. We can watch a movie here, if you want." "That sounds wonderful, see you in a few." I said, a quick goodbye to everyone, and mom gave me an extra-long hug before saying goodbye. I grabbed my purse on the newel post and was on my way.

Once I was gone, and the door is shut tight, Zeni, and Keith walked hand in hand towards the kitchen. "Well, I'm so glad that's finally over." Zeni sighed as she poured iced tea for her, and Keith. "Me too!" Keith agreed. "Thanks." He took his tea and drank.

"I'm also very proud of you too." "Why? All I wanted to do is run that bastard into the ground." "Because you held your own. You taught Reesa, and all of us, as a matter of fact how to hold your temper, and not let anger get the best of you." Zeni smiled, "That is why I'm proud."

Keith reached over and took her hand loosely. "Thank you for that. It took everything I had not to jump over the bench and beat the shit out of him." The doorbell interrupted them. "I wonder who that is. It's getting late." Zeni wondered as they retraced their steps from a few minutes ago and opened the door. Ted Booth stood on the other side. "Sorry to bother you, but I wanted to make sure Reesa is doing better."

The Way Life Used To Be

"Don't be sorry, please come in." Keith offered. They sat at the kitchen table with another iced tea for Ted. "Thanks." He lifted his glass. "I'm proud of both of you, and of Reesa too. She is a very brave young lady." Zeni nodded. "Thanks. I'm just so glad it's over. It's nice to you to come to the trial." "I would not think otherwise. I have made it my goal to make sure he stays locked up for the entire sentence. I would make it longer if could make it stick. As far as I'm concerned, he doesn't deserve any time off, good behavior or not."

Keith smiled, "I agree, keep in touch, okay? I want to see him in jail for the rest of his life too." "Will do. How is Reesa? Hopefully feeling better." Zeni answered. "She seems to be doing better. Her best friend Carla invited her over for dinner, so she is not here. I will tell her you asked about her."

"Good. I'm glad she is not wallowing in her room reliving moment after moment. Getting out and seeing friends would be my advice too." Ted finished his iced tea and declined wanting another. "Thanks anyway, but I don't want to take up your entire evening. I should be going." He stood up to put his glass in the sink, then to head home for some dinner. Zeni stopped him after a silent agreement from Keith.

"Please don't. We would both like it if you had dinner with us." "I would love it." While Zeni fixed some spaghetti, and meatballs, Ted, and Keith sat on the front steps with the door opened to let in some fresh air. "Thanks for the invitation. I must admit you have the nicest family I have met in a long time."

"That we do. Zeni, and I have been married for almost twenty years. Every year has been better than the last. At least until this one." Ted said, "It's still the best. Just stay strong, and together, and you will all get through this." Keith smiled. "You married? You sound as if you speak from experience."

That made Ted smile too. "I was married for seven years. I lost my wife two years ago. We didn't have any children, and I regret that sometimes. That's why I'm envious of yours." That made Keith happy rather than jealous. Something about this man spells trust.

"What happened to your wife if you don't mind me asking?" "I don't mind. She died of lung cancer. Funny thing is neither of us ever smoked, but her previous job had a lot of smokers. Probably is second hand, but it still hurt like the devil." "I bet, I don't know what I would do without Zeni, and the kids. They are what keeps me going."

"I can see that. You have the most beautiful bunch of ladies in your life." Keith nodded, "That I do. My ladies are my life." Zeni called out from the kitchen that dinner is ready. That ended any more heart to heart talks.

Ten minutes after I left, I was knocking on Carla's door, and she answered wearing black leggings, and a long red t-shirt that came to her mid thighs. Her hair in a long ponytail, and swung back, and forth as she hugged me. "You look a lot better." She complimented letting me in. She closed the front door softly. "Thanks. It was a horrible month, but I'm so glad not to have to go to court anymore." We began walking arm in arm towards the kitchen that contrary to my house is to the right of the front doorway. The living room stretched towards the back of the house and is only one-story.

"It smells wonderful." I complimented as I took a sniff. We entered the kitchen. There are two pans on the stove that had lids, and something simmering inside. "Good, we are having tortellini. It's an old family recipe." "I can't wait." I rubbed my hands together. "What can I do?"

Carla looked around the kitchen in a complete circle, flipping her hands up. "I guess nothing., and you're my guest. Sit your butt down and wait to be served." I giggled for the first time in a long time. "Thank you for being my friend, I love you." I wiped a tear from my eye, and she smiled.

"Ah, now we're getting sentimental. After all, what good would I be if I was only here for the good times? Now I said, sit." She snapped her fingers to the table which is decorated in a peach satin spread, and had two plates, silverware, and glasses full of Diet Pepsi.

We sat down five minutes later to cheese tortellini with a white cheese sauce, and garlic bread. Carla waited until the meal is half over before asking. "So, I have waited long enough. How did the whole court thing go?" I swallowed a hunk of garlic bread before answering and wiped my mouth with a napkin. "Well it's easier than I thought. Greg had to sit by his lawyers, and not near me. Even though he pled guilty before the trial started, I still had to tell my side."

I took a drink of my Diet Pepsi. "The prosecutor kept asking him why he did it, and all he would do is hang his head like he is ashamed. As soon as the jury left to deliberate, he kept staring at me, and did this weird smile that creeped me out." I demonstrated the look.

The Way Life Used To Be

"That is creepy." Carla agreed. "Mom, and I kept asking each other why he would do something like this after robbing the store. He must be nuts." "That he is, all that matters now is they lock him up. I only wish that I could continue working at Hankins." "Why can't you?"

"Because it would be too hard. All I would think about is Greg, and that alone scares me so much. I wish it never happened, but it doesn't do any good for wishing." Carla shook her head. "No, it doesn't. But it doesn't have to control your life. You can get counseling and get better so the thought of him doesn't make you vomit."

I laughed again. "That might help to throw up on his ugly face. It would make me feel better if nothing else." We finished eating, and I helped wash the dishes. "Want to watch a movie? It's not late," Carla offered while putting a dish towel in a drawer.

"Sure." I agreed. Two hours later, the movie finish and feeling so much better, I thanked her once again, and walked home in the dark. I no longer have to worry about being alone at night. That brought a smile to my face, and I will finally get a good night's sleep. Seeing my family all together brought a bigger smile. This is the way it should be.

Chapter 5

DeVry University
September 2000

I sat at my desk staring at a business management book, and the words swam before me. I don't want to study. I want to get the hell out of my dorm room and have an evening out. Looking around the room, I smiled at Carla's closet. She has her clothes spread on the floor, and very little hanging up where they belonged.

After four long years of high school, one year of college, and no dates I started my sophomore year. It's already near the end of the month and the leaves are just starting to fall. I glanced up from the book, and shook my head at the mess, and about that first year as a freshman. When we were scared, giddy, and so excited all at the same time.

I decided after many thoughts what my major would finally be. Business Management. I went from something in teaching, to nursing, to nothing. I was ready to give up. By the time I started my junior year, I chose business. I spent more, and more hours in the summer at Starlights washing dishes and serving.

I got to know a lot of the regulars and even remembered their preferences. It showed in the tips I got. I served a lot of them. Seeing all those dollar bills stacking in my coin jar is too much to bear, and I always ended up spending every dime on clothes, and jewelry. Mom promised when I got my degree, she would devote most of her time to making me co-owner along with Mark. It would take a while, but I'm always up for a challenge.

The Way Life Used To Be

I kept in touch with Sara as she, and Mark are hot, and heavy now. Any day we will all hear of their engagement, and I for one am so happy for them. It's in the middle of my senior year when I got the letter in the mail telling me they accepted me to the DeVry University right here in Fort Worth. This way I will be close to home, but on my own at the same time.

The school is about forty-five minutes away. They also accepted Carla. She however had no idea what she wanted to major in. Just being in the same school is enough to make both of us so happy. We decided to be dorm mates. Our house is called Lindlay Hall and had three stories. We were on the third floor which pissed us off some since we would have to climb the stairs multiple times a day. Guess it's one way to get some exercise. It had been such a long three years getting here.

Years of intense counseling and going repeatedly to Hankins with my family until I attended on my own. I am fine. It never made me want to work there again, but it felt better to walk in there, and back out with my head held high and my heart in my throat. I made sure that throughout high school the mask is on. It made for less gossip that way. It will be strange being a freshman again, but this time is different. It's college, and time to grow up.

I was putting away pencils, and other stuff, mom, and dad had bought me for when classes started. The front door burst open, and Carla ran inside. She yelled "I love this place," and flopped onto her bed. I laughed, "Your nuts." "Nope, that I'm not, I just walked around campus, and the library is just huge. It has four stories, and books galore. I'm so excited."

She lay on her back and flopped her legs in the air. "Why are you excited about reading?" "Because I've decided to be an author. Reading books upon books is just the place to get me started." I shook my head and popped open a soda. "You had zero idea what your major is last week. Why an author?" Carla blushed, and said, nothing.

"Carla?" Still nothing. "Who is at the library? and how much does this who have to do with your decision." "I don't know his name." Carla giggled. "He is at the nonfiction counter working, and he gave me the biggest smile. He has the straightest, whitest teeth in the entire world, I think I'm in love," she decided, and grabbed a can of root-beer from our mini fridge. It's a present from Mark to have in our room. We both hated warm soda. "Did he ask you out?"

Sandra Gutierrez

"No, but he wanted to. He started to speak, and then a bunch of stupid girls showed up giggling, and acting stupid, so he forgot about me." "Are you going back there?" "Oh yeah," she sighed, "and next time Reesa, you're going with me. You have just got to meet him. Just don't ask him out." "No chance of that. You know more than anybody my love life is nil." Carla jumped off the bed and wiggled her butt, "and that has got to change, let's find you a man." She is already heading for the doorway when I shot off the chair in hot pursuit.

"Don't you dare, I'm not ready for that thing right now," Carla replied, "and you'll never find out unless you try. It's been long enough on your celibacy trip, let's go." "Oh, all right." I sighed giving up this argument as I grabbed my purse, and a jacket. "No need for coverups, leave the jacket here." Carla grabbed the coat from my arm and flung it over the desk chair. "This way you can show off your elegant shoulders." She teased.

We ran out of the room giggling like teenagers. It reminded me so strongly of our river swim days. I missed my younger years, but thoughts of Greg were still in the front of my head. It's what stopped me from finding a boyfriend. When some good-looking boy would get up the nerve to speak to me, I'd run in the opposite direction every time.

It earned me a snobby reputation, but I couldn't help it. I never wanted a man's arms around me or get close ever again but try to explain that to an overly horny teenager who couldn't think beyond making it to home base. We burst out of the dorm hall, and into the sunshine.

It's a perfect seventy-five degrees, and it felt so nice. I lifted my head, and the curls bounced over my shoulders gently. "This is so much better than our room. Let's move outside. We'll live under a tree or something." "Sounds perfect. You hungry?"

"A little." I shrugged my shoulders. "Here's a pizza joint. Smells good." We walked inside and were told to find our own booth. We sat down in high-back chairs. Our stomachs growled together while we sniffed at the delicious garlicky aroma. They decorated the place in black, and red, and is very homey. "So, did you decide on your classes yet?" Carla asked. "Yep. I'm taking business management, calculus, poetry, and some general reading class for the freshman electives." "Sounds heavy, I have to register tomorrow."

A waiter arrived, and we ordered a medium meat lovers pizza. It's close to dinnertime, anyway. "So. Whatever happened to you, and Taylor?" I am dying to know the latest gossip regarding those two. The

The Way Life Used To Be

past few months Carla barely said, two words about him. "Not much." Carla shrugged. "We took a break for a while to see how things go once, we started college, and since he's up at NYU, it seems a little pointless to stay together when we can't."

"Besides it's a long way to travel for such short visits." "Makes sense. does that mean you're free now?" "I guess so." Our sodas arrived, and we took long drinks, "and since that guy who shall remain nameless, and works at a certain library kept looking at me, I'll pursue that avenue. At least for now." I smiled, "I can just hope that I'll be that lucky someday."

"You will, I heard that Greg is still locked up nice, and tight. No signs of being released any time soon. It's time to fall in love." "Not yet. I need to concentrate on my studies, and not some stud." Carla laughed. "Just you wait, I paid attention in high school, and you could have had man after man. I know how much Greg turned you away from all that. I'm hoping that he won't continue to dominate you even from behind bars."

The pizza arrived, and we dug in. "I paid attention in school too. People were looking at me, and not just because of Greg. I remember now what he said, right before they led him away in the handcuffs. I'll get even." I don't know who all heard him as I am the closest one to the doors leading to the cells. I'll never forget the look in his eyes, and the words he said. It's on my mind constantly even three stupid years later." I took another bite of pizza.

"I sat through so many counseling sessions they were coming out my ears. All it seemed to do is make me realize this wasn't my fault. I wasn't picked because he loved me or even wanted me. I was in the wrong place at the wrong time. I've even forgiven myself for not being able to yell for help. I froze, and he knew it," I said.

Carla finished her pizza and sat back. "I didn't mean to sound insensitive." I shook my head. "Well thanks then. I just meant that I know better than many people, except your family, what pure hell you went through. I'm just hoping that it won't be your life. Running scared doesn't get you very far."

"Not far, but it's gotten me to this point. Greg hasn't defeated me. Not now or ever." "Good to hear., and now that we've made complete pigs of ourselves, want to explore around campus with me?" The pizza pan is almost empty with only a few pieces of meat left. "Sure," we scooted back, and drained our glasses before paying for our dinner, and stood once again in the warm sunshine. No need to waste good soda.

"Where should we start? This place is huge," I asked. "Library?" Carla asked and shot a look of attempted bravery at me. I smirked back at her. "Sure, any reason?" I asked. "None." We strolled across campus. We passed our dorm hall, and one of the three dining halls before coming to the library. It's a brick three story building on a grassy hill, and it overlooked the same river we used to swim in. It's now several miles to the east.

Carla opened the large wooden doors, and we stepped inside to space. It's quiet, and a little drafty. Two floors up is the nonfiction, and history section. It's also where the gorgeous guy worked. Carla peeked around a corner and saw him at the checkout counter surrounded by four girls. They were all clamoring around the desk with their chest pulled way out front, and the buttons on their blouses strained with the effort.

I looked at them in disgust. It's obvious what they were doing, and the guy staring at their boobs is making no secret of it. He looked like a player. Not a team player. An "I" player. Someone who knew he is all that and made no secret of it.

I nudged Carla who is still gaping with her mouth wide open. I wanted to leave the library right then, and there. As I looked around, it seemed I am the only one who wants to bolt. This guy didn't remind me at all of Greg, but there is something that spelled wrong. He looked a little like Taylor with the blond hair, and a deep smile, but that's where the similarity ended. The guy had short blond hair perfectly comped, and a wide smile full of straight white teeth.

He looked fake, and plastic. Carla looked dreamy. Like she couldn't wait for her turn to flirt with him. The guy turned in our direction and cocked his head in a greeting. He had a smirk on his face, and he seemed to drink me in. He stared at my face making me feel uncomfortable. Like he is sizing me up or something. The smirk faded when did nothing but look back at him.

I looked disgusted, and I didn't respond like the other girls. Carla remained mesmerized by him and continued gaping with her mouth wide open. The guy never looked in Carla's direction. He is nothing like Taylor. I had full intentions of telling Carla that first thing.

I waited until we left the nonfiction section, and it wasn't until we were back outside that Carla spoke. "Oh my God. Don't you think he just perfect?" She sighed and flapped her hand against her forehead. She strained her eyes back towards the library hoping to get another glance.

The doors however were shut tight and cut off her view. I glanced over at her and was hesitant to speak the truth. Who am I to tell her the guy is a plastic doll? "Well?" Carla asked when I remained silent. "Isn't he beyond freaking gorgeous?"

"Um, sure, I guess. I didn't get a good look though," I whispered. "Want to go back?" Carla asked, and started jumping up, and down. "No, he looked busy." "He's so much more beautiful than Taylor could ever hope to be. I just know he will ask me out soon. Did you see the way he is just staring at me?" "No, sorry I didn't notice. However, I noticed the many sets of boobs dangling in his face. Not much else could get through."

Carla waved a hand. "They're just a bunch of silly girls. None of them stand a chance." "Carla, I have to be honest. He didn't look you at all." "But..." "No, let me finish. I don't want to hurt your feelings, but I got a good look, and your right. He's nothing like Taylor."

"This guy is a big fat fake., and a huge flirt. It means you, and Taylor are meant for each other, college or not. Whatever separates you right now is insignificant. He's it for you." There, I said, it. Carla just looked at me with a blank stare.

She then smiled but looked crushed for a minute. "This guy is nothing to take a second glance over." I stuck my thumb behind my shoulder. "I've already forgotten." "I didn't realize that. I should write to Taylor, and work things out." "That would be best., and best for me right now is to end this day and go to sleep. I'm exhausted."

We hurried back to our dorm room where Carla started a letter that went well past midnight. I fell asleep almost as soon as my head hit the pillow. I'd decided I would like college. The rest of the year flew by, and by June, school is over for the summer, and I joined a seminar which started July 15th. It's only two weeks long, but it is applied towards one business credit.

I grabbed it as soon as I could and remained at school since the seminar would start soon. I'd still have plenty of time the rest of the summer to enjoy myself. Carla had already left for home, and I thought for sure I'd die of loneliness. I had little time to visit anybody. Bessie cheerfully reminded me time, and time again how neglectful I am becoming.

Sandra Gutierrez

I spent my evenings delivering takeout from the dining hall and eating my meals with the company of a twenty-inch TV for company, and a computer. Could life be any more boring? I thought I'd never find someone special after everything I'd been through, but fate dictated otherwise. I used last Thanksgiving, and Christmas breaks from school to go home, and most of it is spent at Starlights learning the ropes, and cleaning tables. I didn't have a boyfriend, and that is fine with me. I am happy, or so I convinced myself.

There is plenty of time for dates once school is over, and I had my hot degree in my hands. I spent the weekend before the seminar is to start with my family, and dad barbecued steaks. It was definitely better than any dorm food, I told Mom over, and over. "Did you expect any different?" Zeni teased. It's so nice to see her, she held back any tears, and regrets she had by keeping a smile on her face, but never quite reaching her eyes.

I noticed, "No, I didn't. Why aren't you happy Reesa?" I finished my potato salad, and sat back with a smirk on my face, and my hands folded across my chest. "I'm happy." Zeni sighed and looked into my eyes. "Most of the time. How are you enjoying your summer?" She asked and smiled. "Boring so far. I have a group project starting next week though. It should pick up in excitement."

"Important?" I nodded. "Very. It counts towards a credit, and I could use all the credits to graduate as soon as I can, so I'm hoping to do well." "Well. Keep me posted. Any romances yet?" "Not even close. Don't worry, you'll be the first to know if that changes."

I glanced towards Bessie who is in a deep conversation with Jeremy Hathaway. Mom followed my gaze, but said, nothing. Bessie is laughing out loud. She had her head tilted upwards, and she looked so happy, and at ease. I'm jealous that I didn't have that sparkle. If I wasn't so picky about boys, I'd stand half a chance.

"They sure look happy, don't they?" Zeni observed nodding towards her younger daughter. "I suppose so. I was just thinking I'd like a little of that myself. Someone to share my evenings with that will be there for my difficulties."

"You will, I know it. You know it too." Mom reached over and patted my cheek. "Yeah, I guess so." I said, without meaning it. I got up from the lawn chair, and helped myself to a soda from the cooler, and popped open the top, and wondered closer to the back door where Sara sat smiling from the steps. She looked very content.

The Way Life Used To Be

"Hey college girl. How's it going?" She smiled and patted the cement next to her. She had cut her hair, and now it just reached her shoulders. It made her look years older, and more mature. I wondered sometimes what all I missed while being in school. "It goes." I sat down and stretched my legs. It's a beautiful day, and I had worn a sleeveless sundress that showed off my tanned shoulders.

Sara closed her eyes and drank in the warmth. "I love it here, it's so peaceful, and comforting. I spend most of my days here, and even some nights." She said, this with a sly smile in my direction, causing me to gasp. "You, and Mark?" I whispered, and Sara giggled, "and when did this start?" "Several months ago. Mom, and dad were a little shocked at first, but they've come to terms with it. It's made things easier than having to sneak in during the middle of the night and running up the stairs as quiet as possible."

"Ever get caught?" "Every time, but mostly by dad. He wasn't too hard on me though. Mom had a harder time coming to terms." I noticed she didn't tell her own mom, and dad. The way Sara thought of them as family is sweet. I didn't mind at all. "You find anyone special yet?" Sara asked taking a drink of her Coke. I shook my head. "No, and the possibilities are getting slimmer, and slimmer. I just realized I've been in school for an entire year and have yet to have a single date."

Sara shook her head. "You don't give yourself enough credit. Just because you are picky, and have every right to be, and should be, you'll find someone soon. I predict within the month." She kissed two fingers up to the sky. "I swear." I laughed. "That may be a hard promise to live up to since it's summer, and not very many pickings." I am lying about that, but I had to admit, I'm not looking very hard.

"You might be right. I take back my promise, and re-promise you'll find your love by Halloween. That enough time?" She teased. "Plenty. I'm up to the challenge." "That's my girl. I want to be the first to hear about it." Sara said

"That's my promise. Thanks, Sara, for making light of this. It's not light. I know how hard this has been for me, and I will always feel responsible. I didn't see what that asshole was doing while I manned my station." She stood there with a smile on her face and didn't interrupt. She pointed a finger at my mouth which I shut without comment and then I opened it again. "But I should have known what was happening. I didn't have a clue, and I feel so bad still that I did nothing., and now you can speak."

"I will not bother to contradict you." She began, and I looked Sara straight in the eyes. I hadn't realized until that moment how special she is becoming to me. Almost like an older sister, and best friend at the same time. It's so different from my relationship with Bessie. "I guess I didn't realize how much this has affected you except my family, that's where my concern ended. I never knew about how much it still bothers me. I thank you sincerely for your love, and friendship. I couldn't ask for any better for my brother." I finished and smiled. "Better for me."

We hugged, and a few tears escape my eyes, and fell down my cheeks wetting the collar, but I didn't care. I shut my eyes tight. I was so thankful how much we all loved each other. The weekend went by so fast. By the time I got back to school, I was depressed. I faced another two weeks of studies before I could even think of another visit. That Monday, Sara's prediction came true. I met Paul Whitfield.

The seminar turned out to be more helpful than I could ever have imagined because of Paul. We became partners during the first week when we were asked to form groups for a major presentation that would take place at the end of July. Afterwards, we faced a month of bliss, and no classes until the fall semester started. We started dating almost immediately. Every day with him is better than the one before. I'm going to be a sophomore. I'm half-way to getting my degree.

Once September started, we were still together. I for one had never been happier. I only hoped he felt the same way. We ate together in the dining halls almost every night. Not the best place for a date, but neither of us cared much. Just being together is enough.

I am still too scared to do much other than hold his hand and let him kiss me a few times. I liked him more, and more. He seemed to know without saying that I wanted to go slow. It's true we'd been going out for a little over two months now, and it's approaching October already. He however remained a gentleman. Caring, loving, and the perfect first boyfriend for me.

I stared at the wall and thought for once I'd love the quiet to get some reading done with nothing, but a Diet Pepsi for company, and all the quiet I could hope for. My brief trip down memory lane is necessary to keep me sane and realize how time flew. I didn't want to waste time with Paul. Carla is out on a date with Taylor. She left close to two hours ago, and I am still reading the same page.

They started communicating by letters, and by the middle of our Freshman year, they were back on again, and Carla never seemed

The Way Life Used To Be

happier. I only hoped I would be that way too. The sooner the better. Paul always brought a smile to my face, but the happiness is slow in coming.

I was realizing how little we know about each other. He never opened up on his past and I had to wonder sometimes if he is so ashamed of it, he couldn't bear to tell me about it. "I felt the same way when Taylor, and I first started dating." Carla explained before she left. "All I wanted with him is happiness, and now I have it. In his last letter he wrote, he said, he's been talking with Greg's younger cousin Carl. They go to the same college and have a few classes together. Carl's close to graduating. Greg's been saying he's turned over a new leaf and is looking forward to getting out of prison soon."

"Soon." I interrupted. "How soon? He still has seven years to go, and that's only with good behavior." The fear is back. All it took is Greg's name. Carla saw my face, and the panic in my voice. She jumped up and hugged me hard. "Honey, I'm sorry, I didn't think. Don't worry, Greg is still locked up, and even though he will be up for parole, it doesn't mean he'll get it. I'm sure he is just dreaming about the day he's released. Carl is majoring in Criminal Justice or something like that. Who knows? Maybe he will make sure Greg does more time. Wouldn't that be a kick in the pants? Now enough tension. Let's have dinner."

"Sounds good. However, if Carl is anything like Greg, maybe he'll free him before he is even up for parole." I whispered. The panic is fading, and my color is coming back. "Even God has his limits. Carl isn't any more special than anyone else. Your color is looking much better now." Carla kissed my right cheek.

This is a good sign. I didn't break down and cry for the first time in years. I had a panic attack and handled it without falling apart. Progress. The phone rang, and I grabbed it assuming it's Paul, and muttered. "Hello?"

"Reesa! Guess what?" It's Bessie, and she sounded so happy. Gone is the terrible teens, and the mood swings that drove everybody nuts for years. Now she is mellow, and so much fun to be around. I missed her now. "What's up Bess?" "I've been invited to the spring dance, and I don't know what to wear. When are you coming home so you can help me pick out a dress?"

I checked the calendar and found Veteran's Day weekend is the first available time to come home for a visit. There was no test scheduled. "May third. The theme for this year is Spring Fling. Isn't that the cutest name? Jeremy Hathaway asked me to go with him, and I'm so excited." Bessie sighed and smiled at the thought of going to her dance. Jeremy is her very first boyfriend in high school, and they missed last year's dance as they only started dating in June.

"I remember him from the Fourth of July party. He's cute. You sure you want to get your dress now? The dance isn't for months." "Uh, huh, so, how's college? Is it hard?" Bessie had no intentions of going to school once high school is over. she is a senior this year and couldn't wait to be done. "Not yet, I just started classes just a few weeks ago though." I didn't want to tell anybody besides Carla about my increasing feelings towards Paul. At least not right away. I didn't want any teasing over it.

I hoped that it was him on the phone, but I held in my disappointment as I realized Bessie is still talking. "You might feel differently later. I didn't think I'd enroll, but I feel so different now, I love this" I ate a few potato chips, and drank from another Diet Pepsi I found in the back of the fridge hidden by a stack of lunch meat, and cheese.

It's the last one, and that alone made me swear. Now I'd have to go to the Safeway to get more. The store however is just down the street, so it wasn't too bad a walk. I tried walking there in daylight hours just to be safe. The sun is just starting to set. Bessie told me "Just don't get your hopes up. Anyway, Susie, and Jenna are here, and we're going to the movies soon. See you later." "Bye, kiddo." I said. I hung up the phone. It's nice to hear from her, and she sounded so much more content now. It's easier to talk to her now without all the crying bouts. I am looking forward to seeing my family again.

I glanced at the desk and realized the soda is almost gone. I got it over with and ran to the store to restock before I had a caffeine shortage. After all, I never developed a taste for coffee, and am not likely to start now. I grabbed a sweatshirt as it's still warm even at night. It just wasn't warm enough for just the T-shirt I am wearing.

I headed downstairs, and down the block. The sun had just set, and it's not dark yet. I hurried so it would still be light out when I got back. I didn't enjoy going there all by myself, but I couldn't depend on Paul or Carla to hold my hand every time.

The store is bright, and airy when I reached it. I walked straight to the drink aisle and picked up a case of 24 sodas. That should last for a least a few days providing Carla didn't steal any if she ran out of her

The Way Life Used To Be

root-beers. I rounded the corner to the checkout line and found Paul at the registers. He was reaching back for his wallet and didn't appear to notice that I placed the box on the counter before reaching for him.

"Hey. What are you doing here Reesa?" He asked giving me a quick kiss. He looked pleased to see me. I tipped my head up to kiss his neck and smiled. "Nice to see you. I ran out of sodas." I studied him while he paid for his groceries. His tamed blond hair is wild, and he looked tired. He turned back to me once he handed the clerk his money. "Why are you out in the dark?"

It pleased me he is worried about me. "I couldn't concentrate once I realized I was out of soda. Besides it's not that dark yet. What are you doing here?" I challenged. The sky is now a brilliant purple and pink. It's pretty from what I could see looking out the windows.

"I ran out too." He held out two Cokes. "I have a test on Friday, and I needed caffeine." I realized just then how much I loved his face. He had a dimple on his left cheek, and that made him seem more handsome in my eyes. A ball cap covered his hair flipped backwards, and some strands stuck out the back. He looked like he had just gotten up from a nap.

"That soon?" He nodded, "I guess the instructors here don't waste any time." I said and made him laugh. The dimple became more pronounced when he did. "I guess not." He grabbed his bag and waited for me to pay. I tossed a five on the counter, and grabbed the change, tossing them in my jeans pocket. "Ready?" He asked. "Sure. Thanks."

I followed him out the door, and we started meandering back to school. He took the case from my hand and transferred it to his right hand along with his bag. He reached for my free hand with his left which I gave. "You know. I never asked you what your majoring in."

"Something with Education. I'm not sure what yet. I enjoy working with kids." "I don't have a lot of experience with that myself. Only with Bessie if that counts," That made him laugh. "I'd say so. How's she doing, and when am I going to meet her, and your family?" "Maybe sooner than later. She called me tonight to say she's going to some spring dance. made me jealous having to be stuck in school instead of having fun."

"I know the feeling. All last year I was so alone, and now it's different. I don't know what I'd still be doing if it wasn't for you," he said, and turned his head to give me a kiss on the side of my head. It made me smile. "I feel the same way. My first year was spent getting familiar with being on my own, and now I feel the same as you. Like I don't know any more how to be alone. I never want to be alone again. I'm so thankful we met."

He smiled widely and swung an arm around my shoulder. "So, tell me more about this dance your sister's going to. Is it important, like a high school initiation or ritual or something?" "Spring Fling. That's the name of the dance. There's a special dance every spring at our high school. It's a tradition. The name changes every year. According to the most popular vote, it becomes the chosen theme. Every may instead of leaving flowers on a doorstep to declare your love, the guy asks for your hand in dance. It's not a huge deal or anything. Bessie just seems so happy to be going. I'm going home next month to help her pick out her dress."

"I thought you were going to say marriage." He teased. "No such thing. It's a formal though. Bessie's going for the first time with her boyfriend Jeremy. They've been going together for a while now, but just since June. They missed the previous dance. He's never gone before either. Since it's their senior year, they decided to go for one special night before they both graduate. Obviously, he didn't have a chance to leave an invitation. I don't think Bessie cares."

"Sounds like a lot of fun. Did you ever go?" He asked casually. He realized just then how much he wanted to know about her past. Surely, it was wonderful, and high school was fun for her. I shook my head. "No, I didn't." I prayed he wouldn't ask why. It's none of his business anyway no matter how much I had come to care for him.

"Not that interested." I commented lightly. "No, no, I spent most of my time studying to make sure my grades were the highest I could achieve. I didn't have time for much else." There, that is a good enough answer. We continued walking in the balmy night slowly enjoying the quiet, and peacefulness the evening brought. The moon shone brightly overhead illuminating a path for us to follow. There wasn't anybody, but us on the sidewalk. Once we reached our dorm, he continued walking with me up the stairs still carrying my case.

I unlocked the door and opened it to find it empty. "Where's Carla? Out for the evening?" He asked looking around at the mild disorder. "Probably with Taylor." I said, Truthfully, I didn't care that she wasn't home. I like my privacy. At least some time. I glanced at my desk and realized again how much studying I still had ahead of me. "They engaged yet?"

The Way Life Used To Be

"No, At least far as I've heard. I expect I'll hear about it any day though. They've been together forever, except for a short time, in our freshman year. She had a hot flash for a librarian." That made him smile. "A scholar. I can't picture it. You sure that's Carla?" That made me giggle.

He turned to face me and held my face in his hands. He rubbed his thumbs over my cheeks. I closed my eyes savoring the touch of his hands on me. "You always make me smile." I said, softly tilting my face towards his. He rubbed the same cheek with his own before lowering his head and kissed me gently. I had just gone from liking him to deeply caring. I am falling in love for the first time in my life, and it scared me. It made me feel wonderful all at the same time.

As soon as he left, Carla burst in the door, and headed straight for the closet for a pair of shoes to change into. She started throwing clothes around in frustration making me smile all over again. This is such typical behavior for her. Once I said her name about three times, she finally popped her head out from the closet. She is visibly upset that she couldn't find her red pumps.

Only those shoes would go with the strapless red and black silk dress she had just bought for her much awaited dinner. Taylor is waiting patiently downstairs. He is going back to New York in two days. They wanted to have a romantic evening first starting with dinner. "What's with the grin?" She asked.

"I think I'm doing it." I said, breathlessly. "It, you're finally having sex?" She said, it both as a question, and a statement at the same time. "No," I playfully punched her on the shoulder giggling like a giddy teenager. "I'm falling for him." "I'm so happy." She hugged me hard. "You look happy too. Is he the one?" She held her breath, hands in front of her mouth. "I think so, I've never felt like this before, and your very perverted." I teased referring to Carla's earlier comment. "That, I am, but Taylor appreciates me for it. Sorry. Go on. You were in bed?"

That made me laugh out loud. I truly loved my best friend. "No pervert. When he was walking me home tonight, I started feeling it. I don't know if this is the real thing or not." "You don't need to know. When it's right, you don't have to question it. You just enjoy it. Now. When you finally take the mattress plunge, I want to be the first one to know about it. Every single detail and don't hold back."

"I'm pretty sure that will be a long time in the future. I wouldn't even know what to do. Do you?" Carla shrugged. "I'm not sure. All I have for experience in that area is Taylor. Speaking of the love of my life, when we go back for Thanksgiving break, he's coming for dinner. My mom can't wait." "I bet. We're planning on dinner with Bessie, and her new boyfriend, and Mark, and Sara. It'll be a full house."

"You should ask Paul to come keep you company. Show him off to the family. Use this chance to meet everybody during the time of thanks, and crap. But seriously, how's it going with Mark, and Sara? Planning a wedding anytime soon?" Now it's my turn to shrug. "I haven't heard anything. Sara just enrolled in some community college. She wants to take a few business classes for her new job. She's been promoted to head cashier at Hankins, and she wants to go for assistant manager soon."

"Ambitious, that's impressive she's wanting to make more money. I'm glad they're still together." "Me too. I can't wait until we get to go home." I said, "bringing Paul?" Carla asked casually. She got up and headed to her dresser for some nylons. "I might, I've talked my ear off about him to mom, and she's been practically begging for me to bring him home. This is a major holiday though. He might want to be with his own family."

"You never know till you ask. See you later." She said, cheerfully, and headed back out. Once she left, I placed the sodas in the fridge so they would at least be cold. I turned around quickly when the phone started blaring in my ear. So much for the quiet. I sighed and walked quickly to my desk. It's mom, and her voice made me smile. Studying could wait for the time being.

"How's everything?" I asked, "Quiet, I like having the house to myself. Bessie just took off with Jeremy, Jenna, and Susie to see a movie." "She told me that earlier. What do you, and dad have planned?" "He's not home yet. Pete needed some help with one of the dishwashers. It's making a weird clanking sound. Something may have gotten loose." "I'm surprised Pete, and Lisa have stuck it out this long. They may be your most loyal employees." I said, I'd always liked them.

I would never forget how willing they were to take over when I was in the hospital. I remembered now that Lisa made me a basket full of bath soaps, and bubble bath that was sitting on my dresser when I was released. I was still upset about everything, but I made it a point to tell her thank you, and she kissed my forehead, and said, we are her family. If the situation were reversed Lisa knew she could count on us to help

The Way Life Used To Be

her. "So far they are. Completely dependable, and close as family. I don't ever want to be without them."

"I doubt that will ever happen. How's their baby doing?" "All over the place. Natalie just turned two. She loves to run through Starlights. She always has a ton of energy." "Sounds like a busy life." I commented. "It is, but it keeps things from being dull. Your dad just got home. I'll call you soon." "Okay." I hung up quickly. I am already looking forward to seeing them. I smiled to myself as I set the phone back on the cradle.

Seemed like everyone is growing up fast. Especially Bessie. It's so much nicer to talk to her now that she is calmer. I hope this is like turning over a new leaf. If it's only temporary, I'd be more than disappointed. I remember when she first started the eleventh grade she got into a fight after school. It was with one of her so called best friends Janie Mitchem, who started a rumor about Bessie, and one of her ex boyfriends.

It was only yelling between them, and they both ended up with a week of after school detention. Bessie bragged about it for a while, but like all drama, it eventually dissolved on its own. I crossed my fingers she had matured. Ten minutes later, I finally got down to business. I opened a book to write some notes. It remained quiet the rest of the night.

Sandra Gutierrez

Chapter 6

Ted Booth entered Starlights for a quick dinner. It's still blistering hot for October, and the aroma from the soup is enough to bring anybody inside the doors. The front doors were propped opened to welcome the breeze, soft as it is. Plus, he wanted to visit Keith and Zeni. It had been quite a while since he had chatted with them. He wanted to hear how well Reesa was settling in college.

"Hey Ted." Zeni greeted from the counter. She had just taken a customer's order and glanced towards the doorway. "Ham, and Swiss as usual?" "Hey back, and yes please." He greeted and searched for a corner booth. They were well on to first names now, and he found how much he loved their restaurant. Loved their whole family as a matter of fact. He also ordered the same sandwich every time he visited.

Keith was in the kitchen, and Mark was nowhere around, so he didn't get a chance to say hello. Zeni appeared minutes later with a plate with a ham, and swiss sandwich, and a bowl of today's soup, Chicken noodle. "Sit down please. He gestured to an empty seat across from him."

"Sure, it's quiet for the moment. Mark had to run to the store, and Keith's busy doing inventory so it's just me. How's it going?" She asked sitting in the chair he offered. "Pretty good. Ressa settling in okay?" He took a bite of his sandwich. "Yep, she was here for a few days this summer. She seems to love school. Bessie just got done talking with her yesterday, and she sounded so happy."

Ted nodded quietly. "That's good, she needs to be. This might be the best thing for her to gain some independence, and happiness." He took another bite, then dipped into the soup. Zeni took a drink of the iced tea she brought with her.

The Way Life Used To Be

"I know your right. It just makes me so sad sometimes when I walk by her bedroom, and she's not there. I just can't wait until Thanksgiving since she promised to come home. She'll also be here next weekend. Bessie needs her help to find a dress."

Ted finished the sandwich. "Dress for what?" "A school dance, I forget the name, but it's a formal, so she needs a dress, and shoes. Macy's is having some big sale, and Reesa promised to come home to help her. Your welcome to have Thanksgiving dinner with us as well." "Sounds fun, it will be much better than the frozen turkey dinner I'd planned on." Ted smiled wiping his mouth with his napkin.

"That won't do. We're planning on eating at four. That should give us plenty of visiting time before dinner is served." "I'll be there. What can I bring?" "Pumpkin pie if you'd like. You don't have to bring anything though. This is our invitation. I'll have time to make a pie along with dinner too." Ted told Zeni "I was raised to contribute. I'll bring the pie, and anything else I can find. Not sure if you'll like my baking."

"We can't all be gifted in that area." Zeni teased. "Did I tell you Reesa has her first boyfriend?" "No, when did this happen?" "Right after Fourth of July. she met him at school. His name is Paul. I'm going to see if she wants to bring him too. Get the first initiation over with. Keith and Mark will have fun with it." Zeni smiled.

"It may get brutal. If he has a sense of humor, he'll take it all in stride. May even be worth keeping for a while." "I take it she's doing much better, no more nightmares?" Zeni nodded. "Much better. She hasn't mentioned Greg for months now. I'm certainly not going to be the one to bring it up and stir the pot."

"Don't blame you much there. I haven't heard anything new on that subject, but you'll be the first to know when I do." He took a drink of his iced water to wash down the last of his soup. "As much as I don't want to know, I need to." A couple came in she jumped up to take the order herself. "Sorry, I have to go. Duty awaits." She smiled as she grabbed an order pad from her apron.

Ted smiled too as he stood up. "I need to check by the station really quick. Thanks for the sandwich. I'll be in again soon." He took the tray to the counter and waved goodbye with one hand. "Good. I'll have it ready." She said, glancing over her shoulder as she hurried to the couple. Once the restaurant was closed for the night, and they had dinner, the phone rang. Bessie was out again, and so was Mark.

Zeni assumed she'd have to take a message like always. "Hello? Mama?" As soon as Zeni heard who it was, she started crying. Would it always be like this? Happy she was in college, and sad that she is at the same time. She wiped her face. "Hi baby. What's new?" She settled herself in her favorite rocker and tossed a blanket over her legs. "Not much."

"Bessie's been bugging me pretty much every day about that damn prom dress. I wish it was done, and over with already. I just got done eating dinner, and I'm still not too fond of dorm food." "Like I keep saying, there's no food like Starlights. It would be a sad ending if dorm food took the spotlight. Bessie's been nagging me about that too. I keep telling her she has months to get prepared, but she's insistent."

That made me giggle and miss her so much it hurt my heart. "I love you mama." Zeni couldn't speak. She started crying again, and the tears ran down soaking her collar. It took everything she had not to beg her daughter to come home, and just forget about college. "Mama?" She again dried her eyes as best she could and grabbed a Kleenex to wipe her nose.

"I'm still here." She said, in a voice not her own. I could hear it. "Mama, are you still sad?" "Yeah. I guess I am. I'm happy for you at the same time. Just hearing you makes me lonely. I can't wait for Thanksgiving. Are you bringing Paul with you?" "I still haven't asked. I'll do it next time I see him. I just want to enjoy the weekend first. I need a break." I'm hoping Bessie wouldn't ruin it for me.

"I for one am looking forward to it. What's Paul going to do while you're gone?" "He has a final due on Tuesday. He wants to spend the entire weekend studying for it. I'm coming on the bus Friday afternoon. My last class is at two." "You've found a smart one. I like him already." Zeni smiled into the phone. "I hope so. Mama, what was it like when you, and daddy first met? Is it all happy times, or did you have regrets?" I asked.

"It's a lot of both and everything in between. At first, it's a physical attraction as we were both in college, and partying was big at our campus. Along with a lot of sex. None of us were concerned with diseases, and such. Not like now. You haven't gone that far, yet have you?" She sounded panicked, and it made me giggle. "No mama. I asked because of Paul. I'm falling in love with him, and it scares me." So much for keeping my feelings to myself.

The Way Life Used To Be

"That's a normal feeling. I was the same with your dad. He was not my first love though. It scared me all the same. When he proposed I panicked, but I got over it? I guess that's the bottom line here. I pictured what my life would have been like without him in it, and I wanted him in it. Am I making sense?"

"Yes, you are. Thank you for that. I should go now. I have an early class in the morning." Once Zeni hung up the phone, she glanced outside, and saw the sky is a bright pink. That meant the sun is about to sink so she sat on the front stoop with only herself for company and watched the sky turn black.

Once the sun is completely gone, and the first stars started twinkling, she noticed a young man walking down the block. As he came closer, she recognized him. "Hello Trey, how are you?" Trey glanced to his right and smiled. "Pretty good. How about yourself?" He stopped walking, and stopped at the foot of the steps, looking down at her. She looked sad. "I'm well. Just enjoying the evening."

"It's a nice one, that's for sure. I've just finished my last delivery. My pickup is parked down there." He nodded towards his truck sitting at the end of the block. "Why don't you come sit for a minute?" She invited. "Sure. Thanks. How's Reesa enjoying school?" "So far so good. She's on her second year already, and only two more to go."

"Time flies. Before you know it, she'll be graduating, and be back home again." "That's what I'm hoping for." Zeni smiled at him. He settled more on the steps and smiled back. "Wow. It's sure a beautiful night." "Sure is. Every time I get antsy or troubled, I come out here, and watch the sun go down. It calms me down every time and makes me realize how lucky I am to live here."

"Me too, I'm looking forward to spring already. Get those fruits, and berries growing." "Just so you keep on delivering to Starlights. Keith and I love your berries. The raspberries are my favorite." "Mine too. It's hard to stop eating them once they ripen. We got the barn built. Dad, and I will exp, and our business starting in March." Trey said.

Zeni looked surprised. "We just might have to ask for more of your business. What are you raising?" "Cattle, and pigs. A few chickens too. Mom wants to redo the living room, and the only way to help her do that is to increase our clientele." "Well, we're on your list. Just let me know when you're ready to start. I have a weakness for fresh eggs."

"Will do, say hi to Mark, and Keith for me. I should get home soon." He got up. "Sure. Have a good night." She waved and smiled as he started walking the rest of the way to his truck. She liked him. He is always so sweet. Trey reached his house in ten minutes. He parked the truck and tossed the crates near the porch.

"Hey Ma." He greeted as he walked in the door. Cynthia poked her head around the wall separating the kitchen from the downstairs bathroom. "Hi, are you all done for the night?" "Yup, dad should be getting home soon." He took off his shoes and walked over to his mom to give her a kiss on the cheek. He headed upstairs to change clothes and start a load of laundry. Cynthia turned back to the kitchen to finish dinner.

The kitchen is finally updated. It took three years of hard work, and now all that is left is a new living room set. She is thinking of a soft brown leather couch and recliner so she could enjoy the evening news while she rocked. Pipe dreams. But if she could get a new kitchen, a new living room wasn't far off. She flipped the burgers and got the French fries out of the oven just as Jacob came home.

Trey changed from his overalls to a pair of old jeans with holes in the knees, and a tan T-shirt. It's getting chilly at nights now, but not quite sweatshirt season yet. He glanced out the window of his bedroom and saw the barn.

The barn that took four months to build. He remembered years ago when he asked his dad about expanding their business to include chickens, and cattle. They could deliver eggs, meat, and even milk if they raised dairy cows.

Jacob broke down after hearing complaint after complaint from Cynthia about her house. The least he could do is improve it if they had to live there year after year. A place where they could be proud to live in. The first thing Trey did is hire a carpenter named Bret Schmidt to help build the barn. It took an entire summer to finish it. He included enough stalls for four dairy cows, six cattle, and a dozen chickens that had their own house.

Trey is responsible even though his dad is the one who gave the final okay. Jacob still spent most of his time with the produce area, so Trey is pretty much on his own. He also ended up spending a lot of time with Bret who grew up in Ohio and moved to Fort Worth four years ago. He didn't live anywhere near Trey, but they were close to the same age.

Bret is only six months older, and in much better shape. Trey realized this as he looks at his arms and found the muscles starting to

The Way Life Used To Be

lack. That sucked in the late fall, and winter when the only work is feeding the animals and hauling hay, mostly.

They became close friends by the end of the summer and tried to spend time outside the farm as often as possible. The phone rang and interrupted his thoughts. It's Bret. "Hey dude." He yelled. "Where are you, and why are you shouting?" Trey wondered. "I'm partying. Why don't you come and join us?" "Where?" "With Jan. She, and her roommate Sherry are having a move in party. Why don't you come and help us celebrate? You know where the East Glenwood Apartments are? They moved into the north side. First floor. A21."

"I know where that is. I'll be there. Just want to have a quick bite to eat first." "Don't, we're ordering pizza." "Alright, thanks, I'll be there in a few." Trey changed again into jeans with no holes, and a gray, and black striped T-shirt. He said, a quick goodbye to his mom who barely notices, and just gave a quick wave, and headed to his truck. It's a Ford pickup with more rust spots than actual paint, but he loved it, anyway. He gunned the engine and tore down the street with the company of George Strait on the radio.

It's very dark, so he almost missed the entrance to the apartments where Jan, and Sherry were moving into. He saw Bret outside with Jan, and they were already getting in on, but were still fully clothed. Thank god for small favors. He pulled into a parking stall and slammed the door. He smiled as he crossed the lawn.

"Hey, get a room." He teased. Bret, and Jan drew apart, embarrassed to have been caught. "Bout time." He teased as they slapped each other on the back. "Hey Trey." Jan Delucci greet as she smiled over her shoulder. She is glad to see him. He, and Bret seemed to be close friends, and she is always happy to see him. She tossed her long blond hair over one shoulder. She is tall, and tanned. Bret is a good match for her with his bronze colored hair, and huge arms, he is all muscle.

"Yeah, yeah. Hi Jan, how are you?" "Fine, almost everybody's inside. Help yourself to chips, and soda. Pizza just arrived so it should still be hot." "Thanks, I will." Trey lifted one hand in a thank you gesture, and headed inside where he heard music, and a dozen men, and women walking around the living room. Three of them were sitting on the couch eating Fritos, and ranch dip, making a mess on the carpet with the crumbs.

Sandra Gutierrez

He looked around, and noticed how clean it is, minus the crumbs. They had a brown, and plaid couch that faced a TV on a basic black stand. There is a wooden coffee table with half a dozen pizzas sharing the top, and a brown recliner. Everybody seemed to be couples. Several of them had their arms around each other and were oblivious to everybody else.

It's about time he had a girlfriend too. He climbed the carpeted stairs and found two bedrooms side by side with people filling both rooms. They were in awe over every piece of furniture, and knickknacks. He found Sherry amongst the guests, and she called a quick hello to him over her shoulder, and turned back to her friends, and current boyfriend. He had his arm draped around her shoulder and looked smug.

Trey is even more jealous. Not of Sherry or even Jan. Just because he is and could be. Good god. He is almost twenty-two, and still single. His high school sweetheart is long gone, and he hardly thought about her anymore. It wasn't as painful as when their engagement ended, but sometimes it still hurt. He didn't want a one-night stand with just anybody. He wanted someone special. Like Bret, and Jan. Sherry, and her man. Zeni, and Keith. Even his own mom, and dad.

While he is brooding over this, Jim Stevens came in all smiles, and a Coke in one hand. "Hey man, took you long enough." "For what? I just got here half an hour ago." Trey said, sipping his own Coke. "That isn't nothing man. I've been outside with the beautiful Lisa." He grinned. He is still homely looking with a crew cut that did nothing to improve his looks. It also may account for the lack of girls knocking on his door.

"Does she know she is outside with you?" "It so happens she did. Is slightly inebriated, but she'll remember me come morning. I don't have her last name though." He frowned. "That is a deliberate move on her part." Trey wanted to be gentle about that fact, but Jim was not the type to pussy foot around any situation. He wanted the truth always. "Did you get her phone number at least?"

Jim reached into his pockets and came up empty handed. "Damn, why are you always right?" "Struck out did ya?" "I'm thinking so. She's gone too. Damn, why does this always happen to me?" "Same reason it happens to me. Want to blow this place and go somewhere else?" "Don't have to ask me twice. You know what? I'm sober. I've had nothing, but Coca-Cola all evening, and I still can't score. Must be something wrong with the world right now." Jim tossed his empty can in the trash and grinned again.

The Way Life Used To Be

"Let's blow, want to say goodbye to everyone first?" "I feel a little rude eating their food and splitting with more than a bye." "They'll move past it. I'm sure of it. They're still outside anyway so I doubt our absence will be sorely missed." "You got a point there." Trey pointed a finger in his direction and tossed his own soda away. He waved a goodbye to Bret who waved and shrugged as they sped off.

"Back to my earlier conversation, is there something that repels women?" Jim asked. Trey is about to laugh when he saw it. He shook his head instead. "My friend, I thought that same thing about an hour ago. Even wallowed in my own depression briefly." "You out of it now?"

Trey nodded as he made a right turn. "About, I guess. You remember Jennifer Emery, right?" She is the high school sweetheart Trey was thinking about. "I do indeed, used to think she was nice, and just for you." "Now you don't?" He entered the freeway.

"It's not that I don't. You know what they say about high school sweethearts right?" "That it's high school." "That it's fake. High school, and sometimes even middle school I guess is a bunch of drama and getting together then breaking up just as fast. Hell, it's common for couples to only last days before moving on. It's immature, and stupid, I would have loved high school. You had to go there, pull decent grades if you could, then come home to study, and hang out. I guess I regret so much sometimes I never got to go."

Trey thought about his comment. It's the first time in months he thought about what Jim had gone through. He wouldn't wish it on his worst enemy. "Do you have regrets?" Jim nodded. "Some, I guess. It's still a very sore subject. In a roundabout way this is why I've never succeeded in a relationship."

"I don't think one has anything to do with the other. We're getting older, but not ready to settle down yet. It might just be as simple as that." Jim is silent for the rest of the trip. Trey parked in front of his house to check on the plants, and animals for a while. "I will take your suggestion under advisement." Jim said.

"You don't have to take it to heart. All I'm saying is don't settle. I'm single, and most of the time I'm happy about it. It's the other times I feel like something is missing." "My friend, I feel like that every damn day of my life. I talk a lot about girls, but I know where I stand with them. I just like to joke a lot. Beats crying out my sorrows." "I'd like to say I know what you're going through, but all I can do is lend an ear."

"It's fine you know." Jim said, "I've had my share of troubles, and broken hearts, and everything you could think of in between, but I'll find my way on my own. I may need a push in the right direction now, and again, but I'll get there, eventually."

Trey draped an arm around his shoulder and squeezed it. "I don't have a doubt you will. I'll always have your back. I'll be there for you no matter what." "I guess I know that. That might be why I haven't lost it completely yet. I know who my friends are." "That should be a country song title." Trey teased. He checked on the chickens and tossed several handfuls of corn over the fence.

"Probably already is." Jim chuckled. He tossed in a handful of corn himself. Trey locked up, and Jim headed home after that. It's a mile or so away, but he didn't care. He wanted some time to think about all of this in silence for a while.

"Guess what?" Carla screamed. "What? and why must you yell?" I asked while pouring over some books at my desk. I am getting a major headache, and the words were slurring. "Taylor is coming for a visit." Carla squealed, and clapped her hands together, flew, and bounced on her bed.

"When?" I am trying to sound happy for her, but the headache is intensifying by the second. "Friday. I have two days to prepare. What should I wear? Where should we eat? Can he sleep here?" She fired one question after another. "Wahoo. Slow down. One question at a time. Take a deep breath." I advised. Carla took in a short breath and whooshed out again. "Now start over. Wear an outfit that will knock his socks off. Eat anywhere, but the cafeteria. Yes. He can stay here. Just be quiet while you get it on."

Carla laughed. "Oh. I can't wait. Let's go through my closet." She jumped up from her bed and ran to the closet. She flung both doors open and dropped to her knees. Carla flipped through a few outfits before squealing. "I found it," and brought out a mint green sundress that is mid-calf length with spaghetti straps. "Isn't it pretty?" "Very, Taylor will love it, and love even more taking it off."

I teased, "Whatever happened to the red thing you brought home a few weeks ago? I seem to remember you rearranged the closet looking for a pair of red shoes to wow Taylor."

"Now you're talking. I forgot about that." She dove into the closet and came out seconds later with the very wrinkled red dress dangling from one hand. "Thanks a bunch. Take some aspirin or something for your headache." "How did you know?" "Look at yourself. You look like shit." "Thanks, I have to get ready for class." I said. I popped three Advil's into my mouth and washed them down with bottled water and waited for them to take effect.

"Why do you look so gloomy? You're seeing Paul in a few minutes. Smile." "Fine, fine. Oh, I forgot, I'm going home this weekend to help Bessie. I won't be here when Taylor arrives. Tell him hi for me." "I will. Where are you going shopping?" "Macy's for sure. After that I don't know. Depends on where Bessie will strike it lucky. I'll be taking the four thirty bus home and should be back by six on Sunday. It'll be nice to get away for the weekend."

"You'll love it, their sales are magnificent, and you'll save tons of money. You should splurge and get yourself something while you're at it. Wow Paul." Carla suggested with a twinkle in her eyes. "I'm not sure if money is a factor. This is Bessie's first high school dance, and I'm pretty sure dad will have no budget in mind. I'll think about something for myself while I'm wondering the aisles. I promise." "Tell everyone hi for me. Got to go." "Will do, I've got to get to class myself." I hugged her quickly and rushed out the door.

Once I was done with my last class, I sighed with relief, and ran out, and into the dorm room to get ready. I had already said, goodbye to Paul who stated about fifteen times how much he would miss me. I smiled as I realized I would miss him just as much. I still hadn't asked him about Thanksgiving. I promised myself I'd do it as soon as I got back. I packed a suitcase and left the dorm without saying goodbye to Carla. She is saying hi to Taylor by now.

I'm still jealous of the love they shared. I boarded the bus at twenty-five after four. I chose a seat by myself and laid the suitcase to the left on the seat. This wasn't the kind of bus where stowaways are required. If the bus isn't too crowded, that is. I opened a book and read while the bus made stop after stop.

We didn't arrive at the Fort Worth Bus Depot until six fifteen. For a ride that normally took only half an hour, this is pushing the limits of patience. The sun shone, and I realized I'd be just in time for dinner. Starlights is only three blocks away, so I hurried past a few shops, and waved hello to the owners. I arrived at the restaurant smiling, and breathless.

"Reesa!" Mom yelled from the register and rushed over to take me into her arms. "My baby." "Hi mama." I reached up to press my face into her neck. "Tell me everything. What's new? How's classes? How's Paul?" She asked in an offbeat funny way, after she pulled away. She is still holding me by my shoulders. She looked like she couldn't wait to hear every detail.

"Slow down mama. Not much is new from the last time we talked. I said, my goodbyes to Paul before I left. I love my classes, and Carla, and Taylor are spending the week together. They plan on spending the weekend in bed so I'm glad I'm not there." I grabbed a soda from the dispenser and sat at a barstool. I put my suitcase on the floor next to me. "Order up." Zeni yelled placing a plate full of a meatball sub, and potato salad on the counter, and rang the service bell.

She smiled as she walked through the swinging doors into the kitchen. I grabbed my drink and followed her. She started making more sandwiches. "Okay start with classes. How are they going?" "Pretty well so far. I have finals in two weeks so I'm nervous. I hope I do well." I took a drink and looked around. It's busy, but as always, they had things under control.

"You always do. Get enough studying time in?" She asked, and headed to the refrigerator to pull out turkey and roast beef. "I guess so. There's always time for studying, but not always time for doing it." "Paul have something to do with that?" Zeni teased as she lifted an eyebrow and grabbed a hoagie roll. she started slathering mustard, and mayonnaise with one hand while holding the roll with the other.

"Partly." I smiled at the look on mom's face. "Okay," I am already missing him. I didn't think I would this soon after stating how much I needed a break. "That's what I thought. Is he coming to Thanksgiving?" She added potato salad to the plate. "I haven't asked yet." I admitted.

"Order up." Zeni called again, and handed a plate filled with a club sandwich, salad, and fries on the counter. "I'll get it. What table?" "Six, thanks honey." I grabbed the plate, and a handful of napkins, and headed to a corner table where a couple is sitting very close together. The girl reminded me of Sara with the deep blond hair, and a pretty smile. The guy sitting next to her didn't ring any bells. Still, they looked good together.

"Sorry about the wait." I apologized, and they both jumped up smiling sheepishly. "Here ya go. Anything else I can get you?" The couple shook their hands, and the girl smiled. "No, but thanks. This looks good." "Your welcome."

The Way Life Used To Be

I smiled and headed back to the stool where Mark is leaning over the counter waiting. "Mark!" I yelled and threw myself into his arms. They came around my waist and lifted me clear off the floor. "Hi Reesa, and how's my college girl?" he asked setting me back on my feet and smiling.

"Busy, how have you been?" I asked hopping back on my stool. "Where's Sara?" "Sara's been looking forward to seeing you again. She said, that talk you two had last July is special to her. She's like one of the family now. Said she'd see you tomorrow. She has the late shift tonight." I held my breath thinking he would state plans for marriage, but he remained quiet. Maybe it would take a while longer.

"I'm glad you two are still together. It gives me hope for my future." "You never know what'll happen. You going to the house?" "Yup, you need anything for dinner?" Mark smiled. "That brings back memories. You might want to ask mom or dad first." "Ask dad what?" Keith asked coming out of the kitchen with another order.

"Trey, your orders up." He nodded towards the plate sitting on the counter. The restaurant is almost empty by now, and Trey had long gotten used to getting his own plate. He didn't mind, and still left good tips, regardless. "Thanks Keith." He grabbed the plate. "Hey Rees. How's college going?"

He patted my back for a second with his free hand. "So far so good. How're things with you?" I turned in the chair, so I was facing him rather than on the side. "Couldn't be better, thanks, Zeni." He held up the plate. "Keep enjoying school Rees. It'll be over before you know it."

He smiled as he turned back towards Brad, and Jan who had finished their sandwiches, and were watching him. "Who is that?" Jan asked nodding in Reesa's direction. "She's cute, and a very nice waitress." "Teresa Harris. Goes by Reesa. She's Keith's, and Zeni's daughter." He answered taking a bite of his sandwich.

"You know her very well?" She is hoping he'd say yes and ask her out. It had been years since he was with someone decent, and the girl at the counter is a bouncing ball of energy, but in a good fun way. "More so now than when we were in high school. Mostly when we'd deliver here, it would just be Zeni or Keith. Sometimes Mark, but not often. I think this last year she's been around a lot more. She's making her major Business Management."

"Taking over?" "Soon, Zeni talks once in a while about her, and Keith taking the big retirement plunge, but they will wait awhile." Trey answered finishing his sandwich. "So." Bret said, folding his arms, and changing the subject since Trey was not catching the hints. "When are we going to add horses to the barn?"

"What?" Trey asked with a questioning look on his face. "Why horses?" "Adds a nice mix. Plus, I love thoroughbreds." "I'd love to raise some, but we don't have the money right now." "So, when would we?" Bret asked taking one of Trey's fries. "Soon as one of us wins the lottery. Horses are beautiful creatures. They are also expensive." Trey answered ending the conversation and finishing his potato salad at the same time. "Ready to go?" They all left together, and I smiled behind their backs, and turned my attention back to dad answering his earlier question.

"I was wondering if you need anything for dinner." Keith answered after a brief hesitation. "No, but thanks. Why don't you head home now? Bessie's been asking where you've been for the last two hours." I laughed. "I've only been off the bus for half an hour."

"You know your sister. Melodrama at its finest. Go on." He laughed and squeezed my shoulder. I headed home and thought about how different my life is now. I felt in a large part a visitor, and not a daughter. That is silly, so I forced the idea out of my head, and jogged up the stone steps, and opened the door to silence.

"Bessie?" I called, and heard faint noises upstairs, so I rushed up the carpeted steps, and followed the noise to Bessie's room where she stood by her bed fingering a white slip, and blue high heels. "Hey you." I greeted from the doorway. I smiled as Bessie turned around. "What took you so long?" She demanded. "Look at my shoes I picked out."

I stepped further into the room and sat down on the bed. I hardly made a dent in the still firm mattress. "They're pretty, but how do you know they'll match your dress?" "The color is midnight blue. There are plenty of dresses in that color. I've already called Macy's, and JC Penney's. They have four dresses on hold for me to try on. Even if I can't find something in that exact color, the saleswomen said, they'll find something else that'll compliment my shoes."

"I guess you've got it all figured out. I can't wait to go shopping. What time do you want to go?" I rubbed my hands together. "Right after breakfast. That'll give me time to have a morning cup of coffee first." "I've never understood how you can drink that stuff."

"You wouldn't, however, you would understand habits. Especially the bad kind called Diet Pepsi." Bessie teased and turned back to the

The Way Life Used To Be

bed to grab the shoes and put them in her closet. "I know of no such thing." I folded my arms in front of my chest and stuck my chin out. "We all have our vises." I said, as Bessie continued looking in my direction. I changed the subject. "Are you going out with Jeremy later?" "On your first day here after not seeing you for months, and months. What kind of sister do you take me for?"

"It's been three months, and you're the best kind." I reached over and hugged her. Tears started flowing down my cheeks. "Hey. Hey. What's with the tears?" She asked wiping one away with her thumb. I swiped at my eyes. "I don't know. My love for college is huge, but I'm so homesick. I never thought I'd feel like this."

"Like shit huh?" "Yes." I wiped my eyes again and dried my palms on my T-shirt. "Want to help me with dinner?" "Now you're talking." Bessie rubbed her hands together, "and just so you know, it's been just as hard on us with your gone even if it is to get smarter." "Us?" I asked. "Everyone, especially me. Second place is mom, I guess. She talks about you a lot, and she's so proud of you. Almost as much as me." She teased, glancing over her shoulder, and smiling at me.

"Thanks Bess, I needed to hear that." I squeezed her neck, and we walked side by side down the stairs. We headed straight towards the kitchen. "So, what should we make? I'm at your disposal." Bessie asked. "Fried pork sandwiches. We can make a green salad too." I said, after looking in the cupboards, and refrigerator. "Sounds good. Is Paul a good cook, and why didn't he come with you. We're all dying to meet him." She took a pound of ground pork from the bin and tossed it on the counter.

"I left him at school this time. I needed this time alone, so I didn't bring him with me. I'm a little scared too of everyone's reactions. I don't know if he cooks or not since we don't have kitchen privileges at school. It's either a microwave or the dining halls. You'd think I'd be gaining some weight by now." I glanced down at my stomach and pressed a hand there.

"You won't have a problem with the family meet thing. Dad, and Mark will tease him a little, but that's what they're good at. It's an icebreaker thing with them." "That's why I'm scared. Paul has a good sense of humor, as he has to put up with Carla's jokes. He never complains about it." I got out some oil and started pouring some into a skillet.

"Well that's something right there. So how hot is he?" That made me laugh as I started forming patties. I didn't respond though. I started blushing giving me away. "That hot?" I blushed harder because I'm already missing him. I wished he was there with me.

Bessie glanced at my stomach and found it flat as a pancake. "You might be right about losing some weight. You might need a double dosing of dessert." She put the oil back in the cupboard. "The fried sandwiches will hit their mark. I can just about guarantee it." The pork started sizzling. "So besides being hot, how serious is it with him, anyway?" She asked getting out some lettuce.

I shrugged. "Not very. At least not right now. We've only been together for a few months so it's hard to say." I cut up some tomatoes and tossed them into a white bowl along with some chopped up lettuce. "You look happier." "How can you tell?" Some green onions joined the salad mix. "Your face is serene." She flipped the meat to cook on the other side.

I laughed again. "Serene? That's a word I've never heard you use." Bessie laughed too. "I'm improving on my vocabulary skills. You impressed?" "Highly," "You have a glow now. I know it as I have it too. I love Jeremy more than ever. You're not pregnant, are you?" She whipped her head towards me, making her curls flap against her cheek.

"Might be a little hard when I've yet to sleep with him. Are you thinking of marriage yet?" I asked. I've never heard her talk this way. Bessie shook her head. "Not yet, he's been hinting around, but hasn't yet popped the question." "He will soon, and you'll say yes." "Damn right I will." Bessie slammed the spatula on the counter, and a little grease flew off, and landed on the floor. "Oops, I guess I'm not the world's best cook yet. Why haven't you, and Paul hit the sheets yet?"

I shrugged. "Not ready I guess." "Just for the record, mom's happy for you. Dad also seems to be coming around. He did the whole, I'm not ready for this, and all, but he's getting used to the idea. Mom's always smiling when she talks to you on the phone. You'd think she is the one who found Mr. Hottie." I chuckled, and placed the salad bowl on the table, and got out plates, and silverware. Ten minutes later, everyone was home, and like always dinner is on the table. It's almost like old times.

Looking for Bessie's dress proved to be a nightmare. We walked the length of the mall from Macy's to JC Penney's to Sears with no luck. I am ready to scream by the time we left Sears. No dress, and Bessie was showing her impatience. We took a break and have some lunch. "This sucks, big time." She pouted folding her arms over her chest and stuck out her lower lip.

"That's the little sister I know, and love." I teased digging into my chef salad. "That's not funny, I thought for sure Macy's would have my dress. They even had two extra picked out that would go with my shoes." She dangled the blue heels on one hand and ate a fry with the other. "What am I going to do?" She wailed.

"Quit spilling ketchup." I advised, pointing to a red glob on her pink shirt. "Again, not funny." Bessie looked down and moaned. "Oh. Your serious. This is one of my favorite shirts too." She dabbed a napkin on the blob and made it worse. "Oh shit. Now it will stain." She threw the napkin on the table and tossed the fries aside. "I'm not even hungry."

"Well I am, be just a few minutes, and we can continue." I popped a tomato into my mouth and chewed. "Can you go any slower?" Bessie yelled and tapped one foot. She is drawing the attention of several shoppers who stopped eating to stare at us. "Careful, you're attracting an audience." I nodded to a few tables. "I'm done now, are you ready?"

"Yes, I've been done for hours." Bessie scooted her chair back, and grabbed her shoes, and purse. She was already heading for the nearest clothes store by the food court. The store employees chose several dresses for Bessie to try on. I moved a lot slower, and fingered several pairs of earrings, and bracelets waiting for her to emerge from the dressing room. I ended up putting the jewelry back. I didn't have any desire to buy anything anymore.

"Ready." She yelled, and came out wearing a sleeveless midnight blue, and off-white silk dress that came to just below her calves. The skirt flowed in two layers and swished while she slipped on the heels. "It's perfect." I complimented because I meant it, but also because I didn't want to keep shopping.

"You don't want to keep looking?" Bessie turned around to look in a mirror and admired the way she looked. She turned in a complete circle, and the bottom of the dress followed her move. "No, I don't. In case you were wondering, we've already been to three stores. I'm done." The sales lady approached us. "That looks nice on you."

She complimented and smiled. "Cash or charge?" She was determined to make a sale. "Cash." Bessie answered, and headed back into the dressing room to change back into her jeans, and T-shirt. Half an hour later with the dress tucked away in a dressing bag, we entered the house. "All done? Let's see." Zeni asked getting up from her rocker.

Sandra Gutierrez

Bessie unzipped the bag half-way. "Oh. That's so pretty." She fingered the material. "I can't wait to take pictures." "You must wait awhile." "I have no choice, but to. Reesa, it's getting late, and you have classes tomorrow." "Don't remind me." I groaned and headed upstairs to pack the few clothes left on the bed. Once Bessie was out of hearing range, mom entered my room to find out how our day was.

"Need some help?" She asked walking into the bedroom where my suitcase lay on the bed. I thought for sure I'd be able to spend the next night here, but with classes first thing in the morning, and the bus schedule I would have missed two classes, and I didn't want to be absent so early in the semester.

"No, I'm just about done. I didn't even have time to unpack much. Only my jeans I'm wearing right now. I don't have even enough to warrant washing a load." I zipped the suitcase and dropped it on the floor next to my sweatshirt so it would be easier to grab when it was time to leave.

"How was the mall, anyway? I take it from Bessie's attitude it went well." I frowned. Zeni smiled, "and giving your attitude, it didn't." "I shouldn't feel small as Bessie is so happy now that she found a dress. At lunch, she was not a pleasant person to be around."

"I can just about imagine. How bad was the tantrum?" Mom sounded amused and concerned at the same time. She was also thankful she wasn't the one to have suffered. "Bad, I thought she would resort to throwing things, but we limited the damage to ketchup on her shirt. I thought for sure I would get hit over that one." I smiled and grabbed my purse to set on top of the suitcase.

"You don't have to put up with her outbursts." She advised. "I keep telling myself that. She ended up staining her shirt after waving around a French fry full of ketchup. I thought I'd feel sorry for her, but I just don't. I've been given a break from all that while being at school. Being here was not the perfect weekend I'd expected."

"I'm sorry for that." "I know you are, and it's not your fault. I'm glad I have to leave now, and it's not to get away from you, and dad. I hope you know that." "We do, I have to admit you can handle her better than I can. I've tried so many strategies, and although she's mellowed out a lot since her early teen years, she's still hard to handle."

I shook a finger in her direction. "Got that right, and onto juicer subjects now that the melodrama is gone for the moment. Did you ask

The Way Life Used To Be

Paul to Thanksgiving?" "I will as soon as I see him again. I'm scared that he'll say no, that it might be too soon to meet the parents."

"If he did, I wouldn't judge him for it. This is a big deal meeting the entire family. He might be uncomfortable no matter what." Zeni lifted herself off the doorframe and took the suitcase as I was leaning down for it. I took the sweatshirt, and a purse with the return bus ticket in the front slot. I closed my bedroom door, and we started walking down the stairs.

"Have you told him about Hankins?" She asked as we reached the bottom. "No, I've talked about every other subject imaginable, but not that one. He won't understand." "You never know unless you try. If you're falling in love, which you are, you need to be open about everything. Keeping secrets is never a good thing." "I hear you." I said. "Is he shy in general?" "No, he's on the quiet side for the most part. At least until he gets to know you. He's not into college parties or getting drunk."

"Sounds responsible. How're Carla, and Taylor doing?" "They're still together. I think she will marry him someday." "I'm surprised they haven't already taken the plunge yet. Is she getting good grades at least?" We made it to the front door, but I was reluctant to get back on the bus. This was always the hardest part for me, even though I was looking forward to seeing Paul again.

"Mostly, she doesn't care, which seems like a waste of money." I smiled behind one shoulder as I opened the front door. Dad, and Mark came out from the kitchen to say a last goodbye. I hugged each of them and turned to go out the door.

By the time I got back to school and started classes I was piping mad that I hadn't heard from Paul all week. I had my speech about Thanksgiving all planned, and he hadn't shown up for a single class. Our assignments were close to being due, and I fumed that he would just dismiss both me, and his schoolwork.

I stepped into class on Thursday and found him sitting at his desk smiling. "Hey." He greeted. "Hey back." I sat down and forced a polite smile on my face. I hoped it hid my true feelings. "Where were you all this week?" He looked awful and pale.

I felt guilty for the mad feelings, and my polite smile turned into a genuine concern. "Flu. Major letdown. I'm now best friends with my toilet. We had quite a few, heart to heart talks." He teased, making me laugh. "How is your weekend? Did Bessie find her dress?"

Sandra Gutierrez

"Yes, she did, she will look beautiful. I'm glad I got to go home for a while, and even more glad to be back in the grind." I opened a book and turned a few pages until I found the chapter we were on. "That's good, hopefully she has a blast. I'm glad you had fun." He commented.

"I did mostly. You look like your about to have another conversation with your toilet. What's it going to be about this time?" I teased. "The best way to puke without touching the sides. I haven't thrown up in a while though. I'm over this damn bug, sorry we haven't talked all week."

I laughed while we waited for the instructor to grace us with her presence. "I'm staying out of that one." "I don't blame you." "I'm glad you're feeling better." I smiled. I was just as miserable, and lonely as he is. This would have been the perfect opportunity to invite him to Thanksgiving, but the door slammed shut showing class is about to begin. I turned to the front of the room to pay attention to the instructor.

"Good morning class. How is everyone today?" The instructor interrupted. "I need you to form your groups for the skits by Friday. I know that only gives one day, but I only have three groups. The rest of you need to get moving. They need to be at least two people, and only four. I have the sign-up sheet." She tapped the notebook next to her.

Once class was dismissed, we signed our names, and walked out together holding hands. The sky threatened rain, and it was cold outside. I am regretting not bringing a coat to wear. "Want to go to the library? We can prepare for our skit." No time like the present. If we started right away, we'd have a decent chance for a good grade. "Sure, we can do a repeat performance of the last five minutes." I laughed out loud.

"Actually, that is a good idea. I'm sure the rest of the class is just salivating with jealously." We started walking together. He had one hand on my shoulder. I loved it when he is close to me. "We can do a comedy act. Who says it has to be serious or even make much sense? We can toss ideas back, and forth until we come up with something."

We are enjoying each other as we continued talking as we reached the library. He held the door open for me as always. I loved his manners. "Want to go to a movie soon?" He asked as we made our way to the third floor. That area of the library is reserved for studying and is empty for once. That is nice. I hated big crowds. "I'd love to." I answered him already looking forward to it.

The Way Life Used To Be

"Friday sound good?" "Perfect." I smiled up at him. We found an empty table near a window that overlooked the river. "I love the water." I could barely see the river from the library window, but I knew it was there.

"You spend a lot of time there?" He never once went swimming in a pool, much less a river. He had every intention of fixing that soon. He however didn't know how to begin explaining his own upbringing. He envied everyone who had a wonderful childhood.

"Before I started college, Bessie, and I used to go swimming in the river all the time. Carla came with us a lot too. It was a summer ritual with us." "Sounds like a lot of fun. When do you want to go with me?" "Soon as you ask me. Of course, you might want to wait until the weather is a little warmer. Might freeze a limb or two now." "You're probably right."

"You want a soda? Then we can get started if you like." He asked nodding to a machine. I nodded, and he returned with a mountain dew for himself, and a Diet Pepsi for me. "Who came up with Bessie for a name?" He asked. Sam had a lot of nicknames for him, and he always loved visiting him during school breaks. Surely, he had never heard of the robbery, and I didn't know if he would turn in disgust or if he would understand. I never talked about this other than the few selected people. I didn't want to lose him over something like this.

"My dad did, he loves nicknames, and he also came up with mine. I've never gone by Teresa except when I first meeting someone." I answered. "You were never Teresa to me." "Your privileged, I've always been more comfortable being called Reesa, so that might be why." "So, when am I going to meet everybody. Bessie sounds like a unique person."

"She is that, even at her worse moments, I don't know what I'd do without her. I've come to terms with it though. I'm so looking forward to graduating. I'm already picturing myself owning Starlights." "Are you kicking out your parents already?"

I shook my head. "Only when mom takes the plunge into retirement life. Mark will still be there. He used to say college is in his future, but he won't ever attend. He's been working with my parents since he was fifteen, and he wouldn't be very happy anywhere else. He used to say he had bigger, and better plans for his future, but he's blowing smoke."

"I can see his point of view. If it wasn't for my Uncle Sam, I probably wouldn't have tried either. He was the one who gave me my scholarship from his firm," he said after taking a drink of his soda. We still hadn't touched our assignment, but neither of us noticed or cared.

"What firm?" I asked. "Presauret, and Eggert. My uncle, and his best friend started it back in the eighties. They still have an active practice but are also talking retirement." "Sam? Samuel Presauret?" I asked surprised and pleased to hear his name again. "My uncle represented you." He stated matter-of-factly. "Sam used to talk about you, and your family. How brave, and strong you all were. I can see why. You need that family bond to make it through the tough times."

He turned my hand over and kissed the palm. "I was at the courthouse the day they sentenced Greg. I sat near the back since Sam, and I had plans to have dinner that night, but he didn't know what time they'd be done. I saw you at the front pew with your mom, and dad. I never approached you though. I was there only as a visitor. Once the sentence was read, and it was all over, we went out to dinner as planned. I'm sorry, but I never gave it a second thought. I can tell that you do."

"Why didn't you tell me you already knew me?" I asked. All this confused me. "Because when I was at the trial, you looked right at me. You waved to Sam as we left the courtroom. I assumed you knew this whole time who I am." I listened to him with my mouth cracked. "Sorry, I don't remember much about that day except for being elated Greg would get punished for what he did. I'll never forget what your uncle did for my family. Are you still close?"

He nodded finishing his soda. "Very much so. I'm visiting him during the Thanksgiving Break. You should come too and say hi. He would love to hear from you." I was so relieved he opened that book first. "I'm glad you brought that up. My mom's been asking when she will meet you and wanted me to ask you to Thanksgiving Dinner. The whole family will be there. Should I tell her no? That you have other plans?" I asked.

He shook his head in response. "No, I'd love to come. I have a chance to get to know them. Sam's going to a club for dinner. He does that every year so I'm free. He's never put on a Thanksgiving spread in his life." "You made that an easy decision." "I aim to please, ready for dinner?"

I glanced at the wall clock and found it was almost five. Early for dinner, but my stomach was already growling. We gathered up our books

The Way Life Used To Be

and got ready to leave. The afternoon seemed to fly by. "Sure." "Okay. Meet you in an hour?" He asked, and I nodded.

Once we got outside, we went our separate ways. It was ten minutes later when I reached my dorm room. I was running the whole time so I wouldn't be late for dinner. I flung open the door to find it empty. Shit, I wanted to tell Carla about my talk. I'm so proud at the way I handled things. I didn't even panic this time. She is probably making plans with Taylor.

I changed my clothes and made it to the dining hall with two minutes to spare. It's almost six by then, and I am starving by now. I picked out spaghetti, and meatballs with garlic bread. I also made a small salad before exiting the kitchen and entered the open dining area. I scanned the crowd, and didn't see Carla or Paul anywhere, I hated eating by myself.

I got a drink from the fountain and sat at an empty table towards the back wall and started eating. I didn't even bring a book for company. "Sorry I'm late." It's Paul rushing towards me with a smile, and an apology. "That's okay, I just got here." I replied smiling back at him. He sat down and ate a bite of his hamburger. "Man am I hungry. I didn't realize how late it's getting."

"Me too." I started eating slower. I'm almost done, and I didn't want to sit there with nothing to do. "Hey guys." It's Carla. "Hi, want to join us?" Paul asked gesturing to a seat beside him. "Sure thanks. Reesa, I just got done talking to Taylor. He's coming down here Friday and will be here about four. I can't wait." She started doing a butt boogie in her chair causing both Paul and me to smile.

"You look happy. You can't even sit still. I may not be there when Taylor gets here. You might have to say hello for me." "Why?" Carla asked. "Because we're going to a movie. Come to think of it, we haven't had a date in quite a while." Paul answered. He smiled at both of us before he started eating again.

"Cool, what are you going to see?" She took a bite of her lasagna followed by a drink of her Coke. The dinner itself sucked, but it's food so it's hard to complain. Paul shrugged. "Not sure what's playing right now. I figured who cares right?" He earned two nods to his question and finished up his dinner. He pulled his chair back. "Reesa, I'll call you soon with details. That okay?"

"Yeah, are you leaving already?" I'm disappointed even though I had long finished the spaghetti. I'm enjoying the evening with my friend, and my boyfriend. "I need to study. Will you walk with me awhile?" "Sure, she will." Carla answered for me with a smug smile. "Have fun." Paul, and I left together hand in hand.

"It sure is a pretty night." He smiled up at the sky. The stars were bright, and twinkling. "Sure is." I agreed. "Are you sure about Thanksgiving? I can tell my mom no for this time. Her feelings won't get hurt." "I said, yes, and I say what I mean. I've heard so many stories that not to meet them would be a sin." "Sin?" I raised an eyebrow.

"Would go against proper protocol. I'd love to meet everyone, and if they are half as easy going as you, it'll be a piece of cake." "I'm hoping so. I'm sure dad will take you over to Starlights. Give you a chance to check out their pride, and joy." "I hope so." We reached the first floor of the dorms, and instead of heading right up to my room, he stopped walking, and turned so he is facing me, and gathered my face in his hands. He kissed me. It was like the wind is whispering across my cheek.

I closed my eyes and held my breath. I'm falling head over heels in love with him, and instead of scaring me like I'm convinced I would be, it felt so right. So right that I didn't want to tell Carla right away. I said, goodbye, and told Paul I'd walk myself up the stairs. Once he was gone, I waved to his back, and started walking by myself away from campus, and towards the water. I wanted some time alone to think about what had just happened.

I realized that he said nothing personal about his own family other than Sam. I hoped he wasn't embarrassed about anything. I wanted to ask him, but something kept me from opening my mouth. If it's important, he'd eventually say it. I reached the river and looked west. I expected to see Starlights, and my house. I was lonely for the first time in two months, and I thought about walking all the way home just so I could see them.

The water is black, and still. It's beautiful, and peaceful. I slipped out of my sandals, and stepped off the bank, and onto s, and. The water is rippling. I'm tempted to camp out here instead of heading back to my room. I dipped both feet into the water and gasped at how cold it is. I kept my feet beneath the waves thinking at the same time how wavy my own life is. It's close to nine when I finally got up and headed for my room. I am confident my family would accept Paul.

Chapter 7

"**M**ama!" I yelled. "What is it? You sound happy." Zeni asked. She had just finished dinner and is starting the dishes when the phone rang. She set aside the small side as she settled in her favorite chair to enjoy her talk. This would be a better one than last week, and she wouldn't be crying.

Keith is upstairs, and she said, "Say hi for me." He was getting ready to go to a movie with Mark, and Sara. Zeni declined saying she had a headache. "I am, oh mama am I ever. I have news." "Well don't keep me in suspense. What is it? You, and Paul aren't planning on eloping, are you?" I giggled. "Not yet. I'll let you know." "Better not. At least not until you get to know him a hell of a lot better. Did you ask him to Thanksgiving?" "I did, and he said yes right away. He said he's looking forward to meeting everyone."

"Improvement." Zeni laughed, "Seriously though, I'm glad he's willing to meet us instead of wanting to avoid it. We'll make it as painless as possible." "Good, see you in a week." I said, goodbye, and bounced up, and down on the bed waiting for Carla to come back so I could share my news.

I'm in love with Paul. I love his name, his face, his heart, his everything. Carla's only concern is how long it would be before we made it to bed together. It made me laugh at her directness. I wish I had her confidence when it came to boys.

Our skit was a success which is a wonder as we only spent about half an hour preparing for it. We finished this project right before the holiday weekend began. On Wednesday afternoon the day before, Paul drove both of us to my house. "You will love my family." I sighed as I lay back in the seat to enjoy the ride. "They sound nice. I'm a little nervous though." He held up a hand to show me the tremble. "I expect A little nerves. You want to meet them first or see your Uncle, and we'll meet up later?" I asked grabbing my purse from the floorboard.

"I'll go in with you first." "Did you forget they invited us for dinner tonight?" "I will stay at his house with him while we are here, and he's looking forward to having a beer with me. Should be interesting." He stopped the car at the curb. "Oh yeah. I forgot about dinner. The all-important getting to know your ordeal, you ready?" I asked leaning over the seat to grab my overnight bag from the back seat. "You make that sound like I'm in for a torture fest." He teased. I smiled. "Let's go, I'm ready as I'll ever be." He is less happy at the thought of meeting the family now. It sounded like a good idea four days ago, but now they were here he wanted to go back.

That is until the front door opened, and he stepped inside to warmth and a house full of people all talking at once. "Get the plates to the table." Zeni said. Mark reached in the cupboard above the stove. "No, No, The ceramic ones in the cupboard over the sink." Keith told Mark. They were all in the kitchen getting ready to set the table, and their voices could be heard way out in the living room.

"Hi. I'm Mark." Mark extended his hand to Paul with a smile. He, and Sara moved into the living room when they heard the front door open. "Hey Reesa." Sara opened her arms and gave me a hug. "Hey back." I returned her hug. "This is Paul Whitfield. Paul, this is my older brother Mark, and girlfriend Sara Bevins."

"Fiancée." Sara corrected and stuck out her left hand. Her ring is made of white gold, and it sparkled in the light. "When did this happen?" I gushed and grabbed her hand to pull it closer to my face. "That's a doozy. I'm so happy for the both of you." I complimented and released her hand. "Hey Reesa. This Paul?" Bessie bounded down the stairs with a kiss on the cheek for me and stared with a wide smile at Paul who stood in the entrance taking all of this in.

"Hey you, hi Jeremy." I kissed her back and turned my attention to Jeremy who is standing next to her. He had an arm draped over her shoulders. He looked right at home. They smiled at me. I took Paul's hand which had turned clammy. He still looked dumbfounded, and not at all sure what to make of us. True, we were so friendly, and outspoken, and I had a feeling he just wasn't used to it.

Paul looked more than a little scared. "Come meet my parents." I offered and took him into the kitchen where Zeni stood by the table

The Way Life Used To Be

filling glasses and tossed a greeting over her shoulder before she realized Paul is standing next to me.

She turned around the same time as Keith who extended his hand, and said, "Hello Paul. It's nice to meet you." "Nice to meet you sir. Ma'am," Paul nodded once he could speak. "It's Keith and Zeni. Nice to put a face to a name." Zeni said, with a smile. "Come here, baby." I folded myself in her arms, and dad came around my back, and held me tight. Paul watched with a small smile on his face. His heart started beating again. It would be okay. He realized at that moment she is a mama's girl.

"Mama." I whispered, and mom let me go. "Dinner is just about ready." Conversations flowed like the food. Paul helped himself to a taco shell, and Bessie handed him a bowl full of hamburger meat. "Thank you." He said, smiling at her. "So. How long have you two been going together?" Bessie earned a sharp nudge in her side. "Hey," she said, to dad, who is frowning in her direction. "I am just making conversation." She sounded like the Bessie from years ago, and we were all prepared for another sulking attack. She knew how long we've been together as I told her every chance I could on every single update.

She however surprised us by shrugging and turned her attention to Jeremy who is well used to her mood swings by now. Mark came to Paul's rescue because Paul just sat there. He isn't sure how to deal with all this. "What are you studying?" He asked, as Paul swallowed some salad. "Something in Education. I'm not sure what my exact major will be right now, but I love school, and I hope to get a job in middle or high school. The younger grades scare me just a little." He smiled.

"That sounds inspirational. I had a lot of fun in school myself. I just don't want to work in a college." Mark replied and took a bite of his taco. Paul nodded. He liked Reesa's older brother. "I didn't think I'd like it either, but now that Reesa, and I are together, it's a lot more enjoyable." I blushed and remained silent. Paul's comment however earned smiled from all around like, everyone knew the secret, but refused to share it with me.

Paul found he enjoyed this the more the evening wore on. We all talked at once, and nobody minded when someone else interrupted with a comment or a suggestion. The conversations just flowed. They included him like he was one of them, and he loved the closeness they shared. Dessert was chocolate cake with ice cream, and everyone could barely stand up afterwards. "Reesa, let's talk." Sara grabbed my hand while Paul waved us off with a smile.

We strolled upstairs to my bedroom. I wandered over to the window while Sara sat on the bed. "I miss home." "I bet, how is college besides Paul?" "Lonely, and exciting at the same time. I miss home so much it hurts sometimes, but I love my classes, and getting to know other people. There are also no memories of Greg there." I said, leaning my head on the windowsill.

"It's a totally different atmosphere than high school. There's no drama filled hallways with people breaking up every second of the day or hour." "That's one thing about high school I don't miss. You don't have any memories of Greg?" She asked.

"Well, I guess there's one. The prosecuting attorney Samuel Presauret is Paul's uncle." "Wow, Is that hard for you?" Sara pulled a blanket over her as she settled on the bed. "Yeah, I did good though. I was shocked, and wanted to panic, but I held it together." "That's good."

"How're you, and Mark doing?" "Wonderful as always. I enjoy being here. Never a dull moment." She smiled as she twirled the ring around on her finger. "We will stay in my apartment for now. He's already started moving some of his stuff over there. It's been a busy couple of weeks." "I bet." I am a little sad that Mark is leaving. It's for the best, but I wished it was me that is moving out. Sara is the right person for him, and I'm happy for them both.

"Dad is a little concerned we were moving too fast, but for once Mark stood up for himself." "Did Bessie make it about herself?" "No more than normal. She had a crying fest that lasted a week about a month ago or so. Bessie, and Jeremy got in their first fight, and to hear Bessie tell it, all men are assholes, and belong on the bottom of our shoes." She shook her head. "I'm not sorry I missed that one. When's the wedding?" I asked to change the subject. I'm hoping Bessie is done being a bitch.

"Next New Year's Eve, that's over a year away, we wanted to take it slow, and have it perfect. Plus, my Grandfather agreed to walk me down the aisle. He can't make it till then." She explained. "So, tell me. How did my brother propose? I didn't understand things were this serious between you?" I asked. "The traditional way. We had gone to a movie a few weeks ago. I don't remember the name or much about it, but when it was over, and I tossed the drinks in the garbage, he turned to me right in the theater, and proposed in front of many people."

The Way Life Used To Be

"Were you embarrassed?" I interrupted. "Not at all. They cheered us on, and I started giggling before he reached into his pocket, then he asked me to be his wife. It was a very special moment for us. I shouted yes, and I pulled him close to me, and French kissed him in public. Everyone clapped, and then we came home to tell mom, and dad. They were shocked. They hid it pretty well. Mom is making my cake for me."

"Your mom?" "No, Yours. I don't speak with my parents anymore. Ever since Mark, and I got together, I've called Keith and Zeni, Mom, and dad. They've been there for me in so many ways that my own haven't." She sounded sad, and happy all at the same time. "There's always room for one more sister. Welcome to the family,", I reached over, and hugged her hard.

"What happened between you, and your parents? Is that why your grandfather is walking you down the aisle?" I asked as gently as I could. "Not much that I remember when I was younger. Remember that talk we had in the lunch room right before you were stabbed?"

"Most of it, something about a customer who is rude, and got kicked out." "That's the gist of it. Once I was over it, and realized it wasn't my fault, I ran home to repeat my story. I was feeling better about standing up for myself and wanted to share it. My mom was there, but my dad hadn't come home yet. I told her about it, and she called me a bitch." "Why?" I asked realizing this is the first time Sara had opened up to me in the four years she, and Mark were together. I never thought to ask about her own upbringing. It made me realize how little I knew her, and how much I wanted to change that.

"She said, I should never have said something so inappropriate, especially in the workplace. I tried to explain myself, but she said, not to bother. It's inexcusable that I would have the nerve to speak with a customer in that manner. She was ashamed of my behavior, and when my dad got home, and she repeated what I told her, he took me to the shed, and beat me with a belt."

My eyes became wide, and tears filled them. "Oh my god. Over that?" She nodded. "I'm so sorry Sara. I never even asked about any consequences. I was just so happy you started talking about Mark. That's all I fixated on." Sara waved a hand. "It's over and done with. After he told me to pull up my pants, I packed a bag of clothes, and ran away that very night. They didn't even bother to come looking for me. This was not the first time he raised a hand to me, but I made it the last."

"That's awful." "Yeah it was." Sara nodded in agreement. "I just never realized it until recently how much. My God when I look back now, I was sixteen years old. Almost an adult, and I shouldn't have had to worry about getting whipped every time I turned around." "Sounds like child abuse to me. When did it start?" I'm more than a little shocked at all this.

"I remember when I was little, it seemed we more like a real family. I don't remember if he spanked me or even yelled at me until I was a little older and had a mouth to fight back with. I had no brothers or sisters so that might have been a blessing or a curse depending on how you look at it. I must have been six or seven. That is the first spanking I remember."

"Still seems like abuse to me. Did your grandfather know about it?" I asked trying not to sound too angry. I tried to picture a parent. any parent losing control so badly, they didn't know how to stop. "No, I didn't tell him until years later. He said, how sorry he was that he didn't know his own son is a child abuser and wanted to bring up charges. It's too late now."

"He knows it as well as I do. That's why he offered to walk me down the aisle. I told him about the engagement a few weeks ago, and he said if he didn't walk me down the aisle, and give me away, he would never forgive himself. I want him to be there. I need him to be there. He's the only family I have now, and I also think this is his way of forgiving himself for what I had gone through."

She took a deep breath before continuing. "I realize now that it's child abuse. I didn't know it at the time even though all the signs were right in front of my face. When Mark, and I first started dating he touched my face with both hands, and I flinched so hard like I was waiting for a slap, it shocked him. I ended up telling him what happened.

"He was convinced he did something wrong. He made me tell him the whole story, but it didn't do much good." It made me realize what Sara saw in Mark. Mark saved me, and I'll never forget it. It was a very similar way Mark saved Sara as well. He just might not know it. "Why not? If he abused you, and your mom allowed it, they should be in jail." "Not enough evidence. I wasn't even allowed any counseling, and by the time I turned eighteen, and was officially on my own, I realized I had been doing so for some time. I just realized how down I seem."

"Tell me more about school." Sara asked wanting to change the subject. It's still so painful. "No, Finish your story. My moods are up,

The Way Life Used To Be

and down too, so I can handle it. More, I want to hear it." I said. "Okay,", Sara said, and continued after a minute. "Right after the beating in the barn I packed my things. I had nowhere to go. I had no money, no house, no nothing. I wondered the streets for a few hours and ended up at Hankins. Mr. Hankins was in his office and saw me walk in with my bag of clothes, and nothing else. I'm convinced to this day he felt sorry for me even though he denies it."

"He moved me into his spare bedroom. He gave me more hours at the store, so I'd have more money when I finally got out on my own. I've had my apartment for three years now." "I'm impressed and awed at the same time. When I got my first job, my only job, I never realized how generous he is, and still is." "He is. He asked about you about a month ago. Wanted to see when you graduate if you'd come back, and work for him again." Sara said.

"I'm still in shock. Tell him thank you, but Starlights is where I belong. It's my roots." "I can see that. I'm jealous of your family for so many reasons. You are all so much more connected than mine ever was. I've disowned my parents so when I call Keith and Zeni, my mom, and dad, I mean it." I reached over and hugged her hard. "I'm not jealous of that."

"Paul seems nice and talk about hot." Sara gasped and patted her heart with one hand. I laughed. "Speaking of Paul, I think it's time we head back downstairs." We thought he might be suffering, but he wasn't. Paul was having a good time talking with Zeni, and Keith in the living room. It's lit by only a table lamp, and the TV turned on low to the local news.

"Has Reesa told you about Starlights?" Keith was asking, as I made my way into the living room to sit down next to Paul. He put a hand around my shoulder and rubbed gently. "Yes. Several times. I'd like to see it. That way I can put a place to the name. Hey you." He greeted. "Have a nice visit?" I nodded and smiled. "We can go tomorrow afternoon. Dinner is not until four, so there's plenty of time." "Sure. Thanks." "Don't be late for dinner. Remember Ted is coming." Zeni told Keith who nodded. "Promise. We'll be home on time."

They both stood up, so it seemed a good time to end the visit. Paul glanced at his watch and found it was almost eight. "Well I guess I'll see you in the morning." He kissed me gently and then headed over to Sam's. I shut the door behind him and headed upstairs myself. Once everyone had settled down for the night, I found myself again unable to sleep. I also realized I hadn't felt this way the entire time at school. It's almost like, the attack is happening all over again, and I am reliving it. Maybe it's this place. This house I loved so much.

Maybe it's wrong to come here. I tossed, and turned for almost an hour before giving up, and getting out of bed. I stood by the window with my forehead pressed against the cold glass. It's quiet outside. No dogs barking. No kids screaming and having fun during the brief break from school.

I turned away from the window. I thought about a cup of hot cocoa like when I was little. That always made me smile plus sleep better afterwards. I crept down the stairs, careful not to wake anyone. I stepped into the kitchen, and mama was at the kitchen table. "Mama? What are you doing up?" "Waiting for you. Here's your cup." "Thanks." I took a drink. "Nice. You remembered marshmallows." "Always. Now onto serious subjects. How well do you know Paul's family?"

"I took another drink before answering. "I found out Samuel Presauret is his Uncle. He wants me to come visit for a while tomorrow." "The prosecuting attorney?" Zeni asked feeling shocked. I nodded. "Small world. Are they close?" "It appears so. Sam is the one who gave Paul a scholarship from his firm so he could go to college. I know little about his own parents though. What were you guys talking about earlier when I was upstairs?" "Not much to be honest with you. Just about school, and Keith and I compared our days in college. That seems to have changed little from what he told us. About his parents, they're not so nice people."

I shrugged my shoulders. "I hadn't thought about that. They might not be. Bessie seemed a little odd tonight." "Bessie's Bessie. She's grown up a lot in the last few years. Every now, and then when she's feeling jealous, her ugly side comes out. I wouldn't worry too much about it." Zeni waved a hand in an absent don't worry about it gesture. "I don't most of the time. I'm just trying to get good grades. That's my focus, but I don't stop worrying about my family."

"That's dad's, and my job. I'm glad you found someone to bring light back into your eyes again. That's what I want for you. Love, and happiness are essential to a happy heart. School is important, but love has no comparison. It's what makes you feel alive, and important." Zeni pressed a hand to her heart, "and special." She finished her drink. "Thanks mama. I understand now." I reached up to hug her and pressed my face into her hair. "Good."

The Way Life Used To Be

"Now enough of the serious subjects. I'm off to bed honey. Always remember when you need to talk, I'll be here for you." She smiled as she rinsed the cup in the sink. I smiled back at her and gave her a kiss on her cheek. I headed back to bed where I fell asleep as soon as my head hit the pillow. Maybe that's all it took was a good heart to heart to sleep at night.

I woke up the next morning to a cloudy, and cold day, but it didn't matter. Paul was here, and it made getting out of bed easy with him waiting for me. "Where is everyone?" I asked once I got out of bed and was downstairs in the warm kitchen waiting for breakfast. Dad is at the stove scrambling some eggs, and other than him, the kitchen is empty. "Off doing everyone's own thing. Mom reminded everyone that dinner will be at four, and anybody who forgets will go hungry without sympathy or tears." Keith smiled as he spooned eggs onto a plate.

I laughed, "daddy, you always make jokes. Mom made that particular punishment just for you." "You know. I think you might be on to something." He placed the plate in front of me. "Eat." Thirty minutes later Paul arrived. My plate was empty by then, and I had already put it in the sink. I kissed dad, and told him to have fun, and we left together. Once we were out of sight, we held hands, and kissed.

"I've wanted to do that all morning. All yesterday come to think of it." Paul said, wrapping his arms around me. "I meant what I said, last night. I like your family. Thank you for including me." "I'm glad you like them. It would have been a very tense, and uncomfortable situation otherwise." I teased taking his arm. "What do you want to do now? Take a walk or something?"

"Sounds good." He smiled at me, and we started walking leaving his car by the curb. Once we reached the river, he asked "Is this the same one at school?" pointing to the water. "The same." We walked along the bank for a few minutes saying nothing. It's nice not having to say something every single minute. We reached a small park. It's empty. At this time of year, we rarely used the park. We each sat on a swing, swaying while we lifted our faces to the sky. "I love the fall." I whispered with my eyes closed.

"Me too, not as much as summer though. It's drier than anything, but I love it anyway." I swung a little higher until my feet left the ground. "Who saved you before?" I gave him a blank look. "I mean, when you were stabbed, who saved you?" He asked as gently as he could. "My brother, when I was lying on the floor looking up, and wondering why the hell nobody came to help me, I saw my brother. You should have seen his eyes." I shivered for a second while he looked at me waiting to hear me out. "It's hard to describe them. I swear they were red, and not a brilliant sunset red. They were fire. Pure hard angry red. I've seen nothing like that before."

Paul is quiet for a while. I have. He didn't say it out loud. "That explains why he's so protective of you. In a similar way as your parents are. That must have been hard when you enrolled at school. I should be sorry, but I'm not. I'm glad we met, and even gladder we're together." He leaned over, and we kissed. "Gladder is not a word." I teased.

"It is for me." He teased back. "You ready to see Sam? He's been asking about you." I nodded, and we left for his uncle's house. It wasn't even noon yet, so we had plenty of time. Ten minutes later we were in Sam's kitchen enjoying iced tea while he asked how I was doing. "So much better now. I have you to thank for that. I don't know how I would have gotten through everything if he wasn't convicted. Simple community service wouldn't suffice either." I sounded bitter I'm sure, but Sam smiled.

"It wouldn't have. I haven't heard of any parole hearing, so no news is good news." "I'm still hoping he gets denied and spends the rest of his life there. That's just one dream I keep hoping will come true." I finished my tea and declined a refill. "Keep your fingers crossed. You never know." Sam smiled at me. "It is good to see you. Paul's right. You look happy now."

I blushed and glanced at Paul who was sitting with one leg crossed over the opposite knee and smirking at me. "That's right," he agreed. "You do. You should see your face right about now." "I'll pass on that. Thanks." I am still blushing, but neither of them seemed to mind. "So. How's the rest of your family doing?" Sam asked. "Right now, they're busy getting dinner ready. Overall they are both very well." "Good to hear. School's going okay I take it?" "So far so good."

We continued talking until almost two when Paul realized before I did how late it's getting. He gave Sam a quick hug, and we headed back. Once we were almost home, I pointed out Starlights. It's dark. Our house already smelled delicious with the turkey bubbling in the oven, and Zeni is peeling potatoes. "Smells so much better than our cafeteria." I said, giving her a hug. "It should, are you going to the restaurant too?" Zeni started chopping the potatoes and dumped them into a pan.

The Way Life Used To Be

I shook my head. "Nope, I'll leave that to dad to handle. Can I help?" I gestured to the stove. "I will never turn down an offer. You can finish peeling, and I need to start on the stuffing." She smiled as she reached into the refrigerator for some onions and began chopping. Once the room filled with the scent of onions, and our eyes started watering, I asked. "So, do you like Paul?"

Zeni turned from the stove. "Yes, we do. He seems like a very nice, and polite young man. I'm glad you're together, and we one hundred percent approve." "Good, it scared me when I brought him here that he would be subjected to the third degree, and lots of staring, and uncomfortable moments. It hasn't been like that at all, and Paul was enjoying himself." "I wouldn't worry about him, and dad. He knows what he's doing, and I can tell he approves."

"What do I approve?" Keith asked entering the kitchen and gave Zeni a loud smack on her neck. "Stinks in here." "It doesn't stink. That would be your homemade stuffing you're complaining about. In response to your comment, and eavesdropping I am telling Reesa you approve of Paul, and don't you dare say otherwise." She pointed a wooden spoon in his direction.

Keith grinned. "Wouldn't think of it. We're getting ready to go." He said, "Just make sure your back in an hour. Dinner will be ready, and the punishments will be plenty if anyone is late." She attempted to look stern, but Keith could see right through her. "Promise?" Keith teased and patted her on the butt causing her to laugh out loud. "Yes, I promise. Now Scat." She giggled. "We're leaving, Paul you ready?" He shouted disappearing out of the kitchen, and headed towards the living room where Paul waited, talking with Mark.

"Let's go, it's closed for the night, but I can give you the grand tour. Mark, are you coming?" "No, I've had enough of that place for a while. I need a break." He sounded weary and headed upstairs where Sara was waiting. They left together, and Keith drove the two blocks to the restaurant that stood on the corner block. It's black, and unwelcoming. That is the part Keith hated. It looked so much different in the daytime when the lights were on, and customers filled the tables.

"Reesa pointed it out to me earlier. I expected some Mom, and Pop place. At least that's what I had pictured in my head." "That it's not. Zeni, and I started this way back when it's just an old garage. Took years to complete, and a lot of hard work, but as you can see it's all worth it."

Sandra Gutierrez

He stopped the car, and they both got out, and locked the car doors. He unlocked the back door to the kitchen. "This is where Zeni, and I spend most of our time. It's clean now but try to picture the middle of the day, and customers from wall to wall wanting their food pronto. This place looks like a tornado then."

Paul looked around and saw their life. This is the life he wanted. Keith noticed. "You know you will tell her soon." He advised. Paul nodded. "I know." He said, nothing further. It's new to him they care so much.

He wondered around the kitchen in silence and stopped when he reached the register. There were several framed pictures of our family. Some old, and some new. "How?" He asked. "Not sure how. You just have to say it. I will not ask what you've been through, although just between you, and me, it's all over your face. You just have to say it. Force yourself to get it out. You'll feel better for it."

"Your right." Paul said and smiled. "I can see why Reesa's so proud. I will make myself a customer soon." "Looking forward to it, I have to brag now. Zeni makes the best salads in the world." Paul raised one eyebrow. "Absolutely. I wouldn't lie." Keith pressed a hand to his heart. "I swear by it," and grinned. "Then I'll definitely be coming here. I can't say no to that." Keith checked his watch, and it's almost three thirty. "Zeni will have my back any moment now."

"Yeah. I'm ready. Thanks for showing me your place. I can see why you love it." "Besides my family, this is my next best love. Let's go." They returned home with five minutes to spare. They were greeted by Zeni, and a big plastic spoon she is waving in their direction. "See." Keith poked Paul in the shoulder. "How much she loves me." "You are almost late." Zeni scolded. "Almost doesn't merit spankings." Keith kissed her on the cheek. "How can I help?"

"Flattery will not be getting you anywhere. You can finish whipping the potatoes." She kissed his forehead. While they finished getting dinner on the table, the doorbell rang, and Mark is the first to answer. "Ted! Come in. Dinner is just about ready," he greeted Ted. "Smells great in here. I'm starved." He handed the pie to Mark who carried it into the kitchen to place in the refrigerator until dessert time.

"Mom, dad, Ted is here." He yelled from the kitchen. He shut the front door and then headed to the dining room where everyone was seated waiting anxiously for the turkey to get carved. Keith is standing at the head of the table. "Ted, thanks for coming, and sharing this day

The Way Life Used To Be

with us. You bring my pumpkin pie?" "Absolutely. I had to buy it from Safeway, but it still looks edible. Where should I sit?" "Right here." He pointed to the only empty chair next to him with me on the other side.

"Hey Reesa, how are you enjoying school?" He asked after taking his seat and kissing me on the forehead. "You're looking so much better lately. Hey Paul. What's happening?" He gave Paul's shoulder a squeeze without waiting for me to answer him. "Not much. I haven't seen you in quite a while." He smiled. "Been busy. How's Sam?" "Busy too. I'll tell him you said, hi next time I see him." "Please do, Keith you going to carve the turkey, or shall I do the honors?" He teased. "Never, my job, and pleasure. Everybody, please hold hands while I say grace."

Once all our hands were linked Keith bowed his head. "Dear Lord, we thank you for another wonderful year, and having everyone we love, and cherish here with us today. Please watch over Reesa, and Paul, and make sure they come home safe for Christmas. Lord, we also thank you for all this food, and for the extra hands that will gladly pitch in to clean this up." That brought several giggles. "We also wish for everyone here on earth to have something to eat on this glorious day. Amen." He sat down and smiled at his family. "Let's eat."

Paul spent most of Saturday at Sam's for a longer visit, and to have lunch together. "I heard from your Mother." He said, the defenses went up regardless into full gear. "By phone?" Sam shook his head. "I didn't want to say anything yesterday. It was by letter. She's been released and living with some friends. I guess they helped her get a job at a goodwill store. It's only part-time, but it's a start. She seems happier now."

"I bet. Sam, I don't hate her, nor do I love her. She did nothing for me so..." He said, nothing further. "I didn't tell you that expecting you to go running to her with open arms. She knows there's no going back." "So why did you tell me." Paul asked confused by this turn of events. "In hopes you could someday like her again. She wronged you in every way, but hopefully she's matured. You sure have." "Didn't have a choice in the matter. Sam, I'm glad you told me. I really am. This gives me something to think on." "That's all I can ask of you. Now what do you want for dinner?"

Paul smiled while they went out for a change. I left with Sara to see her apartment since I was both bored, and curious where she lived. She drove us, and fifteen minutes after we left the house we turned into a driveway, and she parked the car. I had time to view the place while she grabbed her purse and locked the doors.

They made the apartments of wood painted a deep red with a brick foundation. It looked nice, at least to my young eyes. It had three stories, and she walked to a set near a fence at the back of the property and climbed one set of stairs. She lived on the second floor. She unlocked the door that was painted the same red as the building, and we stepped inside.

It's small with only one-bedroom. She did however make the effort, to make the place homey. She had a worn brown plaid couch and a wooden coffee table that had a vase of plastic flowers, and a vanilla spice candle on a brass plate. It's pretty and made the room pretty.

The kitchen is basic with a white refrigerator and matching white stove. It's clean with nothing, but a toaster on the counter. "You must enjoy living here." I stated smiling at her. "When I first moved here, I spent the first two months sleeping on the couch instead of my bed, and kept a chair pushed against the door jamb. I was so thankful to be away from them, and so scared at the same time. I was convinced they both would come after me and drag me back home. I had it all planned out in my head how I'd get such satisfaction from kicking them out."

"Sounds like it would have been." I said, still standing in the living room near the couch. "After that vision, I felt better about moving out. I stopped sleeping on the couch and placed the chair back where it belonged. The longer it went without them beating down my door, I began to miss them. I had no one who cared about me except for Mr. Hankins. I wanted my parents."

"I've never known abandonment. I wouldn't know how it feels. Wouldn't want to. I know love and have seen it first-hand. Mark used to talk about past girlfriends every so often. He had a smile on his face when he did, and yes, I'm happy for him. None of them worked out as you can see." Sarah smiled at that. "I never had a high school boyfriend before him. I don't know if that is my fault or just the way it's supposed to be. Once we got together, I was happy for the first time."

"I can relate, at least to the boyfriend part." "I hope we can always talk like this. Even if you, and Paul get married, and have tons of kids, and move away. Just promise me it won't be too far." "Done." I agreed, and we shook hands on it. "You want to see the rest of this place?" "Sure."

She showed me the bedroom where I saw some of Mark's boxes in the corner. I guess there is a lot more to do before he would officially be moved in. She kept her closet like mine with clothes piled on the floor, and it made me smile that I wasn't alone in my housekeeping skills. We left afterwards so we could enjoy dinner as a family. Paul, and I would have to leave in the morning. It's the best weekend from start to finish and I am already looking forward to coming home for Christmas break.

By Sunday morning, Zeni is again full of tears. I grabbed my suitcase from my room and met Paul at the foot of the stairs. "Mama," I scolded wiping the tears from her cheeks. "Can't help it. I am just getting used to having you home again, and now you're leaving again." "I know, but you'll see us again in less than a month. Christmas is just around the corner."

That brought a smile to Zeni's face. "I didn't think of that. Paul are you coming too?" The comment is directed over my shoulders. "I'd love to and thank you again for inviting me. Reesa, we'd better be going." Paul hated to leave, but it's getting close to eleven, and he wanted some time to settle back in before classes began tomorrow. "I know, dad, take good care of mama, and everyone else." I reached on my tiptoes to give dad a hug and kiss. "You know I will. Now be gone both of you." He teased.

Paul, and I arrived in plenty of time to unpack, shower, and change clothes before meeting at the laundry room to wash our clothes from the weekend. "Need some quarters?" "Nope." I patted my coin purse. "Mom filled up my purse before we left. It's nice, and heavy." "Good. Let's wash." While the clothes spun, and the scent of the laundry soap filled the room, we sat on two empty dryers, and held hands swinging our arms gently.

"Thanks again for inviting me to meet your family. I had a wonderful time." "Good. I did too. How did you like our restaurant?" "Nice, I can see why your parents love it." "I'm looking forward to getting my degree so I can be there all the time." "I'm looking forward to getting mine as well." "Do you know what grade you'd want to teach?"

"I'm hoping to be a math teacher. For middle school, but I'm hoping for high school. I'd love to teach Algebra or even Trig." "That sounds ambitious, and a hell of a lot of hard work." "It is, but it'll all be worth it in the end. It's just a lot of boring classes the first couple of years as I need to get the basic courses done first. After that it gets interesting." "Yeah. For me too. It's time to switch to the dryers." I pointed to the three washing machines that had just buzzed.

Sandra Gutierrez

Once the dryers started, Paul turned to me with a smile on his lips. "What?" I asked. "Nothing. Just enjoy spending quality time with you." "You call this quality time?" I teased as I hopped up on an empty dryer. "I aim to please. Want to be lazy and go out to dinner?" He asked. "Love to." I remembered our movie date we had last week, and how special that is.

"I can pick you up at six." He offered glancing at his watch. "Laundry's just about done, anyway." "I'll be ready. Dressy or casual?" "Dressy. I want to show you off." He leaped off the dryer and reached over to hug me. He pulled me closer, and whispered "I love you, see you soon." It's thirty minutes later when I'm dressed in a blue sleeveless sundress with open-toe, high-heeled sandals.

I put on some lipstick, and eyeliner when I heard a knock at the door. "Ready?" Paul asked when I let him in. I put the makeup away and turned to face him. "Wow. You look incredible." He complimented. "Thank you for noticing. Yes. I'm ready." I did a little dance in a circle and made him laugh.

He drove for a few minutes before he turned a corner to Highlands. It's a seafood restaurant that also offered hamburgers, and steaks. He found a parking spot near the front door. Already it's busy. A long-haired blond waitress led us to a booth. Once we were seated, and gave her our drink orders, Paul turned to me smiling. "I mean it. You look so beautiful." I blushed and smiled at him.

He took both my hands in his. "I'm the luckiest guy in the world." "That makes me the luckiest girl, and I'm sitting across the most handsome man in the world." I reached over, and we kissed. "I'm having such a wonderful time so far." "You haven't seen anything yet." He said, smiling. Our food arrived, and we ate, already looking forward to afterwards.

"This is much better than the dining hall." I said, enjoying my meal. I finished my steak and slid the empty plate to the edge of the table near his. I looked around, and saw it was still fairly busy, which meant this place made quite a bit of money. Everyone looked happy.

Our plates were removed, and Paul paid the bill while I waited at his side. He then led me out of the restaurant and held my shoulder as he opened my side of the car. "So. What's next?" I asked looking up at him. "A surprise, you'll see, buckle up." I buckled myself in, and he walked around to the driver's side, and sat down.

The Way Life Used To Be

"Where are we going?" I asked eager to see what he had planned. "Questions will get you nowhere." He lifted his chin. "I've been sworn to silence." "Fine, be that way." I crossed my arms and pretended to pout. "Don't you worry my darling. You'll be pleased." He shut off the car at the gate leading to a small park by the river. I waited until we left the car hand in hand, and Paul held the gate open. "What did you do?" I whispered. It's very dark, and I thought for sure we would get lost.

We crossed a short walkway, and I gasped at what was in front of me. A blanket is spread facing the river, and two candles were lit on either side of the blanket causing a soft glow. "Paul this is wonderful." I had my fingers near my lips, and Paul lowered them with his hands. "Surprise!" He whispered and gathered me in his arms. "You like it?"

I looked up at him. I put my arms around his neck and drew his face close to mine. "Yes. I love it." "Sit." He gestured to the blanket. I settled myself with my legs crossed, and Paul sat across from me smiling. "You okay?" "Of course, I am, this is the nicest surprise. When did you have time to set it up?"

"About an hour before I came to pick you up. I remembered how much you love the river, so I wanted the perfect end to a perfect date." "You couldn't make it any better." I reached over and gave him a soft kiss. "I'm glad. I'm just sorry that in the whole time we've been together, we never had a night like this."

He just realized that most of their time together had been dinners in the dining halls, and many talks. Something pretty much buddies did. He thought about what Keith advised. He wanted to tell her more than anything. This just didn't feel like the right time, but it would be soon. He promised that.

"I don't mind." I didn't. My studies would always come first, but I didn't want it to. I wanted him to be first. We looked out over the water and watched the small waves crest and fall. It's mesmerizing, and special at the same time. By the time he drove me home, I'm relaxed, and lay my head against the headboard.

I am in love. Sure thing, classes resumed the following day. I studied as hard as I could so I could enjoy myself next month. Christmas is always special in our family, and now it's even more so. I called Sara who assured me the wedding is still scheduled for next New Year's Eve. Even though there is so much time to prepare, she is anxious about it. She couldn't stop talking about the food, the dresses, the decorations. Every subject possible is discussed. She even made the dresses herself, and they were almost ready to be fitted.

On December 23rd we again drove to my house where Sara dragged me to her bedroom to try on the dress. Paul dropped me off at the front of the house and headed to Sam's. He hadn't visited or called since Thanksgiving and was feeling bad about the lack of communication. He'd meet me at the house in about an hour. I smiled when I heard about it.

"Beautiful." Sara sighed. "My wedding will be so beyond perfect. All I need to do is hem the bottom." She crouched down on the floor, and started lifting the bottom, and sticking pins in every three inches. "Don't make it too short." I was looking in the mirror so I could see what Sara was doing. She had a bunch of pins in her mouth so she couldn't speak. "Why are you doing the fittings now if you're not getting married for another year?"

Sara took the pins out of her mouth and placed them on a table. "Because I have a list a mile long. This is something that can be checked off first." The dress is every bit as beautiful as Sara had described. The sleeves were puffy and ended right above my elbow. It's tight fitting at the chest and flowed loosely ending at mid-calf. I am wearing heels so Sara could get an appropriate measurement. Sara stuck the last pin in. "All done, turn around."

I turned in a complete circle. "All even?" "Absolutely. You doubt my skills?" She giggled. Even she couldn't pretend to be insulted. "Never. I look hot." "That you do. Is Paul downstairs? He needs to see you looking beautiful." I shook my head. "Paul will visit his uncle for a while and meet me back here in an hour." I took the dress off and put it carefully on a hanger so Sara could sew the hem. I put on my own jeans, and a sweatshirt.

"Good, that gives us time to gossip. How's the sex?" I laughed out loud and covered my mouth with both hands. "Funny." I am not very comfortable with this subject, and it showed on my face. "Funny as in I love the sex or..." Sara let the suggestion hang. "You're a dirty girl." I teased. Then I said, "As in I don't know." I stopped laughing and flopped down on the bed next to her. I swore I was the last virgin on the face of this earth.

"I thought by now you'd already hit the sheets." I shook my head. "Nope, and Paul hasn't even brought the subject up. I think he might be as nervous as me." She said, again. "I'm not sure. Yeah, we've kissed

The Way Life Used To Be

a lot, and hugged, but that's about it." "You should change that, and the sooner the better. I know for a fact; love makes the world go around, and Mark, and I have plenty of it."

"What's your secret. The love thing between you two?" I asked. Sara thought for a minute. "It not anything that is obvious. We've had our share of fights, but we never go to bed angry. I remember one fight was about my dad. I thought Mark was going to slap my face for it. I wished my dad dead because of all the beatings. I misread Mark's intentions as he wanted to kill my dad himself for doing that to me." "I'm guessing he didn't follow through on his own ill-advised plan?"

She shook her head. "Nope. But I still wish he would. When Mark's hand flew up, I flinched, and backed away. That's when I knew I misread him. He wanted to touch my face and tell me it would be all right because I had him, now. That's the secret." "I'll remember that. Speaking of love, Paul should get back soon." I hopped off the bed and wandered downstairs.

Paul had a good talk with Sam. He convinced him that after five, and a half months of dating Reesa, he should tell her what his childhood was like. They sat at Sam's kitchen table which was messy, and Sam didn't apologize for it. He had too many other things to worry about than a clean kitchen. He poured both of them Cokes and sat down for a heart to heart.

Paul took a long drink of his Coke and sighed. "You sure?" He asked one more time. He was still scared about telling her what he'd been through. Surely, she'd never leave him, but would she never want to hold him again? "Yes. She deserves to know what you came from, and who you are now. You got to know her pretty well, and her family too. Speaking from experience, it says a lot to being open about your past."

"I always thought to leave the past in the past. It's the here, and now that matters." Paul stated. "In a way it does. But think of it this way. You wouldn't have a present without a past and you wouldn't have a future without a present." Sam advised. "That's deep." He teased smiling down at Sam. He towered over him by at least two inches. "I know. Now you've dawdled here long enough. Go see her." Sam practically pushed him out the door.

Paul left after giving him a thump on the back. He hadn't realized until then that he is closer to Sam, than he ever could have been with his own father. It made him smile to know he had his own family. Paul hopped on a bus and sat down in an empty seat looking out the window and smiling. He is feeling so good, and right. He left the car at Sam's since it needed an oil change, and Sam had a discount at the local Chevy dealership.

"Reesa!" Keith yelled. "What daddy?" I bounded down the stairs with Sara following a little slower. "Can you shred the cheese for the tortellini?" I entered the kitchen and snuffled. "Yum. Where's the cheese?" "Frig." He pointed to the lowest shelf, and I grabbed the shredder, and a knife to open the plastic wrapping on the cheese. "When is Paul arriving?" "About ten minutes. He's taking the bus here." "Why didn't you go?" "He wanted time alone to visit his uncle. I didn't want to intrude." "Understandable. Thank you for helping."

He grabbed the shredded cheese and added it to the pot boiling on the stove. "School still going okay?" He asked stirring the cheese. I shrugged. "I guess so, I have finals as soon as our vacation is over. I'm not looking forward to them." "You'll do fine. You always do." He smiled and turned down the stove. "I've only had one set of finals so far; I'm including High School too." He kissed my forehead. "You'll be fine." He repeated. "Thanks daddy. How're things at Starlights?" I am getting excited about working there and wanted to know about every development no matter how little.

Keith added the noodles to the boiling water. "It's good. Mom hired a delivery driver. He starts in a week." "Who?" "Jim Stevens. He came by when we put out an ad the same day and was hired on the spot. If I think about it, that's the first-time mom hired someone without a formal background check or even references. Mark's word is enough." "As it should be. I've always liked Jim. Very nice, and friendly at the same time. He'll do fine for you." That reminded me I hadn't seen Jim for a while now. I hoped he is still doing okay.

"We've always liked him too. Had a few rough spots here, and there, but then again who hasn't?" "Have you, and mom always been this way with each other? Flirtatious and teasing?" I asked. "Maybe. I haven't thought about it, to tell you the truth. I can tell you my parents were close to the same way, so it's what I've always grown up with. Probably something I don't think twice about, but mom has always been a good sport. Takes my teasing in stride. I joke a lot, but just so you know, it's no joke how much I appreciate her."

He smiled as he took the noodles out of the water and set them in a straining bowl. "Almost done. Why don't you call Paul and let him

The Way Life Used To Be

know we're just about ready?" "Okay" I said. I walked outside to sit on the front porch to enjoy the last rays of sunshine while I called Paul. The voice mail picked up, so I assumed he is still talking with Sam. I surprised him by meeting him at the bus stop, and headed down the sidewalk, so I'd be there when the bus stopped.

The bus took its sweet time going from Sam's house to the depot. Paul got off two blocks from the house. There is a convenience store next to the bus stop, and he stepped inside for a quick drink. Five minutes later, drink in hand, he is whistling as he waited for another bus to take off and started crossing the street. There is not another car in sight, nor anybody on the sidewalks. Most of the businesses along the street had already closed for the day.

The light started blinking half-way through, so he hurried his steps, and is just about to the other side when a car came hurtling through the intersection, and hit him full in the side, making him turn around a full one eighty degrees. He is knocked to the ground. His head hit hard on the pavement. The car sped around a corner and disappeared. His soda spurted all over the road as he lay there not moving.

Blood starting gushing from his head. His eyes remained closed. People came rushing from all direction's moments later after hearing tires squealing and started talking all at once. "Hey buddy. You okay?" "He's so hurt." "I don't feel a pulse." This came from a gentleman who wore a suit and is kneeling on the ground. He held two fingers to Paul's neck. "Anybody see what happened?" He asked glancing around at all the people gathering close. Nobody responded, but he got several shakes of their heads.

"He's not breathing." He mumbled. Then louder. "Call an ambulance." "I'll do it." A woman offered, and gave a brief description to the operator, and then kneeled on the ground near Paul. She started crying and is sniffling as she kneeled there not knowing what to do. I saw the bus stop and hurried my steps so I could be there when Paul got off the bus. I didn't have my watch, so I had no idea how early I was. I crossed the street and saw a crowd in the middle of the road and frowned.

I moved slower towards them, and I didn't see Paul anywhere. There were a dozen people all gathered around. Some were standing, and others sitting on the ground. Two men parted ways when they saw me, and I saw him just then. "Oh No," I screamed, and fell to my knees. I couldn't get anything else out after that burst. I couldn't speak. I was screaming inside no, no, no! My mouth is wide open, but no words spilled forth. I rocked back, and forth with my hands over my mouth. Tears slid down my cheeks and fell on my shirt dampening it.

Paul lay on the ground unmoving. He is quiet. Too quiet. Three paramedics were hovering over him whispering amongst themselves. I held his left hand that lay in mine. I will him to wake up. There is so much blood around him, and his eyes remained closed. "There's still no pulse." One paramedic said, sadly. "There's nothing else we can do. Are you kin?" He frowned in my direction. I shook my head, unable to tell him.

"Reesa It's daddy," he said my name so I wouldn't be startled. He bent down next to me. This time it's dad who came for me. I felt his strong arms try to lift me up. I remained seated with my legs folded beneath me. He then slid down and gathered me in his arms. I leaned against him. "Are you his father?" The paramedic asked as gently as he could. He needed to transport him soon. "No, I'm not. This is Paul Whitfield. Sam Presauret, his uncle is next of kin." "Thank you, sir." The paramedic nodded and flipped open his phone when Keith gave Sam's phone number.

I rocked back, and forth saying nothing. Paul would notice how worried I am and open his eyes. All would be okay again. I sat there for another half hour with my father's arm still around me. My own arms were folded against my chest. The sun started lowering, and I shivered with the cold, but didn't move from my spot.

I lifted my face to the stars and closed my eyes and opened them to the sun shining brightly. So bright it woke me up. I snapped my eyes opened and looked out towards the window. The summer weather is so perfect. Perfect for my wedding. It's my wedding day. After ten long months of being with Paul, he proposed last spring, and of course I accepted. Not only were Mark, and Sara going to be happy. I was too. I am getting married to the love of my life. My first true love. I threw back the covers and bounded out of bed.

Chapter 8

I ran down the stairs and found Paul waiting at the foot of them with his arms outstretched. He gathered me into them and held me close. We kissed like there is no tomorrow. My wedding day. "Ready?" He whispered smiling into my eyes. "As I'll ever be." I am wearing my wedding gown. Endless white satin gathered around my feet as he lifted me up and encircled my waist with his hands.

He looked so proud, and happy as he stared into my eyes. "Let's go," he said, and led us outside where the guests waited. My wedding day. Once I stepped outside, and the sun shone bright in my eyes, I closed them. I opened them again to find myself still in my bed. The sky is cloudless, and the sun is shining. I rubbed the sleep from my eyes and knew. It's just a dream. Paul isn't dead. Not with a dream like that. I could still picture it.

The guests smiling. Paul looking so alive, and happy. No way is he gone. I sat up in bed just like my vision and found my parents in the doorway. Once dad saw me come awake, he excused himself to finish making breakfast. Mom stayed in the doorway watching me. Her eyes were dry this time, and she had her arms crossed. "Reesa, you slept a long time." Zeni said, as she moved from the doorway to sit on the bed.

I was sitting near the edge with my Legs dangling. "Mama, It's just a dream." I said, "Paul's not dead. Oh mama, he must be waiting for me." I darted my eyes from her to the doorway and back to her again. My closet door is shut, but I could picture my dress hanging there, just waiting to be worn. I tried to stand up, but she held me firmly.

"Reesa, what dream? You know what happened yesterday. Paul is gone." I shook my head wildly. "No, don't you see? We're getting married. I could see it plain as day. That's why I know he's not dead."

Zeni shook her head. "Honey snap out of it. I know your sad, and we are too. Paul is dead. A car hit him yesterday. You were there." She would not let me be led by false hope.

I screamed. "Liar, why are you lying to me?" I threw the covers back and jumped up intending to prove my mother wrong. What the hell is wrong with her? Mom grabbed me by the waist and forced me to turn around. "Reesa stop." She said, "I know you're still in shock, but it's time to snap out of it." I wiggled out of her hold, and ran out of the room without another word, and down the stairs. I grabbed the rail at the bottom and used it to spin myself towards the kitchen where I could smell breakfast cooking.

Keith stood at the stove crying and trying to make scrambled eggs. They were already turning a nasty brown, and didn't even look appetizing, but he is determined to make things back to normal as soon as possible. He didn't want another month of misery like I had five years ago. "Dad." I yelled and made him jump. "What Reesa? Why are you yelling?" He turned from the stove ready to embrace me. "No dad." I pushed my arms out in front of me. "Where's Paul? We're getting married, and he's late."

Keith looked so puzzled that I was about to yell again when Zeni appeared in the doorway. "Keith. She's in shock. Somehow she's convinced she's having a wedding today." It might have sounded comical on any other occasion except for this one. She sat at one of the kitchen chairs. "Quit talking about me like I'm not here. I said, where's Paul?" I yelled and tried to leave the kitchen. "Reesa stop yelling," mom said, and rose to gather me in her arms. She looked into my eyes and spoke. "Honey, I know you must feel sad, and we all are, but Paul is dead. He died from a hit-, and-run yesterday when he got off the bus."

"No, Paul's...." "He's gone" mom interrupted still holding my face in both hands. "He's dead. It's time to face reality and stop the dreaming. Paul's not coming back." "He's not." I whispered realizing I was dreaming about the wedding. It's all coming back to me. Paul lying on the ground, blood gushing, and him not moving. I also remembered sitting there on the ground long after they transported him to the morgue feeling empty, and not sure what to do now. Dad stayed with me, and that spoke volumes. He didn't leave. Just sat with me not saying anything.

Mom saw the change in my eyes and kissed me. "Honey, I'm so sorry for your loss. I wish more than anything to take it all back and give

The Way Life Used To Be

Paul back to you. We can't, and as hard as it may be, it is time to move on. Paul wouldn't want you to wallow and live in the past." "How would you know? You got to know him." "From the little things you said, and your face when you said, them. Believe me when I say how easy it would be for you to keep reliving every moment, and live for them, but it's not healthy."

"Might not be healthy, but I can't imagine not being with him. It was only for a few months, but I feel like he is my whole life. I don't know what to do now." I started crying again and didn't bother wiping the tears away. I miss Paul already, and it had not even been a full day. "You live, that's what you do. It'll be so hard for a while, and even a long while, but you hold your head up high and you move forward."

"Easier said, than done, but I'll try." "That's all we can ask. Now, Paul's funeral is in two days. You'd better get dressed. Get some laundry done so you'll have a nice outfit ready." She advised. I am still wearing sweatpants, and a T-shirt, but I had no desire to want to do anything but go back to bed. I wanted to forget everything for as long as I could. "I don't want to go. I want to remember Paul as he was. Not lying in a box."

"That would be cowardly, and you're not a coward. Dad, and I will be right there with you, so you don't have to go alone." "Thanks, and I know I'll be there even if I don't want to be." I couldn't believe I was thanking her for something like this. It isn't like I am being given a present. "That's my girl. Now get dressed, and remember, no matter where you are, and whatever you might be feeling, it's okay to cry."

I headed back upstairs with a heavy heart. I knew it was the right thing to go, but I didn't want to. I was dreading it so much I thought I might get sick. I made it to the dresser and found a pair of jeans to change into. I also needed to find a black dress to wear to the funeral. Just thinking of it made the tears start again. So hard, and fast I couldn't control them. I ended up throwing the jeans against the wall, and that brought Bessie to the doorway.

"Reesa?" She whispered. She waited for me to turn around. I was slumped against the wall with my hands in front of my face. I didn't respond to her. I wanted her to leave me alone to deal with my grief. I wanted her close to me. "Reesa?" She said, again a little more loudly, and strolled into the room, and towards me where she joined me on the floor.

"How can I help?" She asked and drew my arms away from my face. My eyes filled with tears, so she started crying too. Bessie couldn't help it. She had never lost anyone, and this is my first boyfriend. She didn't understand how she could handle anything if something happened to Jeremy. Bessie wiped at my face with her open palms, and I opened my eyes. They were so sad, and empty. She almost lost it again. So much for being stronger for me.

"What can I do?" She asked, and I took a deep breath. I opened and closed my mouth without saying a single word. Bessie could wait. She drew both of us up and led me back to the bed. She sat with me like she did years before when I was released from the hospital. The TV is off, and neither of us suggested turning it on. "I don't know what I'm supposed to do now." I said, Bessie turned her head, so we were face to face. "I don't know either." She said, and it made me laugh. It's a fake one, but still.

"That makes me feel better than a pat on the back. I'd rather have your honesty than any lie Bessie." "I don't know what you're supposed to do. If I were in your shoes, I'd throw things around just to make me feel better. Then I'd eat gallons of ice cream until I got fat and stopped caring." Bessie stated and smiled wickedly. "Okay, I lied. I'd still eat the ice cream just because. I guess what I'd do is move forward. You can't stay still wishing for tomorrow to never come." Bessie said.

"Thanks Bessie, thanks for being there for me." "I'd be nowhere else." She kissed my cheek and stayed in the bed until well after the sun went down. I realized when the moon is shining that I never got dressed. There is always tomorrow. Soon enough, my two days of mourning is up, and I woke up with a heavy heart at what lay ahead of me. I didn't want to go to the funeral, God forgive me. Why couldn't I just say my goodbyes now and forget the whole thing?

I am doing it for Paul. I found two black dresses in the back of my closet on hangers. I handed one of them to Bessie as she didn't have one of her own. She even helped me with my hair, not that it made any difference. I didn't bother using any makeup. With all the tears it would only make smudges on my face, anyway. "Finished." She stated. "Look." I turned to the right so I could see my hair in the mirror. "Looks nice. Thanks," I said, and studied my face. It's sad, but tearless.

Maybe I could get through today, and then tomorrow. Each day would get easier, and easier. That's what I had to keep telling myself. "I like it." I said, "That's better. You'll be okay. I'll be right by your side."

The Way Life Used To Be

Bessie advised and turned me around. "Promise." She held up a pinkie. I laughed a little. "See all you need is a little humor." I held up my finger. This is the hardest part. The not knowing what to expect. The rest I could handle.

I thought I could handle anything that came my way. That's how we were all raised. When you get knocked down, you don't wallow in it. You dust yourself off, take a deep breath and step forward. I was wrong. The funeral is the hardest. I sighed, and followed behind dad, and next to mom as we made our way to the front pews and sat down. The hall is just starting to fill, and I wanted it to be over even before it began. I wanted to lie down in my bed and not think about this.

I raised my head determined not to cry and saw the casket for the first time. It's oak and covered with white flowers. It's open at one end, but I couldn't bring myself to stand up, and say goodbye. How could I look at him like this? "Honey." It is mom, placing a hand on my elbow. "Don't you want to talk to him." No, I wanted to scream. I don't want to say goodbye. "Mama, I don't want to."

"Go say hello. You'll feel better for it." "Aren't I saying goodbye to him?" I wondered out loud "No, you will say you'll see him soon." "When?" I knew the answer, but had to ask it, anyway. She put an arm around me and kissed my cheek. "Someday." She whispered and smoothed my bangs away from my face. I smiled to show her I am trying and realized she is right as always. I got up and approached the alter.

I looked down at Paul knowing he would never wake up again. Somehow, he looked peaceful laying in the coffin with white silk all around him. I reached a hand towards the coffin and touched his cheek. "Hello Paul. I hope you can hear me from heaven. I hope you are looking down smiling at me. I can't smile yet. Probably not for a long time but know this." I blew my nose before continuing. "You were my very first love, and I'll never forget you as long as I live. I love you, and I'll see you soon," I whispered.

I leaned over and kissed his cheek. "Goodbye." I whispered and turned towards Mark who had remained at my side, one arm around my waist and led me to the front pew where the rest of the family waited. I hadn't even known Mark was there when I said goodbye, and I leaned back into his chest. We sat down together and waited for the service to begin. The priest walked to the front of the church and offered his condolences. Once we prayed, he asked for anyone to come up, and say a few words.

I didn't pay attention until an older man in a black suit, and tie walked to the podium, and looked up after several minutes. It's Samuel Presauret. Paul's uncle. He looked straight at me and smiled. "Let me start by saying that Paul is more than just a nephew to me. He is the son I've always wanted and never had. He is my whole life, and reason for living. I'd never have thought I'd be the one speaking at his funeral. I'd always thought he'd be the one speaking for me and not have too many ugly things to say." He paused while there is soft laughter from the audience.

"I guess what I'm trying to say is I love you Paul, now, and always. Don't get in too much trouble up there." He raised his head and saluted. "I'll miss you." He stepped down and looked towards the audience. His gaze locked on me again, and he smiled, and nodded. Once the funeral was over, and they lowered the coffin into the ground, I threw a red rose into the hole, and backed away, tears running down my cheeks.

I felt bad that I said nothing when the opportunity was given, but I couldn't. I only hoped that Paul could read my thoughts now. "Honey," it's mom. "We're going to the restaurant for a while. Do you want to come?" I shook my head. "Not yet. Something I have to do first." I wanted to see Paul's uncle. "Okay. Don't take too long." The church is located close to Sam's house. It's within walking distance for sure. I took off without realizing I am in heels.

I'd regret that later, but for now I didn't care. I walked almost a mile before I saw Samuel Presauret's house. He is sitting alone on the cement steps. His head is folded in his hands. I approached not sure if he wanted my company right now. It was different last month. Paul was with me then. He looked up and smiled. "Hey you. Long time no see." The smile didn't reach his eyes, nor mine. "Hey back. I don't know what else to say right now." I admitted, and he patted the seat beside him. "Why don't you sit for a minute. Want a soda?"

"No thanks." I shook my head. "I'm not sure I should be here." I'm uncomfortable suddenly. It was a lot easier before. "I'm sure! Before you guys came to see me last month, Paul told me all about you. I didn't put the Reesa he referred you to as the same Teresa Harris I represented six years ago. You have changed little, except for changing his life." He stopped to take a drink, and I remained silent. I had the strongest feeling I was about to know all of Paul's secrets even though it's too late.

"You look happier though." he observed. "I am," I answered. "I think though he had a lot of sadness built up inside. Every time I'd talk

The Way Life Used To Be

about my family, and how close we still are, he said, nothing." "I'll say it for him. This might take a while though. You want to come inside?" It's so cold outside, but he hadn't noticed until just then. I nodded and followed him into the house.

We sat at the same wooden kitchen table. He ignored my previous decline for a drink. He poured both of us fresh Diet Pepsi. "I seem to remember from Paul that this is your favorite drink." he smiled. "It is, Thank you." I drank to swallow the lump in my throat that grew bigger. Any second, and I would cry again. "Well, I'm not sure where to begin." He waited for a minute before speaking again. "I guess it started when Paul turned around two. His dad Tim always had a mean temper, and Paul was too little to say anything."

"Tim tried at least a little when Paul was a baby to control his temper, but he always ended up taking it out on him." Sam choked as he remembered it. "It got worse, and worse as Paul grew from a baby to a toddler. He was so into everything like most toddlers are. His mom Tiffany is my younger sister. She never once came to Paul's defense even when Tim would beat him bloody.

Only thing that stopped them was a when a new neighbor moved in, I guess when Paul was six or seven. I can't remember." He stopped talking to take another drink. Somehow talking about him made the pain a little less. His eyes remained dry. I sat opposite him, my drink untouched, and my fingers folded together on the table drinking in everything he was saying.

"Anyway, this neighbor was a teacher, and young, and pretty. I forgot her name though. Anyway, she had only been there about a month and heard the screaming through the walls of her house and called the police. They arrested both Tim, and Tiffany on the spot for domestic violence, and both of them had bruises, and cuts, and lo-, and-behold they chose me to represent the state."

"Ben Richards was the defense attorney for them. They wouldn't speak against each other and were insistent on being tried together. A love story at its worst. After the trial was over, Tim ended up with fifteen years behind bars, and Tiffany for twelve for child abuse, and attempted murder."

"Murder?" I gasped interrupting. "Yes murder. Paul is laying in his bed covered with bed sores, and no clothes on when the police found him. Neither Tim nor Tiffany mentioned a child when they were led away, and since Paul hadn't made a sound, the police had no idea he was even there. I had no idea either. I assumed he is placed in temporary care and is well taken care of while they awaited trial."

"How long was he alone, and how could they not know he is there?" I asked taking another drink, trying to swallow the lump. It remained. Somehow, I knew it wouldn't go away until I was done hearing this story and am out of there. "He was hiding in a closet under a pile of clothes. The police knocked on the door when Tim, and Tiffany were in the living room getting drunk."

"He didn't make a sound when they searched the house, so the police didn't even look in the closet. There is no reason to. He didn't even have his own bed or dresser. He shared two dresser drawers that were in their room for his clothes. Paul slept on the living room couch. There weren't any signs a child lived there."

"Not even a toy. He had nothing. He is alone for almost a week. It breaks my heart still today when I think of him all alone in that house. The same teacher who reported the yelling is the one who found Paul." "How?" "By looking in his bedroom window. Once the sun would lower, Paul is smart enough to turn out the lights before going to bed, but he forgot one night, and that teacher saw them on, and got curious."

"She left her house and tip-toed across the lawn when she saw Paul in the window. There weren't any curtains at the time, and she didn't think twice. She ended up running into the house, and grabbed him, and hauled him to her own house. That's when CPS got involved. You know who they are?"

I nodded. "Once the report was made, they added the attempted murder charge to the child abuse charge. That's when I got involved. Once they were sentenced, I took Paul in as my own, and raised him ever since. I never adopted him, but he is mine, nevertheless. He may have had a shitty beginning, but he grew up into a damn fine man." He couldn't go any further. I remained quiet for a while. It's quite a story, and I knew now how hard it was for Paul to say anything. It made sense, but I was still sad to know all of this now that it's too late.

"How did he live being alone for a whole week?" "By eating stale crackers, and dry top ramen. That is about all that was left in the house. There is plenty of water, but no juice or sodas. He did what he had to survive, but it still makes me furious, and sad, every time I think about it." Sam took several deep breaths and wiped his eyes. "He was planning on telling you this the day he was killed. He came over here to talk to me, and I convinced him that he had to let everything out. He was so

The Way Life Used To Be

fond of you, and your family, and I told him about Greg. Apparently, he already knew you."

"I knew he was coming over here to talk to you. I drove to the bus depot to meet him when he got off the bus. I was too late though. I still feel so bad that I was mad at him for being late to dinner. I didn't have a chance to say goodbye." "He knew, just like he knew how much I love him. I want you to feel free to visit me anytime." "I will. Thank you for telling me all this."

"I still regret that Paul never got to, but I appreciate it all the same. I should go now. We're having a private service at the restaurant, and I'm sure by now everyone's wondering what happened to me." Sam studied me for a while. "You know, you've grown into a very fine, and responsible woman. I keep remembering the trial, and how sad you, and your family were. That look is gone now."

"I was sad for a long time. I'm still that way, but for a different reason. I loved Paul, and always will. I'll never forget him or you. Thank you for sharing his story." I got up and put the empty glass in the sink. Turning around I wiped my eyes, but tears kept forming. "I should be going. I'd like to visit again though." "I'd be disappointed if you didn't. Go see your family and realize that family is what holds the bond. Never break it."

Once I left, I thought about Paul, and what his childhood must have been like. I would never know the pain of a belt or neglect and wouldn't wish that kind of pain on anybody. It made me miss mom, and dad. Just thinking of them is enough to make me want to hop on a bus that dropped me off at the same place Paul died. I didn't want to think about it, but I did anyway. I drove home for a minute to change into something a little more comfortable and slipped off the heels in favor of some sneakers. I left the house, and head towards the restaurant where my family waited.

As hard as it is to return to school, I had to. I still wanted my degree, and the only way to get it was to force myself to attend that first class without Paul. It's almost a week since the funeral, and I took my sweet time packing. It would be hell to go back to school without him. I tossed a pair of jeans into the suitcase when I heard a soft knock at the door.

It's Bessie. "Need any help?" "Sure. However, I don't want to leave. The thought of returning to school is something I don't want to think of." "I'm sure it is, but if you don't, chances are you never will. Then how would you get your business degree?" I smiled. "You've got a point there. I started this school, and now it's time to finish it. Can you grab that stack of jeans?"

We worked side by side until the bed is empty, and all my clothes are packed into the suitcase. Paul's empty suitcase is stacked against the wall by the door. I hated looking at it and kept glancing, anyway. I doubted the hurt feelings would ever go away. I looked away and tackled the dresser. I put nail polish and lipstick back into a travel case.

"You all done?" Bessie asked as she flipped her hair over one shoulder. The room looked so bare suddenly. "Yup. Now I just have to leave." "If it were summer, I'd tell you to forget the packing for now, and let's head over to the river. Skip going back to school for a while." That is a better plan. "That'd be nice. It would only delay the inevitable though. Come on. Let's go downstairs."

Each step felt heavier, and heavier with my suitcase in one hand, and travel bag, and purse in another. I couldn't face throwing Paul's suitcase away. I shoved it into a closet with the hopes of when I returned home for good, I could look at it with bittersweet thoughts instead of a lump in my heart.

Fat chance of that happening though. I placed the suitcase by the front door and searched for my parents. It would be even harder to say goodbye to them. The living room is pitch dark without even a single lamp for light. I found them in the kitchen. They were whispering to each other and drinking lemonades.

"I'm ready to go." I announced. Zeni, and Keith glanced up, and over their shoulders at the same time. "You sure?" Zeni asked. "You could stay for one more meal you know." "I'm not even hungry, but thanks. I'd like to make it back to the dorms before it gets too late. I have classes first thing in the morning." Nothing like enjoying getting back into the swing of things. "I have to do one more thing though."

"What?" Keith asked getting worried at the look on my face. It wasn't anger, but I looked determined. "I have to talk to Ted. I need to know if he's found anything on the hit-and-run driver that killed Paul." "What good would that do if there weren't any witnesses, or any description on the car." Zeni asked approaching me. I put a hand up blocking her from saying anything else, because I wasn't ready to hear it yet.

"I have to try, he said, to check back in every few weeks, and I intend on doing just that. I will have an answer, and I don't care how long it takes." I turned to walk out the door, and neither mom nor dad made any further attempts to stop me. Ted however had no more information than he had a week ago. The tire tracks left at the scene belonged to either a ford or Mazda.

Maybe a Chevy Camaro. There were about eighty percent sure on that, and that is pushing it. Absolutely nobody offered any information or confession, which is what Ted is hoping for even though it's a long shot. He told me not to give up hope, and to keep in touch.

Something may change, and I would be the first to know about it. "I'm so sorry to hear what happened. I'd always liked Paul from the time I met him. He must have been seven or eight, and was accompanied by Sam, and he looked scared. Paul carried his school books. He held them tight against his chest and was frowning. He was moving in with Sam that week. I saw him off, and on after that, during breaks. He didn't deserve any of this." I nodded to him, and said, thank you. I headed back home to finish getting ready to go back to school No answers, and no hope.

I glanced back one more time before boarding the bus that would take me back to school. I dreaded it so much it took all my strength to climb the steps and find an empty seat. I didn't want any company, so I stared out the window pressing my forehead against the glass as the bus driver closed the doors and began moving.

I ended up opening a book and kept it on the same page reading the same words over, and over. They became a blur with my tears. Big fat drops fell on the pages, ruining the typing, but I couldn't care less. The weather outside match my mood. It's gloomy, and cold. Typical weather for the middle of winter, but it did nothing to improve things. Several of the passengers glanced at me but were too polite to comment on the crying. I wouldn't have answered questions, anyway.

The ride ended twenty minutes later. I left the bus with the one suitcase, and walked three blocks to the dorm, hating every step. The suitcase felt like lead, and it also made me realize that when we made the trip for Christmas, Paul had driven us. His car is still at Sam's, and he is trying to decide if he wanted to keep it or sell it. It's quiet when I walked in, and I half hoped Carla would be there for some company.

I realized I needed to be alone for a while. I put my clothes away and didn't even bother to go down to the dining hall for dinner. My stomach is growling, but the thought of food made me feel sick. I grabbed a Diet Pepsi from the refrigerator instead. I took a drink while trying to decide how to spend the rest of my evening. It's so quiet with the other dorm members still enjoying the last of their vacation.

Carla is with Taylor, and I had no desire to join them, even if I knew where they were. The cold drink is refreshing to me, and that is enough. I wanted nothing else, so I tossed some jeans in a drawer, and slammed it shut as another round of tears started. I left the suitcase on the floor with clothes still hanging out of it and rushed down the stairs. I didn't run into a single person, and that is fine with me. I wouldn't know what to say, and I didn't want to try.

I opened a door that led to the courtyard and drew in a deep breath and sat by myself on a bench with my Diet Pepsi in one hand and thought about how in the world could I finish school. Even getting through the week sound like hell. I sat with my head down and swinging one foot.

I wished for this all to be a dream. This had to be a nightmare. The worse one imaginable. I even closed my eyes and willed myself back to a week ago when Paul, and I would spend Christmas together. I realized we hadn't even had time to pick out presents for each other.

I also realized that my family hadn't celebrated Christmas as we always did. Paul's death ruined that holiday for me forever. I opened my eyes and came to the painful conclusion this is no dream. I am by myself at school where it's the loneliest place on earth. True enough, classes resumed the next morning, and I threw myself into my studies.

Thank God the communications class I shared with Paul would be over soon. It's the most horrible hell ever to keep turning back expecting his arms to come around me and hold me close while we pretended to pay attention.

By March I was in a different set of classes, and I am looking forward to spring. Only three more months, and I would be home for the summer. On a Friday night, I was studying for a final when the phone rang in my ear, making me startle. "Hello?" I said, "Reesa!" it's Bessie, who sounded so happy. "Hey Bess, what are you up to?" I tried to force myself to sound happy even though it exhausted me. Four solid days of finals and studying for them had wiped me out.

"You sound tired. I'm getting married." She said, in the same breath. "To Jeremy." "Who else would you be marrying silly?" I teased. "I'm so damn happy. We set the date for June fifteenth. That's the same day we started dating. Will you be home?" "Yeah, my last final is June

The Way Life Used To Be

ninth and I'll be home right after. I can't wait." I only wished it was summer now.

It would be so much nicer to be home with my family, then here alone. "Me too, will you be my maid of honor?" "Be glad to, and for the record, I'd have been so disappointed if you asked someone else instead." "Wouldn't dream of it. Dad's already crying."

I grabbed a bottled water out of the fridge and twisted open the top. "I'll bet, how is mom handling it?" I hated the taste of water, but there isn't anything else to drink in my fridge. I'd restock some sodas tomorrow. They held no classes on the weekends. "I've got the floor plans already. We're having the reception here at the house in the back yard. Jeremy, and I've made it small. Only about twenty-five people."

"Why so small?" "Cause neither of us want a big shin dig. Mom keeps wanting to push for fifty or more, but we're standing firm on this." "Good luck with that. How's everything else?" "Quiet, mom, and dad are still at the restaurant, but they should be home soon. Sara, and Mark are out somewhere so it's just me." "Where's Jeremy?" "Home. We might get together later though. I'm not sure yet." "No plans?"

Bessie shook her head. "Nope, I've got two finals to study for though and then I'm all done next Friday. After that it's graduation, and I'm done with school forever." "Still no college?" I was still getting used to the fact that Paul is gone.

It's hard for me to hear Bessie's happiness, and plans for a wedding when my life is in such turmoil. "Nope, I never want to continue school once high school is over. Jeremy's planning on going to a trade school or something." "Maybe he'll try for something a little more challenging. You should to." "Not likely. I'd like to start a family right away. As soon as we're back from our honeymoon, I plan on stopping the pill." "That's soon. Maybe you should wait until Jeremy is finished with school and has a decent job first." "I'm sure it will take a while. I just can't wait though."

I smiled through the phone and grabbed a handful of Doritos from a bag on my desk. "You sound like you have everything all planned out. I wish I did." It's as close as I could get to talking about Paul without doing it. Bessie understood, however. Lately we seemed to have that in common. Knowing what the other is thinking without having to say it. The same as couples who have been together forever. "You still miss him, don't you?" she asked.

"So much I don't think I'll ever stop." Two tears run down my cheeks. Damn it again. It's been four months, and it feels like yesterday. "You will someday. It'll just take time." Bessie advised taking a bite of her hamburger. No one else is home. "What is this? You're suddenly the older sister?" I teased, taking another Dorito.

"No, That's your job. Mine is to advise and be your shoulder." "I'll take any advice right now. I hate being here." "Then come home. Your room hasn't been touched, and it'll bring a smile to mom's face. You can go to a trade school or something closer." "I don't think I could get any closer. I just need to remind myself I only have a little more than a year to go. It's almost April, and school will be out for the summer in two months." "Just in time to help me with my fittings." "Isn't it cutting it close? Your wedding in less than a week after I'm done with school for the summer?"

"Most everything else is done. Mom wants to do the flowers, and Jeremy's mom is our caterer. She's not even charging us anything. She said, this is the least she could do, and since she doesn't have a lot of money for a gift, she is insistent on this. It's her wedding present to us." "Sounds like you have everything under control then. I'd be happy to."

I'm sad again, remembering my dream right after Paul died. It's so real even now as I thought of it. "Good. As soon as you get home, we'll get it done. I'm having my dress outfitted at David's Bridal. You will love it." "I'm sure I will. What does the bridesmaid dresses look like?" "Pale peach, yours is more of a deep peach with ruffles on the sleeves, and they go off the shoulders. It's floor length." Bessie said, finishing her burger, and started on her fries.

"Sounds pretty. I'm looking forward to coming home for the summer." I ate another Dorito. Licking the cheese stuff from my fingers, I glanced down at the books, and sighed. It's time to get back to studying, even though I am enjoying talking more. It helped keep my mind off Paul, even if it's only minutes at a time. "Me too, I'd better be going." Bessie finished her fries and placed the plate in the sink. She'd do the dishes later.

I folded the bag of chips. "Ok, I'd better get back to the books." I hung up and returned to studying. Two minutes later, the front door slammed open. "Hi stranger." Carla said, "Are you doing any better?" I spun the chair around until I was looking at Carla who stood there. "I'm doing okay. What have you been up to?" I pointed to the bags in Carla's arms. "Besides shopping that is." "That is, I love to shop. I bought some new heels for my next dinner date with Taylor. He's coming down again Friday. Do you want to come with us?" she asked dumping the bags on the bed.

I shook my head. "No thank you, but you have the best time." I struggled not to cry as I thought of Paul, and how this would be a perfect double date. "Are you thinking about Paul?" Carla asked, and I nodded. "I thought so. But come with us, anyway. Maybe it'll help you." "How. Nothing I do helps. Every waking moment I have I spend thinking about him. If only we were going to Bessie's wedding together. If only we had that one Christmas together, if only we had more time. There' are a lot of ifs."

A tear dropped onto my cheek. "It's been four months, and there's no improvement." "I think there is. Maybe nothing very noticeable to you or obvious, but I see a lot of improvement. Your smiling more often, and the tears come less. I don't think you'll get over him, and shouldn't, but I think you're moving on more than you think you are."

I reached up my arms to hug Carla. Holding her close, I squeezed my eyes shut. "Thanks." I said. Carla kissed my cheek and held me at arm's length. "Your welcome, remember I will always be here for you, whenever you need, and whatever your mood." "I don't deserve your friendship, but oh God am I glad to have it." I sighed. I didn't cry. That one tear is it. Maybe Carla is right. I am moving on.

I ended up going to the movie with Carla, and Taylor, and enjoyed myself more than I thought I would. After scarfing down a large popcorn by myself, and a large Diet Pepsi, it surprised me to find myself hungry. "Want to get something to eat?" I asked them. Taylor answered. "Sure, what sounds good?" he smiled at me. "Pizza, I don't care where."

Suddenly I was dying for a meat-lovers with extra cheese. "Sounds good." Carla said, and we started walking from the theater to Pete's Pizza House. "Isn't that where we ate our first night here?" Carla asked pointing to the restaurant. "I guess it is." I answered looking sad and trying not to show it. It reminded me that the very time we had dinner here, and talked about our futures, and how much I was moving forward from that attack from Greg. Now I had to do it again. How?

Sandra Gutierrez

Chapter 9

June 9,2001

It's one week before Bessie's wedding. I am finished with my sophomore year. It was long, hard, and half over. The morning of my final test I woke up happy, and sad all at the same time. Bessie is getting married, and all I wanted since I heard about her wedding is to have Paul there with me celebrating. It didn't matter to me in the least he died before she announced her engagement.

Speaking of engagements, Sara, and Mark decided not to get married. Her grandfather had fallen ill, and she didn't want to get married without him. After a few months passed her grandfather is feeling better They decided they enjoy living together and wanted it to stay that way. She still wore her ring which I never understood why. I also didn't have the heart to ask. It's none of my business, and I figured they had their reasons, and maybe loving each other is enough for them.

I finished my last exam and jumped for joy. Once I calmed down, I realized I was in the middle of the courtyard, and it's full of students. Not the best time to dance around like an idiot, however half of them were doing the same thing I was. I tossed my books on the bed and smiled at the dresser. Time to pack so I could go home for the summer.

First thing I did is empty my underwear, and sock drawer. I realized once I pulled out several handfuls how messy I had become in these last two years. I started out having specific pairs, and in a specific order. Now everything is strewn about with little organization anymore.

I shrugged my shoulders, and thought, oh well, there is always next fall to start over again. I folded a pair of jeans in a box and jumped a

The Way Life Used To Be

little when the door opened. "Hi Reesa, all done for the year?" It's Carla, and Taylor. They were holding hands and attached at the hip like always. "Yup, just a few more clothes, and I'll be out of here." I reached up to kiss both their cheeks. Taylor had gotten a little taller these last few months and is filling out nicely. Carla had a hard time keeping her hands off him.

"Well I still have one more final, and Taylor, and I'll be on the very next bus home. I can't wait." Carla danced a little and kissed him full on the lips. I smiled as I folded two sweaters followed by a pair of jeans. "I feel like I'm leaving for good." "I wish, only two years to go. I can't believe how fast it's gone already." Carla sighed and leaned against the doorway.

"I know the feeling." I zipped a suitcase. "All done, my bus will leave in fifteen minutes, so I'll see you when you get home," I said. I'm sad but didn't know why. I left the room with a smile, and carried the suitcase, my purse, and two boxes in both arms as I headed for the stairs. I walked all the way to the bus depot without looking back at my dorm room. I knew if I did, I'd want to return to the comfort of my room and skip out on my summer break. This year I wasn't joining any seminars so there is no reason to stay.

I realized how heavy those items were after only two blocks, so I was grateful when the bus loomed before me, and the driver rushed to place my boxes, and a suitcase under the bus near the doors. I grabbed a seat by myself and was thankful the bus wasn't crowded.

That meant peace, and quiet as I stretched my legs, and sat with my back against the window. I pulled a book out of my purse along with a Diet Pepsi. I settled back to enjoy the short ride. Mom, and dad had offered to come, and get me, but I'm determined to remain as independent as possible. Plus, it would do me good not to depend on them too much. I opened the bottle and took a sip.

The ride home this time is short, and I stepped off the bus, and grabbed my suitcase, and boxes. I ran the few blocks home. The house however is empty, so I tossed the suitcase on my bed, and refused to think of six months before when Paul was here to spend Christmas with us. This would be a good visit this time. Bessie's wedding is no minor event.

It just occurred to me I never asked about the Spring Fling. It must have gone well since they were getting married in a week. That is a lot to do in such a short time with just getting done with high school, and a wedding a week later. Bessie is never known though for waiting. I made a mental note to ask about the dance. My room is just like before. Empty and smelling neglected. I dumped the rest of my stuff on the bed. I peeked into Bessie's room to get a look at the dress, but it wasn't there. At least in isn't in plain sight. I didn't want to paw through her closet.

Bessie isn't in her room either, so I was a little disappointed she isn't waiting on the clock like before when she picked out the prom dress. I smiled as I thought of the prom, and headed down to Starlights to see if mom, and dad were still there. I wanted to say hello to everyone.

I shut the front door and raced to the restaurant where a bunch of voices could be heard from inside. It's close to five, and in the middle of the dinner rush. I couldn't wait to jump in and take my mind off the last six months. "Reesa!" A voice shouted, and I turned towards the kitchen where Bessie stood hopping on one foot, then the other. She had her arms outstretched.

I ran to Bessie and was enveloped in strong arms that held me tight. It made me feel even more thankful to be out of school when I had this to come home to. "You look worn out." She said, studying my face. "I don't quite know how to handle all the compliments." I smiled at her making her giggle. "I'm feeling so nervous. I will throw up soon." "Better get it out of your system now than in front of our family, and closest friends. My sister the bride." I teased her.

She looked so damn happy. "I'm still trying to get used to the concept. I'm sorry I wasn't at the house to meet you. Mom, and I were discussing flower arrangements before the dinner rush started. Guess it'll be awhile now. Come on, sit with me. I need your opinion." She rushed me to a seat where a glass of ice-water sat just waiting to be drunk. I ignored it. I was not thirsty.

"Now, down to business." Bessie didn't waste any time. "What do you think of white, and peach roses with baby's breath?" I studied the mini white flowers. "They're awful little, aren't they?" "They're supposed to be. A lot of florists use them for fillers." I picked up a rose and smelled it. "Then I think they'll look perfect. Did you or mom pick these out?" I'm curious how they got peach roses, but only mildly so.

"Both. I wanted lilies at first, then mom said, lilies remind her of funerals, and are not the happy flower. She wanted these instead." She pointed to a pile of the pale peach flowers. "What is it I want?" Zeni asked planting a kiss on my head, and settling herself in an empty chair,

The Way Life Used To Be

a glass of lemonade in her hand. She smiled at me. "You glad to be done for the summer?"

"Like you wouldn't believe. I made the honor roll this last quarter." I couldn't help but brag a little. "You can say I'm very proud." Mom hugged me, turning her attention to Bessie. "Baby's breath with Roses." Bessie said, smiling. "Reesa, and I were discussing the flower arrangements, and I needed another opinion."

Mom glanced at me raising one eyebrow, "And what is your opinion?" "That I know nothing about flowers, breath or otherwise. However, those look just fine." Both mom, and Bessie followed my gaze. "That's our first choice too. Guess we're not the only ones with good taste." Zeni smiled and again looked at me. I picked up the glass of water and took a small drink.

"There's a good girl." Keith smiled approaching the table and placed a kiss of his own on my head. He is busy in the kitchen making two plates of meatball subs, and fruit cups, and came out to say hi. "How are you, honey?" He asked and chose a seat next to his wife, "choosing flowers? I'm so glad I don't have to be part of this." He is so glad they limited his responsibilities to giving his daughter away. He liked Jeremy, so it's an easy one.

"No, dad you don't, but you have the distinct honor of walking me down the aisle. Think you can do it without a tear?" "A bet? I love a challenge. Keeps me looking younger. You're on." He shook Bessie's hand. "Seriously, though. Did you settle on something?" He glanced down at the roses. "This. What do you think?" Zeni made a quick arrangement. He nodded. "Good choice." He smiled and grabbed a drink from the dispenser.

"You'd think a pile of dandelions would be a good choice but thank you anyway." Zeni laughed. "I'm crushed." Keith pouted and pointed to his own chest. "I'm being serious," he stated without a hint of a smile although all three of us could see the twinkle in his eyes. "Sure dad." I whispered. "You guys just about done for the night?"

I glanced around, and it's emptying out. Only three customers are left, and they were all just about done. It would be time to close soon. As I glanced around, I saw the couple Trey was sitting with last fall. They were alone this time however the girl saw me, and waved using three fingers, and smiled. I waved back then turned back towards the table.

"I'll help with the dishes." Anything to get my mind off Paul. I jumped up to grab a handful of plates, and two glasses. I got as far as dumping them in the sink before the tears started. I grabbed the edge of the sink, and bawled, tears flowing down my face, and landed on the plates, making soft plops along with the water.

Mom followed me in. She stood there for several seconds in the swinging doorway, then came to me, and wrapped her arms around my chest. Mom buried her face in the back of my neck. She didn't say a word, just held me close.

"Mama, when does it stop." I whispered once I could get my breath. "When does it stop? Make it stop." I kept my eyes closed, and my hands gripping the sink. I took several deep breaths. "It gets easier, but stopping completely, No," She said, still holding onto me.

Dad also followed us, and stood near the doorway, one hand on the hinge. Slowly he made his way towards us. "We'll help as much as we can, but you have to do your part too. Just remember it's your sister, and we know you love her more than anything. Enough to make it through her wedding. I however have taken a bet, so I have no choice, but to not cry." Keith said, chuckling. That made me laugh a little too. "There you go. That's all you need is some humor."

Dad kissed the top of my head and ruffled my hair. "If you can do it, I can too." "That a bet?" "Absolutely, and now I should get back to Bessie. She's been waiting, and none too patiently." I patted dad's arm and headed back to the table. I didn't realize until I was in bed that night, I never did the dishes as I'd promised.

One week later, Bessie got married right on schedule. Zeni got her wish of seventy people all seated around on plastic chairs she, and Keith borrowed from a local church. They were waiting anxiously for the bride to appear. Bessie stood in her bedroom with her hair pulled back with a barrette. It had a peach rose with some baby's breath mixed in, and it looked pretty. The rest of her hair fell down her back in curly wisps. She looked stunning.

I was still wearing old shorts so I wouldn't get anything on the dress while I was helping with her hair. I felt a little useless since I didn't have a clue how to do it. I had gotten into the habit of just pulling my hair into a ponytail most of the time. It's an easy way to handle all the curls.

Bessie is the one with the talent, so she ended up going most of it herself. I attempted to talk to her about starting college, but she turned a deaf ear. I wished sometimes I had Bessie's goal of not only being a housewife but also being happy with that role.

The Way Life Used To Be

I'm satisfied with my little efforts, so I turned to my closet where my dress is hanging in a dressing bag. My shoes were on the floor. They looked uncomfortable as they were three-inch high heels. I changed, already regretting having to wear nylons. They would make my legs sweat before an hour passed. I shook my head as this was not the time for complaints. Sometimes we must sacrifice for the ones we love.

I stood next to her and looked in the mirror. My hair is also pulled back, and I held my younger sister's hand. "Today is the best day of your life." I said, I leaned over to touch her cheek with my own. "Only because you're here to share it with me." Bessie answered smiling into the mirror. "You look as good as me." She complimented. She is so happy, and ready for this marriage.

I turned her to face me. "Not even close but thank you. Now time to get married and make me a huge promise. Always be happy." Bessie almost started crying. She blinked to prevent any tears from falling. "I will." She said and kissed me full on the lips. "You be happy too." "I'll try."

We strolled downstairs arm in arm and met dad who is waiting at the foot of them. He was dressed in a black tux and looked very handsome. Zen was already seated in the front row waiting for the ceremony to begin. Her eyes were misty, but tears hadn't fallen yet.

"Ready?" he asked taking Bessie by the elbow. He smiled down at his younger daughter who was smiling at the alter where Jeremy was already waiting. "As I'll ever be." She answered. I moved ahead of them so l could take the arm of the best man waiting at the front door. We didn't know each other, but we smiled, and headed down the steps as soon as the music started.

The ceremony itself was short, and sweet just like Bessie wanted. As soon as they said, the "I dos.", and gave their audience a modest first kiss as man and wife, the reception started. Both Bessie, and Jeremy opted to have several tables set up in the back yard so when the wedding was over, the guests could just move their chairs to the tables. They wanted everything to be outside.

The weather was perfect. Mid-eighties temperatures, and the wind blew. It wasn't too hot or cold, even at six in the evening. Our family was seated at the head table closest to the dance floor. One of Jeremy's uncles had a platform he let them borrow for the day. As soon as I sat down, I realized I was alone. Sara made her way to her seat and sighed.

Sandra Gutierrez

"Are you doing okay Reesa?" She asked. I shrugged my shoulders. "I guess so." I glanced around and saw the dancing had already started. There wasn't a live band, so Bessie had CDs she, and Jeremy made on a large stereo system. It wasn't too loud, so it prevented people from being able to talk with each other.

I looked back at her. "It's hard sometimes to keep a smile on my face." "Nobody said you had to. Too much smile, it might crack your face." She teased, and I laughed out loud. "Thanks. I needed that." Mark arrived and set three glasses of punch on the table. "Hey you two. What'd I miss." "Nothing, just girl talk. You wouldn't be interested." Sara answered smiling. "Girl talk is overrated. Yeah. You're probably right." he agreed and smiled. He reached over to place his hand on my arm that is draped on the edge of the table.

"You're okay?" he said, and I nodded. "Okay then. Sara time to hit the floor." "Let's go." She agreed, and they left the table with a smile over their shoulders for me and started dancing. I looked around and saw the sun is about to set. It didn't dim the excitement though as couples danced and laughed. I had never felt so alone. I glanced around and realized I was the only person who didn't have someone at my side. How more pathetic could I get?

About as pathetic as Trey. He is standing in the living room at Brad's, and Jan's. They were having another one of their get together. Trey had a slice of pizza in one hand, and the other stuck in his jeans pocket. He too glanced around the room and found it full of people. He knew a handful of them, but the majority were Jan's friends. Brad, and Jan were nowhere to be seen, so he ate his pizza. Trey didn't want to stay but didn't want to leave either.

He thought when he is done eating, he'd have to occupy his attention. He took another bite. "Hey Trey, what's happening?" He turned looking over his shoulder. "Hey Jim, how's it going?" he smiled at him. Jim always had a smile on his face, and today is no different. He is glad he showed up so he would have someone to talk to.

Now he isn't the only one alone. Jim had so many nice qualities but finding and keeping a girlfriend wasn't one of them. That crush he had on his old neighbor went unrequited. She never gave him a second glance, but Jim bounced back just like always. However, he is enjoying his job at Starlights. Keith recently gave him a raise, and he made good tips delivering.

The Way Life Used To Be

Jim's younger cousin Tamara is Jan's close friend, and they are hovered in a corner, gossiping about Tamara's latest crush. Trey realized that Jan had been there for quite a while. When he first arrived, he hadn't noticed. "Good, good, I just gone done with my last delivery, and I swear to God I never want to go back to that house ever again."

He shivered as he helped himself to a Coke. He smoothed back his short hair, but it gave him something to do. "Why?" Trey wondered as he got a Coke for himself to wash down the pizza. They remained standing close to the kitchen where it's less noisy. There were a few people lounging around the table, but most were still in the living room.

"There was about half an hour to closing. I had a delivery about an hour before that, so it was a slow evening. I was just sitting there shooting the breeze with Pete. He can sure talk, mostly about how adorable Natalie is. I agree with him on that one. That is one girl with an energy level that doesn't lessen. Anyway, he is just about to start the last load of dishes for the night, and he gets a phone call. It isn't anything special or anything."

Jim continued, "just two club sandwiches with the home fries." He stopped for a minute to take a drink and take a piece of pizza for himself. Pete, and Lisa were still working at Starlights, although Lisa had reduced her hours because they would have their second baby in a few months. "Anyway. He continued munching and talking at the same time. The house is somewhere on Hamilton. I don't even remember now the exact address, but it doesn't matter. I knocked on the door with a bag in my hand full of hot sandwiches, and the door opened after my tenth knock. I was ready to leave when the door opened, and I wished I had left."

"The doorway filled with a gigantic woman dressed in a see-through white gown that had pearl buttons down the front. Half the buttons are undone, and her breasts were spilling out. They were the size of these." He lifted his hands, and made them the sizes of melons, and placed them on his chest. "I just about threw up on her."

"I made sure I averted my eyes as I handed over the sandwiches. I almost forgot about the money until I got to my truck and had to retrace my steps where they were giving me a live show. She handed over a ten and mumbled to keep the change. I was so relieved, I jumped in my truck, and sped away as fast as I could. I'm still shocked at what I had the un-pleasure of seeing."

Trey smiled as he enjoyed the recap. "Get back to Starlights in one piece?" Trey asked taking another drink of his Coke. "Almost didn't make it. Next time they call, if they do, I'm refusing to deliver." "I don't blame you. Anyway, I'm assuming you're done for the night?" Trey asked, finishing his pizza. "Yes, thank God. I have tomorrow off to so two good news in a row. I'm looking to hook up tonight." Jim threw his empty Coke in the trash and rubbed his hands together. "Wish me luck." You'll need it Trey thought not able to voice it out loud.

He loved Jim like a brother, and almost as much as Brad, but the chances of finding true love, and in this place is slim to none. This is like a bar. It also made him realize how long it had been since he had someone of his own.

Trey kept chalking it up to the responsibility of managing the farm to the lack of single women knocking on his front door to the simple fact he is waiting for the one special person to fill his heart. He didn't want a one-night stand, or worse yet someone is in it for the money, not that he had a lot. He just wanted someone decent, and nice who had the same values.

The thoughts started to depress him. He eventually left. He said goodbye to only a handful of people. Jim isn't anywhere around so he got in his truck and started the engine. He realized he had nowhere else to go. Once he reached his house, he sat in his truck for several minutes trying to find a reason to go inside his house. Even his mom, and dad were out having dinner together.

He slammed the door and continued standing there. Pathetic. He told himself. He turned at the sound of footsteps on the sidewalk "Reesa?" he questioned and squinted his eyes. She is wearing a dress, and looking beautiful, and lonely. I popped my head up.

The wedding is long over, and I didn't even dance one time. I spent most of my time nursing a glass of champagne that Bessie insisted I drink, and I rubbed the stem over, and over, letting the liquid become warm, and the bubbles stopped being bubbly.

The weather is perfect. The wedding itself is perfect, and I was so bored with very few people to talk to. I ate some prime rib, and about five different salads. I ate by myself. Jeremy's mom went all out with her catering this meal, and it's good. Once I'm done eating however, I couldn't stand it a minute longer. I spent two hours staring at all the people dancing and having a wonderful time. I said, a quick goodbye to Bessie, and gave her a hug. She is still so happy; she didn't bother asking me why I am leaving. I slipped away and started walking. I passed the

The Way Life Used To Be

closed restaurant, and continued down the block in my dress, and heels. I kept my head down

"Hi Trey, what are you doing here?" I questioned and stopped my pacing to face him. I forced a smile on my face. He is wearing jeans, and a T-shirt, looking comfortable as always. "I think the question should be what are you doing here." He smiled out one side of his mouth and I never realized he did that. The smile became real. "This just happens to be my house." He nodded toward his house.

"I guess it is." I wasn't paying very close attention. "I've just come from a wedding, and I don't have the faintest idea what I'm doing here." I flipped both hands out to my sides and then rested them on my hips. "Bessie's?" "Yup, and it was so nice." "So nice you're here instead of there?" He questioned trying to figure me out. "So nice I couldn't stand it any longer. I watched my little sister get married, and all I could think of is that I want what she has, and I don't have it. Why don't I have it?"

I asked expecting not to get an answer. "Same reason I don't. I just came from a party, and Jim is on the search for yet another love of his life and knowing him he'll never give up until he finds it, and I'm here alone." "Knowing Jim, he's already found her," I chuckled. "Is the party that boring?" I asked. The thought of going to one sounded like a lot of fun.

"I had a Coke, and pizza. I skipped the beer, and now I'm here at my house. Yes, it's that boring." He reached for his Coke on the hood of his truck and took a drink. It's warm, and flat, and he didn't care. He finished the can and crumpled it using one hand. "I can relate. I was sitting by myself watching the rest of the world get close on the dance floor until I had enough. I walked away from it and started walking towards here."

"Here is a good place to be. You made a good choice. No date you left behind?" "Nope, I went solo, and just for the record, being alone sucks." "I agree, I've stood here longer than I should have. I have the animals I need to check on before it gets too late. Do you want to join me?" He asked holding an arm out. "You finally got your barn built?" I asked surprised. I knew he is planning on expanding their business, but I never expected it to be this soon.

"Yep, this is my last step of many things to do during the day. We got chickens, cows, and pigs. Come on and help me." He offered again. "I should change first." I glanced down at my dress and realized how

Sandra Gutierrez

dirty it would get if I played in the mud. I don't think Bessie would be too thrilled if the dress got ruined.

He followed my gaze. "Yeah, that'd be a good idea. How about this? Go home, and put on some old jeans or something, and meet me back here. I wouldn't want you to mess up a dress that means a lot to you." He teased making me giggle. "Okay, be right back." I hurried away without waiting for his response. I ran back to my house feeling good for the first time all evening. For the first time in six months. It's June, and I was home for the summer. I would help with animals. Life couldn't get much better. Screw getting married.

The house is quiet when I reached it, and I rushed up the stairs. I threw off my dress and kicked off the high heels. The shoes bumped against the wall and came to rest near the bed. I left them where they landed and tossed the dress on the bed. I'd hang it up later. I tore through my dresser, and ended up with a black T-shirt, and blue jeans that had holes in both knees. Otherwise they weren't in bad shape, I told myself holding the jeans up in both hands.

It isn't like I was going on a date. I took out the hair piece and placed it on the bathroom counter with a lot more care than I used on either the dress or the shoes. I put on my sneakers and tied them. I left the house just as quiet when I entered it. Everyone must still be outside having fun, I assumed, and walked as fast as I could back down the same sidewalk, I walked an hour ago.

He isn't by his truck, and the house looked black, so I assumed he is still outside. I made my way around the back of the house, and towards the barn. Chickens greeted me first with their clucking, so I bent down to say hello. "Hey guys." I said, so I wouldn't startle them. I smiled as I watched. Two came close to the fence where I was kneeling, but not close enough for me to touch.

"They won't bite." Trey advised as he approached me. He had a bale of hay in both hands and is smiling. "Promise?" I asked. He nodded. "How do you know?" I remained kneeling. He tossed the bale of hay inside the barn doors, and into one stall. He came back out and bent down. "Because I know they won't. They've bitten no one. Not even a nibble. I've been taking care of them for a while now."

"Every morning when I first come out here, I gather the eggs so we can sell them. This one here is Luther. He's the boss, and I've had him the longest. He's my favorite. His girlfriend is Lissy. She's over there." He pointed to a chicken sitting by herself by the fence opposite where I

The Way Life Used To Be

am sitting. "He's cute." "Cute?" He laughed. "Did you just say my rooster is cute?"

I started laughing too. "Yes, he's cute. When did they become boyfriend, and girlfriend?" I asked. I was enjoying this. It's obvious he is attached to them, and it made me smile wider. "Yeah, I guess he is. I got Luther when he was still young. He was maybe two or three months old and was my first purchase. I bought him from a farmer in Dallas. I started adding other roosters, and chickens."

"I bought Lissy about six months ago or so. She was raised in a farm that had been closed for animal cruelty. She along with a bunch of others were starving. They had to put most of them down. They couldn't even use any of the meat to sell."

"There isn't enough meat on them to begin with. Lissy is one of the lucky ones. Once she came here, she thrived. Luther befriended her, and to this day, I'm not sure why. He might have felt something was wrong and wanted to make it better."

"Since the day she came to live with us, she, and Luther have never been apart. They even sleep together inside the barn at night. I tried a few times to separate them, but it didn't work. I wanted Luther to mate with some other chickens. He won't leave her side." "That's more than most people have with relationships. Maybe even better." I said, "Some I guess." He stood up for a minute to toss some corn onto the ground. "Every morning when I come out here, he's waiting at the gate for me."

"He waits for me to give him a few pets, then he goes about his day. At the end of the day it's the same thing. I come out here to check on everything, and to say good night. He's at the gate waiting." The chickens found the corn and attacked it like it's their last meal.

"That's nice, It's nice. I take it you don't butcher them?" I asked. He didn't look offended which made me feel a little better about being blunt. He shook his head. "Not them. The only animals used for meat are the pigs. I use the chickens for eggs, and the cows for milk, and cheese. You'd be surprised how many people love fresh milk, and cheese compared to store brands."

He glanced at the chickens who had finished eating and looked content. "I guess they're what gets me up in the mornings, and to bed at night. Without them I'd still be plucking fruit, and vegetables, and doing the same damn routine I've been doing since I was ten. That's why Bret, and I built the barn. I needed a change." I stood up so I could take it all in. "This is an awesome place to live. I'm jealous of what you have." I didn't realize until that moment how much I meant it. He was focused, and happy all at the same time.

He never once complained about what was handed to him. It's meant to be. He loved what he did. I wanted something to motivate me. Something to give me the same drive he had. I just had to keep thinking in only two more years I'd be done. This September I'd be a junior.

Trey stood up too and brushed the dirt off. I looked around where the berries were growing and sniffed the air. It smelled so damn good. I raised my face and drew it all in. I've known him for the better part of ten years. He is not only a farmer he is a contented farmer. It's all over his face. He leaned against the fence with his arms crossed and had one leg bent at the knee. It's a casual gesture.

"How are you jealous of me?" He asked when I nodded. "Because you have focus. I want some of it." "You will, only a few more years left right?" "Right. Junior year starts the beginning of September, and I can't wait to be done. I'm ready to take over Starlights right now." I thumped a fist to my hip. "All good things come to those who wait," he advised. "Yeah, yeah." I mumbled. "Come on back." he said, holding out a hand.

I took it and followed him around the barn. We were greeted this time, by a black, and white cow who had its head over the railing. "This is Albert." He stroked the cows head, and neck with his free hand. The cow started waving its tail back, and forth. Albert pushed his head further into Trey's hand for more love. "He's so gorgeous." I let go of Trey's hand and reached out to touch the cow too. The cow instantly responded to my touch, abandoning Trey, and turned towards me.

"He's a she." He leaned his head towards mine to explain what he meant. "After I got the chickens, and roosters I needed, Bret, and I finished back here so we could add stalls for sows, and bulls. I spent close to a month signing various paperwork for them and had all the sows I needed. I wanted one more bull though. I called around and found one in Spring Texas."

"It's far, but it's the only farm that had a bull to sell. I got the paperwork by mail and signed all the forms. Once I made it to Spring, it was close to sunset, and I saw the truck pull around with the bull inside. I couldn't see much of anything. All I could see is the head bobbing up, and down. I already had a name picked out." He glanced back at Albert who is now eating some grass.

"Mom felt the need to give them all names. I never asked why she did, but it's her thing. Now I don't know if any other name would have been right for her." "But if you thought she is a he, why would you keep her? You needed a bull." "The truck doors opened, and she started walking down the ramp. I knew right away it was a heifer. When she reached the bottom, I held out my hand so she could get to know my scent. She licked my hand."

"That's all it took?" "That's all, I thought about saying no for about two seconds. One look at her deep brown eyes took care of that for me. I didn't have the heart to. I took her home, and she's been with me ever since. I got a bull about two months later from the same farmer. Apparently, he felt so bad about the paperwork bring mixed up, he gave me one for free as compensation. He didn't even ask me to return Albert. So. All's well that ends well."

"That's a nice story. Do you have any you raise for meat?" I asked keeping my gaze on the cow. She stood there with her tail swishing. He nodded. "When they get too old for producing milk or the bulls can't mate anymore, I take them to Brad's grandfather's place. He butchers them for us, and saves us lots of money on hamburger, and stuff. As far as Albert is concerned though, I don't think I could ever kill her even if she gets too old to do anything but lick my hand. What it comes down to is she's my baby." "I sometimes wish we had a dog or a cat in our family" I said.

"I used to when I was younger. Now I have everything I could ask for." He glanced towards the house. "So that's the story of Albert. I haven't changed her name. She responds to Albert. She had a calf last week." He nodded to a calf that was lying in the grass. I followed his gaze and smiled. "They're so cute as babies." I whispered. "Yes, they are. He doesn't know how to walk very well. He's stubborn though. He'll be okay. I helped birth him, and Albert licked my hand when he came out, as a thank you. I think she is that grateful so no, I'll never get rid of her. I'll never kill her either."

"Your biased." I teased. "Got that right." "You mentioned earlier how many people love fresh foods. I take it you sell it?" I asked placing my arms on the fence. The moon is out strong. I had no intention of saying goodbye anytime soon. He also seemed to like talking to me. It made me feel guilty that I was enjoying this so much more than the wedding.

It's small of me to place more emphasis on this rather than on Bessie's big day, but I did it anyway. "We do sell fresh foods. We've gained quite a few customers with all the additions we've made, since we finished the barn. I told my dad several years ago that this would do it. He doesn't like to admit it, but he knows I'm right." "At Starlights too!" I said looking over at him.

He is looking straight ahead though. He nodded. "Did you know Keith and Zeni were our first customers?" "No, I didn't. I haven't always wanted to be in charge of that place. Back a few years ago when I first started working at Hankins, I thought my future comprised, becoming a manager for one of their departments. I remember having all these hopes of being a bigwig supervisor, but that is shot." "Why? Hankins is awesome, not that Starlights is any less. After what happened to you, one can't blame you for wanting a change of scenery."

"I guess that's one way to put it. Anyway, after they released me from the hospital, I knew I could never work there again. I did however make it into the store without breaking down when I got my first and only paycheck." "Improvements." He said, the concern, and warmth on his face remained. It made me feel better. "Yeah it is, I concluded that Starlights is where I belong. When I enrolled, I chose business management. It made the most sense."

"I agree, dad always felt bad they never had the money to send me anywhere. They couldn't even afford trade school. Chances are I would have never attended even if the opportunity presented itself." He shook his head. "Sorry. I got sidetracked. We started selling produce once we got enough crops to make a profit. Dad, and I traveled from store to store to pitch our prices, and added restaurants to our list, asking for their business. We had samples, and pamphlets complete with the cost and how our food could raise their clientele. They would make more money so it's a win-win situation, but we got turned down again, and again."

"We did this for an entire week until we were both ready to call it quits. Obviously, it would not happen. Then two weeks later we stepped into Starlights. We thought for sure we would hear the same rejection and thank you anyway speech. Zeni opened the door to us and smiled. That is a first, since nobody before showed any enthusiasm."

"Zeni didn't even look at our pamphlet. She decided she wanted our berries. That's when they started offering the fruit cups with the sandwiches she makes." He remembered how thankful they were to have been given a chance to see their farm make a profit.

He also recalled his parents talking a few days before that happened. they were considering selling the l, and, and house if they didn't get a yes

The Way Life Used To Be

soon. It was that serious. Trey was depressed at the thought of losing everything they all worked so hard for. "I never knew how you started business with them. I just always knew you did." I said, "It may be why your family is so special to us. Keith and Zeni gave us a chance, and they started spreading the word about us."

"Now look at all this." He spread his hands. "All thanks to them." "Mostly thanks to them." I corrected. "You started this. Where are the pigs?" "Around the corner. You sure you want to go over there? It's messy with all the mud." I was smiling. "Of course, I want to." I pushed myself off the fence and followed him to the north side of the barn where I smelled them, long before I saw them. "Your right, they stink."

He laughed. "Yes, they do. Most of it's from the manure and slop they eat that causes the smell. You get used to it after a while." He opened a gate, and we stepped into mud. "You might run your shoes. Want to borrow some boots instead?" He offered. I looked down and shook my head. "No, I'm okay. These are play shoes anyway."

He opened another gate and led me to an open doorway. "Well. Here they are." "Did you name them too?" "No, mom wanted to, but I talked her out of it. I'd probably get too attached to them if she did." "Because you have to kill them." I turned towards him. I realized what he was trying to say. It was a question made into a statement. "You might be right." He turned to close the gate. "It's getting late. It is time to lock up for the night. I don't want to keep you." "I'll help you." I offered.

Half an hour later all the doors were closed, and the gates locked. All the animals are safe and sound. I declined his offer to walk me home. "Hey Reesa?" Trey called when I started to leave. I turned around and stopped in the middle of the sidewalk. I am once again facing him. "Did tonight help?" "More than you know. Thank you for sharing all of them with me." I left with a smile on my face. Trey left to go inside, to think about tonight. He hadn't realized this is the longest conversation he'd had with anyone. It made him feel good.

I sauntered home thinking about all the animals. It's so peaceful on the farm. So different from my life. I opened the front door, and once again realized it's still dark. I was gone for over an hour, and nobody noticed. They are probably still outside in the backyard dancing the night away. I didn't want to join anyone. I just wanted a few more minutes to myself.

Sandra Gutierrez

Chapter 10

April 26, 2003

Now it's my graduation day! My Bachelor of Arts degree in Business Management is in my hands. Bessie is over eight months pregnant with her first child, and looking round, and happy. She made it a point to send me pictures every month so I wouldn't be left out. I never had the heart to tell her I wouldn't. When she was just over five months along, she asked me the question that made me grit my teeth.

"Reesa, you just have to do this. Be my coach. Please with lots of sugar on top." She begged, making me feel obligated to say yes. "Bess, I'd love to help you. I mean it. I can't wait to be an aunt." Now where the hell did that come from? She would see through my obvious lie and get me off the hook.

Great, I said, when she didn't. I had just obligated myself., and that statement reminded me of Jim. I was wondering how he enjoyed working for mom, and dad. So far neither one made any comments to me. I guessed that is a good thing. It's time to stop the daydreaming and get back to the task at hand. I had all my clothes packed in boxes, and my desk cleared out.

Carla still had some packing to do, but then again, she still had two more finals to go. She wouldn't be home for at least another day or so. Speaking of graduating, she didn't pursue her brief fantasy of becoming an author. I had to chuckle again at the librarian she ogled over. After that first day, neither of us saw him again, so that may have been a blessing in disguise.

The Way Life Used To Be

If Carla had gone out with him, I would have supported her, but deep down I would expect him to break her heart. That made me appreciate even more she saw what I saw and never spoke of him again. Who knew? He didn't have enough brains to finish, so he dropped out. That thought made me smile.

Carla however majored in, Home Economics. She wants to teach junior high. I want to I say I envy her choice, but the thought of being around all that drama day after day is not something, I would have any patience for. She has piles of folders for it and would apply as soon as summer ends. I am so proud we both stuck it out to the end.

Once the ceremony is over, and the diploma is in my hands, I didn't look back. I put all my stuff in the trunk and hopped in the back seat of my parent's midnight blue Toyota. They had just gotten it four months ago, and it's already Zeni's new baby. She insisted on driving, and Keith being as good natured as he is, let her have the wheel. "All ready?" she asked shutting the trunk. I packed it to the roof with my clothes.

The rest of my things would be delivered to the house by the end of the week. I'm that eager to be done with school. I couldn't imagine that four years is gone. No more school. It brought a smile to my face as I shut the car door and leaned back to enjoy the ride back to the house.

"I'm more than ready." I sighed and glanced out the window to stare at the dorm hall. It looked so abandoned already, but I refused to have sad thoughts. All about the future now. Zeni pulled away with a smile, and we headed home. We pulled up to the house forty-five minutes later. I jumped out of the seat and began pulling out boxes from the trunk.

"You can do that tomorrow honey." Zeni offered. "It's your first day back, and you have time to relax. I'll help you first thing in the morning." "No mom. I've never been a procrastinator, and I have no intention of starting now." I smiled, and grabbed one more bag, filling my arms, and headed to the house.

Zeni sighed again and grabbed a few bags herself. It only took three trips, and I am regretting my impulsiveness as I stared at my room with bags, and suitcases strewn all over the floor, and on the bed. Oh, well. Not like I only had a weekend and had to return to school soon. I couldn't believe that I'm finally done.

In the morning I am planning on going straight to Starlights. Mom is going with me, and we were both excited. I knew it would take a few years for her to get the guts to retire, but dad is eager to have some relaxing time. I glanced down at the mess, and walked right by it, and headed for the window seat. It's the same, but different, I am different. A college graduate, I couldn't help but smile, I did it.

The sky outside is cloudy, but warm. It would rain later, but I didn't care. I was home again, and here to stay. Hopefully in a year I would start looking for my own place. If I proved myself, I'd be able to do it sooner. I truly loved the house, but now that I am a college graduate, the next logical step is to get my own place.

A one or two-bedroom house or an apartment would be a better option for my first place. There is nothing, but my bed, dresser, and many clothes to decorate it with, but that also gave me a goal. To be fully prepared with furniture, and dishes, and such by the time that moment came. Surely mom, and dad would support that.

The first drops of rain started falling, hitting the window with a vengeance when I pulled myself away to clean. "Reesa you're here." It's Bessie who flung herself into the room, and into my arms. "About time." She is wearing a flowered silk maternity blouse, and shorts that had one of those special waist bands. Her hair is pulled back, and she looked so happy. "I know it, hey you want to help me?"

With two people attacking the mess, it would be done in half the time. I just had to keep in mind her protruding stomach and make sure she didn't over-exert herself. "What are you doing here, anyway?" I asked. I'm surprised to see her since she moved out right after the wedding "Welcoming you home as always. What do...." she gasped at all the boxes, and bags on the floor, and regretted her offer to help? "Reesa this is a mess."

"Stating the obvious, but seriously, I need help." I whirled around and grabbed Bessie by the shoulders. "Please." I begged. "Not the puppy dog eyes." She groaned, and I smiled. "Not the puppy dog look." She groaned louder. "Fine, fine." she threw up her arms. "How the hell did you manage to collect all this?" She bent down to attack one of the bags, sorting clothes that looked dirty from the clean ones.

"If you're thinking I spent most of my time shopping I didn't. Believe it or not I left with most of this, and unfortunately it came back. I can't seem to get rid of anything." I bent as well and opened a suitcase. "This is for the dirty clothes, and this is for clean." I pointed to two laundry baskets. We started tossing clothes, and when both were full to the brim, I stood up to start a load.

The Way Life Used To Be

While I was gone, Bessie continued plowing through clothes, and had two more loads ready when I came back huffing, and an empty basket in my arms. "Here you go." She announced cheerfully. After three loads were done, and the clothes neatly folded, and put away, we decided to be done for the day. I was getting sweaty, and feeling like I'd done way too much, way too fast. I should have paced myself a little more. "What do you want to do now?" I asked pushing a handful of hair away from my sweaty face. I studied Bessie. She is holding her lower back. She didn't seem to be in too much pain.

"Swim." The rain stopped, and it is still so hot outside. "Just the right answer. Let's go." Ten minutes later, dressed in shorts, and t-shirts we were walking down towards the river. You could see the huge lump that protruded from Bessie's stomach, although she didn't say much about it. I couldn't help wondering if she is worried or having second thoughts about having kids so soon. Of course, it will be a little too late to be having second thoughts now that it's almost over.

"You want to get Carla?" Bessie asked pointing towards her house. "She's not even home yet. Still packing. She should be here tomorrow though hopefully. She's not quite done yet." "Did Taylor graduate yet?" I nodded. "He's been done since March. Already has a job with Hewlett Packard. Carla's excited to be done soon so they don't have to have more of the long-distance relationship thing anymore." "I don't know if I could have handled it, that's for damn sure." Bessie stated.

"Well, I have to give them credit. They stuck it out for four years, so I'm guessing they can make it through anything." We reached the river, and didn't I even wait to get used to the coldness, but jumped right in, refreshing myself. Bessie had to take it a little more careful now that she is pregnant. I dove in, and came up, hair in my face, but smiling. I needed this more than I thought. "Thanks for going with me today. I guess I needed a break."

"That's my girl." Bessie kissed my cheek and then tossed some water in my face. "That's my wet girl." she giggled. I giggled back and realized she is right. I'm feeling better. I swam from one side to the other, dipping my head back, and letting my hair trail behind me. It didn't occur to me until just now, I hadn't gone swimming the entire four years I was attending school. I'm out of shape, as I began treading water.

I glanced to the shore where we stowed our towels and found Bessie near the edge, poking her foot into the water, but venturing no further. She must be taking it easy. Her hair is loose and flowing down her back. She had taken out the hair tie. I swam back to where she is standing. "Are you doing okay?"

She smiled in my direction. "Mostly I get feelings of tightness now, and then, but my doctor says that's most likely just Braxton Hicks contractions. I'll know what the real thing feels like." "Sounds painful already." I said, trying not to frown. "It's no picnic, but I want this, so any pain is worth it." "What are you doing tonight?" I asked. "Not much. Jeremy doesn't get off till nine, so it's just me." "Sounds perfect, want to go out for fast food?" "Absolutely." Bessie laughed out loud.

We called it a day as far as swimming was concerned and walked back to the house. Or rather I walked, and Bessie waddled. She made me smile as she trudged along with me. When we reached the house, she stayed downstairs I rummaged through my boxes for a pair of shorts, and T-shirt.

I skipped a shower since I was both starving, and I had someone waiting for me. I settled for tying my hair in a ponytail and skipped down the stairs. I wrote a quick note, and we left in her car. She looked out of place with her stomach almost touching the steering wheel, but she also didn't seem to mind.

She parked in front of a Zips Restaurant, and we walked inside where it smelled good. Five minutes later I am eating my burger, and fries like I hadn't eaten in days. Bessie picked at her hamburger claiming she just isn't that hungry. She just wanted to spend time with me now that I had all the time in the world. Sometimes I had to remind myself I wasn't on a mini vacation anymore.

I ate everything, and even finished her burger so nothing would go to waste, then dumped the paper liner in the trash and the tray on top of it. She left after we arrived home, and I headed upstairs to get ready for bed. Mom, and I were going to Starlights first thing in the morning. True enough, the very next morning I am at Starlights by seven with mom right next to me. Dad opted to have a quiet morning to himself while we discussed renovations. Mom unlocked the kitchen door, and we stepped into quiet.

"This is nice." I commented; I wore comfortable blue jeans with a white T-shirt that showed off my thinness. "You've lost weight." She stated unsmiling. I turned around frowning. "That's supposed to be a compliment." "Only when it's for the good. Good thing you're back

The Way Life Used To Be

home now and can get some meat on your bones." She didn't like the way I am looking right now.

I was pale, and more disturbed than I let on. We sat at the chopping counter, and she poured herself a cup of coffee, and Diet Pepsi for me. She lifted her mug, and I smiled. "Thanks mama." "Always welcome. I thought you'd have developed a habit for coffee by now with college, and stuff. I know that's when I started it. The caffeine did a lot at keeping me awake during finals."

"I guess I never thought about it. I have my one bad habit, and that's enough I guess." "How was dinner last night?" "I was a pig. Bessie didn't have much. I don't think she is feeling very well." "She probably isn't. Now here's our new menu." Zeni pointed to some papers scattered on the counter. "What do you think?"

I glanced at the papers. Breakfast sandwiches including bagels with sausage or ham, cheese, and a rolled over scrambled egg, and English muffins with the same options. Both came with home fries or hash browns, and a cup of fresh fruit, and berries. "You still get the fruit from the Matthews farm?" "They are by far the best. We've also expanded, and added fresh eggs since they've expanded, and added on the barn."

Just saying that seemed to bring Trey, and Jim to the back door. Both of us jumped a little at the sound of the door opening, although Zeni recovered first. "Morning you two. Jim what are you doing here on your day off?" "Keeping Trey out of trouble." That earned Jim a jab in the ribs. "Like you need to." Trey countered setting two crates of eggs on the counter. "Fifteen dozen, today right?" "Right, Reesa, you will love these. I swear they're five times bigger than any eggs you'll find at any store."

I leaned over the crates to study the eggs. "I think you might be right." I smiled over the crates at Trey who is leaning over the counter writing on a pad. "Where's your dad?" Zeni wondered taking a drink of her coffee. Trey glanced up from his pad. "Didn't you hear yet? Dad had quite a few minor heart attacks last year and finally retired much to mom's relief. He's much happier being a homebody although he would never admit it. Bret, and I are in charge now."

"Sorry, I didn't hear that. How many attacks did he have?" "Three, he ended up in the hospital right around Christmas time, and that is the last straw where I'm concerned. I became the parent for a while, and nursed him back to health, but I also clarified that he is done managing the farm. He fought me tooth and nail, but as you can see, I made him realize." Trey smiled trying not to panic again. He had almost forgotten how scared he was to find his dad on the living room floor passed out and not breathing. Trey decided then, and there to make his dad retire. He of course helped with getting the food ready for delivery, but that's as much Jacob could handle anymore.

"Three is a lot. I'm sorry to hear that. Is there anything we can do?" Trey shook his head. "I mean it, anything, you just ask." Zeni offered getting up and hugging him. I watched this remembering our talk by the barn. Trey didn't bring it up, so I chalked it up to a nice visit, but nothing more. I studied the new menu instead not wanting to pry into his personal life although he didn't seem to mind mom's questions.

Besides the two breakfast options, there were more afternoon choices. Barbeque beef on whole wheat toast or roll, chicken teriyaki on a hoagie roll, and deep-fried pork on rye. I remembered the pork sandwiches Bessie, and I made when I came home for that weekend before Thanksgiving and wondered if that's where the idea came from. The meal had turned out well I recalled.

Trey finished writing his total. "Well, that's it. Eighty-seven even. That's for the eggs, eight pounds of strawberries, and six pounds of blueberries, and forty pounds of potatoes." He tapped a pencil on the counter making sure he forgot nothing. "Wait here." Zeni asked and disappeared for the company checks. While she was gone, I remained seated looking at the menu, suddenly tongue tied.

Jim came to the rescue. "Hey Reecie Peecie, you going to join me on deliveries?" he teased. I smiled. "Not yet. Ask me next week." "You lost your chance." He laughed making me laugh too. "You guys changing the menu.?" He pointed to the menu I had still spread out in front of me. "Soon, mom, and I were just discussing some changes now that I'm done with school, and I will be here a lot more often now." "I heard you got your degree. Take what seven, eight years?" Jim teased laughing. "Ten, I'm a very slow learner." I teased back.

"Shows. Just kidding, we love you." He kissed the top of my head and smiled. He had let his dark brown hair grow longer, and no longer sported the buzz cut he had for so long. This is a much better look. His face is still clean shaven, and it seemed he'd always have the baby face look. Trey is looking at the menu too. "Hey these look good, Jim you should try some of these soon." "Happy to be the guinea pig." Jim offered "Reesa, are you going to open for breakfast?"

The Way Life Used To Be

"Not yet, mom, and I have some final plans to make first, but that's the plan. You want to be the twenty-four-hour delivery driver, on call all the time?" "Make some good tips that way. Hey, Trey you should start driving with me. Make twice the money I'm making now." "The way you drive, we'll most likely end up in a ditch before we make it to the first house." "Yeah, you're right. Besides you might hog the tips."

"Never mind, I retract my offer." "It isn't even sincere, but Reesa these look good. You going to make them or is Zeni still in charge?" "Mom, and dad for now. I'm hoping in a year to take over, and they can retire for good." "Must be a lot of work, but you'll be fine." he winked at me as Zeni came back through the double doors to find both men hovering next to me. "Here ya go Trey." she handed the check over and sat down again. She took a small sip of her coffee.

It sounded like a dismissal, so they said a quick goodbye, and both Trey, and Jim left with the empty crates in their arms, still teasing in that brotherly way they seemed to have. Once it was quiet again, mom turned to me. I was still watching the empty doorway. "So, which one do you like?" she asked nodding towards the door. I whipped my head around and was red with embarrassment. "Neither, let's get back to work."

"Liar", she said quietly, but left it alone. Mom had a strong suspicion it was Trey, but let it be. She did however remember right before she met Paul for the first time, and she, and Trey sat on the front steps enjoying small talk, how nice he, and Reesa would look together. Nothing seemed further from that happening. At least not then, but now is the time. "Where were we?" "This." I pointed to the menu. "I like the new choices."

"I do too. If it all goes well, we'll be opening for breakfast in two months. It might take a while for word of mouth to bring customers in that early, but it shouldn't take too long. I'd like to hire a second server if it looks like too much to handle, but we'll see how things go. If it comes to that, you're doing the interviewing." "Why? I know nothing about interviewing." I sounded a little panicked. What did I know about someone's intentions of working there? Whether he or she would last long, get along with the other employees or be trustworthy?

"Because being a manager has its perks, and hiring, and firing is one of them." "You ever fire anyone?" I asked trying to think of anyone who didn't work out. Nobody came to mind. "Twice. This was way back though, when we just offered lunch options. You must have been about six or seven. it's hard to remember. Bessie, I know wasn't even in school yet. She must have been four or five I'm guessing." "What happened?" I asked, hopping down to get another drink.

I sat back down seconds later. "There was a young girl named Trina who applied for a server position, and she seemed nice, and hardworking. She was blond, had a mile-wide smile, and fake as that blond hair. I hired her on the spot as she passed the background check. She seemed like such a responsible person."

"Her first night, she ended up calling in sick, and dad, and I had to bust our butts for six hours covering for her. It was a nightmare, and we didn't end up getting home until about nine at night. Luckily, Mark had put you, and Bessie to bed already so when we got home, all we had to do is conk out. I was so proud of Mark acting as a surrogate parent. He was only eight, and in third grade. He fed you guys cereal for dinner and tucked you both into bed. I doubt you remember that, but oh lord, I never will forget."

"The next morning, she showed up all perky, and full of apologies. I am still steaming mad, and it showed. Three nights later she pulled another call out. I fired her the next day, and she left threatening harassment on our part, and how it's against the law to fire someone for that reason. She even had the police show up that afternoon, and we spent the entire day explaining ourselves."

"That is an even bigger nightmare. I made a vow to make it a practice to only hire someone on a probation period first, then a review. If it all works out from there, it's a win-win situation for both of us." "How long is the probation period?"

"Depends, usually we know within a month if he or she will work out. There was another employee, but this one we had to charge with theft. It was a nightmare." Zeni said, getting yet a third cup of coffee. "Well don't hold back. Tell me what happened." I asked just a little eager to hear the story. This is not only entertaining, it's educational for me. I wanted to know how my parents handled every little incident.

Zeni sat back down and added creamer. "This happened about when you were eight or nine. Again, I don't remember the exact year, but I remember the mistake." She drank about half her cup in two swallows. "This was a young man this time, and he like Trina started out wonderful. So full of energy, and eager to learn." "What was his name?" I asked.

"Tony Phillips. He didn't grow up around here, and said, he is from back east somewhere. I don't remember the town he listed on the

The Way Life Used To Be

application." "Probably made up." "I wouldn't doubt it. Anyway, he started out fine, and showed up every morning eager to start the day, and always is the last one to leave." "I thought you, and daddy always locked up?"

"Back then we didn't always. We had three young children who needed our time, and attention a lot more than the restaurant did. It seemed to work out okay until we started realizing the till is getting short every morning when we counted the days total." "By how much?" I finished my third soda, but didn't want to get up, so I just played with the straw, and empty glass.

"By pennies at first. Less than fifty cents so we chalked it up to a little carelessness by not counting the correct change from the night before. It stopped for a while, and we were right on for about three weeks when Keith noticed it happening again." "By pennies again?" "More, by two or three dollars, and then it started increasing to over ten within the month. By the time we both figured out it's Tony who is pilfering the register, he is gone out of town with our money in hand. To this day they have never caught him." "How much did he end up stealing?" "Just over five hundred dollars. I think if we hadn't figured it out when we did, we would have lost so much more, and have had to shut the restaurant down."

I thought it was a lot of money to lose, especially when you depended on it to make a living. "Well, I'm glad you didn't. That's quite a story. Two in fact." "I'm telling you because one, I trust you to not spread this. Two, that when you hire someone new, what to watch for." "Thanks for telling me. Did you have any hesitations about hiring Jim?" Zeni shook her head. "No that's one I didn't hesitate in the slightest. Not just because of Mark, and their close friendship, but he's a good person. His parents are worthless shits, but he's a good person despite that." "What happened?" I'm afraid of the answer. What if it's just like Paul?

Mom knew though what I was thinking. "Keith and I knew Jim's parents from high school. They were sweethearts since the tenth grade even though at the time Keith and I weren't even dating. By the time we graduated, Keith and were in fact dating, but Jenna, and Richard were now talking marriage."

"It's a match made in heaven, we all thought, and when Jenna was pregnant with Jim, she seemed like she was so happy. I ran into her a few times shopping for baby items, crib, playpen, and such. Spent money like it was candy." "What was it like once he was born?" "Awful." Zeni waited a minute before talking again. She looked at her empty coffee cup, and ran a thumb up, and down the handle.

"I'll get you a new cup." I offered. "No, but thanks. I've had enough." "Anyway, where is I?" "His birth." "Oh yeah. The first year is okay. Jim is a very colicky baby, but he grew out of it quickly. He always had a smile on his face, much like he does now."

"When he was about two Jenna, Richard, and Jim came into the restaurant for some lunch. She left him in a high chair while they ate their food. He was crying and reaching for their plates. It's obvious he is hungry., and Richard got tired of it, and slapped his hand. That made it worse, and dad kicked them out with half their dinners on the plates. Didn't even charge them but told them never to come back. Some customers were shocked at him. They've never seen him act that way, and neither had I, but I let him do it."

"What happened when they got home?" I asked hesitantly. This is so similar to Paul's story. I'm afraid of the outcome but wanted to hear it. Needed to know why Jim is so happy all the time, given what I had just heard. It just made little sense. "Jim was beaten by his father."

Mom looked at me. "I know what you're thinking, and this kind of abuse happens all the time, much to our disappointment. It started with spankings on his bottom, but he couldn't stop with just one slap. That beating started a pattern that got worse until Jim became a teenager and finally had enough. He had long stopped smiling, and became disrespectful, unruly, and I had to do the one thing I hated most in life. I had to kick him out of Starlights."

"Jim was trying to instigate a food fight. He left in a huff after yelling at us that we had no right to tell him what to do. He continued that pattern for a while when he had had enough and snapped. Jim was fourteen when he beat his father down." "I'm impressed, I didn't know he had that in him." I tried to picture him losing control, but I couldn't. "I'm impressed too. Jim never got very tall and was teased by his dad for it. Unfortunately, he didn't know his own strength. He beat his own father to death."

That stopped my smile. "He did?" "He did, spent two years in juvenile detention, and his own mother tried to declare him a murderer, but when the truth came out about the abuse, he was released on his sixteenth birthday, and spent a few years getting to know himself again.

The Way Life Used To Be

He spent some time in a rehab facility to gain control of his emotions. He apologized to us, and we accepted it."

"We knew what he is going through and don't hold grudges for that kind of behavior. He knew it, and started coming by a lot more often, just to help Mark with the dishes, and they would talk. Finally started becoming the man I knew he could be, and he had a smile on his face again. Never reached his eyes though. Have you ever noticed?" She asked.

I hadn't. I remember when I first started at Hankins when he would come in with Trey, and they acted like brothers most of the time, teasing, and just plain having a good time. I didn't even pay attention that he never went to high school, or if he did eventually, never talked about it. "How in the world then did he, Trey, and Mark end up being such close friends?"

Zeni shook her head. "I'm not sure how that all came about. All I know is once he found his real self, he came into the store with an application one day, and Keith and I hired him. He got his GED, but never attended high school. He couldn't, not with his record, but he certainly deserved to." "Yes, he did. You hired him all based on Mark's friendship?"

I'm amazed once again at her generosity, and for her ability to be nonjudgmental. "Mostly, we'll never forget that toddler who cried for his food." "Or the adult who doesn't." "That's right." Zeni smiled. "I believe you understand now." "Thanks mama, yes, I understand." "I thought you would. Now let's leave this joint for a while and get some breakfast. I need a change."

"Reesa. let's go." Bessie shouted from the bottom of the stairs. She is impatient as always. It's May now, and Bessie had just under a month to go before her due date. The weather is turning steamy, and I am just buttoning a short sleeve blouse to wear for her visit. I had no intention of dressing up, even for a doctor's visit. I am, however wearing a jean skirt so that had to count for something. At least I wasn't wearing sweats.

Her appointment is in half an hour, and she didn't want to be late. I agreed to be her coach and didn't have a clue what to do. Bessie hoped that seeing the doctor would help me overcome any doubts. "Reesa!" she shouted when she didn't get any response and started stamping her foot. I am putting on my shoes as quickly as I could and is already regretting my decision to be the coach. Why did I say yes?

Sandra Gutierrez

There is so many other things I could be doing, and I groaned again. "Coming." I shouted just a little, and tied my shoes, grabbed my purse, and slammed the bedroom door. I stomped down the stairs and came face to face with Bessie at the foot of them.

She had her arms crossed and tapped her fingers. Her stomach is belled out, and I had a hard time feeling sympathy for her. Having babies and dealing with the whole married thing is beyond my thinking. After all, I'm still single, and no prospects on the horizon.

"Finally." she said, "Let's go." "I don't know why you have to be so damn grumpy." I pouted getting into the driver's seat, and Bessie settled herself in the passenger seat, and smiled. "I'm not, I'm late." She said, "You still have twenty minutes. That is no reason to yell at me. We have plenty of time." I backed out and headed down the road at a very reasonable speed. "You are going so damn slow." Bessie yelled and thumped the dashboard for emphasis.

"Am not. See the speedometer?" I pointed to the gauges and smirked. "Push the pedal to the metal." I laughed and was quite amused by this. Even more amused when we reached the clinic with a full ten minutes to spare. "See, we were almost late." She tapped the dashboard. "Exaggerator." I slammed the door and followed Bessie inside where we are promptly told to have a seat, and the doctor would be with us shortly.

Bessie lay comfortable on the examining table with an ugly gown covering most of her. She was reading a magazine. "You need any help with anything?" I didn't have a clue what to do. I could only hope that when my time came, that Bessie would be the one doing all the work. I made a very poor coach, but nobody seemed to mind. I paced back, and forth with my head down, and my eyes closed. If only Bessie would change her mind and let me be relieved of this intense responsibility.

I sat down, and crossed, and re-crossed my legs every thirty seconds while Bessie watched looking up from the page of the magazine. She had a smile on her lips and chuckled. I'm already bored. I had to stop myself my sighing out loud several times, and we hadn't even been there half an hour. The sun had disappeared behind a cloud leaving the room darker, when Bessie's doctor came rushing in full of apologizes for being late.

I remained seated thumbing through a magazine while Bessie was examined. I kept my face in a page, and read the same sentence repeatedly, just waiting for this stupid exam to be over. Then I could go

The Way Life Used To Be

back to the house and be normal again. I was hungry already, and the thought of a big bacon cheeseburger made my stomach growl.

"Sorry, Bess, but I am running late. Let's look just to make sure everything is fine. Your due when?" He glanced down at the notebook and tapped a pencil. "Three weeks, you must be excited?" He took her temperature, and blood pressure. "As always everything looks good. Still taking the vitamins?" "Of course." Bessie smiled.

They made her very sick, but she took them faithfully, anyway. "Good." He smiled and looked back up from his notebook. "Let's get this over with so you can get on with things." He checked her pulse, heartbeat, and did a quick ultrasound then drew some blood. Bessie always hated this part and looked away while he stuck the needle in. "Looking good. Just one more follow-up visit in three days, then a final checkup in two weeks, and then that should be it."

"You ready?" "As I'll ever be." Bessie smiled and sat back up again. "Can I get dressed now?" "In about an hour. I have to send this to the lab, and if everything checks out then you can go." He turned to his desk and noticed me sitting there for the first time. "You must be the older sister. I'm Jeff Hendrik." He held out a hand which I shook. "I'm Ressa, it's nice to meet you." I greeted. This man is very handsome with his coal black short hair, and million-dollar watt smile, but I wasn't sure what to do about it.

I glanced at his left hand, and there was no ring. There isn't even a shadow of a ring that he may have worn before. Then again that didn't mean much as lots of men are married who don't wear a ring to advertise it. He had a scattering of freckles on his nose, and cheekbones, and was very tanned. Seemed fit too, from the little I could see. "You going to stay here, or can I interest you in a cup of coffee. The blood test will take a while, anyway." He asked pointing to the tube.

I nodded. "Sounds nice." I put down the magazine and followed him out the door We headed to the lab. Jeff disappeared for a minute with a quick apology and came back seconds later. He took off his lab coat and hung in on a hanger. Underneath he wore a black sweater, and tan slacks.

We didn't speak until we reached the cafeteria. "Please sit. Cream, and sugar?" he asked after pulling out my chair. "Actually, I'm okay. I just wanted to get out of that room." I smiled with relief. "I assume you haven't had kids before?" He asked. I guess I looked young, but then again Bessie is only twenty, and about to have a baby.

"No, I haven't, and I think I just made the biggest mistake by agreeing to be Bessie's coach." "I don't think so," Jeff said, adding sugar to his coffee. "You sure you want nothing." "I'm fine, but I'm scared. I have no idea what I'm doing. Bessie is wrong to ask me." "I don't think she is. She's a talkative one, that's for sure. I don't see her asking if she isn't confident about it."

That made me smile wider and feel just a little better. "Thanks." He seemed nice so far. The cafeteria is warm, and not very crowded. They geared this section of the hospital towards births, and newborn care. There are only a few people sipping drinks. I wondered if they all worked here. "No problem, now that we've gotten the uncomfortable introductions over, tell me about yourself. Bessie's been vague on details." "What details. Don't tell me she's been talking to you about me?" I'm mortified Bessie had been talking about me behind my back.

"Just that she had a beautiful older sister who is single, and she is hoping we'd hit it off." he said, grinning, and taking a drink of his coffee. "She talks too much, although she is right about the single part." She replied "You forgot beautiful. As far as hitting it off, we seem to be off to a good start." "You might be right. Now your turn." I gestured with one hand. "Tell me about yourself." I smiled finding I am enjoying this small talk.

I crossed one leg and swung my foot waiting for him to answer. I pulled my hair back in a ponytail, and I wore no makeup. I didn't expect to meet anyone today, so I took no special care with my appearance. "Well, I'm twenty-five, and as you can see, I'm a doctor. This is my first year as primary physician. Last year I was an intern for this very hospital." He smiled as he realized how much he had accomplished in so short a time. "I'm impressed. Twenty-five, and already a career man."

My heart already started beating faster. I am already having feelings for him, and we just met. What did such things say about me? "I graduated from high school two years early. I also graduated from college and got my master's degree all within six years. It takes the average person seven or eight at the least and that's if they push themselves., and I'm bragging now, aren't I?" I shook my head. "Not at all, I'm just impressed. It took me a full four years just to get my basic business management degree. I feel less educated now." I teased, smiling, and enjoying myself.

"You hungry?" He asked. "I can get us something really quick." "No, but thanks." "Well, soon we can have dinner sometime." He

The Way Life Used To Be

invited taking a drink of his coffee. "Thanks, I'd love to." Why not? He is so good looking, and friendly without seeming pushy. I think it's about time I start to look forward to the future. "I'll call you then. Bessie is forward enough to give me your house number already." "Of course, she did."

I will kill her when we got home. "Well, we should get back to check on her." He pushed his seat back, and I stood up too. We walked back to Bessie's room where she lifted her head at the sound of our return and smiled. "About time." "Right on time." Jeff answered. "Let's finish so I can get on with my life." He teased. "Reesa are you coming with Bessie again?"

"Yes, one of the many perks of being a coach." I smiled as Bessie left to get dressed. We were on our way home ten minutes later. I couldn't help but breathe in a sigh of relief. "I'm so thankful that's over." I reached behind me to strap on the seatbelt. "You make a sucky coach." Bessie smiled over her left shoulder. "I know, you know, mom, and dad know, so why in the everlasting hell am I doing this?"

I flipped both hands in the air. "Keep your hands on the wheel." Bessie advised. She was resting her head against the headrest with her eyes closed and still smiling. I glanced over. "How do you know what I'm doing behind closed doors?" "Behind closed lids, and I don't need my eyes open to know what you're doing. It's all right here." She tapped her head. "You suck." I pouted, and headed out of the driveway, and towards Jeremy, and Bessie's house. "You want to come in for a minute?"

Bessie asked leaning forward to get her purse from the floor. "Sure, but not for very long. Mom has big plans for the evening." "What could be more important than spending time with me?" She pointed a finger to her chest and then unlocked the door. It's silent inside as Jeremy is still at work. "I have no idea." "Want to see the baby's room?" Bessie tossed her purse on the couch. The living room is tiny as the rest of the house is, but it's all they could afford on Jeremy's salary. Bessie didn't care though. It's their very own.

We passed the living room, and mess of a kitchen down a hall past the bathroom, and two bedrooms at the end. She opened the door to the left. "Tada." she gestured, and we walked into a half-done crib, two blankets on the floor, and a three-quarter done dresser. "You need to finish this." I advised, running my hands down the crib and smiling.

"Baby will love this." I turned around. "When it's done." "All in due time." Bessie chuckled. "Plenty of time to finish this."

"Three weeks is not plenty of time, and you could have the baby sooner than that. If I were you, I'd get cracking." "Yeah, yeah. You are such a nag, and what does mom need you to do, that warrants spending so little time with me?" "I've just spent the last two hours with you. What more do you need?" I thumped both hands to my forehead. "Not that I didn't enjoy every minute." "You're my coach. Plus, you're my sister, and you need to suffer along with me." "That, I'm doing with pleasure., and onto mom, she needs to go over more of the new menu options."

"We're thinking of starting to offer the new sandwiches by next week." "That can wait, this can't." Bessie pointed a finger to her stomach. "Bess, I'm sorry, but I'm doing the best I can." I closed my eyes suddenly weary at being pulled in two different directions.

Bessie sat down next to me and watched my face. "I'm sorry Rees." she whispered, and I opened my eyes, and frowned. "No, I'm sorry. I made a promise, and I'm keeping it. Now tell me what I can do for you?" I asked wiping a tear away. It's stupid to cry. I made a promise and will keep it even if it killed me. Mom could wait. "Tell me what you thought of Jeff." "Very nice, and hot, and why did you talk about me?" "Why not?" Bessie shrugged. "He's single, your single. Match made in heaven." "Hardly," I said, sarcastically. "Why not? Do you not see a future with Doctor Hotty?"

I laughed out loud. I could always count on Bessie when I needed to have a good laugh. She lifted herself off the couch and walked into the kitchen for some drinks. She came back into the living room, and settled back on the couch, her feet tucked under her. "I just met him. I can't look that far ahead. Besides you referred Paul as Hotty, if I recall." I tipped my head back to lean against the couch.

"I call them as I see them. About Jeff. Give it time. It'll all work itself out eventually." "I guess it will. Now tell me more about Jeff." I sat back with my eyes closed again. I'm feeling relaxed again. I wasn't planning on going back until her final checkup. That summed up my duties. Bessie took a drink of her iced tea before answering

"Like I said, he's single, and so easy on the eyes. Very nice and seems interested in you." "I seem to remember, he mentioned you giving our phone number. Is that intentional?" I asked. "Yes, I figured you'd never take the plunge." "You've got a point." I pointed a finger in her direction. "Is he nice?" "As nice as anyone I've ever met except for the almighty Trey. Jeff is twenty-five, and if I wasn't married, I'd go for him myself. That's how hot he is. I only call him Doctor Hotty in my head. He might get an ego otherwise." "I'd have to agree with you there. He told me how old he is when we talked. I must think about this more." "Yeah, you think on that."

"What did you think of the baby's room?" "It looks nice, especially once everything is ready. Speaking of which, I'd get started on that if I were you. Much to do, and so little time to do it in." I pointed a finger in her direction. "I guess so, I don't dwell on it or anything." "Maybe you should. You're about to have the awesome responsibility of a tiny human." The thought of it still scared me, and for the life of me I can't figure out why it isn't having the same effect on her. I reached down just then to grab my purse, and on that note, I need to talk with mom. Big plans.

I kissed Bessie on the cheek and left. The house is quiet when I arrived home, so I cleaned my room before it got too out of control. Most of my clothes had made their way out of the boxes. The rest of my things arrived a few weeks ago, and were promptly placed in the corner, forgotten about until now.

No time like the present. I smiled to myself as I changed from my canvas shoes to tennis shoes, and an older pair of jean shorts. An hour later, three boxes were emptied. I could see more of my floor. I decided that is enough for one day. Plus, it's getting close to dinner, and mom still isn't home to go over our latest ideas. I wandered downstairs and searched through the refrigerator for something to make for dinner when I found a package of chicken breasts.

I got out a pan, and the oil when Mark poked his head in. "Hey." "Hello to you too. Long time no see." I cut up the chicken on the cutting board and added it to the pan sizzling with oil. "Such a long absence," he teased. "Why aren't you home with Sara?" I found a package of fettucine noodles in the cupboard. "She's got the late shift tonight. Won't be home for a while."

He moved further into the kitchen. "How did the appointment go?" "Not horrible." I smiled at him over my shoulder. "Although I'm glad I'm not in Bessie's shoes. But to give her credit, she seems to be taking all this in stride." I started the sauce for the fettucine while I was talking to him. "She wants this baby. Has a lot more to do to get the room ready though."

"That she does." Mark agreed with me. "I have to say, I like her a lot better now, than when we were teenagers." He stepped to sit in one of the kitchen chairs. "Remember all those tears?" He shook his head, remembering how every day was a challenge. "Fondly." I said, sarcastically.

I started boiling the noodles. "Most of the time I'd be relieved when she'd lock herself in her room and shut the rest of us out. I would deliberately knock softly and disappear quickly if she didn't answer within a few seconds. Low of me I'm sure, but desperate times call for desperate measures."

"I wonder how she'd enjoy being talked about like this. It's not fair, she has no way to defend herself." "Yeah, but it's a wee bit fun." I smiled. "So, you enjoy being done with school now?" He asked getting some plates out of the cupboard. "I do, and I don't if that makes any sense?" "Perfectly, you feel you've accomplished something, and your missing something at the same time." "Got that right." I got out a straining bowl for the noodles. "Is it small of me to like her better now?" "Not small. Maybe a bit mean." He teased, laughing.

I poured water over the noodles, and transferred them to a plastic bowl, setting it on the table. I smiled at him not saying anything further. I started realizing at that moment how well he understood me. Mom, and dad arrived home thankful as always dinner is ready. Mark ate with us so it's close to old times, but not quite the same. Once dinner is done, and I was back in my room working again. I realized at that moment how lonely I was just then. I'd have to change that, and soon.

Guess there is no time like the present. I am half hoping Jeff would call for the simple reason I'd have someone new to talk to. Then again, I wouldn't know what to say. I called Carla but got her voice mail. I realized I hadn't talked to her at all since school ended. She must be busy filling out applications. Hopefully she'd find a job soon. I know she's eager to put her skills to work. Even Bessie didn't answer when I called her. It's out of desperation, but she didn't have to know it. I gave up and worked a little more on my room. All it did is make me want my own place. I'm tired of living at home.

Chapter 11

It turned out to be two weeks before we could add the new sandwiches to the menu and get them printed. "At last." Zeni sighed and slapped her palms to her forehead. We were sitting in the kitchen at Starlights and looking so relieved it's ready. The place is closed, and quiet as we talked. I for one would miss this. It's nice to have mornings to ourselves. That would end soon. Mom had me helping in the dining room. I was also her backup in the kitchen for a while, until we got the new schedule under control.

I hadn't even had time to talk with Jeff again. Although he asked about me, the next time Bessie went in for her appointment. Bessie made it a point to remind me each time. I didn't feel too horrible since we talked on the phone several times. He is so easy to talk to, but we had yet to go on a date. I remembered his half-hearted attempt to go to dinner, but I didn't take it seriously. "What's on your mind?" Zeni asked taking her palms away from her face and getting up for a cup of coffee. "Jeff." I whispered. "Bessie's doctor Jeff?" "Yep, he's on my mind."

"Been on my mind and continues to stay on my mind. What the hell is wrong with me?" I put my own palms to my forehead, and swung my head back, and forth in frustration. "Are you dating yet?" "No, I just can't stop thinking about him. So again, what's wrong with me. I can't get someone out of my head who's only a casual acquaintance."

That statement is true, but I wanted to get to know him better. "I don't know how to answer you except that you've found someone to replace Paul. Instead of thrilling you, it's terrifying you." "You got that right." I pointed a finger at her chest. "What do I do about it?" "Enjoy the feeling. Wallow in it." "I'm seeing him on Tuesday. This is Bessie's final visit before she either gets induced or goes into labor naturally."

"Then you have two days to find something to wear." "I have a closet full of things." "Something new to wear."

"I know for a fact you haven't bought yourself anything new for a long time now, and contrary to popular belief, having nice things doesn't make you selfish. Go shopping. Have fun. We can finish this afternoon. We have a big day tomorrow." "Yeah, I know. What time do you need to finalize everything?" I asked setting the half full bottle in the sink and tossed the empty bottle in the trash. "About three, bring back the outfit so I can check it out before you go home."

"You seem confident I will find something." The front door opened, and we both heard "Reesa!" at the same time. Carla must be finished submitting applications. I got excited that she was here. She could go shopping with me. "It's Carla." I smiled jumping down. "My savior." I kissed mom on the cheek. "Coming." I yelled. "Hey stranger." She greeted, giving me a hug. She was wearing black leggings, and a long tight-fitting red and black sweater that clung to her curves.

Like me, she lost a ton of weight in school, and it looked good on her. I am still trying to gain some of mine back. Carla suggested lunch and since I hadn't seen her in weeks, I jumped at the chance. She drove straight to the mall where the food court is so conveniently located. We sat at a table eating chef salads and talking about where to go next.

The food court is located upstairs with windows surrounding two sides. The sun shone in making the place seem hotter than it was. It's full of people, all intent on shopping, and eating. The noise was too loud, so we ate in a hurry. "Tell me about Jeff." She whispered grabbing me on the arm. "I heard he's hot." "What did Bessie tell you?"

I groaned and drank my Diet Pepsi. "Exactly that. He's hot off the hotness factor, and he's smitten with you." She wiggled her butt in the chair, eager for the juicy details. I smiled as I studied her. She had recently gotten her hair cut, and it framed her face nicely.

She looks comfortable in the pants, and sweater just as I am wearing jeans, and a T-shirt, but she also looked confident. Her curls even though they were shorter, still exploded around her face as she bumped up, and down in her chair, barely able to control her excitement. "Hot yes, smitten I'm not sure about," I answered. "Is he nice at least?" "Seems like it. We've talked almost every night on the phone." "Maybe next time Dr. Hotty will ask you on a real date with real drinks, and real sex." I couldn't help but laugh. "That's Bessie's name for him."

The Way Life Used To Be

"Why do you think about sex so much?" I didn't want to tell her Jeff already asked me to have dinner. Besides like before it sounded like a 'we must get together sometime.' A moment that would never happen. I hoped that isn't the case. "Because you don't. One of us has to be responsible about this." "Yeah, yeah. You ready to shop?" "Thought you'd never ask. Where first?" "Sears, and Victoria's Secret." Carla whispered and laughed at my look. "Just kidding, let's go." We threw away our plates and headed for the escalator.

Just for laughs we drove to Hollywood's, and Victoria's Secret which sold skimpy night clothes that we admired. I even fingered a few outfits liking the silky feel. We ended up leaving with our laughter barely contained. Half an hour later, laden with a short sleeve silk summer dress, and wrap-around sandals, I was feeling giddy. In two days, I am seeing Jeff again, and I was excited, scared, nervous, and everything in between. Carla waited until we were in the malls parking lot before whispering. "I'm getting married!", and did a butt boogie, and giggled uncontrollably. "Invite Jeff."

I dropped the bag, dress, and shoes. "What did you say?" I asked turning to face her. "Married, bring Jeff, my orders." "Married... to Taylor?" I said, before realizing what I said. Who the hell else would it be? "Married?" I screamed. "It's about damn time," I hugged her so close. "Yes, yes, yes." She clapped her hands in excitement.

We reached her car, and I stuffed the package in the trunk. Carla slipped behind the driver's seat, and put on her seatbelt, and I followed with my own. "Do I look different to you?" I asked studying my face in the rear-view mirror. I even turned my head from side to side to get different angles. Carla turned to study my face "Your lonely," she said as she turned back to the road. "We will fix this, you, and me. Let's go to my house."

She drove carefully, which is new behavior for her, and I leaned back to relax. She pulled into her driveway ten minutes later, shut off the car, and I left my bag in the trunk while I followed her inside. "I'm surprised you haven't moved in with him already," I observed as we walked past the kitchen, bathroom to her bedroom which I could already see is a disaster area. "You forgot how to clean."

Carla giggled. "I'm on a mission." She ran a hand through her hair and settled them on her hips. "I can see that," and I thought I, was bad. "I thought by now you'd have moved in with Taylor?" "Still working on it. I have some things over there, but I guess I have ways to go. If you, and Jeff get together...." I smiled at her. "I'll tell you first." "That's my best friend in the world. Want something to drink?" She offered already heading towards the kitchen.

She poured lemonades for both of us, and we sat at the kitchen table sipping. "Taylor, and I had our first fight in a long time. It was very intense." That shocked me as they hardly ever fought. "What about?" "A coworker of all things. I'm convinced she wanted him, and Taylor would be unfaithful, but just goes to show you how insecure I can be. All is well though. We had incredible make up sex." "Always the best kind," I said, before realizing I wouldn't know.

For once Carla didn't tease me. "I never thought I'd be the insecure one. I play the game of confidence, and well, but I have my doubts same as anyone." "I hear you; I do too, and that's a big fat scary reason I'm hesitant about a new relationship," I admitted. "It can be. I won't beat around the bush, but is it so scary, you don't want to try? I want to see if there's a future."

Carla smiled "I should get you back." I agreed remembering how early I needed to be up in the morning, so we left. Once we reached Starlights, I grabbed the bag, and shoes from the trunk, and headed inside saying a quick goodbye to Carla. She looked at me with genuine concern before leaving for her own house. "What did you get?" Zeni asked wiping her hands on a towel. She tossed it on the counter and headed towards the door where I stood holding my bag.

I handed her the bag and skipped to the fountain to get a drink. "That's pretty," she complimented, and gave it back to me I folded the dress and placed it back in the bag. Setting the bag on the floor next to a table, I sat back down, and took another drink. "I think we're ready to start tomorrow I have nothing, but good feelings about this, and we need to be here by six thirty. I hope it doesn't take too long to get used to the earlier hours."

I groaned. "I knew this was a bad idea. I must get a good night's sleep." Maybe I'd skip tonight's talk if Jeff ended up calling tonight. "Better get home then. I think dad has dinner done already, so this should be an easy evening." She got up to turn out the dining room lights, and I walked into the kitchen to make sure everything was turned off and locked the back doors.

Once we were home, Keith had dinner on the stove, and said, it would be just a few minutes. That gave me time to get to my room, so I could have a few minutes to myself. I turned on the light and smiled at

The Way Life Used To Be

the mess. A clean freak I wasn't, but the clothes on the floor and bed made me smile anyway as I started putting them in my dresser.

By the time the bed is at least empty, I found a place to sit on it. I took the dress out of the bag one more time. "That's pretty," Sara said from the doorway. I put down the dress so she could look. "What are you doing here? Not that I don't love your company." Sara jumped on the bed to admire the dress. "Waiting for you." "Well, I'm glad to see you. How's your grandfather feeling?" "Not so good. He had another stroke, and I've been spending more time making sure he's okay." I closed a dresser drawer and turned around to give her my full attention. I had no idea he got that bad. "Sorry to hear that."

I felt bad for her, and selfish at the same time. "It's not so bad now. He has a nurse round the clock, so it's easier on me now." "That's good. Tell him we're praying for him." I picked up another pile of clothes and started folding. "I will. What's the new dress for?" "Bessie's next appointment." "I heard about it. I for one can't wait until Bessie has that baby." "She's getting on your nerves too?" I didn't mean to sound impatient, but this is typical of her. "Sometimes. I make it a habit to be busy whenever she comes over. It's small of me, but sometimes necessary." I answered for her, making her smile. She looked tired, and now I knew why.

"Sometimes it is. I just feel so tired." She sighed. "I know how it feels to have yourself stretched every way, that you don't have any time for yourself. It's hard to make sure everyone else is happy regardless if you are yourself." That is the best explanation I could come up with. Sara sighed again, louder, and longer. "I should get going." She reached over and hugged me. I closed my eyes looking forward to Tuesday.

Once the room is quiet again, I hopped off the bed, and headed for the closet so I could look at the dress again. I fingered the soft silk and tried to picture asking Jeff to my best friend's wedding, and he says yes with no hesitations, and smiles in his eyes. I let go of the dress and left the room when dad yelled up the stairs that dinner is ready. It got me thinking it is time I left the house too. I'm the last one here, and it's time to leave.

Once I was done eating, I volunteered to do the dishes. The clothes were still waiting for me, but I ended up shoving them to the floor, and got under the covers. Jeff ended up not calling, and I'm relieved. I shut my eyes and snuggled under my covers.

Sandra Gutierrez

Sure thing, Zeni's predictions came true. Five thirty came too soon, and I slammed my hand on the alarm clock, and groaned into the pillow. "This is the stupidest idea." I yelled into the pillow and punched it for added affect. "This is the greatest idea!" Zeni yelled from the doorway. "Get your lazy butt up." she disappeared to start a shower, and I raised my head, hair in my face, and growling at the empty doorway. After two more snoozes, I flipped back the comforter, and sat up, wiping sleep from my eyes, and flipped my bedhead away where it fell right back in my face.

I padded to the dresser where my black jeans, and t-shirt lay. Zeni also wore similar black jeans even though she spent most of her day in the kitchen. An apron when she is cooking covered the shirt, but she is never comfortable in slacks. She spent most of her day on her feet, so she is most happy in black sneakers, and her feet thanked her at the end of each day.

I took a quick shower to wake up. I brushed my hair, and pulled it in a neat French braid, I tied my own sneakers, and headed downstairs. It's six, and we had one hour to be at Starlight's, and ready to serve the breakfast sandwiches.

Word is spreading, and we expected a big crowd which would help sales. "Morning." I whispered as I entered the kitchen where mom, and dad sat at the table drinking coffee, and eating blueberry muffins. "Muffin?" Mom offered with a wide smile, and I groaned. "At this hour?" I plopped into a seat and am handed a glass. "How do you look beautiful at all hours of the day?" I mumbled shaking my head and smiled. "Kitchen pores." She answered taking a bite of her own muffin.

"What the hell are those?" I pulled open the refrigerator in search for something to eat and came up with a peach yogurt. I found a spoon and started eating it straight from the plastic container. "When the kitchen is full of pots, and pans cooking, and the air is nothing, but steam, it does wonders for the skin. Same as taking showers I guess."

She shrugged, and smiled at Keith who is sipping his coffee, and listening. "You can always have coffee." Zeni offered taking another bite of her muffin. "Might give you a wake-up boost." "That's just trading one bad habit for another. I'll just be happy with this." I held up my yogurt, and a glass of orange juice.

The clock struck six fifteen, and both Zeni, and Keith jumped up to throw their muffin papers in the garbage. "Let's go." she said, as she clapped her hands. "I can't wait." "Mom, you are too, happy for your own good. I grumbled." "Fine, let's go." Starlights is mysterious when all three of us pulled up. It's only six thirty, and half an hour to go before opening. The sun is just rising turning the sky from a midnight blue color to various shades of pink. It made me want to keep watching as a sunrise against a cloudless sky in the middle of summer is the best way to start out any day.

Zeni unlocked the kitchen door and turned on the lights. "We need to plug in the coffee pot first." she said, to me. I started thinking someday I'd enjoy the smell of freshly brewed coffee, but I would not hold my breath on that. "You ready?" she asked Keith who kissed her on the lips. "More than. We will kick ass." That's why Zeni's predictions always proved true.

By six forty-five, we had five guests at the front door smiling, and waiting for us to open. They'd been coming for years now and couldn't wait to try the new sandwiches. Zeni ended up opening the doors five minutes early with a smile, and me standing by her side, menus in hand, and seating the guests.

By eight, I am too busy to think about Jeff any longer, and we hit a lull at ten. I sat at the dining counter, water in hand, and looked forward to drinking it. My throat burned from talking so much. I closed my eyes and tipped my head up.

"Has it always been like this?" I asked as I lowered my gaze, and opened the top, and was about to take a long sip, when the back doors opened. "Hey Trey," I greeted, and stood up as soon as he opened the swinging doors. There isn't anyone in the kitchen, so he poked his head in the dining room to seek us out. "You don't have to stand. Stay comfortable." he offered and headed to the fountain for a Coke. "It's okay." I jumped down from the stool, and we went in the kitchen together. He had set some crates on the counter full of food.

"Ready?" "I am." I smiled, and grabbed the notepad mom always used, and a pencil. I held both items in one hand and flipped loose hairs behind one ear with my free hand. "So, how're things going?" he asked glancing towards the dining room. It still looked busy as we had a lot of customers still eating. Everyone looked happy for the moment. "Good, at least for a first day it's good."

"We just started the breakfast menu, and mom ended up opening early. It was wall to wall for a while, but now I'm taking a break." I took a drink of my water. "You starting to have a healthier lifestyle now?" He teased nodding towards my water. "I'm trying to, I can't depend on Diet

Pepsi my whole life. Plus, dad wants me to eat, and drink better. Sometimes I hate when adults know what's best for me."

He drew forward putting his arms on the counter and smiling at me. "Fathers can be formidable opponents." "Especially mine. I love him for it, anyway, and I'm sure he knows it." "So, how's your dad doing?" I asked. "Better than ever. He's still retired and makes noises about wanting to jump back in to help with the farming. Bret, and I have to put our feet down every time."

"Becoming the surrogate parent?" I teased. "When he needs it. Bret put down half for the barn, and dad, and I came up with the other half. Bret feels responsible for him too." I smiled. "That's nice. He sounds like a hard worker." "He's the best. Takes a lot after his grandfather, but he would never admit it." "Sometimes it's hard to admit we're our parents' children." I smiled at him. "So wise." He teased, smiling back at me. "I think you'd like him, and his girlfriend. Her names Jan, and she's a sweetheart. They come in here often. You waited on them once. It was during a break last fall."

"I remember. They had a club sandwich and are joined at the hip. Jan waved to me." "You have a good memory, and yes they are. They are nice people who know how to have fun. They have a lot of parties at her, and her roommates house. Offer pizza all the time." "I guess I make it a point to memorize little details about the customers that come in here."

"They seem to appreciate it. Is that the party you were at when I came to your barn?" I still remembered that night. He had forgotten. "Yes, it is, I do the same thing with our customers., and yes, they are thankful. I also remember Jim had a story about some woman with a cantaloupe chest and came back scarred. Said, he would find his one true love." "Jim's always finding his one true love. I'm thinking the one true love thing doesn't exist." Trey laughed at my comment.

"It might, you never know. There're books all about that same subject." "Did he find the impossible?" I asked hoping Jim found it. Trey laughed. "What do you think?" "I think he came home alone." He leaned a little closer. "Your right. Just do me a favor and not tease him. I think his ego's a little bruised." It's hard to be offended at either of them which I think relieved him. "I wouldn't do that even without that story. I like him." "It's hard not to. Even with all his stories."

"So, how's everything else?" I asked taking a drink. "Good mostly. One if my heifers had a stillbirth. It's messy trying to clean up." "That's awful. Is the cow okay?" "Seems to be. She made this god-awful sound when the calf came out. She started licking it clean and moaned when I had to remove it. It's now happy times."

"That sounds similar, to how a human would react. I guess that mother instinct is in all of us." "I think so too. Well, I'm all done." He announced and turned to his right smiling. "Two hundred fifty-five even." He emptied the crates, then stacked them together. "I'll get the check." I offered and hopped down from the stool. While I am gone, he leaned against the counter, and drew his head down resting it in both hands wanting to call it a day. It's hot, and the crates were cumbersome on his back. Jim didn't want to do any more. He just wanted an afternoon to do nothing. He especially didn't want to face that sow right now.

Trey drew his head up when the doors swished again. "Here ya go." I smiled and hopped back on my stool. I slid the check over, and he took it shoving it in his pocket. "Thanks. See you next week." He smiled and stacked the crates. I had already finished my water, and was heading through the swinging doors, so he stepped backwards through the back door, and headed to his truck.

By six, I am also thankful I wore sneakers instead of flats or even heels as I carried the last of the dishes to the kitchen and wiped down the tables. "All done?" Zeni asked her hands full of soapy suds as she washed plates, and Keith dried. This time of night when there were just a few dishes to clean, they didn't bother using the dishwashers. "Yes, thank god."

I moaned and sat much more on the stool than this morning. My back is on fire, and I wanted nothing more than a long warm bath to make me feel better. "I'd have to say this is a success." Zeni smiled over her shoulder. "The bagels were the most popular." "Yes, I know, I've had plenty."

"Now that you've enjoyed your full first day, you ready to enjoy your second?" Keith asked putting the last plate on the shelf above the sink. "I need a break." I groaned again and started taking off my sneakers. I wouldn't mind just walking around the rest of my evening in bare feet.

"Wait till we get home for that. You'll appreciate my nice thick carpet." Zeni advised. "Ready to go?"

They turned the lights off and headed home. I would walk home, but now that my feet were nothing, but small stabbing pains. I kept my mouth shut, and sat in the back seat, slipping off the sneakers, and massaging my own feet. "Just think, when you, and Jeff hit it off, and start dating, he'll be there to rub your feet." Zeni said, from the front seat, with her eyes closed. She knew what I was doing and smiled.

"You seem awful optimistic. I have to meet Bessie at four tomorrow. As much as it pains me for you to be her coach, you promised her, and childbirth is a lovely thing." Keith advised, pulling into the driveway and shutting off the car. "Why do you have to keep reminding me?" I just wanted her birth thing to be done. "Because someone is counting on you." Zeni advised, sounding serious. "I will take a bath, then I'll be down to help with dinner." I offered and pulled off my socks. "Oh, my sweet baby Jesus." I buried my feet in the carpet, and shuffled up the stairs, Zeni, and Keith laughing behind me, and headed towards the kitchen. The long days didn't bother them, so they started dinner while the water ran upstairs.

I lay in the bathtub full of bubbles and closed my eyes. My feet still ached, but not as bad. My back is still on fire, and nobody there to massage it. The bagels are good, but after three hours of serving the stupid things, I came to resent them every time I saw them on the plate. Like they had little beady eyes and smiles that laughed at me from the plate.

Now I am hallucinating. That is just wonderful, I thought as I lifted one leg that had bubbles falling off and plopped into the water. The water is cooling, and I glanced at my watch and groaned. Seven o'clock on the dot, and that much closer to tomorrow. I sniffed the air and smelled dinner. Time to get out. I climbed out of the tub and got dressed.

Fifteen minutes later, comfy in sweatpants I am sitting at the kitchen table my mouth full of stuffed green peppers. One of our favorite dinners, and one I've never mastered myself. I'd just be happy with dad making them. "I want to get my own place." I announced once I took my first bite.

I glanced around and felt again the loneliness. Both Keith and Zeni looked up startled. "You do?" Zeni responded and smiled. "I think that's great. You know where you want to live?" "No, I hadn't thought about that part. I was thinking, especially last night, how I'm the last child still here.

"Bessie is two years younger than me and has a house. Mark who is older, is on his own. I'm still here, and I need to leave." I took a bite of

The Way Life Used To Be

my dinner. It's delicious, and I am thankful I didn't have to make it. Especially with a day like this one. Zeni reached over to place her hand on my arm. "You need not leave. You want to leave. It's not the same." she advised. "So again, I ask, where do you want to live?"

I opened and shut my mouth. Where did I want to live? Near the river or a lake. Close by the restaurant in one of the many apartments surrounding it. "I honestly don't know. Want to help tomorrow?" I asked hopefully. "After we close, we can go driving to see what's available." "Remember your promise." Keith reminded me as I took a bite of his stuffed pepper.

"Oh yeah. I came this close to forgetting." I pinched two fingers together. "Wednesday?" "How about Friday. Keith can open, and we'll take the morning house shopping." Zeni offered, and Keith nodded his agreement. He liked his children out of the house, but still nearby. It made retirement seem more like a reality now than just a dream.

"Sounds good, I don't know what to look for." "You might be most comfortable with an apartment for now. Something with one or two bedrooms that you can turn one of them to a guest bedroom that one of your most special family members can stay in whenever the need arises." Zeni suggested.

"Don't you mean a roommate?" "No, I don't. You had four years of Carla as a dorm mate, and now it's time to have yourself for your own company, except the valued family member I mentioned earlier." It would be nice for Bessie to have a place to visit, once she had the baby. "I'll keep it in mind." I helped with the dishes, smiling. The thought of getting my own place seemed less scary now. I'm looking forward to it.

The phone rang when I was again settled in my room. I had the lights off, but I'm still awake. "Hello?" It's Jeff, and as soon as I heard him, I smiled into the phone. "How's everything?"

He had just gotten home after getting a takeout pizza for his dinner. He didn't feel like cooking, after putting in a full day. "Quiet" I answered burrowing under. "Any births lately?" "Not a one, I'm glad my day is over though. You sound tired." "A little, all is well though. Anything exciting happen?" "No, just put in a long one, and from the sounds of it, so did you." "It was long too, that's for sure, but a good day." Jeff poured a beer into a glass while waiting for the pizza to get done cooking. He is starving and realized he missed lunch. Not exactly a healthy way to live.

The buzzer sounded interrupting his thoughts, and I heard it through the phone. "What are you making?" I asked closing my eyes. I am getting so tired. "Takeout pizza. It's one of those take and bake things." "Sounds good." I smiled into the phone. "I sure hope so. You ready to come to Bessie's visit. It's her last one you know." He slid the pizza onto a plate, and cut it, using his shoulder as a temporary holder for the phone. "I'll be there." "Looking forward to it. I know Bessie's also wanting this to be over soon." "I can relate."

"Dinnertime." He announced cheerfully, already wanting to eat. "Listen, I'll let you eat, and see you tomorrow." "It's a date. Get a good night's sleep." I smiled as we hung up. By morning, I am frowning all over again. That damn alarm clock is becoming my new worst enemy. Only ten more hours, and I would see Jeff. My heart started beating wildly, and at the same time I am feeling exhilarated, and hopeful.

Seven o'clock came way too soon, but I am greeting the guests at the door with a smile. Looking at the clock only made the time go slower, so it's both a blessing, and a curse. I wanted the day to be done so I could see Jeff, but I also wanted it to last just a little longer so the anticipation would be that much sweeter. "Good afternoon Mr., and Mrs. Cleveland." I greeted to a couple who had been coming for years.

"Hello Teresa." Helen Cleveland smiled. She is one person who never used nicknames and wouldn't start now. I was polite not to comment on it. I seated them stating I'd be back in a minute to take their order. I knew damn well what they would order but would take it anyway without assuming.

This is what I knew from all the time I spent visiting here during school breaks. Take the orders with a smile and move on. Just some light chitchat, then move on to the next customer, never forgetting to check on your assigned tables. Tips were better that way.

I glanced at the clock. One thirty and moving forward. "Order up." Zeni yelled and thumped the bell. "Coming mama." I said, rushing up to the counter, and grabbed two plates of meatball subs on whole wheat buns, and macaroni salad.

"Here ya go." I said, placing the plates down. "Enjoy your meal." I smiled at Helen, and Curtis Cleveland who already dug into their sandwiches with a hasty thank you. By two thirty, Zeni stuck her head out of the kitchen. "Reesa." she exclaimed. "Coming." I said, again a little more wearily, and headed to the kitchen. I held four plates in my hands.

The Way Life Used To Be

"It's almost time to go." Zeni stated and grabbed the plates to place them in the sink. "I'm scared." I whispered taking off the apron. "Your fine. Go home, get dressed, and get yourself a boyfriend." Zeni ordered, "Yes mama." I kissed her cheek and headed out the back door strolling to the house. I had a full twenty minutes, and it only took five to get home.

The house is empty, and dark when I opened the door, and hurried up the stairs to change into the sundress. I didn't have time to re-wash my hair, so I settled on brushing it till it shone, then braided to a nice French braid, and put on silver hoop earrings. No perfume. I didn't want to be that obvious. I tossed my T-shirt, and jeans into the hamper, and walked to the closet in bra, and underwear keeping the bedroom door open. Didn't even worry about it as nobody would come through it.

The dress hung nice, neat, and wrinkle free as I took it off the hanger. I smoothed it even though it didn't need it. It's beautiful with tiny purple, blue, and hot pink flowers. Grabbing the dress, I picked up the sandals, and headed to the bathroom picturing Jeff's face while I put on the dress. It made me smile even wider than I was before. "Reesa?" Bessie yelled from the bottom of the stairs and started waddling up them without waiting for an answer.

"Reesa?" she said, again rounding the corner, and I stuck my head out the bathroom door. "Are we late?" I only had one sandal on. "Let me see." Bessie said, clapping her hands. "Come out." "I only have one sandal on." I repeated and leaned down so I could put the other one on. I stood up just as Bessie made it to the doorway. Bessie grabbed my hand is on the doorframe. "Let me see."

I sighed and stepped out. "Tada." I spread my arms out and slapped them back to my sides. Bessie squealed. "Mom is so right. You look hot. Jeff will be pleased. Let's go." She said, excitedly, and started back down the stairs. "Shouldn't I do something else with my hair?" I turned to the mirror, twisting so I could see the back. "No, you look beautiful. Let's go. I'm so excited."

"I'm coming. Don't get so excited you have the baby at my feet." I advised and shut the bathroom door. "About damn time." Bessie said, taking my arm. "Let's go, Jeff's waiting." She squealed. "He's been asking about you every damn time I go in, but you already knew that didn't you?" She didn't bother waiting for a response, and I kept quiet.

We left the house, and I locked it, and settled myself in the driver's seat. "You nervous?" Bessie asked putting on her seatbelt. It barely fit over her stomach now. "Yes." I said, backing out of the driveway. "But I promised you I'd go, and I'm not backing out." I turned the car and started down the street.

"Why thank you. I'd be lost without my coach." Bessie teased, smiling, and making me grin. "So, what's Jeff like or do you know much about him? I want to know what I'm getting into here." "Besides being the best doctor, I could ask for, he's so nice, and not in the geeky sense. He's polite, easygoing, and of course hot. I think you two will hit it off. He's mature too, something I forgot to mention before."

Bessie continued, "he told me about some of his ex's before, and I thought he would call them bitches or losers or cheaters or something to that effect." "You're so optimistic." I teased smiling, and I supposed they were none of those things? Bessie shook her head. "Nope. not a single negative thing to say. That is why I say he's mature." "I must keep that in mind."

We got out together and realized we were early. We went in any way. It would be a short wait. We sat in the waiting room, swinging our feet, and waited to be called. I sat with my hands folding over each other, and head down with Bessie watching me, smiling. "Elizabeth Hathaway." The nurse called from a doorway with a notebook in both hands and smiling politely towards the waiting room.

"That's us. Let's go." Bessie whispered. As soon as she is in the hospital gown, and on the exam table, I was ready to be done. I glanced at the magazines but didn't want to sit. Bessie is looking at me but said nothing. I could tell something is on her mind, but I said, nothing either. "Bessie how's it going?" Jeff asked walking into the room, smiling.

I had excused myself to go to the restroom, so I missed his entrance. I took a few extra minutes to splash cold water on my face hoping to reduce the redness. "Good, although I'm more than ready for this one to be over. I'm too big, and uncomfortable." She moaned leaning back on the pillow. "Do your worse." Jeff brought the stool over and sat on it with his overcoat hanging over the sides. "I intend to." he smiled. "Just kidding."

He took her blood pressure and listened to her heartbeat when I entered the doorway and looked down at Jeff. I thought about what Bessie said, about the ex-girlfriends, although I hid a smile. He smiled. "Hey there, come back already?" He asked. Like he hadn't been waiting for three weeks, and two days. Like it's nothing. I moved into the room, and he glanced down at the sandals. "New shoes?" They were already

The Way Life Used To Be

hurting, although I am trying not to show it. "No, they're old," I lied, but said nothing more. He didn't seem interested, anyway.

"Well, you're already five centimeters dilated. I'd say about two or three days at the most. You ready?" he asked, and all she did is smirk in his direction. "I guess you are. I'll book a room for you as soon as you call me. Just make sure you're in true labor. No false contractions." He pointed a finger. "Just kidding." He stood up, and kicked the rolling stool back with one foot, and I watched him do it, and it turned me on.

He turned to me smiling. Bessie opened her mouth right on queue. "She'd love to have dinner with you," she said, sitting up. Jeff laughed. "Bess, you are quite the matchmaker." He shook his head. "Always glad to lend a hand," Bessie said, climbing off the exam table. "Yes, you are, however I've beaten you to the punch. Reesa, how about that dinner we talked about? Tomorrow sound good?" "I'd love to." I answered and reached down to get my purse so we could get going. "Let's go so you can get ready." Bessie said.

I glanced at her gown, picking at it with two fingers. "You don't want to get dressed first?" "Little things." Bessie laughed, and headed towards the dressing room down the hall, pleased with herself. Once the room is quiet, Jeff turned to me. "I'll call you when I'm done for the day. Make final plans. It's nice to see you again." he leaned a little closer, and I love the new shoes. "You about ready now." Bessie said, leaning against the doorway dressed in her regular clothes, and holding her purse.

"I've been ready since we got here." I hated this place. Jeff being the exception. He waved goodbye, and headed to his next appointment, and we left the hospital with a sigh from me, and a giggle from Bessie. "Bistro's." She said, as we left the clinic her arm linked with mine as we headed outside, and into the sunshine. "Why Bistro's?" I asked getting into the car. "Damn it's hot." I waved my hand trying to cool the seat. "It's romantic. Perfect for a first date." Bessie put on her seatbelt. "I can't wait until this baby is born."

I placed my hand on her stomach and the baby turned. "What is that?" I yelled whipping my hand away. "You have some serious gas or something." "David's saying hello." "You already named him?" I stared at her stomach wanting to touch it again. "Six months ago, Jeremy's idea." "You didn't have any say in the matter?" I backed the car out. The seat burned through the dress, but I wanted to get home.

"I had plenty of say. I want a boy, and we're having a boy. I made Jeremy choose the name." "You have the perfect relationship. I'm jealous." I pouted, and we entered the highway. "It was perfect for a long time. We had a huge fight last week that made me wonder for an entire night if I made a mistake in marrying him. Took me three days to calm down."

I parked in Bessie's driveway, turned off the engine, but didn't move from her seat. I turned to Bessie who had tears in her eyes. "What happened?" "Let's go inside where it's cool, and I'll tell you." I frowned in her direction as we left the car, and the outside temperature is worse than the car.

Bessie's house is better with a floor fan in the living room, but nothing else for relief. I didn't want to complain. I wanted to hear what is wrong? Why didn't I notice all day that Bessie was sad? Am I that shallow?

Bessie left to get some drinks, and came back with a Diet Pepsi for me, and a bottle of water for herself. At least she had a few good habits. I smiled as she sat down. "Jeremy cheated on me." She said. She took a drink of water to swallow the lump in her throat.

The tears grew bigger. My smile vanished. "Oh honey, why didn't you tell me. I will hurt him." I punched a pillow. "That is his face." "It's my fault, I neglected him for some time now, and put the needs of getting ready for this baby before him. I apologized for it, but it hasn't changed things."

"You are a pregnant woman. Don't feed me that crap about neglecting your man. If he had any honor at all, he would understand that significant fact." "I tried, I thought for sure after the baby is born, he'd realize what he would lose by divorcing me, but it's not that way."

"Then why are you still together. He's an adulterer or some other such word. I can't think of what he is. He's stupid." Bessie pointed to her stomach. "Because of him. Because of his baby, we're still together." "That's no excuse. You can be a single mother..." What did I know about being a single mother? I wasn't the person Bessie should talk to. I should encourage her to talk to a marriage counselor that could give her proper advice.

Bessie interrupted. "No, I won't. Don't say it again. I will not be alone. I don't even have an education." Two tears spilled down her cheeks and landed on her lap darkening the pale blue jeans she wore. "Yes, you do. You have your high school diploma, and you will be a mom. You can get a job, and we'll help you with babysitting. We'll help with everything, anything you need. You have a support team. We're your family, not him."

I hated Jeremy now. How could he do this? He was so close to becoming a father. He broke his vows. Everything I loved about him dissolved right there on the spot. "I'm due in three days. In three short days I will be a mom. I can't think of anything much beyond that. The thought of doing this alone scares the crap out of me. I don't want to do it." She took another drink of water while more tears fell.

"I know." I patted her knee, then moved closer, so I am rubbing her shoulder. "I know." No, a counselor is not the answer. We sat a while in silence until the clock struck five, and neither of us moved. My feet were aching in the new sandals, but I didn't take them off.

By five thirty I am still there. I had no clue how to help her. I'm still sad for her, but I am unwilling to leave her in the state she is in. "When is he expected home? I don't think I want to be here when he walks in that door." I nodded towards her front door. "I don't know to be honest with you. He's been gone the last two days, and…" I exploded. "Gone with his bimbo?"

"I haven't asked where he's been. I think I've been in my own world the last few weeks. It was when I heard Jeff ask you out that brought everything I've been feeling lately to the surface." I took a drink of my soda and placed it on the end table. "Have I been neglecting you?" Bessie reached over to take my hand. "No," She said. "Then in that case, let's make dinner. It's almost six, and I'm starving." "Okay, thank you for staying here with me. I guess one of us has to be lucky in love. May as well be you." Bessie said, sadly, and crossed her other leg. "You think Jeff might be the one?"

"You'll never know if you don't have dinner." "He will be calling me soon to make plans on where to eat." Bessie sighed. "I know that. I was in the room. You can have him choose, which may be the right thing to do, or you could take the bull by the horns, and decide yourself. I just love Bistros. Always have. I think Jeremy, and I can work through this."

"How do you know that? Do you trust him after this? After two days of being gone, and for all you know with another woman?" I hated being so blunt, but I had to for her sake. Bessie shook her head. "No, I don't trust him. Not in the least bit. He is sleeping on the couch because I won't let him in the bedroom. He tried for months to cuddle with me, and I booted him out every night saying I was too tired or too sore. I'm always too something. I think he got tired of hearing it, and that's why he found another woman. I want to blame him for all this, but in all honesty what else is there? I can't kiss him. I can't hug him, and I can't leave him."

"I hope you know what you're doing. Just remember, and don't ever for one minute forget that we all love you, and your room is ready if you need it. Want me to tell mom, and dad?" "No, not yet, I need to. I just don't know when. Say nothing to anyone." "What do you want for dinner?" "Pizza, I'll order it." Bessie wandered to the kitchen to grab a phone book, and I waited on the couch trying to absorb this. I called mom, and dad, and told them I wouldn't be home for a while.

"All done. I got us a vegetarian without tomatoes." "Sounds perfect." I leaned my head back and closed my eyes while Bessie did the same. Sometimes it's nice to do, and say nothing, and knowing it's okay to do it. "Want to watch a movie?" Bessie offered, opening one eye. I nodded.

The pizza came twenty minutes into the movie. We ate, with few words, and I found it's so relaxing. I almost didn't want to leave, but when the movie is over, and it's close to nine, I realized I had to be up early, so I stood up to leave. "I'd better get going. Early day tomorrow. I may not understand everything you're going through, but I'm glad you told me." I kissed her cheek, and she walked me to the doorway.

In the car alone this time, I sighed. I laid my head on the steering wheel thinking if I would have done the same thing. Love someone who broke their vows and not trust them at the same time. Didn't love, and trust go together? Not wanting to dwell on it any longer, I started the car, and headed home.

The house is empty when I arrived home from Bessie's and waited until Jeff's call which came two minutes after I walked in the door. Talk about perfect timing. "Hey there." Jeff greeted. He had just gotten done with rounds, and it's a hot, grueling day. He stepped into his apartment which is just as hot as outside, turned on the air conditioner, and headed to the kitchen to make something to eat.

Nine thirty or not, Jeff was hungry! The hospital cafeteria left much to be desired. He only ate there when there is no time to go anywhere decent. He rummaged through his cupboards, smiling when he found a can of Beefaroni. Hot damn. Cheap noodles. Oh well, it isn't like there is much to choose from as he only had a half full box of cheerios, some instant coffee, and spaghetti sauce with no noodles. Pathetic. Jeff sighed,

The Way Life Used To Be

and dumped the Beefaroni into a bowl, and stuck it in the microwave for a few minutes.

He thought about Bessie's idea of dinner, and it made him smile. Jeff flipped open the cell phone and dialed. May as well start somewhere. "Hey back. How is your day?" I asked hanging up my purse and headed towards the kitchen seeing if anyone is home. I poked my head in, found it dark, and headed upstairs to change into shorts, and to get out of my sandals which were making my feet scream.

I almost sighed out loud when I undid the straps and tossed the sandals aside. I may never wear them again. "Busy." The buzzer sounded. "What are you doing?" I heard the ding. "Making dinner." He looked through a drawer that had a bunch of silverware and found a spoon. That sounded like the talk we had a few days ago. It made me smile. "Would you rather call me later? I will be up for a while."

I offered, grabbing a pair of jean shorts, and a T-shirt. I wanted to take a bath anyway since I didn't have time for one earlier, and the sweat from working, and going to Bessie's appointment is making me feel grungy. "No, It's fine. I'm just having Beefaroni, the dinner of champions."

He got a bottle of water out of the refrigerator and tucked it in his arm. He headed to his couch so he could sit down and relax for a few hours. "I think that's Wheaties, and it's for breakfast." "I don't have any, so I make do."

"Well, it sounds good anyway." I smiled as I found a pair of socks and sat on the bed. The bath would wait for a few minutes. "No, but it's food." He uncapped the bottle of water and took a sip. "What did you, and Bessie do for the rest of the day?" "Hung out at her house. We had pizza for dinner. That is about as healthy as yours." I teased making him smile. "That sounds better. I wish I'd thought of that myself. Would have been easier than that take home a pizza. Are you feeling a little better about the whole birth thing now?"

I shuddered. "Yeah. I suppose so. It's just hard to be her support when I've never gone through it myself. I feel a little out of sorts sometimes." "You're doing fine." Jeff finished his dinner, and shoved it aside, leaning back on the couch. As always, it's so easy to talk to him.

Like I've known him forever. "I try. Duties of the older sister I guess." "Something like that. Have you thought about where you'd like to eat?" "No," I admitted. I didn't want to suggest Bistros. "Just not seafood. Other than that, I pretty much like anything." "How about

Something Meaty? I heard they make good hamburgers." "I haven't been there. Sounds perfect."

"Then it's decided. Is tomorrow still okay?" "Perfect." I am already looking forward to it. "Seven work for you?" "Yes. I'll be ready." I hung up the phone with a smile, and grabbed my clothes, and headed to the bathroom. I would enjoy a few minutes to myself. If Bessie called saying she is already lonely, I knew I'd go over there to help her. I want to put my foot down where she is concerned. I knew I was being weak. That it's out of love I'd never say no. I think Bessie well knew of that fact.

Jeff hung up too, and took the bowl to the kitchen sink, and ran water over it. The next day it's so busy at Starlight's I hardly had time to breathe, much less dwell on my upcoming date. I didn't even have time to pick out something to wear. I didn't have to think about the sandals. That is a very poor decision I made on that one. "Order up." Zeni called and slammed the bell. She is also tiring of order after order, but never complained about it.

I grabbed three plates of barbecued meatballs, turkey club, and roast beef sandwiches, handed them out with more than a smile, and a quick. "Here ya go. Enjoy," before going on to the next order. It's close to five when I hung up my apron, and said, a quick goodbye before realizing when I got home, I never told mom about tonight. Oh well, I am an adult now, and it is high time I did things on my own without having to worry about their approval or even checking in.

I decided just to walk home as mom drove me this morning, and I didn't want to bother them with a ride home. Plus, I wanted some time for myself before my date. For once even Bessie isn't at the house as she is lately. Now I knew why. She is lonely at home and needed company around her. I could just about imagine what she is going through and I felt so sorry for her trying to do the right thing.

I took a quick bath and headed to my room dressed only in panties as I rummaged through my drawer for a dressy type bra. The sun had disappeared from my window leaving it shaded, but still stifling hot. It would be hours before it cooled down enough to sleep tonight.

I found a white lacy bra, a tan short sleeve blouse with mother-of-pearl buttons, and a navy pleated skirt. It's thigh length and accentuated my tanned legs. I frowned at the sandals I had tossed in the closet the night before and bypassed them for white backless pumps. They had two-inch heels, and made me at least a little taller, if nothing else. I laughed as I dressed and brushed my hair deciding on leaving it down

The Way Life Used To Be

instead of the usual French braid. I smeared on some hair gel to keep the curl in and minimize the frizz.

I had just grabbed my purse when the front door-bell rang, causing my breath to catch. I took a deep breath and walked downstairs to answer it. Jeff stood leaning against the doorframe like he didn't have a care in the world. "Hi," he said as he held out his arm. "Hi." I said and slid my arm through his. He led me to the car. It's brick red and had leather interior.

He opened my car door, and shut it gently when I slid inside, comfortable against the softest leather I ever felt. I buckled the seatbelt as he ran around to the driver's side and got in. "You look amazing again." He complimented as he started the car and turned his head to look at me. I had turned my head and found my smile matched his. "I ended up making reservations, not sure how busy they'd be." "Always a good plan." "Always." He agreed.

We arrived at Something Meaty with about ten minutes to spare, but we are promptly seated, and when I glanced around, found it isn't as busy as I had expected. They gave us ice water, and we gave our drink orders to the frizzy haired waitress who had a mile-wide smile and seemed friendly enough.

Once she left, we studied the menu. "I heard they have the most amazing minestrone soup. I'm sure it even beats my mothers." "I'm shocked to hear you say that," he laughed. "She would be too! I must keep that secret from her." I am enjoying myself.

"That might be best." He agreed setting down his menu. I set mine down too. The same waitress reappeared to take our orders, and hand us our drinks She left a second time, and Jeff turned to me. "You look nice tonight. I was expecting to see the sandals again. Those were pretty." "My sandals, and I are not on speaking terms." I took a drink of my iced tea.

"Did you get in a fight?" He teased taking a drink of his own Coke. "Not exactly." I grinned. "I bought them on a whim, and I need to be a little more careful about impulse buying. They hurt my feet too much to wear them again." I admitted. "Then I take it they're shoved in the back of the closet?" "Seems like a nice permanent home. Speaking of homes, where do you live?"

"In the Berkeley Luxury Apartments. They're near Ryan Place." "I've heard of that place. It's off some Golf course, right?" "Close. Colonial Golf Course is about ten minutes away. I can see it from my floor." "Is it a nice place?" I asked. "Very, I've lived there for three years now. They have two, and three bedrooms in the east village, and one bedroom's, and studios in the west village. There's a large seasonal pool separating the two sections in the central courtyard, and a basketball court, and workout area. I spend a lot of time there working out after a long shift, and Bessie wears me out with all her long drawn out conversations."

"She is a talker, but that's why we love her. Tell me more about the apartments." I relaxed my head against the booth and smiled, looking at him. He frowned for a minute. "You want to know more about where I live. Am I that boring of a person? There isn't any other conversation possible?"

I laughed out loud and explained. "Not in the least bit are you boring. I'm thinking seriously of getting my own place so yes, I want to know more about where you live." "Well, the owners are nice, and seem to care about the tenants a lot. Every time I go in there to pay rent, or need to put in a work order, Marlisa, the manager, and co-owner asks about how I'm doing. If there's any new baby pictures she can gawk at." "And do you oblige?" I asked.

"Whenever I can. The work orders sometimes are a little slow in getting completed, but mostly, it's a nice place. It may be why I haven't moved. It's relaxing, quiet, and that's all I'm looking for." He took another drink, "I'd like to show it to you." "I'm already excited." "You want to see it tomorrow? I have the day off. I'd love to spend it with you." "What if Bessie has the baby?" "That might put a dent in our plans, but there's always the day after if that happens. I'm only there to deliver the baby."

"After that, it's all up to the nurses, and of course Bessie. She'll have her hands full for a while." "Yeah, about eighteen years of a while." I smirked, making him laugh. Our salads, and minestrone soup arrived. "That about covers it." "Just about, so as long as Bessie doesn't call, I'd like to see it." I dug my spoon into the soup and took a bite. As promised, it's delicious. "It's a date," he said. He dug into his own soup.

We ate in silence for a while, and it's nice. Not at all uncomfortable as I had sometimes imagined. "This is a nice place." Jeff complimented as he finished his soup and started on the salad. "Yes, it is. I must tell my mom all about it. Except omit the part about the great soup." "Might hurt her feelings? I don't agree. I've tasted her soups, and I have to say it's tough competition."

The Way Life Used To Be

I glanced up surprised. I didn't even know he went in Starlights. He saw the surprise on my face. "I order takeout from there. Usually once or twice a month. I like your delivery guy. Very nice and seems to appreciate my tips." "That'd be Jim. Jim Stevens. Your right. He's like a brother to me." "He seems like he'd make a good one."

I smiled and finished my salad. The waitress reappeared, and placed our main courses on the table, and took the empty soup bowls, and salad plates. It looked so appetizing with the bacon peeking out of my burger. The fries looked wonderful too. "Are there any more kids still at home?" He asked.

I shook my head. "I'm the last, but not for too much longer." "I'm an only child. Not sure if that's a good or bad thing." He took a bite of his burger and chewed slowly. "Sometimes I wish I was too, but then I think of all that I'd miss if I am. I wouldn't be a coach, that's for sure."

"You have a point there. When are you off tomorrow?" "At noon, I have to help open. After the breakfast crowd, Mark will be there at eleven. I'll be free after that. Want to meet at your complex?" "No, I'd like to pick you up. Be all proper like. Noon you said?" I nodded and finished my last fry.

Once again, our plates are cleared, and dessert arrived. Cannoli's which were my absolute favorite. I dug into my cannoli with pleasure. "This is one dish my mother never mastered." I ate a forkful. "Mine either. She is raised on the idea women are housewives, and useless anywhere else. She never held a job, but she is there every day when I got home from school."

"I'm sure I bored her with all my stories, but she never once complained. She is big on boxed dinners. Macaroni, and cheese made with powder is her favorite. I used to crave it when I was younger. She made it for me for breakfast, lunch and dinner for two years straight." "Didn't you ever tire of it?" I asked, but he didn't seem to mind.

He nodded his head with a smile. "From the very beginning. She'd vary it a lot, adding pepperoni, sausage, hamburger, but it's always the same. I never complained though, not even once, and ate every bite every time." He took a bite of his own cannoli and savored the taste. "You love her that much?" I questioned head still tilted, and he found he loved it. It seemed to be a move she did without realizing it.

"I do. She died two years ago from lung cancer. My dad smoked like a chimney his whole life. He's still alive, and she's dead. Never smoked a single cigarette in her entire life." he sounded bitter about it, and the cannoli didn't taste as good now. "I take it you're not close then?" "We get along fine on the surface. He lives in Paris, Texas so I don't see him often. I hide my true feelings very well, so when I come back from my visits, I don't fall apart. At least not anymore."

I studied him while the waitresses removed our dessert plates. He seemed so well in control, like nothing bothered him when everything bothered me. That must take a lot of strength and will power. He paid the bill without blinking an eye and held my shoulder while walking out to the car. He had thought little beyond the dinner portion of the evening, and once I'm seated, he turned to me intending to ask what I'd like to do next. I'm gazing him with my head tilted.

He buckled his seatbelt, started the engine, and sat there for a minute. "Where to?" He started to say "I want..." I said, at the same time, and both stopped, and I giggled. "What would you like to do now?" He asked. "Visit your apartment." I answered. "I'd love to, but you won't be able to see much this late at night. The pool area is already closed, and the workout area. All you'd see is a bunch of apartments, and lights. Not much to admire at night." He answered.

"You're probably right. Do you go swimming a lot?" "As much as I can. It's harder lately because of my schedule. The pools Olympic size and has a diving board. it's heated too. Anything else you want to do?"

I thought for a while, but nothing came to mind. I didn't want the evening to end. I couldn't think of a way to prolong the evening. "Want to go for a walk?" He asked.

When I nodded, he backed out, and headed for Trinity Park which is also near the apartments. Sometimes after work, he'd head over there for a picnic, and unwind. Most of the time, right before sundown, it's quiet. He could feed the ducks that swarmed around him looking for a handout. Or walk along the trail that led toward the Trinity River. It's a long trail that he normally took on his days off so he could enjoy it.

He reached the park entrance and found it empty. That is good. He hated an audience especially on a first date. We got out of the car, and he took my elbow while we entered the park, and the ducks came, quacking.

I squealed, and bent down, reaching out my hand to touch them. "Want to feed them?" He asked. I turned my head. My hand is still outstretched. "You have something for them?" "The park supplies old bread. It's here in a barrel." He pointed to a wooden barrel at the front

The Way Life Used To Be

gate. I jumped up, and grabbed a loaf, then squatted back down, and started ripping the bread in little pieces.

"You must love animals?" He observed sitting next to me and tore his own bread. "That I do. We had no animals growing up, and until I visited a friend's barn a few years ago, I didn't realize what I am missing." I said, smiling. "I had a dog once when I was little. A springer spaniel, and I loved her so much." He whispered. "Her name was Spring, and my mom got her for me on my fifth birthday. I got nothing else, and I didn't care. She was my best friend for fourteen years. She died five years ago, and I miss her almost as much as my mom."

I stopped feeding and turned to look at him. "When is your birthday?" I asked. "April fifteenth. I named her Spring because it was Spring when I got her, and I couldn't think of any clever names that suited her." "When's your birthday? We should celebrate it." He sounded like he is teasing, so I couldn't be sure. He then pointed towards the east. I looked, but it was too dark to see anything. Jeff said, "she's buried in Trinity Pet Cemetery over there."

"Sometimes after my shift I'll get a sandwich or something, and come out here to sit, and relax. Once the sun sets, I walk over to talk to her. We have dinner together so to speak." "My birthday is next month. July 25th. What do you, and Spring talk about?" I asked. He had expected her to tease him which is something Bessie would have done. He didn't realize until that moment how different they were and preferred Reesa's quiet style.

"Work mostly," He replied, and tore another piece of bread. The ducks approached closer. "I tell her how my day was, and what could have gone better when I have a difficult one. She listens, and never judges which is a lot more than I could say for some of my patients. I swear most of them have a solution for every symptom that has nothing to do with each other. It's comical and frustrating at times. Anyway, that's what we talk about. That, and the fact I'm still single, and unfortunately she has no opinion on that."

"Sometimes being single has its advantages," I advised. "Nobody to answer to, nobody to yell at you when you've done something wrong." "Nobody to love." Jeff interrupted looking at me, unsmiling. I stood up, smoothing my skirt. "I think I would have liked her, Spring." I felt sorry for him losing both his mother, and pet all within a few years of each other. I wondered if that is something that would make someone more or less loving? For me, I think I'd be less for the simple fact I already lost someone I loved. I don't feel the same anymore.

"She would have liked you too. She is very particular about the people she let near her, and I think you'd have gotten along just fine." He stood up too, wiping the dirt off his jeans. We put the rest of the loaf back in the barrel and headed back to the car. It's getting late, and I realized how early I had to get up. "Are you getting another pet?" I asked once we are settled, and we were on the way to my house. "Not for a while. I've had a busy schedule for quite a while, and not enough time to care for another dog." "I think you should." I advised once he pulled into the driveway.

He reached to turn off the engine. "Don't bother, I can get to my front door myself, and I have an early day. Don't forget to pick me up." I said, pulling off my seatbelt. He shut the car off, anyway. "Chalk it up to good manners, courtesy of my mother." He smiled and walked me to the front door. "I'm surprised my mom, and dad aren't waiting at the door for me."

I turned to say goodbye. "Hopefully they would approve too. I'll see you tomorrow." He whispered and kissed me on the cheek. "I had a good time tonight." "Me too." I smiled, and opened the front door, keeping it open while I watched him drive away. I touched my cheek, realizing that is a perfect way to end the evening. I sighed and turned to open the front door.

Chapter 12

"So, how was it?" Zeni asked from the living room where she, and Keith were relaxing, and waiting for me to get home. She fully trusted me, but she didn't know Jeff. Didn't know if I would come home happy or sad or angry. Or not at all. They finished cleaning up by six thirty. For once there were no customers who stayed past six so finishing up is an easy task.

They locked up Starlights and drove home. She isn't hungry, so she heated spaghetti from last night for Keith. Once he is finished, she rinsed the plate, and left in the sink. She sat in her favorite rocker watching ER, and staring at the TV, and relaxing, but not paying attention. She kept an ear out for a car pulling into the driveway.

Once the front door opened, she could breathe again. She got the details from Bessie, so she isn't too worried when I didn't show up after my shift. "It was perfect," once I saw her sitting there acting like she didn't have a care in the world. "I will go change into something comfortable, I'll be right back." I dashed up the stairs, and into my room. I turned on the light then leaped on the bed smiling at the ceiling. It's the perfect first date, and tomorrow I am having a perfect second one.

I sat up to take the sandals off and rubbed the bottoms of my feet. They were still sore from yesterday. I grabbed a pair of anklets from the dresser, and unwrapped the skirt, and unbuttoned the blouse, throwing both into the hamper. I'd wash them on my next day off. I slipped into a pair of old black sweatpants, a white T-shirt. I headed back down-stairs where mom still sat, and dad is nowhere. around.

"Where's dad?" I asked plopping on the couch and slipping my feet under my legs. "Went upstairs to relax. Wanted to give us girls time to gossip. So, tell me how it went. I'm dying for details." She put down her book so she could give me her full attention. "We ate at Something Meaty. Had minestrone soup, cheeseburgers, plus to die for cannoli for dessert." "Sounds yummy, I skipped dinner tonight." Zeni sighed and smiled. "Why? You never skip." "Not feeling so good today. Must be a bug or something. Tell me about your evening since you have a mile-wide smile on your face."

I sat down and folded my legs under me. "Jeff is even nicer than I expected from the visit a few weeks ago." "Did Bessie's appointment go okay?" "Fine, although she will pop that baby out any second I think." "Sooner would be better than later. She's been spending a lot of time over here lately. Bessie say anything about why?" "No, she's been lonely for company. I had dinner with her last night after the appointment. Saw the baby's room too." She has a lot of work left to do on that.

"Isn't Jeremy helping her?" "Far as I know. I think it's just the crib that needs to be put together. That, and there are a lot of clothes lying about. I don't think that'll take too long." I got up for a minute to get myself something to drink. Mom followed me into the kitchen where we continued talking at the kitchen table. Much like we did when I was a few years younger.

There had been little time for one-on-one confession, especially with us being opened earlier now. I'm feeling like I had very little time to myself. It's nothing, but work, then come home to bed. This would have been the perfect opportunity to tell mom about Bessie's news, but I kept quiet. Hopefully Bessie herself would say something, and I'd be off the silent hook.

I did however get up to make her some scrambled eggs. "What are you doing eating again?" She asked. "I'm not, you are. No skipping meals. Not on my watch." I wagged a finger in her direction and made her smile. "I guess I need to take my own advice, I'll help you." She started to get up. "No don't, I'm playing mommy." I got two eggs out of the refrigerator and cracked them against a bowl. "You make quite the mommy. What else happened on your date? I'm dying for details."

I grabbed a whisk out of the drawer and started stirring the eggs. "Well, to end the evening, I got a kiss on the cheek." "And that is the best part?" "That is the second-best part." I giggled and spread some butter in a pan. "After dinner, which was awesome, we walked to Trinity Park to feed the ducks. We talked a lot, and tomorrow he's taking me to look at his apartments. If I like it there, he will help me get an application

The Way Life Used To Be

so I can live there too." I'm sure I sounded excited. I poured the eggs in the pan where they started bubbling.

"Are you saying you decided on an apartment already?" She asked. "I don't want to settle for the first available place although having Jeff nearby would be a plus." I slid the eggs onto a plate and popped two pieces of bread into the toaster. "It might be, I'd like to at least meet him first before you take that plunge."

I giggled out of nervousness. "I might be able to manage that. I have to admit; I'm already looking forward to it." I placed a plate before her. "Thank you for being a mommy. You did very a good job, taking care of me," Zeni teased taking a bite of her eggs. "Not practicing for the real thing or anything, but sometimes we need to be taken care of."
"So wise."

She took another bite. I smiled and bent so I was eye to eye level with her. "Thank you, and you'll like him. He's a mama's boy who grew up with a dog he loved and visits every week. His dog died a few years ago, and he walks to her grave, and they talk. That's all we did tonight too once we are done eating. You'd have been proud of me. Not even a good-night kiss except for the one on the cheek when I got home."

"Good. You need to get some sleep since you need be up in five hours. What time is he meeting you?" "Noon," I said, getting up so I could get ready for bed. "We'll meet him then." Zeni got up herself and placed her empty plate in the sink. "See you in the morning," I said. I kissed her forehead and headed to my room where again I couldn't settle down long enough to lie down, much less try to sleep. I sat at my windowsill, smiling into the night, and picturing living at that complex.

Zeni walked into her own room where Keith is lying on the bed, watching the evening news. "Reesa might move out soon." "I'm glad, it's time we had the house to ourselves." Once they are cuddled close, Zeni reached over to touch his cheek before rubbing her face next to it. "Then why does this make me sad. I want her to have freedom, and as much as I'd want to go after her, I'd let her. I may have a few words to say about it, but I'd let her. That's why I love you so much." He kissed her lips. "Mama hen."

The alarm clock is becoming my worst enemy as I slammed the snooze button, and screamed into the pillow, then punched it for added effect. After the third snooze, I opened one eye to find the sun glaring in the window, and I jumped out of bed to close the curtain, shutting out the glare.

Sandra Gutierrez

Once I am dressed, I remembered why I am so excited about today. Jeff. It made me smile as I'm going to see the complex today. I am already falling in love with it and hadn't seen it before. That didn't matter though, I am still excited. I French braided my hair since I didn't want it in my face while working and tied the end with a red ribbon to match my blouse.

I smoothed my jeans and headed out to start my shift. I was walking this morning. That way when Jeff came to pick me up, we could go straight to the complex to check it out. I am already looking forward to noon. The place is dark, so I turned on the kitchen lights, and got several bagels, and English muffins out of the bins, and started slicing. Mom followed me and is already starting the afternoon soups while I got sandwiches ready.

As soon as dad turned the signs several customers filled the doorway. Within five minutes two orders were on the ring waiting to be filled. I quickly plated the orders and slammed the bell. "Orders up." "Thanks honey." he smiled and headed towards the dining room to deliver the breakfasts.

He hurried to take the next table. Once it slowed down, I moved from the kitchen to the dining room to help out until the part-time waitresses arrived. We scheduled them in an hour. I handed plates to customers with a smile, and had six more orders before ten o'clock, and a break finally. I was on my feet for over three hours and dying for a Diet Pepsi.

Dad is in the kitchen helping mom, and there weren't any customers waiting so I grabbed a soda from the fountain and hopped on a bar stool for a few minutes. I guzzled down the liquid with a straw, sitting on my stool, and swinging one foot over the other leg, enjoying the quiet. The lunch rush would start soon, but for now is nice.

I glanced over as the stool next to me became occupied and smiled. "Hey you." Trey smiled back. "What's happening?" "Big day. I'm looking for an apartment in two hours." I said, turning back to my soda. "You tired of living with Keith and Zeni already?" He teased jumping up to get his own soda. He sat back down, and took a drink, waiting for my answer.

I am smiling. "Yes, I'm tired of it. I thought when I graduated, I'd love living back home, but I've been home for two months, and I'm ready to get out." "Where are you moving to?" He is curious, but only mildly so. He had only stopped by for a minute between deliveries. "Not sure yet. I'm checking out an apartment complex nearby, but this is the first one I'm looking at. I don't even know if I'll move yet. I just want to."

"I don't blame you." He wanted to move to, but with his dad's condition he is scared to. His mom isn't strong enough to care for herself, and him, so he had to stay a while longer. He however is thinking of building his own house nearby.

"How're the rest of the animals doing? That cow doing better?" I asked running my fingers up, and down the cup. It's damp from the ice, but I didn't care. He smiled thinking of them. "They're doing good. She's feeling better. Albert's pregnant again. Due in about four months, and Luther got in a fight with another rooster." "Who won?" "Luther. It's neck, and neck for a while, but he once again proved he's the boss."

He smiled at the memory of the two roosters butting heads. "Who is the other rooster?" I asked getting up for another refill. "I'll get it." He offered and is back thirty seconds later. "Where were we?" "Thanks. The loser rooster. What's his name?" "That's a better name than I picked out. His actual name is Petey. He has yet to mate. The other chickens ignore him as they're hot, and heavy for Luther. He has two girlfriends now."

"Two? One is never enough? What kind of name is Petey, anyway? Might be the reason for the lack of sex." I advised, pointing one finger, and smiling. "They're not monogamous. Not like humans are." "Most anyway." I smiled. I am once again reminded of Bessie, and that reminded me, I needed to check up on her, and see how she is coping.

"My mom came up with the name Petey. I never asked how she did, but that's his name. Just like Luther, I guess the name's just stuck. I don't question her. It's just something that makes her happy, so I go along with it." "Sounds like it is, with all your animals you name." I scooped up the empty cup. The clock struck ten thirty. I jumped off the stool to throw away the cup. Four customers just came in, so I grabbed some menus off the rack.

Trey got up too. "I'll throw that away" He offered as he took the cup and threw both in the garbage. "Thanks. see you around," I said over my shoulder with a wide smile for him and went to take the new orders. Trey smiled too as he watched her back and left to finish his day. He also just realized he never told her what he was doing there in the first place.

211

I delivered the food orders, and three more before the noon hour arrived, when Jeff showed up at the same time. "Hi Reesa." He said, stepping inside. The front doors remained open during the summer hours. He looked comfortable wearing blue jeans, and a T-shirt looking right at home. I turned around smiling at the sound of his voice. "Hi Jeff. About time you got here. I've been waiting for hours." I teased, and he laughed moving further inside.

"You by yourself?" He asked looking around. It's empty, which is unusual for the lunch hour, but that is okay with me. It would make leaving easier since I wouldn't be leaving anyone shorthanded. "Reesa!" Dad shouted from the swinging doors before noticing Jeff standing there with me.

"Hey, I know you. Meatballs sub on wheat, hold the onions." Jeff laughed. "Am I that predictable?" "Nah, I just remember certain customers. You are one of them, you should be honored." Keith teased making both of us laugh. This is easier than I had predicted. "Hey Zeni, get out here." He bellowed behind his shoulder. "She's been cleaning the kitchen." "Mom's always busy with something." I took off my apron.

"What am I busy with?" Zeni asked approaching the group and grinning. "Hey, I know you." Keith slapped her on the butt. "Keep your hands off me, you big galoot." She laughed and slipped an arm around his back. "I am popular! You both remember me!" Jeff declared. Zeni nodded. "You guys want a sandwich before you take off?" Keith asked. "Sure." Jeff answered taking me by the shoulder. I smiled up at him. Once dad left to make our lunch, mom stayed with us, keeping her apron on, and folded her arms.

Zeni continued, "I would say it's nice to meet you finally, but since that's unnecessary, I hear your looking for an apartment today." "Hopefully." He answered. "I'm taking her to see my complex, and if things go my way, she'll fall in love with it, and move in soon," he grinned down at me. He squeezed the shoulder he was holding. "Just bring her back in one piece, and Reesa I want all the nitty-gritty details when you get back. Make me fall in love with it too," Zeni said giving me a quick kiss on the cheek. "I like him." She whispered into my hair, meaning it. "Have loads of fun, and I hope you fall in love with it, and him. He's the one." She said, not bothering to sound discreet.

Jeff didn't seem bothered by it. He seemed to enjoy himself. I grinned and kissed her cheek. "I'm thinking so." Dad arrived with our sandwiches in a bag without asking what we wanted. He knew what we

The Way Life Used To Be

liked, and we waved goodbye, and headed outside. "That is a lot easier than I expected." He said as he let out a sigh. "I already like both of them."

"And since you seem to be a favorite customer of theirs, the feelings mutual." I teased. He looked over at her. "Kind of hard to not like sandwiches. Especially when they come with all the treats your mom likes to give. Hey, maybe she can teach me how to make pies."

"She still has to teach me that." The sandwiches smelled up the car, and I wanted to dig in right away. I skipped breakfast this morning on account of nerves, but now that the hard part is over, I am famished. "Your mom is exactly like my mom." He said, "I take that as a compliment." "It's meant to be one. My mom is the glue that held my family together. No, I've never known what it's like to have brothers, and sisters, but she is the glue."

"That pretty much sums up my family, minus the siblings' part. I think it's more my dad who's the glue though. I think they'd be lost without each other, but my dad is the one who keeps us in line. He doesn't hardly shout, but when he does, it's like a storm. Doesn't last very long though, before long it's gone, and peace reigns over us."

We reached the cast-iron gates, and even though the gates are opened, he had to enter a code on the side to get through. "Nice security." I observed nodding my head in approval. I'm already impressed and felt safe. "The owners installed the gate two years ago after they had a bad break in. The code identifies the vehicle coming in. Stopped the crime after that. There've been minor petty crimes here, and there, but that's it. I feel so much safer now, and so will you." He put his hand in mine and linked fingers. In his free hand, he carried the bag of sandwiches, and potato salads.

"You seem confident I'll want to live here." "Of course, I'm confident. That's the bottom line here. What's best for me!" He pressed our hands to his chest and made me laugh. "That's the other reason. Making you laugh." We turned a corner and headed towards the office. "Time to get approved." He stated.

"Shouldn't I look at the apartments first?" I asked, he shook his head. "No need. Let's go." He led me to the office door which stood open, and airy. It had a pleasant vanilla scent, and a woman sat at a desk, smiling at Jeff, and turned for a polite smile at me. "Hey Jeff, what are you doing here handsome.?" She stuck a pencil in her hair and leaned back. "Getting you a new tenant," he said. He eased me forward. "Marlisa, I'd like to meet Teresa Harris."

Marlisa Hudgens smiled wider. She is a pudgy woman with out of control red hair that liked to spike up, but her smile is contagious. She shook my hand firmly. "You want to fill out an application?" She handed over a notebook when I nodded. "So, Jeff. how's work going?" She asked while I filled out paperwork. "Pretty good. I have a childbirth scheduled for tomorrow hopefully." He answered sitting back in his chair and folded his arms. "Anyone I know?"

Jeff nodded towards me. "Her little sister. She's getting induced if she doesn't go naturally." "Is she overdue?" I answered. "No, but by Thursday, she will be, and she doesn't want to wait that long, so she asked for a little help if nature doesn't cooperate. Here are the forms." I handed them across the desk. Marlisa slipped on a pair of glasses. "I'll just run these through the air fax. I should have my answer in about half an hour. You want to wait here?"

"No, but thanks. I'm taking Reesa to see the place. We'll be back shortly." Jeff stood up, and I followed suit while Marlisa sent the information through. We walked along a sidewalk free of any leaves or debris. "It's nice. I like it already." I observed looking down, then back up towards the trees that swayed gently in the wind. "They must have a wonderful groundskeeper to keep the sidewalks and grass this clean."

"Marlisa has a nice lawn crew that does the grounds twice a week. They're top of the line." "Shows. If the outside is any sign, I can't wait to see the inside." I swear he could already read my thoughts. "I can't show any empty units, but I can show you mine. That way you'd have a good idea of the layout." "Okay," I said. I reached for his hand this time which he gave. We strolled, enjoying the fresh air, and sunshine.

"Over here is the pool," he pointed to a gate in the middle of the complex. "You can see it better from the second floor though. Most of the gate covers it from ground level." I strained my neck and found he is right. All I could see is ripples of blue water between the slats. "Can you go inside the gate now?"

"If I had the key. It's in my apartment. Want to see it?" "Of course, although I already want to take a swim. If I had it my way, I'd already be in the water, bathing suit or not." "All in due time," he teased. I backed away from the gate and followed him around the pool area where he pointed out the gym.

The Way Life Used To Be

It looked empty this time of day, but I could see two bicycles, and a weight set from the bottom of the stairs. "Don't tell me you don't have that key either?" I asked grinning at him. "Same key as the pool gate. Also, in my apartment." He laughed and led me to the back side of the gym, and up a set of stairs.

"Ready?" "Of course, don't hold back now." I said, looking over his shoulder so I could see inside the apartment once he unlocked the deadbolt. The entrance way is spotless, and held nothing, but a wooden stand holding a dragon statue, and a coat rack. "This is the kitchen. All units come with a refrigerator, stove, and microwave, built in above the stove. Works well too." "Very economical." I observed looking around.

The appliances were tan, and clean. He seemed like a spotless person, and that alone racked up points. They separated the kitchen from the dining area by a bar, and two bar stools. He didn't own a dining room table because it's just him, and tables took up too much space.

The living room had a single brown leather couch that looked very comfortable and worn in without looking trashy. There is a wooden brown coffee table in front of it with two pictures. I leaned forward to see the pictures more closely. One is a young woman sitting under a tree with a skirt flowing around her ankles. She had long black hair and is beautiful.

"That's my mother when she was still a teenager. She is seventeen when that is taken, and my grandparents couldn't afford any fancy senior pictures, so they took homemade photos for her album. I found that picture in the attic of my mom's, and dad's house. He asked me if there is anything I wanted before he took the boxes full of her things to the dump.

Couldn't stand to look at it anymore is his excuse, so I spent two days going through every box she had and came up with this single picture of her. It's too precious to think of him dumping it, so I kept it. I also found that picture of Spring the winter before she died. Everything else is old books, and stuff I'd never need. I took the pictures and left.

He explained placing the bag on the coffee table. I had forgotten about our lunch, but that could wait. "Ever go back?" I asked peering closer at the pictures. "As little as I can manage. I went there about two months ago for a quick visit, and we barely tolerated each other. It's a very painful visit, but I got through it. Hey next time you can come with me and keep me sane," he offered smiling. He is only half joking.

"I would, just to keep you sane. No other reason." I teased straightening back up. "I like the apartments so far. Do the one-bedrooms look the same?" He shook his head. "No, only one bathroom, and the two bedrooms have one, and a half. They're not as large either, but for one person, it'd be perfect. I prefer the two because I enjoy having space." "Want to see anything else before we have to go back?" "You forget about something?" I asked nodding to the bag. "Oh yeah, wait right here."

He disappeared into the kitchen and came back with two bottles of water. I opened the tab, and took a drink while he opened the bag, and took out our sandwiches. "Thanks." I smiled as he handed me mine. We ate in silence, and again it isn't uncomfortable in the least. I finished my last bite, and crumbled up the wrapper which he took, and tossed everything into the garbage. "You want to see the rest?" He offered.

I shook my head. "I've seen enough so I'm ready when you are." We got up at the same time and headed to the front door where he locked it once more. We headed back to the office. Marlisa is waiting for us with a wide smile. "Back so soon. Teresa what did you think?" "I love it, did my application get processed or do you need more time?" I knew I sounded anxious, but I couldn't help it.

I wanted to live here so bad I could taste it. "All done. You ready to see any of the empty units so you can pick one out?" It's her way of telling me they approved me. I smiled, "am I approved?" I asked. "With flying colors. I have the amounts you'll need for the first month." She pointed to a notebook. "First month is special with two hundred dollars off. Security deposit's only one fifty. You have pets?" "No," I answered. "If that changes, let me know. Pet deposit's two hundred nonrefundable. So grand total is three hundred fifty dollars."

"Can you manage that?" "Yes, that's a lot lower than I expected." "Having that special adds up. I get a lot of calls about them, and this one is about to end, so you've come by at the right time. Speaking of checking out your new home, are you ready?" I jumped up. "Am I ever." Marlisa showed me both a one, and a two-bedroom that were still being cleaned. Both were empty as the tenants had just moved out two weeks ago and smelled like lemon detergent. The good news is they would be ready within a week.

Once Jeff, and I were back in his car, he asked which one I liked better. The prices were both within my budget, but I still liked the two-bedroom better. I had full intentions of making the spare bedroom a guest bedroom so I could have Bessie, and her new baby over for visits. Especially with going through a strenuous time. She'd love it and give her time away from Jeremy. "I'm thinking a two." I replied buckling my seatbelt.

I leaned back and smiled at him. "Thank you so much for taking me here today." He reached over to take my hand and pressed his lips to my fingertips. It's a nice gesture and reminded me how much I enjoyed going slow with him. He didn't seem in any hurry to rush things either. "Your welcome, need any help moving?" He asked taking my fingers away from his mouth, but kept our fingers entwined as he rested them against the armrest.

"Maybe, but I'm sure mom, and dad will help me." I am already picturing how I wanted to decorate my bedroom. It's the rest of the place I had no clue about. "Have you, and Bessie always been close?" I nodded. "Not this close. We've always had a special bond between us, and it's gotten stronger. She was very difficult as a teenager. At a lot of times, but we got through every mood swing. I'm glad I'm her coach even if I don't act like it."

"That makes sense. I think you like it a lot more than you let on. I don't mean the having a baby part. It's the support you give her. She talks about you a lot, that sometimes I want her to stop, she's such a talkative type." "Why don't you?" I don't know why I said, that.

I knew he could never tell her to be quiet any more than I could. "Cause if I did, I wouldn't know so much about you, so I have an ulterior motive in all this," He laughed. We reached the restaurant where dad is just locking up. "You need to help your parents?" He asked nodding in their direction. "Yeah, just a sec." I hopped out of the car, and he followed close behind me.

"How did it go?" Zeni asked smiling at the sight of me, then extended the smile to Jeff. "You came back for seconds, right?" She laughed. "Much as that appeals to me, No, I'm still full, from eating lunch." "I'm moving out." I said. I pressed my hands to my face. "I'm accepted." "Of course, you are." Zeni's smiled widened. "Good news, when?" She is already looking forward to a house with no kids. The feelings from last night were already dissipating.

"Hopefully next week. The apartment I want is being cleaned as we speak. You're not sad in the least bit?" I teased. "A teeny tiny bit." Zeni teased then locked the restaurant doors, and her, and Keith headed to the car. "Are you coming home?" She turned her head waiting for an answer. "We'll be there soon." I said, Jeff opened my door, and smiled as he started the car. We headed back to the house.

"So." Jeff smiled in my direction as we left the parking lot. "Are you getting excited?" "Am I ever." I smiled back at him over my shoulder. "My mom took the news better than I expected. Not sure how my dad feels yet." "I think he's fine with it. Most dads would be in this situation." He turned the corner and headed to the house. "Is your dad anything like mine?" I asked. "No", he said, "He smoked every day."

"It started out with two packs a day and increased to three by the time I had moved out, and to this day he hasn't quit. When my mom passed away, he didn't even shed a tear. I'm the one who cried buckets and is called a sissy over it. I am twenty, and a man, but I cried like a baby when she died." He didn't feel like a sissy anymore, but bygones are scarce. "Did you call him on it?"

He shook his head. "No, what would have been the point? He has his beliefs, and I have mine. I did however squeeze his shoulder when I left with my box and told him no matter what I'll always love him. I don't regret that one small gesture." "It's not small." I advised as we turned into the driveway. "It's huge." "Yeah, I guess you're right. Anyway, I didn't say a word about mom. Just said, what I needed to, and left the house without looking back." "Did he at least acknowledge you?" I unbuckled my seatbelt again and grabbed my purse. "No," "Then that's his loss."

"Your wise for such a young person." He teased opening his door. I giggled as we walked into the house. Zeni, and Keith were sitting at the kitchen table, iced teas in front of them, and whispering. "Did you see the way they were looking at each other? Like they had stars in their eyes." Keith said, Zeni nodded. "Did I ever," she sighed. "Do you think they're falling in love?" Normally she would have never thought of something like that so soon. Times had changed from when she is that age. "I do, and for the record, he's good for her." "I agree."

Once the front door opened, they looked up, and smiled as we entered the kitchen. "What did the apartment look like?" Keith asked. "Well kept on the outside. There's a pool, and weight room I can enjoy when I'm not at Starlights." I said. "What, no more river swims?" Zeni teased making me laugh. "Of course not. The kitchen is white oak, and big. At least big enough for two people. Each unit has a microwave built in over the stove. Marlisa is the manager, and she promised if it ever breaks, a replacement is free of charge providing it isn't intentionally broken." "Sounds nice so far."

"I get one with two bathrooms. The half bathroom is off the master bedroom, and the full is between the two. I'm making the smaller bedroom a guest room so Bessie, and the baby can come, and visit." "What about Jeremy?" "If he wants to come too." I said, keeping my face blank. "When am I going to see your new place?" I smiled. "As soon as you want."

Zeni studied Jeff for a minute. He remained quiet while I rambled on about my new place. "Will she be near you?" She asked him. "Yes ma'am, she's in the same building as mine, and down one flight of stairs. We'll be close to each other." "Good." Zeni said, feeling better, and better about it. "Make sure she's safe."

Jeff nodded his agreement. "You don't have to worry." "That's my job. Mom's privilege. Are you still coming to the birth or did you change your mind?" "I'll be there, I'm meeting her at three unless she needs me before. This is her moment, and I'm there for her." We all walked Jeff to the front door since it's getting late, and none of us had dinner yet. Jeff didn't mention going out again.

Once the front door is shut, and Jeff is on his way back to the apartment, mom, and I sat at the kitchen table talking. "What's going on with Bessie?" She asked not beating around the bush. She had no idea the marriage is in trouble and felt like she didn't know her younger daughter very well. "You make a terrible poker player. Your face is like a mirror."

"Jeremy's cheating." I finally said, and the room stilled with just our breathing. No other sound. "How long?" Mom asked wrapping her hands around her cup and lowered her head. "I don't know, and I don't know if he's still doing it. Bessie just told me a few days ago, and I had to promise not to tell anybody." Zeni tried to take a sip and lowered the cup without taking one. "I'll wait for her," she decided. "So, on to brighter subjects, tell me honestly what you feel for Jeff?" She took a real drink this time.

"When Paul died, I felt like I did too. As far as love is concerned. I'd never find it again. The feelings I have for Jeff are so much stronger, and deeper than Paul, if that could be possible." "I know Paul is your first love, and how devastated you were when he died. I'm glad it hasn't stopped you from trying again." Zeni got up to get another iced tea. "It almost did. The first time I met him, I was nervous about dating again.

He pretty much squelched the nerves right out of me. He's very easygoing and laid back. I think I needed that this time."

"Maybe. Have you met his dad yet?" I shook my head. "No, they're not too close from what he's told me." "Guess they can't always be as perfect as us." Zeni teased causing me to laugh. Zeni laughed too. "Let's go to bed. You have a big day tomorrow playing coach." She stood up and emptied the rest of the tea in the sink.

I growled. "Why must you keep reminding me?" I slapped a hand to my forehead. "Oh, that's right, I'm such a loving, and supportive older sister. What was I thinking when I agreed to that one?" "You love Bessie." She gave me another kiss. "Bed." "Yeah, yeah." I grumbled again, and headed upstairs to my bedroom which stood dark, and lonely.

The moon is glowing in the window, so I needed no other light as I shut the door and lay down on the bed thinking of my future. A baby tomorrow, and an apartment next week. So much to look forward to, I smiled. That alone warranted a trip to the closet. Not something as dramatic as the sundress, but I wanted to look nice for him. He noticed when I bought something new, so appearances were important to him.

I found a jean skirt, and dark blue short-sleeve blouse that is wrinkle free. "Hot damn." I whispered, and set the clothes on the desk, and got ready for bed. Four hours later I got up and headed to the shower. I yawned since I didn't get much sleep. In seven hours, I'd see Jeff again. It almost made the lack of sleep worth it.

At the restaurant, at seven the front doors opened, and our day began. By eleven I had a break with a cup of iced water, and hung out at the counter, still wearing my apron, and swinging my leg in tune to the radio that played from the wall speakers. At one thirty the phone rang, and Keith answered it, yelling through the swinging doors, it's time for me to leave.

"Already?" I said, as I ripped off the apron. "See you at the hospital later. I'll call you." I said, this over my shoulder as I yanked open the back door and ran back to the house so I could change and freshen my hair. Bessie said, she is already at the hospital, but it'd be another hour. I had plenty of time to prepare. The house is quiet and cool when I unlocked the door.

I raced up to the bedroom and changed in two minutes flat. I pulled the rubber band from my braid, and brushed my hair, retying it to a ponytail high on my head. I put on lip gloss. That is my only makeup. I needed nothing else, and Jeff seemed to like it that way. He said, nothing outright, but he also seemed the type to speak his mind and isn't shy about doing so.

Besides, if he didn't like me the way I am, that would have been his loss. I wouldn't be dating him if he was that shallow. I rushed down the stairs, and out the door in minutes, and headed straight for the hospital, my radio tuned to a soft rock station. No country music today. "Hey Bess." I greeted once I entered her room with a large blue teddy bear with a white tie, I picked up at the gift shop down-stairs. Sara is there too in a rocking chair and reading a book. "Hey Sara." I swooped down and hugged her. "Are you coaching too?"

Sara shook her head. "I'm the support. I'm just not needed at this moment," she smiled over at Bessie who is laying in the bed, straps on her belly, and frowning. She didn't even say thank you for the bear. Just glanced at it, then at Sara, and I talking. I glanced at Bessie, and saw the anger in her eyes, and assumed it was directed towards Jeremy. I smiled at her, receiving nothing in return. Jeff came in, coat flapping against his legs.

"Ready to be a mom?" He asked and turned to me smiling. "You ready to move?" He pulled up a stool, and chart from the table. Bessie remained silent, and I smiled making up for her sullenness. "Am I ever. Today too soon?" Jeff checked the straps and did a quick ultra-sound before standing up. "About an hour to go. You'll feel the contractions get more intense. Remember your breathing, and it'll be over before you know it." He patted Bessie's bare knee and turned towards me.

Sara continued to sit and read. "I talked with Marlisa this morning on the way to work. She said, the apartment will be ready sooner than expected. By the weekend, she promised." "I can't wait. I'm ready to move my stuff now." As I clapped my hands, making him laugh. "Need some help?" "Of course, she does." Sara answered. "We're all going to help, except the new mommy here." She didn't mean to leave Bessie out, but she wouldn't be able to do much, anyway.

Bessie wanted to cry. They were making plans knowing full well she couldn't do anything. Her marriage is in trouble, she is having a baby she didn't want, Reesa, and Sara were acting like they were new best friends. Life sucked right now.

It continued as she pushed and grunted making me want to vomit as I studied the pinkish liquid wondering what in God's name is he possibly thinking to make childbirth the grossest thing possible. All it did is make me decide, with great pleasure, to never be in her place. Kids weren't on the menu.

Bessie gave a final push and flopped her head back on the pillow moaning in pain as the baby's head appeared along with the rest of his bloody self. Her face is puffy, and swollen, and small tears of pain leaked out of her eyes, and onto her cheeks where they lay without being wiped away. I'm supposed to be mopping her face while supporting her from the head of the bed. All I could concentrate on is Jeff who is concentrating on the task at hand, and all that blood that leaked out onto the bedsheets.

Jeff placed him on her stomach where she stared in wonder and wished Jeremy for all his faults was the one at her side. He should have been, and would be, if she hadn't thrown his sorry self in the streets last night. That was after he admitted the affair hadn't ended, and then said, he is falling in love. She didn't even ask the whores name. It didn't matter. She is nothing along with him, and they deserved each other.

He still should have been there supporting her, even if he had someone else in his bed. He came into the house to grab some clothes he had left behind last week. He asked, "when the baby is born, can I have a picture?" A damn picture is all he wanted. She shoved him out the door with a pair of jeans in his hand and told him never to come back again. She'd think about visitation later after she calmed down.

However, it didn't make it hurt any less. His job is to be there supporting her, not making it with someone else, and leaving her to pick up the pieces. Reesa is a poor substitute. All she did is stand there making googly eyes at Jeff, and she is supposed to give her support. Some support. She did all the hard work, had to hold this newborn baby, and pretend he is the best thing that ever happened to her, and Reesa couldn't care less. She had Jeff, and apparently that is enough. She held the baby and cooed sweet nothings to his face smeared with blood, and afterbirth. It's the ugliest thing she saw, but said, nothing until the nurse approached to wash him. She lay her head back and closed her eyes. "What a cute baby." She whispered, and opened her eyes again, and watched the nurse swaddle him. Jeff, and Reesa had already left the room along with Sara. She is alone and started bawling the minute she realized it.

She also realized in that moment she is already resenting having the baby and didn't mean what she just thought. It was for Jeff, Reesa's, and Sara's benefit, but they weren't even there. She had never felt so alone as she closed her eyes once again and sighed. She even thought it might be best just to give the baby up for adoption. That way he would be with two people who truly loved each other and could love him unconditionally.

Oblivious of Bessie's anger, and resentment, I made it home followed by Sara. Jeff still had other patients to see, and we wanted to spend some time together. I had seen little of her and wanted to hear all new gossip. Nobody else is home, so I assumed mom, and dad made it to the hospital to visit Bessie.

That would be good. Then she wouldn't be alone. I felt bad I wasn't totally there for Bessie today. Now that I thought about it, I wasn't there at all. My mind is on moving, and Jeff. I'd make it up to her somehow. We went into the kitchen for drinks, and sat at the kitchen table, our feet propped on chairs, and chatted.

"Bessie seems down. I thought she'd be happy to be free of the baby." "She'll never be free of the baby. But your right, she's already depressed. I could see it not only in her eyes, but in her entire body language. I'm just surprised she didn't snap. That's Bessie's usual way to deal with things is by crying, snapping her words, then she's over it." "Doesn't sound like a very mature way to handle emotions." Sara observed taking a drink of her root-beer.

"She's never been one on maturity. I love her to death, but lately it's like she's a teenager again. I know she's been going through hell, but I get so tired of it. It's one reason I loved college so much. I got to avoid much of her wrath." "I didn't, I must have been your substitute." Sara shook her head smiling. "It's not funny, but a few weeks ago she came into Hankins to pick up some groceries. I am in the deli at the time, and said, hi to her as she is walking past with her cart."

"Did she have a moment right there in the store?" I grimaced picturing her. "And then some, she is slamming buns in her cart when I came around the counter to give her a hug. She wheeled the cart in my direction missing my stomach and when I jumped back, she yelled at me to get the hell out of her way. I admit I snapped at her, and she ended up leaving the store with her cart in the middle of an aisle without another word to me."

She apologized later stating it was hormones or something, and I said, "it's okay and I understand." "I can just about picture it. I'm glad I wasn't part of that particular tantrum." "Thank your lucky stars." "I do often. I used to apologize for every mood swing she had when we were younger. I realize now that's not the way to mollify her, but I didn't know any better than. Who knows, she thinks this is acceptable behavior."

Sara took a last drink of her soda. "Oh, I don't know about that. It may well have been hormones talking, but I don't want a repeat. Hopefully this baby is the only one she has for a while." "From your lips." I kissed two fingers up to the sky. Sara left shortly afterwards as she, and Mark were having friends over for dinner, so I washed the glasses we used, and headed upstairs to find some boxes in the spare closet so I could start packing. No time like the present.

Jeff proved to be as good as his word as he lugged up box after box two flights of stairs in the blinding sun, and sweating a storm, but never complained. This is what I wanted, so it's what he wanted. The last item to be moved into the larger of the two bedrooms was the mattress, and box-spring.

Zeni stood in the corner where I placed the dresser, and started folding clothes, and placing them away. It's the least she could do. Keith is in the kitchen putting some of their old dishes' mom insisted I have in the cupboards. Mark ran the restaurant by himself for a while. It's the middle of the week, and slow so they took advantage of the time, and moved my things all within the morning, and afternoon. They scheduled Bessie to be released from the hospital at six, and both Zeni, and Keith volunteered to get her.

Now it's four o'clock, and the day is scorching. We stood in the living room with sweat pouring down our faces and drinking tall glasses of iced tea that Zeni fixed that morning. It's better than water, although I planned on buying a lot of groceries to keep my shelves full. I had a list in my head that I needed to write on paper. I thought about asking Bessie to help me. I decided it would have been rude. She is going to have her hands full for a long time, but I planned on a visit soon. I wanted to know if the marriage had any hope. Is it over for good? Zeni still hadn't talked to her. She is biding her time as well, and even though she had just visited her that morning to see the new baby, she didn't say a word.

Bessie is there by herself dressed in sweats, and she could tell she is crying, but Bessie didn't confide, and Zeni didn't ask. It made for a very short, and uncomfortable visit, and she left after only half an hour, feeling bad, but glad she isn't in the same position. She did however promise herself she would get the truth out of her one way or another when she picked her up that evening. Enough is enough.

She met me at the house along with Jeff. We were talking in the bedroom and packing clothes into boxes. She watched us from the doorway, and we both had their backs to her, intent on we were doing. She hadn't the heart to interrupt. It made her feel better we seemed to communicate just fine, and as she glanced around the emptying room, she wanted to celebrate. I knew she is there watching us, and I smiled.

She backed out of the room, and down the stairs waiting for us in the living room. We had our arms full of boxes and headed out to Jeff's car. After four trips in three cars, we were finally done. The living room only had one loveseat, that they were storing in the basement intending on giving it to the goodwill or dump someday soon, but I insisted on having it. I couldn't afford a couch not having just dumped over three hundred dollars for my rent. Mom agreed without an argument.

She is glad to get rid of the thing, and saved her, and Keith a trip to the dump. "I like this place." Zeni nodded looking around. "Spacious, and airy. Just make sure you dust at least once a week. With the windows right there, you'll get dust build up in no time." "Check." I smiled. "Mama, you don't have to worry." "I know, and I promised I'll try."

"Yeah right, I know how you are." I laughed making her laugh too. Once they left, and it's just Jeff, and myself, I felt self-conscious for the first time in a month. He made it easier by giving me a kiss. A real first kiss that I responded to eagerly. He closed his eyes as he drew his arms around my waist, as I slid my hands into his hair, short as it is. We stood in the living room with only the couch for company and held each other. "Have dinner with me tonight." He invited smiling down at me. He had his arms on the small of my back and rubbed slowly.

"All right." I didn't even bother asking what he is making. It didn't matter. This is a huge first step, and I am looking forward to the future now. Jeff left so he could start cooking leaving me by myself, so I settled my instant loneliness by attacking the bedroom. Mom had put a lot of clothes in the dresser, but most of them lay on the bed in a huge pile taking over most of the space.

I found a pile of hangers in a box, and started hanging blouses, and skirts in the walk-in closet. My first walk-in closet. This is so cool. It's roomy, and I loved it. Once the bed is empty, and clothes put away, I placed the extra hangers in the closet, and started on the kitchen. The living room didn't need any help yet. I put the dishes in the cupboard and tried out the microwave smiling. It worked well. I sipped hot cocoa. It's too hot for it, but I wanted it anyway. It reminded me of all the warm talks I shared with mom. I only hoped that they wouldn't stop just because I am on my own now.

I put away cups humming along to the radio. Jeff drove to the grocery store to pick up the hamburger, and noodles. He made his way to the checkout line and hardly paid attention to the man standing behind him glaring at his back. He paid for the items, grabbed his bag, and left the store without a backward glance.

Yeah, he thought to himself. Big bad doctor strutting his stuff. We'll see how long he struts with a car looming over him, knocking his sweet ass to the ground, and his big head hitting the pavement with a splat. The image made him want to laugh out loud. He had to stop himself from doing it.

The urge came on strong sometimes, and this is no exception. Won't be much longer, he promised. Reesa watch out. Your second love's about to bite the dust.

It's close to five when I finished putting in the cups, and the counters are empty by now. I continued my cleaning streak by wiping down the counters.

There, that is good for now. I put the rag over the oven handle. At least I'm done for a while. I smiled at the clock on the stove. Jeff didn't mention the time, so I didn't know how long to wait. I paced for a few minutes trying to decide. Five fifteen is long enough. I grabbed my new apartment keys, and rushed out, and up the stairs where his door is opened, and the smell alone is enough to lure me in.

There were two candles burning on the fireplace mantel, and a table lamp turned on low in the corner of the coffee table. Other than that, there were no lights except for the kitchen. "Hey there," he greeted from the counter. "Have a seat." He gestured to a bar stool.

"Hey back. You need any help?" I glanced at the bowl of hamburger, but he seemed to have everything under control. "I invited you for dinner, not to help make it." He shook a wooden spoon in my direction. "Make yourself comfortable." He added some chopped onion to the bowl. "Is your new apartment spotless yet?" He teased smiling out of the corner of his mouth.

"No way, however, I had a small success of putting my clothes away. My bed is made, and the dishes are in my cupboards. Not bad for an hour's work." I sounded pleased and made him smile. Jeff sprinkled

The Way Life Used To Be

some bread-crumbs over the mixture and started mixing with his bare hands. He wore a white apron over his jeans, and that alone made me want to laugh. He looked just like a chef.

Jeff rolled several meatballs and placed them in a frying pan where they started sizzling. "What are you making, anyway?" I asked leaning over the counter so I could get a closer look. "If you must know, I'm making us spaghetti, and meatballs complete with garlic bread." He nodded towards a loaf covered with a tinfoil wrapper. "Homemade, and everything."

I laughed out loud and settled back on my stool. "Liar." I am enjoying myself. He is good natured. "Busted. I had to make a quick run to the store. Meatballs are homemade though. I get at least minimal credit." He put some water in a large cast-iron pot and placed it on the stove. Once the water started boiling, he put the noodles in, and turned the meatballs over.

"These will take a while. Want to sit on the balcony for a while. Watch the sun set." He removed the apron and threw it on the counter. "It's barely six. The sun won't set for at least two hours, but yes I'd love to sit on the balcony." He grabbed two glasses of wine, and held them in one hand, and my hand in the other as we stepped on the balcony where he had two lawn chairs, and a matching table between them. They were cheap, but nice. looking. I sat down and accepted the glass he handed me. I had never tasted wine before, but I am open to new things. It isn't half bad, I decided. "You going to get a set too?" He asked sipping his wine.

"Eventually. This feels nice out here. I might have to get a set real soon, so you can have dinner with me out on my balcony." "It's a date," he said. He reached out his free hand to take mine which lay on the table. He brought my fingers to his lips, and kissed them, gazing at me. I had my mouth open savoring the feel of his lips on my skin, and it made me shiver.

He noticed but kept quiet instead of teasing me. "So, tell me, do you ever talk to Spring while you sit out here?" He glanced over. "I did, when I was younger up, I didn't have a lot of friends. It's nobody's fault so there is nobody to blame. Spring became my best friend. She is better than any boy or girl since she never talked back or made me feel bad." "Now I wish I knew her."

The meat started spattering making us both jump up. "Time to finish." He said, and they got up, and he headed back to the kitchen. I sat on the stool with the half empty glass of wine still in one hand. He took the meatballs out of the skillet, and placed them on a paper towel to drain, while he made the sauce. "I feel like I should help." I said, finishing my glass. "And I said No, you're a guest, not the cook. Besides when it's my turn to be the guest, I intend to take full advantage."

He stirred the noodles while somehow maintaining eye contact with me. "How?" I asked amused and tilted my head. "I will sit on your lovely couch and you will supply me with a Coke, smiling as you do so." He said, although his eyes were twinkling giving himself away. "Will I?" I interrupted raising one eyebrow. When he nodded, I said, "Continue." I helped myself to another glass of wine even though I didn't want it and settled back on the bar stool to hear more.

"You will wear an apron like mine. I'd let you borrow this one, but it's too big so if you don't already have one, I'd suggest getting one." "Noted. next?" "You can indulge in a Diet Pepsi while I'm enjoying my Coke. I will allow that small pleasure." He smiled while chopping up tomatoes. "The dinner itself is up to your imagination, but I don't have any worries about that. After we eat, you will do the dishes, as I will do tonight. We will enjoy another sunset on your balcony complete with chairs, and a table which I also suggest you buy soon."

He added garlic, and pepper to the sauce, stirring as he spoke. "Once the sun sets, you will lure me to the bedroom where you will take full advantage of my weakness, which I will protest." "How long?" "Five minutes. After which I will surrender to your boldness, and we will spend the rest of the evening making sweet love until the sun comes up." "All night?" I raised my other eyebrow.

"All night," he smiled taking the noodles from the pot. "When I insist, I must leave for the hospital, you will delay me by promises of more love when I return, and the love story will begin." "Does it end?" He shook his head. "No, it gets better, and better, but there's no end. How does my scenario sound to you?" "All good except for me doing the dishes. I think you should offer, then demand when I push your offer aside. Other than that, it sounds like a perfect evening. I like the bold me part."

"I do too. Time to eat." He carried both plates while I carried fresh glasses of wine, and we strolled back on the balcony to eat. The sun is setting as I took my first bite. "It's pretty from this view." I whispered after swallowing. I wanted no more wine as I am already feeling the effects of it, but the glass waited on the glass table gathering moisture.

The Way Life Used To Be

"Yes, it is." Jeff agreed taking a bite of his garlic bread. "I love eating out here. It's why I haven't bothered buying a dining room table."

"Even in the dead of winter I sit out here in the cold?" I ate another meatball. He is almost as good a cook as mom although I would never admit that to her. "I wear my favorite blue sweatshirt, and sweatpants when I have dinner. The hospital requires the standard blue scrubs, but when I get done for the evening, and get back to my home, the scrubs come off, and the sweats come on. Only then can I relax." He broke off another piece of bread.

"And what about the other seasons?" I asked glancing towards the untouched glass. He followed it frowning. "Have you had enough?" "I think so," I smiled "Tell me about the rest of the year." He got up for a minute without excusing himself, and I followed his backside as he disappeared into the kitchen. His back is just as appetizing as his front and looked wonderful in shorts.

Returning just thirty seconds later he placed a glass full of Diet Pepsi, and ice before me. "Drink," he smiled. "I don't know if I want to see you lose control. I might have to carry you home, and as tired as I am, I might trip down the stairs, and hurt us both. Better be safe than sorry." He smiled back at me and continued eating. "About the rest of the year, in full winter with the clouds threatening rain, I wear a wool coat over my sweats. It's perfect for that time of year. Springtime is a light gray sweatshirt over my clothes, and now in summer much like this one, is just a T-shirt, and shorts."

I glanced down at the jean shorts that showed off tan strong legs and smiled. "Why not the sweats?" Looking at his legs gave me a rush of feelings. I could see the muscles on the back of his shins pulsing, and it's hard for me to stay in my chair acting like a good girl. "Too hot," he said. He glanced at my empty plate. "I see you're still living. My cooking must not be lethal." He took the plate from my hand, and this time I followed him into the kitchen.

Once he turned from the sink, his heart started beating faster as he took me in from the loose ponytail I wore to the pink blouse, and tan shorts. He didn't just think it, he knew at that moment, he was in love with her. I had my head tilted as I reached for him and encircled my hands around his neck as he folded his own around my waist and drew me closer.

Our eyes closed, and we kissed. No chaste kiss on the cheek this time, and not like that first kiss we shared earlier today. This is different.

My mouth opened and welcomed his tongue. I had never French kissed before, not even with Paul during the whole time we were together.

I found I liked the feel of our tongues moving together as he moved even closer and spread his hands from my waist to my upper back while I cupped his face and felt the beginnings of a beard stubble. It's sexy and made me realize this is no boy I am kissing. He is every inch a man, and his muscles bulged as I slid my fingers down his arms feeling the firmness.

His breath hitched as my fingers trailed down to his wrists, and his own fingers tightened against my blouse making me realize what I am doing. I am making him excited. I continued my trip down to the tips of his fingers while looking at his face. His eyes were half closed.

He pulled away looking down at me, breathless, and not wanting to stop, but felt he had to. This is very new, and he didn't want to spoil it by moving too fast. I am smiling and kept my hands on his wrists. He turned them over and captured them in his. He brought them to his face and rubbed the backs of my hands to it. "I love you." He whispered keeping his eyes in that half dreamy state. He had a serious look on his face though, so I knew he isn't making light of this. "I love you too." I whispered back.

Chapter 13

Jeff walked me back to my apartment where we kissed once more at the front door, before I said good night, and he headed inside. We said, we loved each other. I did it. Fell in love for a second time after being convinced I never would again.

I plopped on the loveseat and ran my fingers over the arm rest thinking of Paul. It had been almost three years, and I could now think of him fondly. I'm done crying over him. It didn't cause a stabbing pain in my heart like I thought it would. It did however remind me I need to visit with Ted.

It had been months since I had last seen Ted, and I still had no word on who killed Paul. I'm convinced more than ever it isn't random. No hit-, and-run went on for this long without a single damn clue. I needed answers and needed them soon.

By the time I dragged myself to bed, I didn't even bother changing, but lay down on top of the comforter reliving the evening. It's by far the best dinner I ever had. Jeff loves me. I closed my eyes and saw him through the closed lids. He loves me.

As always, the alarm woke me too soon, and I had to hurry once again to make it to Starlights without my hair being washed, and sleep stuck to my eyelids. "You look like shit." Zeni chirped from the counter where she is slicing bagels. "Thanks." I said, "I love you too." "Why do you look like shit?" She took some eggs from the refrigerator and started cracking them into a white mixing bowl and while we're at it, what happened with your hair? She pointed to my forehead where stray wisps had pressed themselves because of the sweat.

I slapped a hand to my head, attempting to smooth some stray hairs behind one ear, and began slicing cheese. I didn't even notice my forehead. "I got up late this morning." "So late you neglect your appearance?" She frowned in my direction trying to figure it out. "I had a date last night and got to bed late. I'm still presentable so get off my back."

I couldn't even muster the strength to have any merit behind the threat and made mom laugh. "Your pathetic." She shook her head. "Is this date with Jeff?" "Yes, he made me dinner, and it was amazing." "The food or the sex?" I rolled my eyes. "The food. There is no sex."

Zeni lifted one eye in amazement. "How is the dinner?" I finished slicing the cheese, and placed the loaf back in the refrigerator, replacing it with some tomatoes. "Perfect, he's a wonderful cook, and he told me he loves me." I braved a glance at mom who stopped slicing bagels to gape at me. "What did you say?" "That I love him too." "Will you do me a favor?" She asked. "What?" "Invite him for dinner with me, and dad. He's a long-time customer of ours, and I want to know him better."

I looked at her, and she had a half smile on her face, and hope in her eyes. "We didn't sleep together." I said, "I didn't ask." Zeni replied. I nodded and sighed. "Promise not to grill him?" "I promise; however, he might be the type to enjoy it, you never know." She laughed and made me laugh too.

"Do you want to have this initiation dinner tonight or in the foreseeable future?" "It'll be fun, dad, and I already like him. You love each other, and I want to know him better. As far as dinner is concerned, how about Friday at our house?" She was already going through recipes in her head. This would be fun. Today is Wednesday, so it gave us two days of preparation, and time for her to see Bessie. It's high time we got all this tension out, and she was tired of waiting for her daughter to tell her what was going on.

The clock struck seven, and time to open. "I'll ask Jeff," I said over my shoulder. I threw on an apron and unlocked the doors. For once there were no customers waiting, so I expected a quiet morning. That would have been perfect since my demeanor is less than pleasant. I escaped back to the kitchen to let Tamara handle the morning customers. She was a part-time waitress, and very efficient, so I had no problem with it.

Zeni continued chopping up potatoes for potato salad. I returned to slicing tomatoes when the back door opened. Trey, and Jim approached with their arms full of crates. "Then Jan shows up with this redhead she claims is perfect for me, Hey Reesa." Jim greeted, slamming a crate full of strawberries, and blueberries on the counter before continuing "She's twenty-four, and just over five feet six. Jan explains on the phone to me, that when she, and Brad planned the party last Saturday, I'm to show up casual like, and alone, so they can hook me up."

Trey placed a second crate full of eggs on the counter a lot more gently than Jim did. "I met her. She's extremely nice, she's no five feet six though. More like five nine or ten. Jan has some serious height deficiencies." He is thinking this is a deliberate attempt to make Jim look like a fool.

No woman in their right mind would even want to be seen with someone they towered over. That type of situation is reserved for the freaks of nature. At least in his opinion. "Her name is Camille. Jan couldn't stop talking about how adorable she is, and how perfect we'd be together. Any way I get there, and the party's in full swing like all their parties are. I'm alone, and ready to get laid."

I laughed out loud hearing about Jim's women stories and hoped soon he would find someone who made him happy. I thought the world of him. Jim looked down at me. "Reesa you offended?" He teased smiling and looked right back up.

I shook my head. "Never, tell me what happened once you got there. Get lucky?" "I wandered into the living room where it's packed with people, to search for Brad or Jan so I could find my true love. I found Jan in her bedroom with Camille. They were sitting on the bed laughing, and when I walked in, she turned to look at me, stood up to shake my hand, and surpassed my height by two inches. I had to look up to see her." He shuddered making me laugh again.

I wanted to be there, so I'd see first-hand Jim's reaction. "She is wearing heels?" I asked trying to picture it and make the situation better. Jim shook his head. "That is the sad pathetic part of my story. She is wearing sandals. Flat sandals, and she is taller than me. I didn't stay. I made some stupid excuse to leave. I didn't even say goodbye to Jan."

"Did you hurt the girl's feelings?" I asked hoping the answer is No, I never knew Jim to be outright rude to someone's face, but there is always a first time. "No, At least I don't think so. Trey you met her right? Did I make her feel bad?" Trey is leaning against the counter with his back and had his hands folded across his chest. "No, you didn't. I didn't get to the party till about ten, and both Jan, and Camille were on the couch eating pizza."

I grabbed a Pepsi and joined them. "She's very nice, talkative, and no you didn't hurt her feelings. She was matched up with someone else, and happy by eleven. I don't think she's given it a second thought. I don't know the guys she hooks up with, but she's fine." "See." I said. I smiled at Jim. "All's good all around. Now you have plenty of time to find the next true love. She's out there. You just have to give it time, and you'll find her."

Bessie chose that moment to walk in the kitchen, ignore me completely, and said, hello to Jim, and Trey. "Hey Bess. How's it hanging?" Jim asked lifting the now empty crate. "Hanging too low for my comfort." She smiled down at her ample chest. "I know it's best for the baby though." She headed to mom's office and turned on the computer. Jim followed her to the doorway. "Glad that's settled." Trey smiled at me. "Jim, see you back at the house later." Jim waved a hand in farewell. "I should get going. I have customers to satisfy." He pecked me on the top of my head and left.

Once it's quiet again, I got back to work, and placed the sliced tomatoes in a bowl, and started tearing up lettuce. I am concentrating on the task at hand and not paying attention too much else. I already lost almost half an hour listening to Jim. Bessie had shut the office door, shutting me out of their conversation, but instead of making an issue of it, I continued prepping.

By the time I was through for the day, I had no less than thirteen comments about my hair, and different products. I just had to get the grease look out, I am ready to scream, and go to bed without saying a single word to anyone for the rest of the night. Zeni said, she would lock up, so I drove home carefully since I could barely keep my eyes open. These late nights are going to have to come to an end if I'm going to continue working the mornings. Hopefully Jeff would understand.

Of course, he would. He is a doctor for crying out loud. Used to working tons of hours, and no sleep. He had to understand, if I needed to get some rest now, and then. My stomach started growling reminding me I hadn't eaten hardly anything all day. I am too busy yawning and trying to keep my eyes open to bother with stuffing my face. However now I'm regretting not providing my body with the necessary things to keep it running.

I swung into an Italian restaurant that offered a takeout menu, and walked inside, smelling the onion, and garlic, and smiled. I studied the menu not sure what sounded good, and ended up ordering Parmesan

The Way Life Used To Be

chicken, and am back in my car a mere fifteen minutes later. I'd take a nice bath, then enjoy my dinner with the company of a movie, and some good old-fashioned alone time.

I pulled into the apartment complex with a smile and am already looking forward to a night to myself. I planned on lots of nights with Jeff, but not tonight. I climbed the steps with heavy feet and unlocked the door with relief. Stepping inside, I flipped on the living room light, and the room seemed to come to life.

The sofa looked lonely. I should get another couch or a chair or something to make the place look homier. Maybe an end table so at the end of hard days, I could cuddle on the couch or chair, and read a good book with a floor lamp for extra lighting. Sounded nice, and something to buy soon. Right now, all that sounded good is a nice bath and lemonade. I placed the bag on the kitchen counter and headed to the bedroom to find a change of clothes.

I found a pair of pink sweatpants, and a black T-shirt in the dresser, and headed to the bathroom where I started my bath and added some peach flavored bubble bath for added affect. I took a long sip while making my way from the kitchen to the bath where the water is making the mirror steam. Stretching out in the nice warm bubbles, I just lay there for a full ten minutes, sipping the drink, and had my eyes closed, savoring the quiet.

My cell phone rang while I was relaxing, and I opened one eye, and reached for it. "Hello?" I whispered. "That's one tired greeting. Did I wake you?" It's Jeff and made me smile. It's nice he called often. "Nope, I'm sitting here all alone with a lemonade for company." "Sounds pathetic. Want some real company?" It sounded so tempting that I almost said, yes. "Normally I'd jump on your offer, but not tonight. I had about an hour of sleep last night, and I'm feeling the full effects, of the up all night theory. Can I take a rain check?" I took a sip of the lemonade and waited for his response.

He didn't hesitate as I'd expected. "No problem, I do however have full intentions of seeing you tomorrow. No excuses." "None given, one condition though. My mom wants us to have dinner with them Friday." I held my breath expecting him to decline saying although he felt comfortable around us, this is too much too soon.

"Sounds great. What time," He is smiling. He even sounded enthusiastic. He is truly one of a kind. "I must get back to you on that. My mom is insistent on getting to know you better, so if you could oblige, I'd appreciate it." "I'd love to know them better. Not the same way I know you, but you understand." He made me giggle. "There's that sound that makes my day., and how was your day by the way?"

"Busy. I left my apartment without washing my hair." "The start of many terrible things," he teased. "You're not kidding. I had no less than thirteen comments on my sour demeanor, and I think mom's regretting me being co-owner. I might be demoted to a simple cashier or waitress."

"Not a bad career you know. You'd make a stunning hostess in one of those cute little bouncy frilly tutu uniforms that end past your butt. I can just see it now, with the white blouse that's just a little too tight, so when you bend over to serve the drinks, the buttons strain." "You're a funny man. I'm dying of laughter right now." "You love it. How did your day end?" "I came home after being on my feet for the past twelve hours, and now I'm soaking in the tub, massaging my aching toes."

The image made him smile. He wanted to offer again to come over and take care of her. Something about her voice is weary, and a little sad, but he didn't have the heart to ask what was wrong. "You want to hear about my day?" "Of course, I have hours left of my day yet." "It's close to nine already. Only three more hours till tomorrow."

"Don't remind me." I groaned. "I had no idea how late it is." There is no clock in the bathroom, and it also made me realize the water is starting to get cooler.

"I had two deliveries, and both were successful. One boy, and one girl." "Busy day. Are the babies healthy, and happy?" "As they can be, both are swaddled up in warming blankets, and probably sucking their thumbs or nipples right about now." "The image makes me cringe. You just ruined the moment." I laughed. "Then my job is done. I'll see you tomorrow. Don't miss me too much." "I won't, have a nice, and lonely evening."

I hung up with a smile and leaned back in the tub. It's getting even colder, so I lifted myself out, and dried on one of the towels my mom insisted on me having. This isn't too bad as most of my things I now have here, had belonged at home. It isn't costing me much at all.

Dressed comfortably in my favorite sweats, I drained the water, and scrubbed out the tub once it was empty. I had no intentions of letting this place get dirty, and grungy. Once it's clean, I shut off the light, and headed to the kitchen where I placed the takeout bag and put the plate in the microwave. It made the room smell good, and once it beeped, I grabbed a fork, and sat down in the love seat to enjoy dinner. The doorbell rang as I took my first bite of chicken and made me swear. Damn Jeff. I said, I wanted a night of quiet, and he already isn't listening.

I am about to shout to just come the hell in, when I realized I am alone, and had no window peeper to see who is outside. What if it isn't Jeff? The knocking persisted, and I heard a muffled voice. "Reesa open the damn door before I kick it in." It's Bessie, I scrambled up, and ran to the door, flinging it open to find Bessie standing outside with a baby stroller, and bag over her shoulder. "Hey there." I greeted, and Bessie headed inside pushing the stroller. "Meet your nephew, David." Bessie said, sarcastically, sitting on the loveseat without being invited, and took a bite of the chicken Parmesan.

"We already met at the hospital." I continued to look puzzled while Bessie crossed her hands in front of her chest, glaring. "What's your deal now?" I asked following her to the loveseat, a questioning look in my eyes. I thought once she had the baby all these emotional mood swings would be gone. I guess having the baby blues is a fact, and not a myth as I'd always believed. Apparently, it's still in full force, causing me to wish she'd just leave. I didn't have the energy for this right now.

Bessie swung her head in anger. "What's my deal?" She punched herself in the chest. "What's my mother fucking deal? I'll tell you what my deal is. You left me high and dry at the hospital with hardly a word of encouragement, while you were there. I'm sorry I hooked you up with Jeff. It has turned you into the most selfish bitch." She finished and stabbed the fork into the chicken again. "What are you talking about, and why are you, so hell bent, that my world revolves around you?" I asked bewildered.

Bessie's eyes were so angry. I had no idea what I did that pissed her off so bad, and to tell the truth, I didn't much care. Bessie is being a bitch and eating half my dinner at the same time. Bessie slammed her hand on the couch in frustration and made the baby whimper.

She ignored him for the moment and forced herself to calm down. "When I asked you to be my coach, I did so without the slightest hesitation because you've always been there for me. I told you first about Jeremy because I trust you. I didn't care that Jeremy wasn't at the birth because I wanted you there. You were all that mattered to me, and when you got there, what did you do?"

"You spent the whole time with Jeff, and not me. I'm never first with you, and I thought for sure this one time I would be. I'm still not first with you, and I'll never be." Tears started falling down her cheeks, and I realized they were real. Not the normal fake kind she used when she is having a moment. I also knew it wouldn't do any good to deny that I wasn't there for her. I wasn't, and both of us knew it. "I didn't realize." I began. "How selfish I'd become."

"I thought I could deal with it, and not let it bother me, but it does. I don't want it to bother me anymore. I know now how excited you were to be moving out of mom, and dads. Instead of being happy for you, I wasn't. Again, I put my needs first."

I reached over, and put my hands around her neck, and Bessie lay her head on my shoulder, feeling the tears building. "I'm sorry." I whispered. "Yes, you were right that I made a piss poor coach. I'm so happy and relieved to have found my own place. I feel like a grown up now." Bessie giggled. "Seriously, though, I am selfish. I never wanted to be a coach because I had no clue what to do. I didn't know how to support you, but I could have tried."

Bessie pulled away and dried her eyes with the back of one hand. "I'm sorry I yelled." She glanced down at the baby swaddled in a yellow, and blue blanket. He had settled down and closed his eyes now that the yelling is done. She picked up the bundle and lay him in my arms. "Meet David," she said, more softly this time. I folded the blanket back. I held the baby close while he shoved a hand in his mouth and started sucking. "Jeff called earlier when I was in the tub and told me he delivered two babies today." "Were either of them as cute as mine?"

"Sorry, I didn't ask. I came to work without washing my hair, and when I got home, all I wanted to do is relax so I started a bath. He told me about his day, and said, the babies were being well taken care of. It reminds me of this one. How simple it is for them to find whatever's handy to comfort themselves." I moved away the blanket from his head and rubbed the baby's cheek. It's so soft, and warm.

"See. You're a natural." Bessie complimented smiling for the first time in months. Jeremy finally moved all his things out that morning, and they exchanged no words as he walked out of the house they shared, for the last three years.

Not even a goodbye as he slammed the door behind him. He walked to his car without a backwards glance. She cried all afternoon and ignored the baby who whimpered at the tension. Once she was headed over towards Reesa's, the tears were done. Seeing her now, bent over the baby's head, she knew she did the right thing by asking her to be her coach.

The Way Life Used To Be

"How's it going with Jeremy? Did you two work things out yet?" I asked glancing at Bessie. Bessie shook her head. "I was just thinking about it. Earlier this afternoon Jeremy came by after I finished feeding the baby. We are cuddled in the rocking chair just enjoying the quiet, and he came in without warning. I thought once the front door slammed, he would be full of apologies, and I'm so sorry." "And he isn't?"

"No, he isn't. I looked up when the door slammed and made the baby cry. He didn't even look down at him. He didn't look at me even though I am staring at him. He stomped to the bedroom and came out not even thirty minutes later. He had two suitcases full of clothes. He had just shoved clothes in from the dresser. Didn't even have the courtesy to close the drawers afterwards."

"Asshole." I said, taking a bite of my chicken with my free hand. The other is still holding the baby who had fallen asleep in my arms. Maybe I'm a natural at this if the baby is comfortable enough to sleep in my arms. "Fucking A." Bessie agreed taking a drink of her sprite she had tucked into the stroller. "I am low, and desperate enough to consider running after him, and begging him to stay, but I caught my dignity before it flew away from me." "Good for you."

"Are you going to stay in the house by yourself or try to sell it?" "Sell it, I don't want to stay there, but he's entitled to half the proceeds from the sale. I've already started packing some things I don't need. Where are you storing them?" I leaned over to take a drink. The baby snored still burrowed in the blanket. He is hurting my arm. I didn't want to put him down. It's amazing how good he made me feel. All my earlier fears are fading as I smiled down at him.

"He's so beautiful, isn't he?" Bessie sighed smiling at her son. I just nodded. "I rented a storage unit for now. Mom wanted me to use a portion of the garage, and I will soon. I just want to get out of there now, so I rented a space for a month, why? You should save the money. I'll help you." "I appreciate that, and when the times comes to get my stuff out, I'll take you up on that."

I looked at her finally understanding what she is saying. She didn't want to stay in a place that made her sad. "Where's Jeff?" Bessie asked sneaking another bite of my dinner. She is starving and had eaten nothing substantial in almost a week. Not good for the baby's milk, but she is too stressed, and sad to get the energy to take care of herself.

"At his own apartment. I wanted a night alone, however he agreed to dinner at mom, and dad's tomorrow. I expect multiple drama." "I heard about it this afternoon after you left. Mom's all excited forgetting the menu ready. I'm not sure what is on the menu, and she didn't elaborate." She glanced down, and there is only one bite left. "Take it." I offered. "Mom is insistent on knowing him better. Jeff's a very willing participant so that alone gives him major points in my book."

"That's because she's nosy. Good intentions of course, but nosy." Bessie waved the fork in my direction. "Until recently, you've had Paul in your mind right up here." She pointed the fork to her own forehead. "Right up close. Jeff is the first person to bring those feelings where they belong, right here." The fork pointed to her heart. "Keep them there." "I will," I said. "Where are you going to live once the house goes on the market?"

"Back home. My stubbornness only goes so far. I'm taking my old room, and David will have yours so he's still close to me, but I can have a little privacy too. I thought long, and hard about telling mom, and dad that I wouldn't do that. Crawl back home after making such a big to do about moving out in the first place, but I realized that would have been a stupid move on my part. I've been looking for work. I'm using the computer at Starlights."

"That sounds better than being alone. Just make sure you come and visit me a lot." I finished my drink and placed the empty glass on the coffee table. "Speaking of using the computer, did you, and Jim have a nice talk?" "Very, he's a sweetie, almost as much as Trey. He stayed for over an hour talking to me and walked me through the resume process. I have no idea what I'm doing, but I'm giving it my best shot. I want to make my own money for once."

"Once? You mean Jeremy wouldn't let you work?" "I never bothered. He makes good money at the plant, and for now, his child support will get me enough stuff at least where David is concerned. I just want to do something other than being a full-time mother with a little pin money." "I'm betting you do it."

I smiled at her. "Count on it." Bessie got up to throw the plastic plate in the garbage and stood staring out the kitchen window. "This is a nice view." She could see the swimming pool shimmering in the moonlight, and lanterns that hung around the edges, making it look romantic. "Have you gone swimming yet?"

The Way Life Used To Be

"No time yet. I do however have full intentions of fixing that soon. Probably my next day off." "Which is?" "Friday. Only two more days, and I have a whole day to myself. I'm counting the minutes." "Are you liking it here so far?" "I'm loving it. I feel free, and happy for the first time." I smiled and leaned over to place David back in the stroller. He settled down and never opened his eyes. Just moved his head a little to the side.

"Even before Paul?" Bessie asked turning away from the window to sit back on the couch. The baby is still deep asleep. I thought it looked very easy to just cuddle him for a while, then he'd go to sleep. Goes to show how little I knew about raising one. "I think so." I nodded in agreement. "I didn't think I would, but Jeff has a way about him that is appealing, and attractive. I want to know more. He makes me want more."

"That's how I felt about Jeremy especially when we were just dating. The first year of marriage is wonderful, and I couldn't ask for much better, but it's right after the second year started, that he began changing. It might have been some of my fault too." "Usually takes two. I tend to take your side, but it still takes two." I'm seeing Bessie's faults. I know first-hand how difficult she can be, and she is right. You keep pushing someone away, eventually they'll stop coming back.

"I guess you're right." Bessie glanced at the clock and realized it's almost ten. "We should go now. I'm sorry to have kept you up." She crossed over to the couch and scooped up the diaper bag. I walked her to the front door feeling better about our talk. "We'll see you at the dinner, and I'm sorry about earlier. I won't be that selfish ever again." I reached over and hugged her harder than usual. Bessie's eyes filled with tears, but they are sad tears, not like the angry fit she carried for the last several days. She didn't want to leave this place. It's quiet, nice, and so much better than the thought of being back at home.

"It'll be nice to see Jeff again. Give me a chance to apologize to him too. I don't think there's any need for that. I don't even think he took offense. Only reason I knew what is bothering you is because I know you." "Guess you know me a tad better than he does. Have a good night." She reached over to kiss my cheek before rubbing a hand on my face. "I love you." She didn't wait for an answer. She carried the stroller, and diaper bag down the stairs, and headed to her car.

I shut the door and sighed leaning against the door closing my eyes. My little sister is a big sister in so many ways, but at times like these I felt like a counselor, mother, older sister, and friend all wrapped into one. She is getting divorced, and just had a baby, and I could barely keep a relationship going.

Granted Paul is taken away from me before we saw it blossom, but still. Twenty-two years old, and only on my second relationship ever. Most people my age, are married, and having children, but not me. I had one love, and on my way to a second, and I am twenty-two already.

I picked up my empty glass and placed it in the sink. I'd do dishes tomorrow. Already it's going on ten fifteen, and I am so tired I wanted to scream. I didn't even bother to change clothes. I lay down on the bed without turning down the comforter and sighed as the front door opened again. I snapped open my eyes expecting to see Bessie at the bedroom doorway. I smiled as Jeff appeared.

"Hey you," I whispered, and held out a hand. The feelings of wanting to be alone tonight were rapidly diminishing, and I found I wanted his company. "Hey back," he held my hand, and leaned down so he could kiss my fingers. "Time for bed." He lay down next to me facing the closet that I left open, and clothes spilled out, but I didn't care. I turned into him and touched his face with my free hand.

"Close your eyes." He whispered and did the honors himself while stroking my hair. "Your hair feels better." He leaned close and smelled the strands. "It's been washed." I said, with my eyes still closed. "No more humiliation."

"Do you feel better?" He asked stretching his legs. His toes stretched past the end of the bed making him realize how short the bed is, and how tall he is in comparison. Didn't make him care though. I sighed and snuggled deeper into his chest.

He moved his hand from my hair to my back and rubbed gently while I slept. It isn't until morning when the sun poked its ugly head into the window, I realized what just happened. I slept with a man for the first time in my life. No sex, not even any kisses. Just the best back rub I could imagine, and his strong warm body next to mine.

I tried to tiptoe from the bed so I could get dressed, but he snapped open his eyes at the movement. "Good morning," he smiled, and reached for my arm. "Morning yourself, I have to get up." I kissed his cheek, and turned towards the closet, while he sat up on one arm watching.

My backside is to him as I dove for a clean blouse hoping it wouldn't be too helplessly wrinkled. Ah Ha, pay-dirt. I smiled to myself

The Way Life Used To Be

as I found a white silk blouse buried between two pairs of jeans in the corner of the closet. I backed out and sat on my heels analyzing the mess. "You ought to think seriously about organization." He teased sitting up in the bed, smirking.

I turned around and threw a pillow at him. "I don't have time." I stood up quickly with my clothes in my arms and headed for the bathroom. Jeff watched from the bed, leaning on one hand bent at the elbow, smiling. Once the water started running, he got out of bed to look out the window in the bedroom. This view faced the front of the complex where he could see her car in the slot, and not much else. This time of day is silent as most of the tenants had already left for jobs or other errands.

He leaned against the glass, and spotted a man facing a tree, and frowned. This is no tenant, as he wore tattered jeans, and a long tattered black sweatshirt. It's the type of clothes that got his attention. It's almost eighty degrees already, and this guy is dressed like it is winter, and forty degrees outside. He wore sunglasses so he couldn't see his eyes. When the man turned, he looked straight into Reesa's bedroom, and grinned at Jeff.

He raised a hand like he is saying hello and took off at a trot not looking back. Weird, is all Jeff could think of as he watched the man leave. He didn't appear to have a vehicle. Once he was gone from view, the bedroom door squeaked open, and I appeared hair wet, and hanging in ringlets, and dressed in snug black jeans with the blouse tucked in.

I headed straight to my dresser to search for a pair of socks. Once I located a pair, I sat on the bed. Jeff stayed near the window. His head is pressed against the pane like he is concentrating on something. I frowned a little while tying my shoes. He turned from the window and walked towards me. My arms are already opened and waiting for him. "Hi again," he said, looking down at me. He folded me into his arms where I rested my cheek against his chest and rubbed gently.

I looked out the window, but I saw nothing that warranted more than a second glance. "You still love me?" I asked. "Nah. That is a two night ago moment." I giggled into his chest. "More than ever." He whispered into my hair. I lifted my head to look into his eyes which were dreamy, and half opened. I smiled and drew away. "I have to get ready for work before I'm too late. You still up for dinner at mom, and dad's tomorrow?" He nodded in agreement.

"Just don't leave me there to fend for myself. You never know what might happen," he said, rubbing my arms. "Go to work." "Yes sir." I smiled as I backed the car out of the assigned slot and smiled the whole way to Starlights. My hair is presentable today, I got enough sleep that the haziness from yesterday is gone. My eyes were clear and sparkling. He still loved me. It would be a good day. I carried that thought with me as I flung open the doors with a flourish and stepped inside.

Dad is there stirring minestrone soup. "Morning Honey. Sleep better?" He asked stirring with a wooden spoon and giving me half of his attention. He didn't notice much else, but mom did once he left the kitchen to set up tables in the dining room. "You look tons better than yesterday." "I had two visitors last night. Bessie came over with the baby and chewed my ass out." I started to explain while hanging my purse on a hook.

"Why did your ass need chewing?" Zeni interrupted going to the refrigerator and pulled out a bucket of raspberries. "I am a piss poor coach at the hospital, and Bessie made me aware of my selfishness." "As long as you at least apologized, I think Bessie will get over it. Being back home may be just what she needs right now." "I'm thinking you, and dad will never get the house kid free." I chuckled.

"Not anytime soon anyway, but it's all for the best. Jeff sounds like a very nice man. When he would call to order his meatball sub, he mostly got it delivered. I told him to come in sometime and get the order to go. I don't think I've ever seen him sit down and enjoy it." "I'm sure he enjoyed plenty of them. Just in the company of his own place. The more I get to know him the more I realize he doesn't have much of a life outside the hospital." "He may not, given that he's an obstetrician. That must take a lot of time right there." "I'm sure it does. I've found I make a good aunt. I got the baby to fall asleep in my arms."

"Progress. You, and Jeff talking about the future yet?" "No, it's been only about a month obviously it's too soon to be thinking that way." "You'd be surprised how fast it can happen, especially when you've found the right person to do it with. Things can progress fast. Now about dinner tomorrow, is he still coming?" "Willingly. He's actually looking forward to it."

I found I am too. It didn't hurt that he is a faithful customer. Even if he isn't, his easygoing ways would have won them over. "Then he's worth keeping around for a while." Zeni smiled, and placed the fruit cups in holders, and put them in the refrigerator until the lunch menu

The Way Life Used To Be

started. She had decided when we started opening for breakfast that lunch would be available at ten, that way three hours could be devoted to breakfast options only.

She didn't want to have the breakfast portion available all day so both her, and Keith kept most of the menu just it had always been. Friday evening after I finished my shift, I am bone tired. For some reason, I wasn't exhausted like the last few days. It's the dinner I am looking forward to. Now that kept me light on my feet. I helped lock up, and I'm dancing my way out the door. I walked towards the house where I knew Jeff is waiting.

He isn't there yet, so I walked in shrugging my shoulders, and took a few minutes relaxing, and helping with dinner until he arrived. Mom is already in the kitchen mixing up ricotta cheese, and spinach and turned from the counter to say hello. "Long time no see," she teased placing the rest of the spinach back into the refrigerator. "Where's Jeff?" she glanced over my shoulder. I am alone in the doorway, leaning against the door frame, arms crossed with a slight smile on my face. "Probably still working," I said. I entered the kitchen. "You know what I've concluded?" "What would that be baby?" Zeni said, with half an ear.

"How much I hate cooking now that I'm at Starlights all the freaking time! What made you keep on cooking even though you do it all blessed day long?" "Not sure how to answer that one. I guess I don't think about what I'm missing when we have so much. Dinner is a necessity in many cultures, I would imagine it's just something you do. You can have bitter feelings about doing it, or you can just do it. See what I mean?"

"Kind of. I've been very depended on fast food which may account for my sudden increase in weight. That should stop soon." I grinned down at my stomach which I could tell isn't much different from three months ago when I first graduated. "That's a very tempting offer which I'm sure the franchises appreciate, but no, it's not healthy, and even though I think you're too thin to begin with, this isn't the best answer which I think even you know."

I grinned at her, and offered, "What can I do to help?" "Spread some of this sauce in the pan." She pointed to a pan full of homemade marinara sauce that is bubbling on the stove. I grabbed a wooden spoon and began spooning sauce into a glass dish. Zeni added some Romano cheese to the mixture. "I was afraid at first. Of Jeff." She began and began stirring the cheese. "Of you losing him like Paul. I never want you to go through that ever again, but I've also concluded that I can't dictate your life or be afraid every time you find someone. I came to that conclusion a few days ago when you brought Jeff to Starlights. You're not afraid, are you?"

"I guess I'm not. I don't have nightmares about Paul anymore." I admitted. "Progress once again rears its lovely head." "I think you've got that wrong." I giggled. "It, rears its ugly head." "That isn't par with this particular situation." Zeni explained. "Speaking of progress, Bessie's been coming to Starlight's more, and more often. Usually in the afternoons to help me shut down for the night. She finally told me what is happening between her, and Jeremy. She, and David will be here shortly."

"Where did they go?" "To the grocery store, she is running low on milk, and took the baby with her." "So, what's it like having a newborn again?" "Interesting. I am just beginning to enjoy freedom, and that sounds selfish, I know, but I was enjoying it, anyway. I just didn't realize how short lived my freedom would be." Zeni said, filling the shells with the cheese mixture, and placing them in the pan.

"I would never call you selfish. Do you know the sacrifice you've just given to make Bessie happy? To know she has a place to call home again?" I didn't wait for an answer. "You are the most unselfish person I think I've ever had the pleasure of knowing, and that is a virtue all on its own. Bessie told me she is moving back home. I don't think she's proud of that fact, so I didn't comment much on it. Are you regretting your decision?" I asked turning on the oven for the manicottis.

Zeni shook her head. "Not for one single minute. Believe it or not, Bessie has turned into a fine young mother. She is the first person to wake up when David is fussing and tends to him with gentle words. She doesn't yell anymore. She has that mother instinct I was doubting existed for the longest time." "Why were you doubting her abilities to mother?" "I guess I chose the wrong words. I didn't doubt she would be a wonderful mother, but she took a long time to want the baby. I doubted she would love him as much as she does."

"Sounds like you two talked a lot more than I realized." "More lately than before." At that the front door opened, and Bessie appeared with the baby in the same stroller she used when she came to visit me "Hey Auntie." Bessie reached over the handle to give me a kiss on my cheek. "Hi sweetie." I picked up the baby from the stroller to cuddle with him a minute while the manicottis cooked. They were already giving the entire kitchen, and most of the house the most delicious smell. All our stomachs started rumbling.

I bounced the baby with the blanket wrapped around him, and David cooed as he opened his eyes at the newcomer who held him. I sat in mom's favorite rocker, holding the baby in one arm, and an iced tea I grabbed from the counter in the other. I rocked with my eyes closed. The doorbell rang startling me. "Come in." I shouted from the chair. I am too comfortable to answer the door, and I recognized Jeff's car out front.

David gurgled when the door opened. He isn't at all unhappy at the interruption. "Hey you," he greeted coming in to give me a kiss. "You a mother now?" He teased leaning closer. "He's so big already." He touched the baby's cheek with one hand. "Guess I forgot to tell you," I teased back, and lifted my face smiling at him. "Bessie's in the kitchen if you want to say hello."

"No need." Bessie stated coming into the living room carrying a glass of ice-water. "Mom kicked me out of the kitchen. Claimed to have everything in control. Hi Jeff." She greeted coming over to him where he placed a hand on her shoulder. "Hey Bess, enjoying motherhood?" "Mostly, he keeps me up at night so there are no restful nights anymore." "That's common, he should grow out of it in the next few months with a routine. Reesa, hand the baby over so I can see how big he's getting."

I handed over the baby, and smiled at the way he doted over him, and kissed his forehead. "He's already gained four ounces." Bessie said, proudly leaning against the wall. "That's good. You should make a return appointment soon." Jeff advised to nod towards David. "Especially during their first three months, it's important to make at least weekly checkups.

Zeni came out of the kitchen to announce dinner, and saw Jeff standing in the living room holding the baby, and bouncing him, and smiled. He seemed right at home here, and comfortable enough to hold a newborn without seeming squeamish. "Time to eat," she said, quieter than usual, not wanting to startle the baby. David lifted his head at the sound and spit up some formula Bessie had just given him thirty minutes ago.

Jeff washed the mess with the bib and carried the baby to the kitchen where Bessie had a rocking seat all ready, and next to her. It had a mixture of little stuffed animals hanging down for entertainment, and David started batting at the strings. Keith is at the counter gathering plates and smiled over his shoulder. "Hey Jeff, glad you could make it. Sorry it's not takeout this time." He placed the plates in the center of the table next to the manicottis.

Jeff smiled. "Me too, smells good in here, and much better than takeout." He glanced around the comfortable kitchen. So different from his own dad's, although it made him miss it when his mom was alive. She was the best cook along with just about everything else and made him sad. Hard to keep a smile sometimes when he saw all the love, and happiness in this home. "Where's Mark, and Sara?" I asked taking a seat kitty corner from mom and patted the seat next to me for Jeff.

He sat down and placed the napkin in his lap. "They'll be here soon. Sara's just getting off work, so Mark waited around instead of coming here first." "She's still at Hankins?" I asked. "She just made assistant manager of the deli department. Likes it a lot." "All done with being a cashier?" "In a way, she still mans the register at the deli counter for the customers, and she's learning the budgeting, and payroll for that department. She seems to love it so far. She dropped out of school. It's taking too much of her time." "That's nice, I'm glad she's still there. I wish sometimes I was, but I like restaurant management even better."

I smiled at Jeff. The front door burst open, and Mark, and Sara appeared in the doorway, hand in hand, and talking. "But if you don't expand your hours, there you might lose out on your position." Mark argued, leading the way into the kitchen. "Hey Rees." He kissed the top of my head. "How's it going Jeff?" He too remembered him. "Hey kid." He kissed the baby on the top of his head.

"Not necessarily." Sara argued back kissing the baby too, then turned her attention to me as well. She followed Mark to the table, and sat across from Jeff, and me. "I just might not have the responsibility of payroll any longer, but I'll still be the assistant manager. Payroll will just go to someone else instead." "What are you arguing about?" Keith asked, helping himself to some manicottis from the glass dish. "Sara's promotion. She wants to cut her hours by four a week. If she does that, she'll lose part of her position. I'm afraid she'll be demoted after working so hard to get that position in the first place. I don't want to see that happen to her." Mark explained.

He filled a spatula full of manicottis for Sara's plate, then filled his own. "Thank you," she blurted, and returned to their earlier argument. "I'm not in any jeopardy of losing any damn position." Sara wanted to yell at him for not understanding where she is coming from. Between

The Way Life Used To Be

the new job, and settling in their house, she didn't seem to have any time left for herself. Not getting off until seven every night four days a week is getting to her. She had no time alone with Mark, and all they did when she saw him is fight. It just isn't worth it.

"You don't know that. It could be taken away from you with no notice, and then what?" "I'd worry about it when or if the time came. Let's just enjoy dinner, and we can shelve this for another time." It's her way of stopping the argument before it got out hand. They were surrounded by family who didn't need to hear about their squabbles.

Mark sighed, and smiled, "these are wonderful mom." He glanced at Zeni who so far hadn't said, a word, but is sitting back observing her family. All in all, it seemed normal, except for Jeremy out of the picture, and me with someone new. She saw our hands sneak together under the table and smiled. I guess we seemed so right together that she could put any remaining worries out of her head.

"Thanks honey," she answered, and took a bite from her own plate. Once our plates were empty, I took them to the sink, and washed some water over them to soak. I took my place back at the table and took a drink of water. "How long have you been a surgeon Jeff?" Zeni asked, refilling her glass of lemonade. "I'm not," he answered. "I'm a first-year resident. Last two years I was an intern at Fort Worth General. This last June, I finished with my internship, and got offered a position with pediatrics, and neonatal. I wasn't sure if I'd like it, but I've proven myself wrong. I love it more than I planned on."

Zeni smiled at that. He seemed to have goals, and responsibilities. She had a very strong feeling they would be living together soon. She could tell when she glanced at Keith, he was having those same thoughts. Once all the dishes were in the sink, and the table is clear except for the glasses, Zeni suggested a movie. Both Jeff, and I declined stating we had to get up early the next morning. We said, goodbye, and Jeff again said thank you for a wonderful dinner, and we left in better spirits than an hour before. He, and Mark shook hands like friends.

"That was easier than I had expected." Jeff sighed opening my car door. "It might help that I'm their favorite customer." I giggled, making him smile. "Meet you back home," I said. Jeff started his car and backed out of the driveway. I walked back to Starlights, where I left my car. We didn't talk on our phones during the drive, but I didn't mind. I had a long day already.

We ended up reaching the apartments at the same time. He had his arm on the small of my back as I unlocked my door. "Did you have a good time tonight?" I asked, even though it's obvious we both enjoyed ourselves, minus the love spat from earlier. That reminded me I needed to spend more time with both Mark, and Sara. I had no idea they were having issues. "I did. Your mom's a good cook." "Comes with practice." "It was fun, and Mark, and Sara seem to have a good relationship."

"For the most part. I haven't heard them argue this bad before." "It's healthy." He disappeared into my kitchen and came back out moments later with ice waters for both of us. "If you say so." I hate fighting. I'm hoping we would never have one. I chuckled to myself knowing that is all part of being in a relationship. I turned on a table lamp for a little light, not wanting the glare of the overhead living room light right now. This is a little more romantic somehow, and I lit a candle.

Once I turned around, and faced Jeff, he was gazing at me. "What's wrong?" I asked reaching out to hug him. "I want to marry you," he said. It stunned me at first, but only for a second. "I want to marry you too," I said, after thirty seconds of silence. He lowered both of us to the couch where the candle burned on the coffee table. He wanted to know about the comment earlier about Bessie's dilemma.

"When Bessie had her first visit with me, she mentioned you lost someone special a few years back." He said, crossing his knee over the other leg, and leaned back in the couch to get more comfortable. I told him everything starting with Hankins. He listened intently not interrupting until I was finished. "He's still in prison I take it?" "He has a few more years before he's eligible for parole, and I hope to god he gets denied. I don't want him to set foot outside those walls."

My voice is rising, and he could hear the fear in it. "Do you still shop there?" "Whenever I have a chance to. I haven't been there in a while though." The Safeway that is just down the street may be a little more expensive, but it's closer to where I now lived. It made more sense to shop there instead. "Is there any chance it's the same dropout who hurt you, that killed Paul?" He asked switching his leg.

"I still think so, but I've been talking with the detective assigned to my case off, and on for a few years now. He said Greg is still in prison. Couldn't be the same person, but I still have my doubts." "Do you still love Paul?" He asked. I shrugged my shoulders. "Yes, but not the same way I did when I was with him. It's been long enough that I'll always care about him, but no I'm not in love with him anymore."

The Way Life Used To Be

"That's good. I was convinced you still carried a torch." I smiled, realizing at that moment I didn't. He would always be special to me, and my very first love, but I never cried over him anymore. "You're my torch," I whispered. He smiled and lowered his head so we could kiss. I responded, and when he led me into the bedroom this time, I followed without question, knowing what would happen, and wanting it too.

He led me to the bed, and we lay down facing each other, arms wrapped around each other, and kissing. I opened my mouth and welcomed his tongue while slipping his T-shirt over his head, and my t-shirt followed. Both dropped to the floor while we touched each other.

I had never felt a man before in this intimate way. I could see his chest is full of dark colored hair, and it was sexy. I didn't want to seem like a beginner, and he didn't seem to mind my fingers exploring his chest and stomach. He reached around my back, and undid my bra, slipping it off my shoulders, and dropping it near our t-shirts. He moved his hands back to me touching me so I couldn't help, but shiver, and moaned.

His hands covered my breasts before he lowered his head to kiss the nipples which throbbed with anticipation at his touch. His tongue played around each nipple before he took the left one into his mouth, sucking making me throw my head back moaning louder.

He could feel the sexual need running through me. I drew my head forwards again, bringing my hands up from where they lay by my waist. I ran my fingers through his hair as he washed the right breast. I had a hard time controlling my emotions by now

Eventually he lifted his head to look into my eyes, which were half closed. I opened them wider, and I stared into his face as he took my face in his hands and rubbed his fingers over my cheeks. "You ready for this?" He whispered. I nodded as we reached at the same time to our waistlines where I lowered his shorts, and he slipped my skirt from my waist, knees, and ankles, until we are dressed only in our underwear, which is gone in seconds.

I am naked with him. It is exhilarating, feeling him harden against my thighs as I reached down to feel him. He moaned louder and grabbed at my hair. His eyes closed as he savored my touch. My hands are cool as I surrounded him, and stroked up, and down. So, this is what this is like. To love someone so completely. Without hesitations or doubts. Just love everything about the person including his flaws which from what I knew of him, there were none.

Once I am done exploring, I raised my hands to clasp his waist, and he moved me. Now I am under him, and he is on top. I closed my legs around his waist, just waiting for him to enter me. I'm not even scared at this point. I just knew I wanted him in every way in every way possible.

He braced above me, and slowly entered me, while I gasped with pain at first, that dissolved into pleasure as I moved with him matching his thrusts. "Am I hurting you?" He asked, looking down into my face. I had my eyes half closed, and shook my head, as I reached around him to stroke his back, running my fingernails down the length.

I loved this. Loved him. Loved the fact we were making love for the first time. I am making love for the first time in my life and couldn't think of anyone more perfect for me than this man. I came first with a shock to my system, and loud moan, and dug my fingernails into his lower back, while he followed afterwards.

Once he got his breath back, he eased out of me, and flipped on his side facing me, smiling. I matched his smile with one of my own as I placed a hand on his chest. "You sure you still want to marry me after that?" I asked smiling at him. "Nah. I'm good." He teased turning towards the ceiling. I giggled, making him look back in my face. He flipped onto his side, facing me, and cupped my face in his free hand. The other is bent behind his head. "I'd marry you today if I could. I mean it when I Say I Love You and want to spend all my remaining days with you."

"Good." I reached over to smack his lips with my own. "Now you get to sleep with me." "We slept together last night." I flung a pillow in his direction which he evaded with no effort. "You're a lousy throw." He said, smiling, and reached over to pick up the pillow.

"You just don't appreciate my talents." I playfully pouted while lifting the bedspread from the floor where it ended up. "What talents?" He teased. "Just don't quit your day job to start a career in baseball." He raised his eyes as another pillow flew over his head by a good foot and landed by the closet door which still stood open with my clothes bundled in a pile in the corner.

"I have many," I stated, and spread the bedspread over the sides, and flopped back where Jeff is laying, legs crossed, and still smirking. "Yes, you do, which you have just shown in multitude." This time a pillow hit him dead in the face, making him laugh. "No fair, you were right next to me. No challenge." I scooted further down on the bed until

The Way Life Used To Be

I am laying down, and Jeff slipped an arm around my neck, and drew my face towards his for a last kiss.

"Goodnight," I whispered. He kissed my forehead, and closed his eyes, savoring the feel of me next to him. The phone rang as I was drifting off to sleep, and I grumbled reaching for it. "What?" I said, then "Sorry, hello?" "Why are you grumpy?" It's Bessie, she had just settled the baby down for the night and wanted to talk to her sister. "Hey Bess." I smiled at Jeff who kept his eyes closed listening. This is common with them.

"Hey back. I forgot to ask you earlier if you, and Jeff want to go to Big Al's with me tomorrow. Mom, and dad offered to watch David for me." "Just a sec, I'll ask." I covered the mouthpiece with one hand. "You want to go out tomorrow?" "Where?" He asked, opening one eye. "Big Al's. Bessie needs a night out." "Sounds fun," He agreed, and closed the eye, leaning back on the pillow. "He said, yes." I said, into the phone. "What time?" "Early. We can get some nachos first for dinner. Seven?" Bessie asked scrunching her face.

"Sounds fun." I repeated Jeff's comment. "We'll meet you there. Do you care if Carla, and Taylor come?" "The more, the merrier." I said, goodbye, and hung up the phone to snuggle against Jeff's chest which he put an arm on my back and squeezed gently.

Sandra Gutierrez

Chapter 14

"You had sex." I snapped my head up. "No, I didn't." Blushing and therefore confirming the fact I just had sex. Carla waved a fork in my face. "Liar, liar," she teased. We were having lunch at Ron's. Carla called me that morning just to say hello, and when I told her that I had the day free, she grabbed at the opportunity to have lunch and make final arrangements for her wedding. She set the date for September first, which is two weeks away. All the arrangements were being completed, and all I had to do is try on the maid of honor dress.

Jeff had left before Carla's phone call, so I had the place to myself, and planned on reorganizing my closet when the phone blasted in my ear, surprising me. Now, sitting in a booth I blushed giving myself away. "Fine, I had sex." I said, not wanting to talk about it. This is my first time, and I wanted it to be something only Jeff, and I enjoyed.

Carla understood what I was trying to say without me saying it. That's why I loved her so damn much. I told her about Jeff's suspicions about Greg. "I told Jeff about Paul, and he understood what I am feeling. After I told him about him dying, he asked if there is a possibility that Greg is the one who killed Paul." I took a drink of my soda, and a bite of my salad.

"He's not released, is he?" I shook my head swallowing a tomato. "Nope, but that would have been a good theory." I had heard no news at all so Ted's advice of no news being good news deemed apt in this situation. "No kidding. What were you doing this morning? I didn't interrupt any plans, did I?" I shook my head. "Just daily housecleaning. I was about to clean my stupid closet, then you called, and here I am." I waved my fork in the air, "And loving it. Any excuse to avoid chores. So, tell me about your wedding. Everything ready?"

The Way Life Used To Be

The waitress came to get our empty plates and refill our glasses. We had a lot to talk about, but we were not ready to leave. The waitresses, and other staff didn't seem too concerned about it. "I still have to go over the menu with the caterer and pick up the flowers. My dress is ready. Want to see it?" "Is it not bad luck to see the bride in her wedding attire before the wedding itself?" I wondered out loud. "That's the groom." Carla laughed. "You ready?"

I downed the rest of my Diet Pepsi. "Yup." We drove to her house that she, and Taylor purchased last month. It's a single-story brick stucco and had a black wooden front door with plated glass windows on either side. "Elegant," I said. I followed her inside the house were Carla tossed her sweat jacket on the bench in the foyer. "It's a bit messy, so don't be alarmed."

"I remember how you used to be in the dorm room. The closet was a constant mess of clothes upon clothes. None of them were in the actual dresser where they belonged. I see you haven't changed." Carla grinned. "Got that right. The bedroom is down the hall." Carla led the way past a pale blue carpeted living room decorated in a blue, and cream plaid couch Carla had picked up at a discount store two weeks ago. A wooden coffee table covered with empty soda cans, and an ash tray full of cigarette butts.

"Who started smoking?" I asked nodding towards the ashtray. If Carla started that nasty habit, I'd be disappointed. "My cousin Larry. He's visiting from New York to come to the wedding. He's a smoking fiend, and neither Taylor nor I have the heart to ask him to smoke outside so we bought a fan." She pointed to a large fan facing the front door. "It works most of the time too. Anyway. Here's the bedroom." She walked past the living room and grinned at the kitchen.

It too is covered with last night's dishes, piled on the counter, and the dishwasher is open, but empty. It looked like someone thought about doing the dishes but reconsidered. I am glad she isn't the one smoking. We walked down a short hallway to an open doorway where the dress hung from the doorframe, encased in plastic. She unzipped the cover, and pulled out yards of white, and cream.

"It's so pretty." I complimented, fingering the train. It had mother-of-pearl along the edge, and up the back. This would have been the perfect moment to tell her I am getting married too, but something stopped me. This is her moment. "Just needs to be cleaned." Carla said, smiling over her shoulder at me who continued admiring the dress. "Did you ask Jeff yet?" "No, but I will tonight." I had forgotten to ask him.

"Has Jeff popped the question yet?" Carla asked out of nowhere, making it easy for me. "He has, I just didn't want to say anything right away until your special day passed." I said that a lot calmer than I am feeling. "That's super nice of you, but this is your best friend you're talking about." She accused, pointing a finger at my face. She then pressed both hands to it. "I'm so happy for you." She hugged me hard. "Thank you. You're always there for me," I said, smiling at her. "My job, which I take on with pleasure."

We left the bedroom and made our way back to the living room where we sat side by side on the couch. Carla tossed aside a sweatshirt, and shorts hanging on the arm to the floor. "That's not helping with your housecleaning," I advised, smiling at the lack of Carla's domestic skills. "Comes with the territory. I've never been concerned with technicalities." She brushed a hand across her bangs where they fell back over her left eye.

They had a tendency to fall that way, no matter how hard she tried to have different styles. Eventually she gave up on that hopeless task. "Where are you going tonight?" She asked. "Karaoke, at Big Al's. Bessie invited us. She said it's fine to ask you, and Taylor." "We'd love to join you. I want to meet the offspring soon though. Is she taking the baby?" She couldn't wait to start a family.

Thank God Taylor felt the same way. I laughed. "Not quite the place to bring a child. Mom, and dad offered to babysit tonight so she could have a night out." "Bringing a date? My cousins still here, and they're about the same age." Carla is ready to play matchmaker. "I don't think she's ready for that yet. Jeremy just moved the last of his things out a few days ago when Bessie got home from the hospital. He hasn't come by to visit even once. I don't think he wanted a child in the first place and is just waiting for this opportunity to bow out."

"That sucks. Taylor, and I were talking about starting a family soon. I've already stopped taking the pill so we can have babies right away." "Just wait until the wedding is over first. Don't you want time to yourselves first?" "We've had years. Time to be adults now," Carla advised, laughing. "Believe me we've had many talks, and Taylor's not the type to fuck me, and then leave my ass. We're in it for the long run."

"Such colorful language." I teased. "Did you ever tell him about the librarian you had the hots for back in school?" "I did. He understood

The Way Life Used To Be

even though I didn't cheat on him. I don't deserve him." I punched her in the shoulder playfully. "I was with you remember?" Carla nodded laughing. "He is a major player which is why I saved your life before you made a fool of yourself. Trust me you, and Taylor are, and will always be perfect for each other. Do you think I have that connection with Jeff?"

"I know you do, want to have a double wedding?" Carla rubbed her hands together in anticipation and smiling. "I hadn't thought about that, and this is your special day. Your wedding is in two weeks. Wouldn't it be too late?" Carla thought for a minute. "No," she yelled. "It isn't, I still have to talk to the caterer, and we can just make the menu bigger. We need to find you a wedding dress." "No problem. Share my day with me" She wiped her hands on her knees.

"Except for I'm your maid of honor. How's that going to work? And it may not be as simple as just wanting a dress. It needs to be beautiful, and unique, and mine." "We'll use the bridesmaid dress on Bessie. It might need to be adjusted, but that's fine. She can be both our maid of honor, and we'll find you a dress., and yes, it's that simple. Fort Worth is chock full of wedding dresses around every corner." "You think it's that easy?" I asked rubbing my hands together. "What if this makes Bessie too unhappy? She's going through a divorce."

"I think it's about time you make yourself happy for once and not worry about others." Carla advised. "You think Jeff will agree?" I asked realizing she is right once again. "Yes." Carla said. "He will, now, Taylor, and I are planning on speared meatballs, melon balls, barbeque chicken wings, finger sandwiches, and a bunch of other finger foods, sound good?" "Very, I need to make sure it's okay with him, and tell my parents. Wish me luck." "Crossing my fingers as we speak. Let me know as soon as you do so we can shop. I can't wait." Carla did a butt boogie on the couch. She is so excited she couldn't sit still. "A double wedding. I'm so happy." She flung over to my side to give me another hug.

They discussed details about tonight. "Bessie said, we'll eat there." "Absolutely, we'll be there. What time?" "Seven, I should be going." I left after that growing more excited by the minute.

Jeff was already at my parent's house when I pulled up, making me frown. What is he doing there without me? I turned off the car and headed inside without knocking. Nobody is in the living room. I glanced upstairs, but all is quiet there too. Maybe the baby is still sleeping.

Sandra Gutierrez

I rushed up the stairs. Bessie's door was open. She was sitting in her rocker, baby in her arms, and singing, with her eyes closed, and rubbing the baby's head with one hand. "Hey there," I whispered from the doorway. I am leaning against the doorframe. I crossed my arms, smiling. Bessie looked right at home, Jeremy at her side or not. "Hi," Bessie whispered back. "I'm trying to get him to go back to sleep. He just had a feeding." David is bundled in a blue, and white plaid blanket, eyes opened halfway, and looking at his mother.

"He doesn't look that sleepy." I observed moving into the room and leaning down to look at the baby. His eyes moved toward me, and he gurgled. "He likes you." "Babies like everybody." "Not his dad." Bessie sounded sad and lowered her eyes. "Has he even come by to visit?" I went to sit on the bed. "Not even once. I haven't been back to the house since we moved here, so I don't know if he's tried or not, but I don't even care at this point."

"Then you don't know if he's trying to make amends. He might be sorry and wanting to make things right again." I advised. "Too late. Jeff's downstairs," she nodded towards the doorway. "You should go say hello." "In a minute. I have news that you might not take too well." "Tell me anyway. I want to hear some gossip." "It is not gossip! Jeff asked me to marry him!" I held my breath looking for Bessie's reaction. Bessie said, nothing.

She looked down at the baby, then back up at me. I had my hands in my lap waiting for her to say something. She sighed and forced a smile. "Did you say yes?" I smiled. "Of course, I did! I have a favor to ask. Will you be my maid of honor this time?" "I'd love to." Bessie said. "I don't want to make you sad. I don't, but I need you." I reached over and hugged her. "Thank you, honey." I kissed her on the forehead. "I should go see what Jeff is doing."

"Go, I'll be okay, promise." I smiled, and jumped off the bed, and ran down the stairs towards the kitchen as the living room is still empty. I heard voices as I made my way towards the kitchen and stopped when I reached the archway. Zeni stood at the counter with Jeff. He is holding manicotti shells and listening. "and once the cheese mixture is softened, you add the egg, and spinach." "And then what?" Jeff asked frowning. "Your shells need to stay hardened. They'll cook once they're in the oven. You then use this tool."

She grabbed a tube laying on the counter. "It makes the mixture easier to fill in the shells without breaking," she squirted some mix into

The Way Life Used To Be

the shell, and placed it on the glass dish. "What are you doing?" I asked from the doorway. I had a questioning look on my face. "Learning how to cook like your mother." Jeff smiled in my direction. "Your man here is quite talented," Zeni smiled over her shoulder. "Where were you?" "Visiting Bessie upstairs. Baby's getting bigger by the hour."

"No," Zeni shook her head. "Before. Jeff's been here for close to an hour." "With Carla. She's making final wedding plans." I glanced at Jeff who is nodding his permission to tell them. "And mine." Zeni dropped the tube on the floor as she spun around. "What did you say, you, and Jeff?" She clasped her hands to my face and squeezed. "You're engaged?" She whispered, and I nodded, pulling myself away from the doorframe to stand near Jeff. Mom reached me first and grabbed my arms.

I lifted my smiling face. "You approve mama?" "I do." She shouted. "My baby's getting married., and my other baby's getting divorced. Such drama." "You're telling me. I had to ask her to be my maid of honor when she's just moved out of her house." "It's your day, Bessie chose her path and had her day in the sun. Now it's your turn. She'll be okay." She kissed me on the cheek and held my face in both hands while turning her head towards Jeff who is filling manicotti shells like he didn't have a care in the world. "Marry that man."

A few tears fell down my cheeks as mom held me. "I intend to." "Did you ask Keith's permission?" She directed that question to Jeff who is now watching us. "Ask me what?" Keith asked coming into the kitchen. "What the hell are you doing?" He pointed to the mess on the counter. "Daddy," I started to say, and was interrupted. "Sir, I... we have something to ask you," Jeff said. He wanted to sound confident but is stuttering at having to ask the most important person in my life.

"You're pregnant," he stated, then laughed. "Just kidding. Yes, you can marry her," he kissed my forehead. "Nice job, kiddo." "That was easy." Jeff sounded shocked. "Thank you, sir," he held out a hand, which Keith ignored. He pulled both of us into a hug and held us close. "Take care of my baby," he said to Jeff, who nodded. "Well." Zeni is crying. "When do we shop?"

I repeated Carla's offer. "All I'd have to do is find my own wedding dress, and instead of being Carla's maid of honor, Bessie would wear the dress, and be both of ours. That way Carla doesn't have to find someone else on such short notice. All they'd have to do is expand the menu."

"Sounds like a plan. Tomorrow we'll go shopping." Zeni clapped her hands. "We'll start with David's Bridal and go from there if we don't have any luck." "Sounds good." I agreed and turned towards Jeff. "We'd better get Bessie, and head out." It's already six thirty, and our stomachs were already rumbling. "Go on. We're fine. Keith set the table, and we'll have a date."

Jeff, and I took off with Bessie. David had finally fallen asleep, so Zeni, and Keith would have at least a few hours of peace, and quiet. It's a quarter to seven when we arrived at Big Al's, and it's already crowded. We however found one empty table towards the back, and furthest away from the bar, and front doors. We didn't care. Jeff ordered three drinks and brought them to the table.

Bessie took a sip of hers, and sighed, "Oh, I love this." She tilted her head back. "A night of no baby is just what the doctor ordered." "This doctor?" I pointed to Jeff who had an arm draped around my shoulder and squeezed. "Yes, this doctor. Bessie you don't worry about anything except enjoying yourself. No baby worries." He pointed a finger with his free hand in her direction. "Got it?" "Scouts honor."

Bessie kissed two fingers up to the ceiling. "These people seriously suck." She laughed at the duet ruining Tim McGraw, and Faith Hill's "*I need you.*" "Your next." I teased and earned a look to kill. "Am not, I'm entitled to a night of no worries remember? I'll be doing nothing except enjoying my nachos as soon as they get here and making fun of singers." Bessie stated taking a drink of her peach daiquiri.

"What do you think Reesa? Want to give it a go?" Jeff asked at the same time Carla, and Taylor appeared. I shook my head at his suggestion. A public singer I am not. "Hey," she said, giving Bessie a kiss on the cheek. "When am I going to see your adorable offspring?" "Whenever you want, just not tonight. Tonight, I'm free." She raised her hands above her head, "and enjoying every second."

"Good for you. I brought food." She set two gigantic plates of loaded nachos on the table where five hands grabbed at the food. "Thanks," I said with a mouthful of nacho. "These aren't half bad." I swallowed and followed it with a drink of my Long Island Iced Tea. Jeff had insisted I'd like it, and I did. "So." Carla thumped a fist on the table. "Did you tell Jeff about our plans?"

I turned to Jeff who is smiling and eating. "Yes, I did, and everyone's in full agreement. Mom wants to go shopping with me." "Works for me unless you want me to go with you." "She's excited and

The Way Life Used To Be

wants to help. She wants to be a part of this, and since she can't cater or do much else, this she can do." I ate another nacho.

"It's fine, I already have my dress so when you get yours, be sure to bring it by. I have to check you out." She winked, and made both Taylor, and Jeff laugh. I downed the rest of my drink. "That is excellent. I need another." Jeff offered to get me a second drink, but I waved him off stating I could get it. I made my way past bunches of people who were just standing around talking, while waiting for their own drinks. Trey, and Jim were sitting at the bar teasing each other like they always did.

"So, you're still convinced your love is waiting here for you." Trey teased, elbowing Jim in the ribs, and smiling. Jim strained his neck towards the dance floor. "I see her, later." He hopped off the stool. Trey only shook his head, when I approached the bar to order my drink.

"Long time, no see." he said, smiling at me. "I guess so, how are you?" I asked smiling. I am always happy to see Trey, and it showed. "Couldn't be better. I'm keeping an eye out for Jim," he flipped a finger towards the dance floor where Jim is bumping and grinding on some blond. She is loud but didn't seem to mind it though. It's hard on the other dancers trying to stay out of her way as she flipped her head back and laughed.

"He's holding his own." I turned towards the dance floor. "Are you?" He shrugged his shoulders. "I guess so. I've been so busy that I think this is the first time in months I've had any fun." "And are you having fun?" I asked peering closer at him. He looked to the point of exhaustion. He shrugged his shoulders. "Trying to. I should be more like my friend over there," he nodded at Jim who had his hands around her waist, and she was laughing. "Stupid laugh by the way."

I laughed too, and he smiled. "That's a better sound." "I think Jim will be okay, and no, I don't think you should be more like him. I like you just as you are." The bartender handed me my drink. "Thank you." I said. I waved to Trey. "It's nice seeing you." "Always my pleasure," he turned, resting his hip against the counter, and crossed a foot over the other ankle. "I should go rescue him. He's giving me the pleading eye." "Go on." I laughed more and hopped down taking my drink with me.

By the time I reached the table again, the nachos are gone, but I didn't care. The one drink I downed ten minutes before is taking effect. I felt light-headed, dizzy, and a very happy. "Sorry to take so long. You bored yet?" "Nope. Bessie's been entertaining us with baby stories which we are tolerating with great restraint. Didn't she promise a night free of baby talk?" He smiled in Bessie's direction.

She is laughing and clapping her hands. She had just finished a story about David puking up baby formula all over Zeni's favorite T-shirt, she swore a blue streak which was unlike her. It was so comical to watch and hear. "That's right." Bessie held up her empty glass. "Time for a refill." She laughed and bounded up to the bar. When she was gone, I smiled in her direction shaking my head. "She needed this."

"I'll say." Jeff observed. "She's dancing," he pointed to the dance floor where Bessie is in a full embrace with Jim. "Oh my god," I strained over the table to get a better look. "With Jim Stevens of all people," I studied them, and Bessie is laughing with her head tilted back, and Jim joining in. "They look right together," I observed lifting my glass. "Cheers to Bess." I took a drink. "Who's Jim again?" Jeff asked.

"Our delivery driver at Starlights. He, and Mark used to go to school together, so they've known each other for a long time. He's a sweetie." Jeff looked over at them and smiled. "Come to think of it, I never met Jeremy. I don't know if they were happy together, but she looks it now." He observed, still looking Bessie's direction. he turned back to me extending the smile and took a drink. "You want to dance?"

"I want to dance," I agreed, and set my empty glass on the table. "Let's go." We slipped out of our seats, and Carla, and Taylor watched from their chairs as we folded our arms around each other, and I gazed up at him, a half smile on my face, and eyes half closed. "I'm feeling tipsy," I murmured, and was met with a soft smile of his, although he chose not to comment. It's obvious this is just what we needed. A night of fun with no drama. He liked her friend and is looking forward to getting to know them even better.

Once the song was over, and we started making our way back to their table, I smiled at my fiancé. Looking up at him, I find he is looking down at me, a look of complete contentment on his face. By the time it was midnight, Bessie was still going strong on the dance floor, but Jeff, and I called it a night. After all, I had to work at nine, and didn't want to be dragging my feet. When I get done for the day mom, and I are going dress shopping, and I'm excited at the thought of her going with me.

Carla, and Taylor left too, so I made my way to Bessie who gave me a loud smack on the mouth and Jim who kissed my cheek. "Enjoy," she laughed at us, confident that Jim would take her home. He isn't even drinking. Just having a good time. By the time I made it to Jeff's car, I am feeling the full effect of those two drinks. I am lightheaded, dizzy, and so happy. I am also looking forward to a good night's sleep since it felt like only snatches for the last few days. Jeff carried me up the stairs as I giggled. I almost fell when I attempted it myself.

I flung open the door that I again forgot to lock, and Jeff walked in, dumping me on the bed. He laid down next to me as he undressed me while I closed my eyes once again loving his soft touch. My Blouse came first as he undid the buttons one by one until it slipped off my shoulders, and he removed it off my body, and tossed it on the floor.

My closet is still a mess so one more blouse wouldn't make that much of a difference. Bra came next as he reached around my back, and unclasped it, also slipping it off my shoulders. He remained silent so long, and his hands had yet to touch me intimately, that I shivered expecting his hands on me. He felt it and sighed as he reached for me. He fingered one breast, taking the hardened nipple into his mouth while I moaned, and grabbed his hair. It's the alcohol making me bolder, but I arched my neck, and ran my fingers through his hair, sensually while he took the other breast into his mouth much like he did last night.

I moved my hands from his head to his chest, to the bottom of his shirt which I tugged for a minute before pushing it over his head, and dropping it on the floor, near the blouse. He lowered his face to touch mine, and we opened our lips at the same time, and kissed gently at first, tasting the alcohol that made it all the sweeter.

This time, I took the initiative, and touched his tongue with mine, running it over his teeth, before delving deeper into his mouth. He closed his eyes, savoring the feel of me as I reached down to his jeans, and slipped his belt off, and jeans down his knees, and feet, where they also joined the growing pile of clothes on the floor.

He followed suit, and I again took him by surprise by climbing on him, and straddling his waist while he grabbed my hips, and I tossed my head back, shouting his name as he entered me, then drew my head forward until I was looking down. My eyes were on his, as we rode the wave together.

Once it's over, and we were both spent, I continued sitting on his hips, smiling as he looked at me. He had a slight smirk on his face. "So, this is the real you?" He said, running his hands up, and down my rib cage. "Do you like the real me?" I asked shocked at my behavior. I had never felt so good, and so right then right now. I didn't want to go to sleep even.

Sandra Gutierrez

"Very much, so much, I'd like a repeat." "In the morning. I'm drunk, and happy, and I need to sleep." I climbed off him and lay down on top of the comforter. I didn't even bother turning the comforter down. Side by side, we slept with smiles. I almost missed the alarm I had set for seven. Mom had told me the day before she would get the morning prepped by herself. It's Saturday, and is slow, first thing in the morning on the weekends. Everyone had the good sense to sleep in which is what I need to do.

I planned on getting there by nine so I could help with the lunch crowd, and then we'd take off to shop. I couldn't wait, and I had already convinced myself we'd find the perfect dress the first place we went to. There is less than one week to the wedding, and I still didn't have a wedding dress. Not that I didn't try.

Mom, and I traveled to no less than five stores, and tried on fifteen dresses, none of which wowed either of us. We started with the day after Big Al's which I am late for work by close to an hour. I was delayed by another bout of love making. Jeff practically had to shove me out the door, remembering to lock it this time. I needed to pay better attention.

Five stupid stores, and no dress is enough to wow me. I want to scream and cancel my part in the wedding. I am about ready to cancel the whole damn thing, and just let Carla have her special day. This is a sign I wasn't ready for this yet. Carla had everything she needed, so my absence wouldn't make that much of a difference, except Carla wouldn't hear it.

If she needed to, she'd buy the dress herself, and force me into it. Just so I'd shut the hell up as she shouted into the phone, and I ended up hanging up on her for the first time. Of course, I am over my mad thirty minutes later, and called up apologizing. Carla instantly forgiving me for my bout of temporary insanity and laughed out loud

"You'll find something, and if you think about it, five stores is nothing. I bet you five dollars you'll find your dress by tomorrow. Want me to go with you this time?" "No, but thanks. Mom is convinced like you, I'll find it soon. When I told her during my insanity moment that I'm done with this, she told me in no uncertain terms to shut the hell up. I hate my mom," I stated, and thumped my fist on the counter. This caused, Zeni to look up from slicing carrots. We were in the kitchen at the house, and I am talking on my cell phone. I was sitting at the table with a pad of paper, and pen before me, intending on listing new stores to visit tomorrow. Mom is making a buffalo stew for dinner tonight.

The Way Life Used To Be

This would be a new item to offer at Starlights soon, but she wanted our opinion before offering it to our customers. "Your angry again? Didn't we already go that round?" She asked already focusing her attention on slicing. The house is already filled with the smell of onion, and garlic, and smelled so good. Carla however laughed. "Go make up with mommy. I'll see you in two days for fittings. Have your dress by then."

"You are just as mean as mommy. I'll see you later." I slammed the phone down and faced mom who is now slicing celery. "Why are you yelling again?" she added the carrots, and celery to the pot along with potato chunks. "This wedding is the stupidest idea ever. I'll never find my dress, and Jeff will be so embarrassed when I show up in jeans. Why do I have to dress up? Jeans, and a T-shirt sound so much better." I started cutting up the buffalo meat for her.

"Because you agreed to take part, and since Carla's already found her dress, and wants more than anything for you to be part of her day, it's only right for you to find something just as spectacular. You will find it tomorrow. Five dollars is the bet I believe?" "Yes. If I win, I'm ten dollars richer. I like that idea." I smiled as I placed the meat chunks on the skillet where they started sizzling. "You're going to deliberately not find something so you can benefit off your poor friend, and mother?" Zeni pressed a hand to her heart. "I'm offended. Seriously!" She shook her head laughing.

"I have no idea what you're talking about." I feigned innocence as I stirred the meat. "Liar face. You're getting your dress tomorrow." She shook a spoon at me. "No choice." "I guess I'm outnumbered. I'm not going all the hell over the place though. Two stores will be my limit. That'll be seven and that's enough. Otherwise, it's jeans, and t-shirts." Zeni sighed as she added the meat to the pot where the vegetables were simmering. "Dinner's just about ready. Is Jeff joining us?"

I nodded. "In about half an hour. He had the afternoon shift at the hospital today." "He should be right on time then." She started buttering bread to go with the stew. Jeff ended up coming to the house in twenty minutes, and since the stew was ready, and the bread in the basket, all we had to do is sit down, and enjoy.

It's a huge success as Zeni got many compliments, with a definite yes to add it to the menu as soon as possible. She is planning on updating after the wedding is over. That way I could give my full attention to it.

The following afternoon at three o'clock. Keith kicked us both out of the kitchen after yelling until he turned red.

This is such a rare event. Both of us flung off our aprons, looking more than a little embarrassed, and we took off in mom's car to look once again for my dress. "That was a very difficult morning." Zeni observed, backing out of the driveway. She tried to act like Keith's outburst meant nothing to either of them, even though she is crying inside. She let him yell like he just did. One look at his face, and she snapped her mouth shut, and let him.

Once he stopped, she left the restaurant without a further word to him, including a goodbye which is rare. "You're telling me." I sighed and crossed my arms in front of my chest. "He had no right to do that you know." "Yeah, I do, but neither of us have been very easy to live with the last few days. I've tried to be patient and realize how hard this must be for you trying to find just the perfect dress in such a short time. It couldn't have been easy for him either, being forced to listen. He is bound to snap one way or another."

She found a parking space in front of Sears at the Hastings Mall, and we walked through the store without exchanging a single word. We took the elevator to the third floor where most of the clothing stores are located. David's Bridal had a huge sale going on, and was so full of customers, we bypassed it in favor of a discount bridal, and prom store called Elegance. It's close to the food court, so we caught whiffs of different foods while wandering through several racks.

"What do you think of this?" Zeni stated holding up an off-white ankle-length gown with a short train. It's simple, elegant, and had the magic numbers on the price tag. Forty percent off that day only. Zeni dangled the tag while smiling, holding up the dress to her neck. "I like it," I said. We headed straight for the nearest dressing room.

I followed her to the dressing room to try it on. Once it's over my shoulders, and the silk flowed down to my feet, I faced the mirror, and smiled. This is the dress. I flung open the door where Zeni stood right outside and turned around so she could button the back. Once they were all buttoned, she smoothed the dress, and I turned around again, so I faced her.

"Well, what do you think?" I asked when she just stood there, hands on her face, and crying. Zeni rubbed her eyes and held me at arm's length. "I love it," she whispered before more tears started falling. "I love it," I smiled, and cupped her face. "I guess I lost the bet," I laughed, and wiped her tears away. "Mama, I think I'm finally okay." She knew I was referring to Paul. "You're okay," She clasped my hands. I turned to take it off, and once I am dressed back in jeans, we headed to Walt's having the dress dry cleaned. It looked clean enough, but why take chances?

Once I paid for the cleaning, I turned to mom. "What now?" "Now you have the rest of the day to do whatever you want. What do you want to do now?" "Visit Sam, I haven't seen him since Paul's funeral." "Tell him hello from us." I smiled. "I'll call you tonight and let you know how it went." Ten minutes later, I am in my car. I had left parked in mom's driveway, and I headed to Sam's. On the way I saw the park where I had fed the ducks with Jeff. I stopped and visited them first.

I walked through the entrance to the park, and grabbed a loaf of bread from the barrel, and strolled towards the pond. It's such a beautiful day, and I very much wanted to spend the rest of it outside, enjoying the warm rays. Two mallards approached me, and lay down in front of me, burying their webbed feet underneath them, and waiting for some bread. I tore off several chunks and then tossed them straight into the water where more mallards attacked them. Once the bag is empty, I lay back with my feet stretched outwards, lifting my face towards the sun, and closed my eyes.

This is the life, I thought I'd have. I opened my eyes to the sky and saw Paul. "I sure miss you! I'm getting married in a few days, and I still wish sometimes you were with me," I sighed, and stared at the sky. "I graduated. You'd have been proud of me. I'm enjoying my life now, and I have my own place. I'm doing good. See you soon."

I got up, said, goodbye to the ducks, and got in the car, and backed out. I headed back on the freeway, and towards Sam's house.

"Hey Reesa." Sam greeted me. He is tending his garden when I pulled up and smiled. "How are you doing?" "Hi Sam," I lifted my face up, and he kissed my cheek. "I'm doing a lot better now." "Shows. Your all done with school I take it?" "I graduated in June and have been working at Starlights ever since. We started opening earlier for breakfast a few weeks ago. You should come by, and try our new sandwiches," I offered sitting on the stone steps.

"I'd love to. Be right back." He climbed the steps and disappeared into the house leaving me alone for a minute. I leaned back, enjoying the rays warming my face, and neck. "Sorry to take so long." Sam apologized and handed me a glass which I accepted. "Thanks." Taking a sip, I smiled at him. "I'm sorry it's taken me so long to say hello again," I began, and he waved a hand dismissing it.

"I know you're busy, and I appreciate it all the same. I sold Paul's car two months ago. Only got six hundred dollars for it, but not seeing it in the backyard is a lot better for my mood." "I bet, what did you do with the money?" I realized how blunt I sounded, but he didn't mind. It's nice to talk about Paul now.

"I bought a pedestal for the garden, and a riding lawn mower. I had to come up with most of it from my savings. Selling his car helped." He took a drink of his iced tea. "Was it too painful to keep it here?" I asked. "Yes. Every time I'd leave for work, I'd come out here, and see the car in the yard. I'd be happy all morning until I came outside and saw the car. I couldn't take it anymore, so I put out an ad, and sold the car within a week."

I smiled and finished the soda. "I think Paul would have approved." "I think so too. I talk to him sometimes. When I'm done with my practice for the day, and I come home to an empty house. It's hard even to this day, to not expect to hear from him, so I come out here like now, and I work in my garden, and we talk." Sam smiled, and shook his head, lowering his eyes. "It helps."

I studied him realizing how much he is still hurting. "I talked to him earlier at a pond while feeding the ducks. It's the first time I said, hello to him in three years." "And what did he say back?" He said. "I told him I'm getting married in four days. I like to think he's happy for me." "Then congratulations are in order." He reached over to give me a one arm hug and kissed the side of my head. "I think he'd have given his approval."

"Thanks. I needed to hear that. I should go, but I'll visit more often. That I promise." "That I'll hold you to. Tell me about your wedding and don't leave out any details. You'll make a beautiful bride. It'll be a beautiful day for you." He stood up with me and walked me to the car. I said, goodbye with a smile, and started the car.

When I reached the apartment, it's quiet, still, and cool. I breathed a sigh of relief that for the moment, I didn't have to deal with anyone. I headed to the refrigerator for a soda which reminded me I am running low. I'd make a trip to the store for groceries soon, since my cupboards were almost empty. Granted I didn't cook much here, but that is no excuse. I rummaged through what is left of the food and found nothing

The Way Life Used To Be

appealing. I wanted to make Jeff a good dinner, since I'd never cooked for him before so a trip to the store is in order.

I bypassed Safeway. By the time I reached Hankins, it's close to four. The sun is blazing hot. Inside though it's cool, and only two registers are opened. Sara isn't around though, so I grabbed a cart, and started with the produce. I selected some carrots, and celery, bagged them, and moved on to the broccoli, and cauliflower. A stir-fry sounded wonderful, and something I hadn't made in a long time. Now would be a good time to break in my kitchen utensils.

I walked away towards the pasta, and spices, remembering where everything is even from the brief time I worked here. It's like I never left. I even expected myself to stock shelves. I giggled to myself, and located the stir-fry sauce, and noodles. It isn't until I paid for the groceries, I realized I didn't panic. I made it to the store, found all the groceries, and left without a single thought of Greg.

I smiled and headed home to make dinner. On the way my cell phone rang. "Hello?" "Hello gorgeous." It made me happy to hear his voice. "I have a surprise for you tonight. What time are you off?" "An hour. Any chance this is a naked surprise?" He teased, and is met with nothing, but a giggle. "Anything I can help you with?"

"Nope. Just meet me at my apartment when you get home." "Will do, bye gorgeous." I snapped the phone shut and tossed it on the seat. This would be perfect. I'd have dinner hot, and ready when he walked in the door. I thought of wearing nothing, but an apron, making every guys fantasy of the naked chef come true, but thought better of it. It would be my lousy luck it would be a member of my family instead of Jeff coming to pay a visit.

He watched her leave the store with a wave, and a smile. Not too much longer now Bitch. It was worth it following her home last month. He knew she moved out but had no idea where to. Now she is living with the big badass doc. The stupid doc didn't understand what is about to happen. He loved the look on his face when he stared at him through the bedroom window. He waited all night for a glimpse of Reesa naked. It got so bad he pressed a hand to himself to prevent himself from getting too excited. All night he waited to see her and had to see him instead.

Stupid doc is shirtless, and he knew what they were doing. Little slut. Yeah, your nothing, but a useless slut. Big fucking deal you have a degree. That doesn't mean shit, at least to the general population.

I got home in plenty of time to start my dinner. First things first though. I dumped my bags on the kitchen counter, then headed to my bedroom to change into something comfortable.

I giggled as I remembered Jeff's fantasy waitress ensemble. That vision would be waylaid, at least for now. I dressed in jean shorts, and a black T-shirt, keeping my feet bare. I wandered into the kitchen to begin cooking. I got as far as getting the wok down from a cupboard, realizing this is the first meal I made in my new place. The chicken is cubed, and sizzling when my front door opened, and Bessie came in without bothering to knock. I said, nothing seeing the look on her face. She is smiling. She looked happy for once, so I wasn't about to ruin it.

"How's it going?" I asked, stirring the chicken. "I have news, Jim, and I are dating now. Can you believe it?" She squealed. She slapped her hands to her face. "With Jim?" I snapped my head up in shock. "After one night?" "Yes. I've never felt this way. Are you happy for me?" Bessie held her breath waiting for an answer. She spent all night with Jim after the bar had closed for the night, and Zeni, and Keith didn't even question where she was.

Probably assumed she spent the night on Reesa's couch. He proved to be a very gentle lover, and although this isn't her first-time making love, it's obviously his. She didn't mind though, He held her so lovingly. She felt things she never felt with Jeremy. "I suppose so." I began and held up a hand when Bessie hissed. "Let me finish.... Just three weeks ago Jeremy moved out. Do you remember that?"

Bessie nodded, still baring her teeth. "Keep your teeth inside your mouth." The teeth disappeared. "I'm devastated for you. A single mother, and your living with mom, and dad again. You have so much to overcome without having to bring in more. Honey, I love you so much, but you're not in love. You're in love with the idea and don't you hit me." I pointed to Bessie's hand which had fisted and is pounding the counter.

The hand slipped under the counter. I sliced the rest of my vegetables. The broccoli, and cauliflower joined the carrots, and celery in the wok. Bessie took a deep breath before answering. She needed a minute to calm down, as this is so typical behavior of her. "I would not hit you. I just wanted to hit something." She smiled as she unclenched her fist.

"I've never been so miserable in my entire life. When I got married, that was the happiest day I've ever had. I thought this is it. I've found

The Way Life Used To Be

the Love of My Life, and we'll grow old together, and have many kids we'll love, and cherish. That didn't happen as much as I dreamed it would. I tried to be the very best wife I could be, and I failed. I won't fail with David being a mother to him, and I won't fail with Jim."

"Just give it at least six months before you marry this one," I teased, and smiled. I put the noodles on to boil and stirred the vegetables. "Smells good in here. What the hell are you making, anyway?" Bessie leaned over the bar to get a better look. "Chicken stir-fry. I just realized this afternoon I have yet to use this kitchen, and I'm making Jeff a surprise dinner. Think he'll be impressed." I gestured to the stove. "Sure will, where's your chicken?"

I waved a tray in front of her and placed it on the cutting board. "So, are you getting excited about your wedding?" Bessie had leaned back on her stool and folded her arms. I nodded "I even found a dress. It's in the closet." I nodded towards my bedroom where Bessie took off to look. Smiling, I put the chicken in a separate frying pan to cook before they'd be added to the wok. Only twenty minutes to go. Jeff would be home shortly, and my dinner is going well on schedule.

"It's beautiful." Bessie gushed running back and hopped on her stool. "I want lots of pictures. Want me to do your hair?" She asked one question after another without pausing. She sounded just like mom when she did that. I laughed, and added the chicken to the vegetables, and let them simmer in the sauce. "Thank you. Took long enough and I have to admit I was ready to give up on finding a decent dress, but all is well now." I smiled and stirred the noodles. Bess repeated "Can I fix your hair, and makeup?"

I nodded and got out a straining bowl from a cupboard. Bessie would do a much better job on her hair than I would any day. "You think I need a veil or something?" Bessie shook her head. "I have an idea I saw at the mall yesterday in a jewelry store they had these very fancy hair clips that you can add attachments to. I'll pick up something to put together tomorrow."

She jumped off the stool, and around the corner into the kitchen where she stood behind my back and ran her hands through the sides of my hair. "I think we'll do this. Put the sides up behind your ears and capture right about here."

She pressed her thumb near the middle of my head. "Then we'll leave some curls down the side, and the rest hang down your back. Simple, yet elegant. What do you think?" "Beautiful." Jeff answered from the doorway. Bessie dropped her hand in surprise. "Hey handsome." She smiled in Jeff's direction as he wondered closer and sniffed. "I smell something wonderful."

"Your right in time. Sit down." I smiled, and Bessie dropped the rest of my hair in place. "I'll let you guys eat." She felt like a third wheel suddenly even though Jim is expecting her soon. "I wanted to invite her too, but also needed some time alone with Jeff. Bessie made it easy. Jim's waiting so you two enjoy, and Reesa, I'll see you tomorrow." She kissed Jeff on the cheek, followed by mine, and skipped out the door.

"What is that all about?" Jeff asked watching her leave. "She's in love again, with Jim Stevens of all people." I shook my head filling two plates with noodles. "You mean the delivery guy?" He questioned sitting on a stool near where Bessie is sitting an hour ago. "The same as long as I've known him, he's been a skirt chaser. Loves every woman he lays eyes on."

"I'm hoping that Bessie isn't just a passing thing for him. She's already devastated, and I don't think she could handle another break up." I spooned chicken, and vegetables over the noodles, and added more soy sauce. "I have to say I'm surprised knowing what's going on with her she'd be so willing to move on so soon, but maybe that's what she needs to do. Ever think about that?" He accepted a plate, and a glass of iced tea.

I nodded and picked up my plate to join him at the bar. "I have, and I've also not seen her this happy for months now. I love my sister, and I love Jim." "Then that's all that matters. They'll figure out what to do. This is just wonderful." He smiled down at his plate. "Is this my surprise?"

I speared a piece of chicken with chopsticks. "I found my dress with mom, and when I got home, I realized my cupboards were screaming for food, so I drove to the store, and Wala." I gestured to our plates. "I'd made you dinner to celebrate." "Celebrate what?" He finished the last noodle and washed it down with some iced tea. "Are you doing the wife duties with a smile?" He teased.

"Finding my dress. Want to see it?" I giggled. I knew about the bad marriage myth of the groom seeing the bride before the wedding, but I didn't care. "In a minute, I have something to show you first." He smiled as he reached in his back pocket for a box. "Close your eyes." I obeyed without question, and he slipped off the stool to get on one knee.

"Open." I opened my eyes, mouth opening wider, and wider as I realized what he is doing.

"Marry me." He smiled and opened the box. In it is a square-cut diamond surrounded by four smaller diamonds intertwining the edge. It's simple, yet so elegant, and beautiful. He took the ring out, and I had my left hand already outstretched.

It's made for me. It fit perfectly, and when I gazed at my hand, the diamonds sparkled in the sunlight from the living room window, and I laughed in delight. "Thank you." I jumped up from the stool and squatted down to his level where I threw my arms around him and smacked his lips with my own.

"Your welcome." He laughed too, and hugged me hard, lowering us both to the floor where we lay side by side facing each other on the carpet, plates forgotten as I drew my arms around his neck, and kissed him, pressing my body closer to his. He wrapped his own arms around my waist and pulled me even closer until I was on top of him. I again took the initiative and lifted his T-shirt up his chest and over his head, tossing it near the couch where it landed on the arm.

It's so much easier now loving him, and soon we were naked, I am on top of him, riding, and shouting his name, tossing my hair back, and loving every minute of it. By the time we were both spent, I slipped off him, grabbed my shorts, and chuckled as I made my way to the bedroom to find clean underwear. "That is one way to appreciate a good dinner." He smiled following me into the bedroom after rinsing off the plates in the sink. He is still naked and turned down the comforter himself this time.

"It's my way of appreciating you." I giggled grabbing him again and kissed him. "You ready for round two?" He asked short of breath. Good god, she is perfect, he thought as I looked up at him, fingers in his hair, and smiling into his eyes. "Later, right now I want to lie down, and feel you next to me." I drew us down on the bed and did that.

He lay down on his back, drew an arm around my shoulder, and rubbed my back as he had for the last two weeks, and kissed the side of my head. "We will be married soon." He whispered into my hair. "You bet your ass." I whispered back and closed my eyes.

Sandra Gutierrez

Chapter 15

September 1st
Our Wedding Day

The sky is a perfect blue without a cloud in sight. I woke up with a huge smile. My wedding day. Our wedding day, I corrected myself as I forced myself to think of Carla, who is also waking up, and shouting. "Wedding day." She dialed my phone, and I am already sitting up in bed. "Wedding day!" She shouted into the mouthpiece. I held the phone away from my ear. "I know!" I started laughing and jumped out of bed. I am alone this morning as Jeff, and I decided, to honor the tradition that he wouldn't see the bride until the wedding started, and he would be waiting at the alter along with Taylor.

I drew up the blinds and smiled at the scene outside. The sun is directly overhead, and the window is warm. It's a perfect day to get married, and we could start our life together. I was dressed in sweatpants, and a T-shirt for now, as the dress is at the hall hanging in my dressing room. I didn't want to take any chance it would be ruined.

Bessie is due any minute so she could get my hair, and makeup done. I liked the idea of the sides pulled up like Bessie suggested at dinner the other night. I am also thankful Bessie is showing her support. I couldn't even eat anything for breakfast, I'm so nervous. Jeff is gone for the moment and said he would meet me at the hall in an hour, so I only had about half an hour to get my hair worked on.

Bessie, hurry the hell up, I yelled to myself as I paced the living room, willing the front door to open, and Bessie to come rushing in full of apologies. Just staring at the door seemed to work. Bessie rushed in,

The Way Life Used To Be

bag in hand, and all smiles. Jim is right behind her, smiling in return. "Big day Reecie Peecie." He greeted giving me a kiss on the cheek. "You're telling me. Bessie, help." I grabbed my little sister by the arms, pulling her into the bedroom. "Jim, we'll be just a little while."

Bessie apologized, and giggled, glancing over her shoulder, a wide smile on her face. "Take your time. I'm fine," he waved a hand in our direction, and sat on the couch, waiting patiently. He had learned in the few days he, and Bessie had been together that this is typical behavior of her. She had no sense of time, and he was the one worrying they'd make Reesa late on her special day.

"Sit down." Bessie directed to a chair I had placed in front of the mirror. She scooted around, so she is facing the back of my head, and bent down for the hair clip. "Want to look first?" She asked leaning over. "That way you can see the before, and after." "No, I trust you. Just make me look beautiful." I was advised, to sit up straight, and to be comfortable. I already washed my hair from earlier.

"Relax." Bessie said, and placed the clip in her mouth while she ran her fingers through one side, capturing it with the clip, then moved to the other, leaving a few loose strands she'd curl in a few minutes. "Trying to." I took a deep breath, wanting to have eyes in the back of my head, so I'd see what she is doing, but waited none too patiently while Bessie took her sweet time.

She plugged in a curling iron. "Where's your dress?" she glanced in the closet, but it's shut. "At the hall already. I wanted nothing to get on it, so I left it there last night." "Probably a very good idea." Bessie reached for the iron, and placed a few strands of hair in it.

Ten minutes later, she unplugged the iron. "Finished." She announced. "Want to see now." She grabbed a hand mirror and gave it to me. I'm standing up with my back to the floor mirror so I could see the end results. "I love it. You are talented." I tossed the hand mirror on the bed. "You ready to go?" Bessie shook her head. "Makeup?" She reminded and pointed to the chair. "Sit." "I was just sitting. I look fine now." I am getting anxious as they had less than fifteen minutes before we had to leave.

"Your pale. Sit down and be quiet." Bessie ordered and reached into her purse for a compact. "Now you're beautiful." She gushed just a few minutes later, and snapped the compact shut, tossing it, and the eyeliner pencil back in her purse. "I'm a true miracle worker." She complimented herself laughing. "Now we can go, and a whole seven minutes to spare." she pointed to the desk clock. "Plenty of time."

"No, not plenty. I'm getting ready to have a serious panic attack," I yelled, jumping up from the chair. I knocked it on its side. I rushed out the doorway where Jim is now standing waiting for us. "Reecie, you look a picture," he couldn't help tease, as I bared my teeth. "Relax bride. I've known you all my life, and I don't think I've ever seen you look more beautiful. Take a deep breath and make me proud."

"Bessie, you now ready to go?" "Yes, yes. you are both so pushy." She put on the shoulder strap of her purse and opened the apartment door. The hall itself is bustling with activity when Jim pulled up, and I fell out the back seat in a rush to get to the dressing room. Carla is already inside, complete with her wedding dress, and veil, and smiled when the door opened.

"About time," she teased then smiled at the look on my face. "Relax we still have almost an hour before the ceremony will start." "They have told me to relax no less than five times in the last half an hour." I wanted to yell and punch something just because I could. "Then take the advice." She crossed the room to place her hands on my cheeks which were getting redder by the second. "Your fine, your beautiful, and your about to get married," she kissed the right cheek, and rubbed it with her thumb.

"Thanks Carla. I love you." I hugged her, not wanting to get makeup on her dress or wrinkle it. "Where's Jeff?" "Down the hall getting dressed." I took off my T-shirt, and unzipped the cover, holding the dress. "Here, let me button it." It's Zeni standing in the doorway dressed in a pale peach satin floor length dress with matching heels. She had her hair pulled up in a chignon, and looked very elegant, and beautiful as always. "Thanks mama." I smiled and presented my back.

"Bessie did a wonderful job with your hair." She fluffed the bottom. "You're a picture." She filled my face with her hands and kissed me full on the lips. "Mama, you're a picture," I complimented, smoothing her dress. As always, she is beautiful. "I certainly am," Zeni laughed. "Your makeup looks nice." She turned my face left to right, examining it.

"That woman amazes me sometimes what she can do in so little time with so little effort." I put on satin white heels, so I am almost as tall as her. "Okay," Zeni clapped her hands. "We have about half an hour until the ceremony. Need me to do anything else for you?" I looked

The Way Life Used To Be

around the room, and it's a mess, but we could always clean it up once the ceremony, and reception are over.

We planned the reception to take place right after the vows were spoken, and the caterers are already set up so the guests could eat while they visited. "Not that I can think of," I said. I smiled at her. "Jeff should be ready soon." "I'll go check." Zeni left the room as Jeff was leaving the dressing room, panic all over his face. "I forgot the garter," he said. I grabbed his car keys from the coat rack in the hall-way. "Relax." Zeni rubbed his arm. "I can go get it, what store?"

"Dawson's Floral, Zeni, thanks, but I've got it." He patted her arm when I stuck my head out the door. "What's all the fuss about?" I asked. All you could see is the front, and one side of my hair. The doorframe still hid the rest of me.

"Your mom wants to run my errands for me. You look great by the way," he complimented, and came forward to kiss my cheek. "So beautiful. I'll be right back." He left the hall before either of us could object. Zeni turned to go back into the dressing room. "You know it's bad luck for the groom to see the bride before the ceremony begins." she chided, then smiled.

"He only saw my head. Bad luck doesn't play a part." I teased back. Mom smoothed the skirt because she needed something to do with her hands. She turned me around, so I am facing her, and two tears fell down her cheeks. "My baby," she whispered. "Let's get married." Carla watched as she is already dressed, and her own parents were waiting at the front row. Taylor came out of his own dressing room and headed to the alter to wait for her.

Jeff threw the car in reverse, and sped out of the parking lot, and headed towards Dawson's Floral, with a smile on his face, and dressed in his tux. While he was gone, Carla approached me, and held my face in her hands. "I'm so proud of you." "Thanks." I hugged her again. "You ready?" "As I'll ever be. Remember the routine?" I nodded. "To the tee. You, and Taylor will go first, then when you're done with your vows, Jeff will go up to the alter, and I'll follow with dad. That way we'll be at the reception line together." "You learn fast. Let's go."

We left the dressing room and walked down the hall. Jeff made it to Dawson's where the garter is waiting in a cooler. He planned on giving it to Keith before heading to the alter, so Reesa would have it in place by the time she walked up the aisle. Jeff swiped his credit card and grabbed the garter. He slipped his wallet in the back pocket of his slacks.

He'd leave the wallet in the glove compartment of the car when he got back to the hall.

Jeff left the store and headed across the parking lot to his car when a Black Camaro came speeding across the lot, bumped him in the back spinning him around, and knocked him down to the pavement head-first. The car sped off again, around the corner, and the driver gave himself another high five to the air as he disappeared. The sky is still a brilliant blue as Carla made her way down the aisle with her arm in her dad's smiling. Taylor is waiting, tall, and handsome, smiling just as wide, and held out his hand as she approached the alter.

I remained at the back, watching my friend get married, and dad approached on my left. "I will not cry." he whispered, leaning close to my head. "I forgot to bet you." I smiled up at him. "Then I'll be dignified and not remind you." He teased. "Like that'll work. Did you break your promise to Bessie?" "Not where she could see me. I waited until she had that first dance with Jeremy before the first tear fell. Until then I was a man."

"You're still a man." I giggled. "I bet you cry before I make it to the alter." I held up my left pinkie. "You're a very cruel daughter. You know damn well I will lose." He held my pinkie with his own. "Why can't we bet on something else. I know, no more Diet Pepsi for you. That's a sure win for me." "I'm drinking more water now." "You're a damn liar," he laughed into my hair. They announced Carla, and Taylor man, and wife, and turned to the crowd.

"Our turn, let's go." Jeff isn't at the alter yet, and I strained my face to see him. He is running a little late since he had to run to the store first. I wasn't wearing a garter and didn't care. I only wanted Jeff. Keith made it to half-way down the aisle before the first tear fell. "I lose." he whispered, and I looked up at him, wanting to brush it away. "I'm glad you lost this one." I whispered and squeezed his arm with my hand.

We made it to the alter, where again it was empty. No Jeff to take my hand. I started to panic. What if he suddenly changed his mind and bolted? I heard of people doing that at the altar, just leaving their intended. I never imagined it would happen to me. The preacher waited with a polite smile, and all three of us spun our heads around when my Aunt Carmela shouted from the hall.

"There's been an accident." She started running in her high heels in the grass towards the guests, and I knew, just like before, this time it's Jeff. I didn't want to stay there. Everyone crowded around me and

The Way Life Used To Be

hugged me hard. I just stood there with my arms at my sides. I said, nothing.

Aunt Carmella approached me. She looked so sad that she had to be the one to give the bad news. She is crying hard, ruining her makeup. Aunt Carmella is wearing a pink dress, and her blond hair is pulled into a chignon. "I'm so sorry" She said as she rubbed my arms. I nodded. I couldn't say anything back. She understood. She smiled softly and kissed my cheek before heading off to find the rest of my family.

I insisted on driving myself home. I had yet to shed a tear. I was surprisingly calm as I drove from the hall to my apartment. Once I parked in the stall, I lay my head back against the headrest and closed my eyes, remembering Paul. This is so similar. Except I am in a car this time instead of sitting on the pavement. Why is this happening? To lose both men in such a tragic way. Is this my fate? Destined to be alone for the rest of my life?

Eventually I shut off the car and pulled the dress out of the backseat heading to the apartment, dreading every step. The inside smelled musty suddenly, and I turned to ask Jeff to help me air out the place, and realized I am alone. No crazy dreams this time, but I am alone anyway. I made it to the bedroom where I threw the dress on the bed and shouted at it. "Why?"

I debated between leaving the dress alone and slashing it to ribbons. I left it alone while I faced the mirror. The same mirror I was staring through two hours before, having Bessie dote on me. I yanked the pins out, and the curls fell to my shoulders. Throwing them on the floor. I stared into the mirror at my image. "Never again." I shouted to the mirror, and threw a shoe at it, shattering it into tiny pieces.

"Never again. Never again." I yelled over, and over, crumbling to the floor, and buried my face in my hands. My eyes were still dry even though I am screaming to the wall. "Never again." My promise is going well for the first week, anyway. I'm determined to never fall in love again. This is a thousand times worse than Paul in every way possible. I lost my fiancé on our wedding day. How absurd that I wasn't even allowed to have a wedding.

Fate is so beyond cruel, I hated living right now. I remembered being able to say goodbye to Paul at the pond. I didn't even want to stop at the pond this time, even if it would help me get through the day. The ducks seemed to like my company, and I could talk to Jeff through the clouds like I talked to Paul, then maybe I'd have some closure.

Sandra Gutierrez

I didn't notice the sun, warm day or small clouds that appeared out of nowhere. I needed to go through Jeff's things and turn his key in. A task I am not looking forward to. I called Jeff's dad who is short with me on the phone. He did agree to meet me tomorrow afternoon to help me. I tried not to be offended when he hung up without a goodbye, but after this, I wouldn't ever have to see him again.

My stomach started growling, reminding me I had eaten nothing all day, so I jumped at the opportunity to get out of my apartment, and grab some takeout, and kick back, and watch a movie. Ten minutes later I am in the drive through of a McDonalds tapping my thumbs to the radio. Once I was back, I had just gotten a movie picked out, and my dinner on a plate, when Bessie walked in.

I was so thankful for company. I jumped up to give her a hug. "Smells good." She plopped herself on the couch and unbuckled David from the stroller, and lay him on the floor where he gurgled, and started kicking his legs. She reached over to take a fry from my plate. "So, how are things with you?" She asked. "Okay, I guess. I'm not looking forward to tomorrow." I ate a chicken nugget. "Want a bodyguard?" "Now there's a thought." I pointed a finger in her direction.

We ate in silence for a while. I bought extra in hopes she would come see me. I put the movie in and glanced at David who had fallen asleep on his back, and arms flung over his head. Once the food is gone, I tossed the empty bag in the trash and the plate in the sink. That is the nice thing about takeout food. Very little cleaning up to interrupt my day.

Bessie, and David left shortly afterwards after giving me lots of hugs. I knew she was there to check up on me, but I didn't mind it. I turned out the lights, turned off the TV, and headed towards my room.

Yeah, bitch. He smiled as she disappeared down a hallway. Going to say goodbye to your loser doctor. See how much good it does now that he's dead. Big bad doctor biting the bullet on his wedding day. Could life get any more perfect?

Slut is now alone. He wiped fake tears from his cheeks. I'm so sad you're all alone now. Now you've learned your lesson. We'll see. He made a mental note to keep a closer eye. She might need someone to help pull her through this, thus proving how much of a whore she is. As the saying goes, once a whore, always a whore.

True enough, Jeff's dad showed up right on schedule. I made it a point to be in Jeff's apartment ahead of time so he wouldn't pull any surprises. I grabbed his pictures off the coffee table and stuffed them into my pocket. "Well let's get this over with," Tom Hendriks said, after introducing himself. Tom reminded me a lot of, with the black hair sprinkled with gray. He wore a full mustache and looked miserable at the task ahead. He offered me a handshake, and we got to work, exchanging very little words.

It made me glad I thought if the pictures. I didn't think Jeff would have wanted him to end up with them. His dad surprised me when the apartment is empty by putting a hand on my shoulder and kissed the side of my head. "Thank you for making my son so happy." He said, before taking off to empty the trailer at a local goodwill.

I sighed with relief when he was gone and headed back to my apartment to put the pictures on my own coffee table. I took a moment to look at them, rubbing my thumbs over them lovingly. This would be hard, having them in plain sight day after day, but I couldn't stand the idea of them being anywhere else.

December 2003

It had now been over two months since the wedding day that turned out to be the very worst day ever in my life. I still had to shed a tear. Try as I might, I couldn't muster the strength to cry. Jeff is gone. I could very well face that fact. I still couldn't cry over him.

What the hell is wrong with me? I cried oceans of tears over Paul, and now I couldn't cry over my fiancé? I got out of bed looking at his side where he had slept, and his pillow remained untouched, like I am waiting for reality to set in. I would see him lying next to me, smiling, and ready to start each new day.

"This is fucking reality," I said, out loud. I'm sad that this is my life now. I meant what I said in front of the broken mirror. Never ever again would I fall in love. Two men that I loved were taken from me. I would not under any circumstances put a third one through it. I would be alone, and that is my reality. I dressed in black jeans, and a black, and pink striped T-shirt, intending to go to Starlights. It had however been months since I was there that I thought I might have forgotten how to run things.

I tried once to go back to work full time right after the funeral, and it backfired big time. I ended up spending the whole day in the kitchen wanting to cry. I was sent home by an equally sad mom. It nearly killed her to have to have done it, but it's for my own good. I wasn't doing a damn thing except for hovering over the sink sniffling. Mom told me to take a few weeks off to recuperate, and it turned into months. I spent my days alone, wandering the halls, and eating just enough that was necessary.

I looked down at my left hand and realized I had taken off the engagement ring. It would have meant so much to me to be going back to Starlights as a newlywed. If only I was insistent on getting the garter myself. It's a feeling of guilt I would never get over. It isn't until one day I was washing my hair and was getting ready to leave that I thought of Paul. He was visiting his uncle, and, on his way back to me when he was killed. Same with Jeff. He made it to the store, purchased the garter, and is on his way back to me when he is killed.

That is too close a coincidence. This had everything to do with me, and nothing to do with circumstance. It's time for another visit with Ted, but not today. Today I would hold my head high and face my family by working my full shift. It's almost six thirty, and I am bone tired from little sleep. I am determined to get through today. Why in god's name didn't it get easier? Everyone says, time heals all wounds, so why didn't the pain lessen?

I exhaled, grabbed my purse, and left the apartment which looked bare, and neglected now that Jeff isn't there. I drove to the restaurant. I let myself in the back door where Keith and Zeni were already at the counter, slicing tomatoes, and cheese, and laughing. She glanced at me "Feeling better?" "A little. I need to work again. My checkbook is mad at me." "Feeling a little empty?" "Just a tad, I need to go grocery shopping soon too."

I began slicing bagels. Zeni smiled as she returned to slicing the tomatoes and placing them in bins for the sandwiches. By the time it was noon, I was too busy to even think about Jeff. I was right. Staying in the apartment is depressing. This is just what I needed to start feeling better. I also realized I didn't forget what I was doing. I had convinced myself I would. It's like I had never been away.

At three, I said, goodbye to mom, who hugged me, and is feeling a little better herself. Once I am in my own car, the bravado is gone. I put my head on the steering wheel. I willed the tears to come just so I could start to feel better. Why couldn't I just cry this out? Even being held by mom didn't help like it did before. When I was in the hospital all those years ago, just feeling her arms around me started the tears rolling.

The Way Life Used To Be

I raised my head and decided to take a walk. The fresh air would do me good. I'd go grocery shopping some other time. I carried nothing, but my purse, and started walking towards the river. While I was enjoying the water, Trey is not having a good day. He lost a very important client because of the hard-economic times. She could no longer afford the fresh vegetables she had been ordering for her cafe for ten years.

He slammed the tailgate shut and cursed out loud. Thank god there is no one around as the cafe is located outside Fort Worth, and in a secluded area. He only hoped he, and Bret get some new customers soon, so their business could keep afloat. He is thinking too hard. One customer didn't break their business. It would be a different story if they lost several over the next few weeks with no new prospects. Then he would need to worry.

He tossed some empty bins in the truck bed and headed to Starlights. It was late in the afternoon, and he tried to deliver there by six thirty in the morning. Between the customer he lost and three other deliveries that were scheduled ahead of Starlights, he didn't make it there until four.

Zeni greeted him as always. She is never concerned about him. She knew he'd make it even if isn't first thing in the morning. Thank goodness she orders early, so when she is running low on supplies, she'd never have to substitute the menu. It's quiet this time of day with the dinner rush not yet ready to start. It should pick up within the hour.

For now, Zeni breathed a sigh of relief, and is in the kitchen measuring ingredients for tomorrows soup when the door opened, and Trey rushed in full of apologies. "No need to," she smiled in his direction. "It's too busy this morning anyway to concentrate on supplies. Hold on a second so I can get my list."

"Ok," Trey was relieved that she was so understanding. It's quiet in the kitchen, and he wondered where Reesa was. Usually she is here this time of day, but he had only dismissed that thought when Zeni appeared again with a notepad, and smile. He got his total, and she handed him the check. It's close to five, and customers were filling up, so she gave only a thank you, see you soon, and had disappeared into the dining room.

He left shortly afterwards to Carly's Market for his next drop off, and it's pushing six when he is finally done for the night. It's early for once as he normally wasn't done until seven thirty or eight. He shut off the truck and locked it. He headed for the farm so he could check on the animals.

Luther is sitting against the fence waiting for him. He petted his head through the fence, and he bobbed his head up, and down in greeting. "Hey buddy." He spread some corn on the ground which the chickens attacked. He smiled as they always acted like they were starving. He walked around to the pigs, and filled their trough full of slop, and leftovers from their dinners the last few nights. Their favorite is potato skins.

Once they started eating, he wound his way to the cows to say good night. When he got to the gate, he stopped walking. I was sitting on the ground in my jeans, and Albert is laying down with her head near the gate. I am rubbing her head from eyebrow down the length. Albert had her eyes closed and licked my hand. "Hey, how's it going?" Trey greeted entering the barn for the first time that day.

Bret is nice enough to feed them in the mornings. He started digging in a bag for some corn for the chickens and putting the kernels in a bucket. "You wouldn't believe the day I had," he wiped at sweat building on his forehead. "Up at four this morning, and it's been nothing, but go, go, go all freaking day long, and I just got done about half an hour ago. It's going on seven, and I'm exhausted. How're things with you?" He asked glancing at me. He smiled at Albert who looked to be in total bliss. Without waiting for an answer, he continued. "I grabbed a sandwich from Starlight's earlier. It surprised me not to see you there. Saw Jim though. He is all talk as usual."

I continued looking down at the cow and was silent. All that moved is my left hand as I continued rubbing the cow. "I'm talking to Albert," I said. "That doesn't surprise me. She likes you." He glanced at the cow, then back at me, pivoting towards the pigs. "Be right back." He stomped away while I sighed.

What the hell am I doing in Trey's barn. This is his place, not mine so why did it feel so right to be here? Trey returned moments later. "The guys are fine. Just wanted to check on things before locking up for the night. You okay?" He asked looking at me seriously for the first time all evening. "Yeah." I attempted a smile and started to stand up so he could finish. "Stay a while. Albert's obviously happy to have you around. I can say just about the same." He smiled squatting down beside me.

He drew his knees near his chest, and he rested his arms casually over them. "Jim's happy with Bessie." That made me smile. "Is she his current true love?" I enjoyed talking about other people. It's so much easier than trying to talk about Jeff. "You could have a point there." He pointed a finger in my direction. "When I got there, and ordered my dinner, Jim was sitting on a stool waiting for the kitchen to close for the night. Started right out by gushing about how perfect they are for each other. Wants to ask her to marry him already."

"Just the thing to make her run in the other direction." I advised, knowing just how devastated she is over Jeremy's not honoring his vows. "You could have a bigger point. I don't think he'll be taking that plunge anytime soon. I think he's just happy for the first time in his life." "I can honestly say the same about her." I smiled at him, and he reached over to touch my cheek with three fingers. That is my undoing.

I closed my eyes and sighed as tears started flowing down my cheeks. I am helpless to stop it and realized just then what he did for me that nobody else could, even in their best intentions. He got me to cry. He said, nothing for a while. Just stroked my hair, and I leaned into his side. "Just let it out," he whispered. "Let it go until there's nothing left to give."

Loud gulping sounds escaped my throat, and I buried my face in my hands. Trey closed his eyes and sat with me without saying a damn word. Just held me as the storm raged through me. I ended up soaking the side of his shirt, but he didn't care. "You're always welcome here, you know that?" He asked. "I didn't know where else to go," I said, once I got my voice again, and drew away from him.

He unlocked his fingers and kept one hand on my shoulder while I opened up to him. "I can't believe I ended up here." "I can. Albert has that effect on people. I guess I should say certain people." "Who wouldn't she like?" "My veterinarian." "Can you blame her?" "I guess not. She doesn't seem to realize he's there to help." "You're not saying it in the right words." I teased. My eyes were dry now.

"Probably not feeling better now?" "A little, I miss him." "I know you do. I can't say I've ever been in those same shoes, but I know you do." I studied him, realizing he knew what I'd been through. "I never officially met Jeff. I knew a lot about him, courtesy of Carla. She's full of information even when you don't ask for it."

"That she is, we were going to have a double wedding. He was killed by a hit-, and-run driver that same day." There, I said, it. "I know that too. Carla showed me her dress, and pictures of you in yours. You would have made a beautiful bride. She also told me how he died. Just like

Paul." "Just like Paul." I said, "I don't know what else to say right now." Trey admitted feeling at a loss for the first time all evening. "I don't know either." I said, and sighed, drawing my knees up, and folded my hands over them.

"Want to just sit awhile?" He asked. It's a full ten minutes before either of us said, a word. It's so nice. I looked at him, my head tilted. "Why is it you always know what to say?" "Gift I have, tell me about your day." "Well, there's not much to tell. I worked my full shift today, and then I came out here. I have to admit that right now is the highlight of my day." "That's pathetic, even from you. Come on. I'll walk you home."

I placed my hand in his and brushed myself off with my free hand. "My car's at Starlight's." "Then I'll walk you to your car." We started walking, enjoying the quietness as we made our way to Starlights. "Listen," he whispered, closing his eyes. I listened, trying to understand. "Do you hear it? The night, how soft it is." There isn't a sound except for the occasional car honking. Even the birds were quiet for once. "It's nice," I said.

"It's my favorite time of the day. When I'm done with the deliveries, and the animals are happy, and fed, I like to kick back at my house with a Coke, and just sit on the stairs doing nothing at all." "Not even a beer?" I interrupted, but he didn't seem to mind it. "Not even a beer. I like my quiet when I've had a long, hard day like today. It's nice to just drink a Coke and enjoy the evening." "I'm glad you don't party a lot." I smiled at him.

"Never felt the need for it. Next time Brad, and Jan have a get together, Jim said he's bringing Bessie. Wants to brag for the first time in his life." "As he should, she seems to be settling down, and I love them both. They can brag all they want." "Are you feeling a little better now?" "As always you know what I need before I do. When are you having your next get together?"

"Probably next weekend if all goes well. You should come too with Bessie, and Jim. That way you'll know someone and won't feel like the perpetual third wheel." He teased. "Ha, ha", I said, sarcastically. "Seriously, I think you'd enjoy it." "I would. They're nice people."

"The best. I never had a single doubt when I hired Bret to help build the barn. Before I met him though, I assumed he is a typical young lazy man who would have a coffee or cigarette break every five minutes, and not get anything productive done, and most of the work would fall on my hands. His first day there he picked up a hammer and started on the walls. Didn't mention a break once, and I had to force him to put down the hammer to get some lunch."

"Sounds like you judged before you met him." I observed making him chuckle. "I guess I did. Of course, I never told him that." "Did he stay hard working or did you have to kick his butt occasionally?" "He worked harder than I did. Once the barn is finished, he had these crazy ideas of buying horses after the cows, and chickens, so we could start making decent money." "I never met any horses?" I pretended to pout. "I never bought any. Cost too much and I have enough to do as it is. Would have been a nice touch though. I haven't ridden a horse in years."

"You used to?" He shrugged his shoulders. "A long time ago, I guess. Before we moved here, that's for sure. I must have been about five or six, maybe. We lived in Silver Springs then, and one of our neighbors had a huge pasture with several horses. Mom, and I would go riding by the Springs River in the summer, and sometimes take a picnic along. It's a lot of fun." "Your dad never went?"

He shook his head. "Not too often. Once in a while, he'd go with us, but he worked long hours at the mill, and didn't have a lot of spare time. It made mom, and I close though." "I bet. It sounds so nice." "I just wish we had more free time now, like we did then. I wouldn't change what we have now for anything though. It'd just be nice to have more time to enjoy nights like this one." He smiled down at me. We had reached my car, and it stood by itself in the parking lot. He left right after I let myself into the car. I breathed several deep breaths before I started it and headed back to the apartment.

July 2005

Summer can be full of joy or sorrow, depending on how you view things. I guess any season has that affect, but I think summer has the most influence. I viewed it as living. Living in the moment and being happy about it. It's what got me through and continues to drive me. Nothing much else does, that's for sure. It's been almost two years since Jeff died, and the pain of losing him is dim. I've had my family to pull me through. Although I've given up dating, it's turned out to be a positive pull in the right direction.

I am waiting for mom to show up as the menu is about to change once again, and she, and dad had made their announcement they were retiring. After years of hemming, and hawing she decided, and would stick with it, come hell or high water. "Hey baby," mom greeted, rushing through the doors, and joined me in the dining room. It's past closing, and almost eight o'clock, but we were both wide awake.

"What took you so everlasting long?" I teased her and smiled. She is still so breathtaking, that she didn't seem near old enough for retirement. While looking closer, I could see the fatigue wearing on her eyes. "Why do you stare at my pores?" She asked getting a root-beer from the fountain. "I stare at the whole picture. I see tiredness oozing out. What gives?"

Zeni sighed. "It's this place I guess." She looked around hating and loving it all at the same time.

She showed me her ideas, and I promised to come up with my own, and we would have another meeting next week. The kitchen door opened, ending this update as we saw Lisa with her older daughter by her side come through the swinging doors.

"Hi Nana" Natalie squealed running over to give Zeni a hug. She is a splitting image of her mother with the deep blond hair in two pigtails, and freckles everywhere. She loved Keith and Zeni like family and called Keith Grampy. Lisa sat in a chair hands folded in her lap while Zeni, and Natalie went in search of some cookies, leaving us alone. "So, what brings you by?" I smiled at her.

She used one finger to flip some hair behind one ear. She had straight hair, no bangs, and a serious frown on her pretty face. "I'm in trouble." Lisa sniffled as tears formed in her blue eyes. Her lips started quivering. I'd never seen her so upset in all the years she'd worked for us. "What could have happened?" I questioned, leaning forward to touch her arm. "My babysitter stole from me. Stupid bitch."

It would have been a laughable situation if she didn't wasn't on the verge of losing control. "Bitches are stupid." I agreed. "How much?" "One hundred dollars in cash." We had most of rent ready to pay, and I was naïve enough to believe she would never paw through my underwear drawer.

"I had another envelope in the safe, but I didn't have time to move the money from the drawer into the safe before Pete, and I went on a dinner date. We were celebrating our thirteenth anniversary, and when we got home, the bitch is acting nervous. She bolted as soon as I paid her."

The Way Life Used To Be

"She'd been watching the kids for a year now, and you'd think that is time to earn trust." "Sometimes there's never enough time." I advised. "Your telling me. Natalie seemed to like her too." "Come here." I stood up and held out my hand. She took it without question, and we walked through the swinging doors to the office. I sat in my chair and wrote a check for two hundred dollars. Handing it to her, I said before she could protest "Pay your rent and have a better anniversary date."

She got out a "The" Before she lost control. She buried her face in her hands. I hugged her tight and put the check in her pocket. Zeni, and Natalie were sitting at the bar eating cookies, and drinking milk. They both had smiles on their faces and acted like they didn't have a care in the world. I glanced at the plate and managed a small smile myself. The perfect evening snack, I looked from the plate, and met mom's eyes. Mom winked at me.

It wasn't until Lisa, and Natalie left in a much happier frame of mind that I realized I had made my first decision as co-owner, and it felt so incredible. When I was done for the day, and comfortable in sweats, I picked out a movie, and I lay back on a pillow thinking about today. I sighed and got up to make some microwave popcorn. In the middle of the popping the front door opened. I breathed a sigh of relief at Bessie standing in the doorway.

She had a huge grin on her face. "What are you doing?" She asked shutting the door and making her way to the kitchen where I stood at the counter. My elbows were on the counter, and l was waiting for the buzzer to sound. "Not a whole hell of a lot. I'm watching a movie. Want to join me?" "Love to." Bessie clapped her hands, and walked to the refrigerator, and helped herself to a bottled water. She walked to the couch and pointed to her water. "You want one?"

I glanced up. "I'll get it." I wanted to squirt in some flavoring. I found the cherry lime fizz is good. Bessie twisted open the top and walked to the window. The buzzer sounded, and I grabbed a bowl, and dumped the popcorn in. I tossed the paper bag in the trash. I glanced at the clock on the wall, and it's after eleven.

"Why aren't you home taking care of David?" He just turned two a few weeks ago and is a very busy toddler. Bessie giggled turning away from the window. It's very black except for the underground lights illuminating the water and making seem eerie. "Jim's at the house with mom, and dad. He told me to take a night off and is right now sitting in our kitchen feeding him. It is a challenging ordeal, but he's a natural, and a trooper too." She sighed and flopped on the couch.

"You've been taking a lot of nights off." I wondered out loud. She looked tired. "I wanted to stay home tonight with Jim, but I fell asleep in the rocker. Jim woke me up, and I was so startled. David was just waking up from a nap, and I was enjoying the peace. He smiled at me, and told me to come see you, and to take the night off. I'm not tired anymore, and so here I am." She spread her hands. "How have you been doing?"

I sighed and took a drink of my now red water. I reached for a handful of popcorn. "Better now. I met with mom tonight, and I have a much better idea of the changes she wants to make." I took a drink to wash the popcorn out of my teeth and threw the empty bottle in the trash. Once I am settled back on the couch, I pushed the play button on the DVD player. The movie started, and we sat comfortably against couch pillows, and watched.

That is the nice thing about sisters. I didn't have to say a damn word sometimes, and Bessie always understood. Once the movie is over, Bessie gave me a quick hug. She said, goodbye, and she'd see me soon. She wanted to get back home to David and relieve Jim. Three hours away is enough of a night off. Once I shut the door behind her, I locked it carefully remembering this time. I headed back to the bedroom to try again to sleep.

By four in the morning I was still wide awake and staring at the ceiling. The sun started poking through my window at six. I got up for the day without a single hour of sleep. Thank god I wasn't working at Starlights. I remembered that last time I worked without getting a decent night's sleep, and how many comments they made about my appearance. I wouldn't make that mistake again.

I however changed clothes from old black sweats to nice jeans, and a clean white T-shirt. I wanted to see Ted later. I still had suspicions that the Greg found a way out, and killed both Paul, and Jeff. I intended on proving that theory. I jumped in the car, rubbed the sleep from my eyes, and attempted to look presentable as I drove to Starlights.

I wanted a bagel sandwich first and didn't want to make anything at the apartment. After I ate, I would see Ted. By the time I made it to the parking lot, and shut the car off, it's close to nine. It isn't very busy. I'd just go in the back and have a quick breakfast. That way I wouldn't bother any of the customers.

The Way Life Used To Be

I got all the way to the prep counter before being spotted. "Hey baby," I smiled. "Mornin' mama. I know I'm not scheduled today, but I have errands to run. I'm just going to make a quick sandwich." I hurried to the refrigerator before I'm turned around by the elbow. "You can't sit in the dining room like the rest of the world?" "I'm fine in here mama. I don't want a big crowd right now."

"There's not exactly a mob out there. Just two couples, and they're just about done, anyway. Take my coffee with you. Get a drink, and I'll meet you out there in five minutes. We'll eat together." She smiled as she bustled me out of the kitchen, mug in hand. She started making two ham bagel sandwiches. I placed the mug at a corner table. I rushed to the soda fountain for a Diet Pepsi since I was out, and that also reminded me another trip to the store is in order before I headed for home.

"Sorry, honey," mom apologized, and set a tray filled with two bagels, and two fruit cups. "Sorry for what? I've only been waiting for a whole two minutes." I smiled selecting my sandwich and fruit cup.

Zeni took a drink of her coffee, then smiled at me. I was sitting there staring at my food, and not eating, "What's wrong?" "I have to do something later on today, and I'm a little scared." I started rubbing my hands over each other.

"Does it have something to do with Jeff?" She took a bite of her bagel. I nodded without speaking. I picked up my sandwich to take a bite and lay it back on the tray without eating it. "It has both to do with Jeff, and Paul. I need to go to Ted's office today." Zeni put down her bagel. "Why?" "I think Greg killed them. I will prove it." Zeni picked up the bagel again. "We would have gotten word if they released him. He still has a minimum of a year left before he's even eligible for parole. It isn't him honey."

I frowned as I took a drink of my soda. "I need to buy more of these. They were killed because of me, and by God, I'm getting answers." "It isn't you and never has been. It's two very tragic accidents closely related, but it isn't because of you." "Then how was I involved in both?" "By circumstance. I don't see how the same person who killed Paul, knew you were seeing someone else. Then is at the same store Jeff is, killed him, and still hasn't been caught. There are too many holes in that theory."

"There are, but I'm going, anyway. I'll see you later this afternoon." I gave her a kiss on the cheek and dumped the tray on the counter rack.

I am intending on heading straight to Ted's office. I'm trembling, but confident at the same time I would have my answer by the time I left. Just when I got ready to head out, I glanced over to see Jan sitting by herself eating an English muffin sandwich. I was going to wave as usual, but she beckoned me over, and patted the seat next to her.

I walked over there and sat down. I waited while she finished eating. "I just realized we've never had a conversation, but I wanted to introduce myself since Trey is such a fan of your family." "No need." I said, dismissing the introduction. "Trey's told me all about you, and Bret. It's nice to talk. Trey acts like you two are his proud children."

Jan laughed, and I could see why Trey liked her so much. She pointed to the doorway where both Trey, and Jim were coming through, and when they reached the table, Trey kissed her on the cheek. "Where's your better half?" "Already hard at work." She replied making them laugh. "Bret a hard worker?" Jim teased, earning a punch on the shoulder.

Trey turned to me. "And what brings you by on this fine morning? Aren't you off today?" I nodded. "I am going to see Ted in a while, get some answers." Trey made the mistake of frowning at me which caused me to feel defensive, even though I didn't need to. He could tell my mood changed as I got up without saying another word and left without a backwards glance.

He also looked miserable as he smiled over at Jan who is taking all this in, but she could see right through him. The man is over the moon. Jim however spoke up. "What the hell is wrong with her?" Trey shrugged. "I didn't do a damn thing." He knew he sounded defensive but tried to act like it's no big deal. Jim came along with Trey for the rest of his deliveries.

It's for the company mostly, and it got him out of his apartment where it's so depressing most of the time. Jim had plans with Bessie later today, but for now his day is free. He had full intentions of finding out the latest scoop with Trey. He is acting so different lately, and Jim was trying to put his finger on why. That scene ten minutes ago was tense, to say the least. He couldn't remember those two people ever having an uncomfortable moment before.

"Any hot dates lately?" he asked. May as well bite the bullet and get it over with. Trey only glanced at Jim with his right eye. He bared his teeth. "So many I can't keep count," he said sarcastically. Driving up Hotterman's Hill for his next delivery. There is a small mom, and pop restaurant on the top that had an excellent view of the river that is breathtaking. "Liar." Jim teased. "Seriously, who's the current love of your life?" "Seriously, no one." Trey answered sarcastically again. "I don't have time, and you know it." He is looking forward to Tuesday when he'd make his next delivery to Starlights. They were still one of his favorite customers. "You should start making the time. Look how many times I tried, and failed, and I'm finally happy."

"Glad someone is." Trey said, frowning, then reached over to squeeze his shoulder. "Sorry, I'm happy for both you, and Bessie, but Reesa's a different story. She had such a hard time with her fiancé's death and came out to the barn for some quiet time." Trey turned and headed up the hill.

"That is terrible what happened to him." Jim shook his head. remembering. "I heard this isn't the first time." "It isn't. Back when she is in college, her boyfriend was killed by a hit-and-run driver. Now this. It has to be killing her." "Close enough, you plan on being the knight, and shining armor come to rescue her from a life of loneliness, and despair?"

Trey only give that same look. "Reesa could do worse you know." Jim stated. "That she could. She also stated in no uncertain terms that she would never try again." "You could start by being her friend," Jim advised. He proceeded to pop open a can of Coke. "I've been nothing, but her friend for years now. It hasn't gotten me anywhere except for more friendship, and now a fight." "Bite the bullet and ask her out already. Nothin' better than some make up loving." That is something to think about.

I reached Ted's office and was promptly seated minutes later. When Ted opened it and found me sitting there looking like a lost puppy, he scooped me in his arms. "How are you doing honey?" "I've been better. You have time to talk?" "Always have time for you, come in. I don't have any sodas, but want an iced tea or coffee?" "Iced tea is fine." At least it isn't water.

His office changed since the last time I was in here. There is a huge oak bookshelf near the window, and oak cabinets replaced the gray filing cabinets with brass locks. It looked neater. "Looks nice in here." I complimented looking around and smiling. "I decided some time ago this place needs an improvement." "I'd say you were right. I like the new stuff." "Why thanks, now, what do I owe the honor of your visit? Miss me much?"

I giggled. He had a way of making me feel at ease. "Actually, I'm on a mission, and I'm hoping you can help me." I took a deep breath. "Love to if I can. What's on your mind?" He put down his pencil to give me his full attention. He folded his arms on the desk and smiled politely waiting. "I need to know if there is any possibility that Greg Oakes was released without our knowledge."

Ted looked shocked at my question, but not too surprised. He remembered when she first came to visit just over a year ago. "I'd know if they released him," he smiled his answer. "Trust me. I'd be the first to know., and yes, I've had those same thoughts myself." "Any chance there is a case of mistaken identity?" I asked. "I can check if it'll make you happy?"

I nodded, so he turned on the computer, and waited for it to warm up. "So, tell me what's new," he asked taking a drink of his iced tea. "Did you hear about Jeff?" "Yes, I did, your dad told me last time I walked into Starlights. It was about two weeks ago or so. You weren't there, or I'd have said, hello. I had an assignment that lasted almost a year way up north in North Dakota of all places. Here's a word of advice, never move there. Useless state with zip to offer. Is that what this visit's about?"

"Partly. I haven't seen you in a while, and now I know why. I wanted to say hello, and catch up, but I need some answers." Ted studied me a minute before realizing what I needed. I wanted to know if the killers were the same. The computer blipped signaling it's ready. "Well, I'll see if you're right, and if Greg is responsible. I'll have your answer in a minute. Is everything else going okay for you?"

I nodded. He typed in Greg's name. Gregory Thomas Oakes and came up with a match. "Well here it is." he turned the screen so I could see. As everyone, but me suspected, he is still in jail with fifteen months to go before he is eligible for the first parole. Just seeing his information is enough to bring back the shakes. I fought them off and read the information on the computer.

As they advised me, he is housed at Texas State, and the parole hearing is set for September 2006, fifteen months from now. It even stated his cell number A-2011H5. I felt better knowing he is still locked up, but disappointed at the same time. "I am sure it was him." "Like I said, so was I. However, you have your proof in front of you. Sorry honey, but he isn't the one responsible." I sat back slowly in the chair and took a drink of my iced tea. "Well thank you anyway." "Feel better for it?"

The Way Life Used To Be

I shook my head. "I thought I would. But no, I don't." "If I hear anything different, you'll be the first to hear it. Count on it. Don't be so sad though. I don't believe in the least this is the best thing that could have happened to you, and I don't for one second think this is Gods will. Someone is responsible for those deaths, and I only wish I was assigned to finding out who. I will keep you informed if I find out anything." "No matter how minor?" I asked, and he nodded.

I drove from his office and turned a corner to head to the grocery store. I'm getting a caffeine withdrawal in the worst way. Now that that task is done, I felt just a tiny bit better. At least it isn't Greg still haunting me with his ill-advised promise of getting even.

I stopped at Hankin's for more groceries realizing a baked chicken I made two weeks ago, is the only meal I bought in a while. My cupboards were so empty I'm depressed about opening them. I lived on takeout for the most part. I need to talk to Trey. Why he is so disapproving. I thought he was a good friend, but maybe I am mistaken about him. After all it's entirely possible to think you know someone like the back of your hand, only to find out you don't know them at all.

I shook my head and concentrated instead on the task at hand. Grocery shopping is not my favorite thing in the world. I'd rather get more takeout. All good things must come to an end though. My bank account had only five dollars in it. I however had over three hundred on my credit card. That would get me through until I got my paycheck on Friday. It's only Monday, and they were no good, anyway. Just ask Lorrie Morgan, I chuckled to myself.

I grabbed a cart. My body needed some serious fuel. My stomach agreed as it rumbled as I passed the deli and sniffed the fresh fried chicken. This time Sara is behind the counter, and there is only one customer ahead of me, ordering the 8-piece meal. Sara dug out chicken from the bin and placed them in a brown bag. She added a package of dinner rolls, side dishes of mashed potatoes, gravy, and coleslaw. It looked good. The lady who ordered the meal paid. She smiled a goodbye and left with the package dangling from one arm.

"Hey stranger," she greeted as she looked up, and saw me leaning against the counter with both elbows. I tucked my fingers under my chin. "Hey back," I smiled as I leaned forwards, and kissed Sara on the cheek. "What's new and exciting?" "Special on roast beef, and scalloped potatoes." Sara pointed to the whiteboard displaying the days specials. "Sound good?"

Sandra Gutierrez

I contemplated it for a second before shaking my head. "Not tonight, I have to be firm, and buy actual groceries this time." I pointed to the cart which held a dozen eggs, sliced cheese, bread, and a case of Diet Pepsi. Sara leaned forward to examine the contents. "Very healthy even for you," She giggled. "It's nice to see you out, and about. Are you starting to feel better?" I shrugged my shoulders. "A little, I guess. What are you doing tonight?" "Absolutely nothing. Mark's going to a movie with dad, so I have the place to myself. I'm looking forward to some peace and quiet." She slapped the counter for emphasis.

"Are you guys fighting?" Sara shook her head and scrunched up her nose. "Not at all. He's been closing every night, and so have I, so we have seen little of each other as it is. I thought I'd be looking forward to some time alone with him. He's been looking forward to some time away from the restaurant, I'm now looking forward to my own time. What are your plans for tonight? Want to come over to the house?"

"I need to finish shopping first. I have eaten nothing healthy for a week now. Fast food is getting old." I glanced at the cart. "How about we go out for one last dinner? After that you can start your health regiment. I'm off in half an hour." "You sure?" "Very sure, if you're up to it afterwards, you can come over to the house, and we can gossip." I laughed. "You always know how to make me feel better." I got out the scribbled list I had shoved in my pocket.

"I will finish, then I'll call you, and we can meet someplace. Just not Starlights. I want a new place." Sara thought for a minute, tapping a finger to her cheek. "I know." She yelled. "Eduardo's." It's a new Mexican restaurant near our old high school. "Sounds great. I'll meet you there at six?"

Sara glanced at the wall clock. It's close to five fifteen. "Sounds good. I'm so excited." She clapped her hands together causing me to laugh even harder. Yes, she had a knack of making me feel better. She hadn't even asked about Jeff, and that is fine. It still hurt think about him. I shook away those thoughts and concentrated on shopping. I ended up with two boxes of cereal, milk, peanut butter, and jelly, hamburger, spaghetti sauce, and rice along with the other stuff I had in my basket before I saw Sara.

I paid for them with my credit card. I lugged the three bags to the car where I shoved them into the trunk to get home. I wanted to unpack before heading over to Eduardo's. I am looking forward to an evening of company.

Chapter 16

It only took ten minutes to unpack my groceries. I glanced around at the growing mess, and dust growing in the corners. Tomorrow I'd do a thorough cleaning. For now, screw cleaning. I am going out to dinner. Another evening away from this depressing hellhole is the perfect solution. I felt bad calling my first home away from home a hell hole when just two years ago, it was heaven on earth.

Hopefully soon I'd feel differently again and want to come home even if I am coming alone. Once the food is put away, I changed my clothes from jeans to a silk wrap-around skirt, and white silk blouse. No need to dress sloppy as we were going to an upscale restaurant. It's no black tie by any means, but I felt a little better dressing, and added blusher, and eyeliner. I am looking so pale.

I snapped on the lid to the blush and placed the wand back in the bottle. I shut it and carried both items from my bedroom to the bathroom and dumped them in a wicker basket I placed on top of the toilet. It's full of hair clips, ponytail holders, lipstick, and other makeup.

By a quarter to six I am ready. I shut the door with a smile, and headed to the restaurant, calling Sara on the way. She said, she is already at her house, and would meet me inside. We'd get there about the same time. I parked the car at five to six and headed inside where I'm promptly seated by a friendly hostess, and two glasses of ice-water are placed at either side of the booth.

I thanked her and waited on Sara before ordering any food or drinks. They decorated the restaurant in black, and gold, and gave it a very warm feeling. "Hey again." Sara slid into her seat and grabbed her water. "I'm so thirsty." She drained half the glass and placed it on the table a little too noisy. "Your right on time." It's barely past six, and Sara had run from Hankins, to home to change, to the restaurant, and was still out of breath.

She however looked beautiful with her hair pulled back in a French braid. She wore an ankle-length navy-blue cotton skirt and matching shirt. She had a silver cross necklace Mark bought her on their first anniversary around her neck, and it glowed from the overhead lamps.

"I'm glad. I busted my ass getting here." She clamped a hand over her mouth. "Am I not supposed to swear in here?" she whispered and made me giggle. "I don't know or even give a damn right now," I smiled running my finger along the edge of the glass of my water. "What's on your mind?" "I had a visit with Ted this afternoon. I was sure I'd find the answers I was looking for, but nothing happened. I'm not feeling so happy right now."

"I'm sorry, I wish I could find them for you," she reached over to rub my hand. "That's not the only thing bothering me. I think Trey, and I are having issues." I told her what happened. "It's perfectly fine, even healthy to have arguments." Sara advised. "I don't know how to handle a fight with a man." I admitted.

"Speaking from experience, and this is not regarding Mark. He would never lay a hand on me. Probably wouldn't ever think of it. My father didn't know how to resolve issues using words. His fist is far more effective. I learned how, and when to shut up. I could feel the anger building, so I removed myself from the situation. No child, man or woman should know how that feels." She stopped for a minute to take a drink of her water.

"Trey doesn't hit. Neither with words nor fist. He doesn't have it in him. I think it's a misunderstanding, and you're the one who left without talking it through. Trey has been there for you, talking through every emotion you had, and he's still there waiting to take more. Talk it through," she advised.

A blond waitress came bustling up to the table, full of apologies for keeping us waiting, and asked to take our orders. "I'll have a fully loaded burrito with refried beans on the side." Sara said, handing over her menu. "I'll take a chicken enchilada without beans." I smiled at the waitress and handed over my menu. "Drinks?" "Iced tea for both of us." Sara answered, and the waitress smiled, and hurried away, only to return minutes later with our food.

"What's new with Bessie?" She took a bite of her burrito. "I haven't seen her in quite a while." "Bessie, and Jim are still together, and she claims she's in love." "She divorced yet?" "I think she's filed, but nothings final yet. I think they have to have some waiting period to make sure this is what they both want."

"She moved in mom, and dad's right after the baby was born, and I'm not sure why she's still married, unless she doesn't want to take the final step, and just end it all." I finished my enchilada, and pushed the plate towards the center of the table. "This is something that takes more time. I've never been in her shoes, and never will. I do however think Jim is much better for her in all ways." Sara finished her burrito too and shoved her plate towards the middle. "That is the best." She sat back and patted her stomach. "Yes, it is."

The waitress came to take away our plates. We both declined needing dessert. We paid our own bill and stepped out into the starry night. It's close to eight, and neither of us felt tired. "What do you want to do now?' Sara asked placing her shoulder strap of her purse over her left shoulder. I shrugged my shoulders, not knowing what sounded good on a Monday evening.

"Want to see my apartment?" I asked realizing she had yet to visit me. I chalked it up to being too busy. "Sure. I need to stop by the house first though, and change. These shoes are killing me." She flipped out a foot and shook it. The shoe landed near the wall ending up upside down. She left it where it is. "Those don't look in the least bit comfortable," I agreed. I got into my car, and Sara got in hers, and I followed her to their house where it's very dark, and Mark is still at the movie.

They were renting a one-bedroom house, and it is cozy with the living room right by the front door. They had a shabby plaid couch with two end tables, and a rocking chair. Simple, but they loved it. The kitchen is neat, and clean. Sara learned from her years at Hankins how important it is to keep a clean area and extended it to her own housekeeping.

She disappeared into the bedroom with an apology over her shoulder, and I wondered into the kitchen, and peered over the sink. The backyard is lit only by the light from the kitchen window. It only showed about a quarter of the yard. It isn't much, but Mark had bought a barbeque grill two months ago. He placed it on the back patio so they could enjoy dinners outside when it isn't raining.

They had yet to have a barbeque, but Sara was planning to have one, and invite the whole family. That gave her an idea as she is replacing her sandals with tennis shoes, and jeans. She'd mentioned to Mark in the morning to invite Trey too. Sara tied the shoelaces and quickly left the bedroom. She wanted to see the apartment. "Ready to go?" She asked turning off the living room lamp.

I turned from the window and smiled. "Sure, I like what you've done with the house." "Mark, and I painted the kitchen two months ago. I hated that puce green color that is so popular in the seventies. I like it much better now, don't you?" It's now a soft baby blue, and she bought matching window treatments to go with it. It's a lot warmer looking, and both her, and Mark now enjoyed cooking in it.

"It looks brighter in here." I complimented, and we stepped out so Sara could see my place. I equally knew how messy my own place is compared to Sara's and hoped she wouldn't be too judgmental. I used the key code, and the steel gates swung open. I parked in my usual spot, remembering with a smile, I did lock the door before leaving for dinner. Small accomplishments.

Sara followed me in, and squealed the minute we were inside, and the front door is closed. "It's so cute," She gushed, and rushed to the kitchen to investigate. She ran her hand over the countertops clean for once. "You must love cooking in here." I looked down at the spotless counters. "It's okay." Sara swung her head around after peering in the cupboards. "Just okay, I'd love it."

"I have to admit I don't take advantage. Look at my garbage for proof of my eating habits." I pointed to the garbage full of takeout boxes, and bags. Sara peered in. "Not exactly healthy choices." "I haven't been feeling my best for a while now. I did however make an internal promise to myself to better my habits. Which is why my cupboards are thanking me for the food I have generously stocked them with?"

"I think you should spend more time at the house with me, and Mark. Being alone can't be good for you." "I may take you up on that. I thought when I first moved in that I would love having an extra bedroom I could eventually decorate, for an office or guest bedroom or something. I haven't touched it since. I'm thinking of moving again. This isn't as easy as I thought it would be."

"I'd give it a little more time. Get yourself a roommate or something." "Now that's a thought. A stranger sharing my digs, I don't think so." It might be nice for a while to have another person to talk with, but this is my place. I didn't want a stranger in it. "Just a thought." Sara smiled and headed to her bedroom. "Mind if I'm nosy?" "Not at

The Way Life Used To Be

all." I followed her into the bedroom. I tossed the comforter over the bed.

I had shoved on the floor that morning, and I fluffed the pillows while Sara rummaged through the closet. "This is awesome. A walk-in closet." I smiled, and grabbed two blouses, and skirts from the floor of the bed, and shoved them on the closet floor. "Don't be offended about my mess. I haven't wanted to clean in a while." "You don't want to see my closet. I think there are still clothes from when we first moved in heaped on the floor." Sara explained backing out of the closet. "I spend most of my time making sure the living room, and kitchen are always presentable in case company presents itself. My bedroom is a different story. I'm glad if the bed is made."

I smiled in agreement. "I see your point." "I'd better get going." Sara said, glancing at her watch. It's close to nine and getting late. "Mark should be home now. Think about what I said, about Trey." She advised. "I'll think it through. Drive safely." Once again when the door shut, and I was alone. I wanted to leave. I couldn't expect Bessie to come every night to keep me company until it's time to go to bed. I had to be my own best friend at times like this.

I could have called many people, but the only person who came to mind, that I wanted with me is Trey. God, I wanted his arms around me again. He is so caring, and nonjudgmental. I wondered over to the living room window and pressed my face against the sill. I liked the coolness. The pool is still open, and I realized I had never used it the whole time I'd lived here.

There isn't anyone around which would be perfect for me. I'd enjoy a good swim, then maybe I could sleep tonight. I smiled and rushed to the bedroom. I changed from my skirt to a one-piece red swimsuit with a black slash that ran from the left shoulder to right hip. It's cute, and I got it several years ago, but hardly ever wore it. Shorts, and t-shirts were the normal dress for the river swims, but this is different. I am a grown up now, and time to alter my wardrobe a little.

I grabbed a towel from the bathroom and rushed out the door. I ran down the stairs, and across the lawn to the weight room, which is also empty. It's Olympic sized and glowed from the in-ground pool lights. I unlocked the gate with my key and placed the towel on a lounge chair. Even though it's after nine, it's still so hot outside.

I dipped a foot into the water, and it's still warm. I hurried to the twelve feet end and did a quick surface dive into the water. I am right.

It's a little cool. It felt delicious on my skin. I swam using a breast-stroke, to the shallow end where there were a set of three steps leading out of the pool. I sat on the bottom step to catch my breath. I realized how out of shape I am becoming even though I had gained a little weight. I am still thin, and not very attractive in my opinion, but I didn't care right this minute.

I hopped up from the step, and swam back, and forth three times before coming up for a rest. The diving board looked so inviting, but I'd use it next time. I also made an internal promise to myself that I would use the pool for at least three days a week, and the gym too. I'd get in shape in no time.

I climbed out of the pool, dripping wet, and spread the towel on the lounge chair stretching out to enjoy the evening. I closed my eyes, and breathed deeply, smelling the apple blossoms from nearby trees. This is the life I thought to myself. After a few more minutes, I got up shivering. It's almost ten, and the pool area would close in the next few minutes, anyway. That is okay as I'm now completely refreshed.

I grabbed my soaking wet towel, and climbed up the steps, into the exercise room, and was tempted to use one of the walking treadmills, but walked on past, still promising myself that I would use it soon. I opened the door and was back into fresh air. I rushed back to my apartment, growing colder by the second. The night air felt so good when I first left the pool, but now is growing chillier, and clouds started coming in.

I let myself in, and changed clothes into sweats, and a T-shirt. I found it on the bottom of the closet along with the rest of the mess. I settled down on the couch for another movie, and popcorn. I didn't have to be at Starlights until nine, so I had plenty of time, and wasn't tired. Not after that swim anyway.

I felt so refreshed, and better now that I was in water again. It didn't compare to the river, but still. I thumbed through the DVD's expecting Bessie to come barreling through the door, but it remained closed. She is doing just what I suggested and spending more time with David.

Pretty Woman is a nice choice. Old, but good. I stuck it in the player. I grabbed my popcorn and didn't even bother this time to dump it in a bowl. The bag would do fine this time. A fizzy water completed my dessert, and I settled down to the quiet, and watched.

I didn't realize I fell asleep until it was almost midnight, and I was slumped over the edge of the couch with one leg on the floor. The

The Way Life Used To Be

blanket is bunched around my ankles. Half of it is on the couch and half on the floor. I shut the DVD player off and decided what the hell. I didn't want to make the short trip from the couch to my bed which beckoned me. I grabbed the blanket off the floor, spread it around me again, and settled against the pillow. I smiled. It's a good evening.

Yeah, he thought watching her from the pool where he stood for the last three hours. She had no idea she is being watched while she spread her slutty legs in the pool, touching herself while she pretended to swim. He had followed her every moment until she lifted herself up to touch herself yet again on the lounge chair. He had gotten excited as he imagined her wetness as he was gliding inside of her. Just like he saw Jeff do from the living room window. Once a whore, always a whore he always said.

He'd watch closely. Surely, she'd be moving on soon. That kind always did. He'd be waiting. He is always waiting.

The sun isn't as bright in the living room as it is in the bedroom, so I didn't have to squint my eyes against the glare. I should switch locations. My bedroom could be out here, and the living room cramped into the bedroom area.

Now that is a thought, I chuckled to myself. I pulled myself up off the couch. I was not enjoying the sore muscles that accompanied it. My back, and legs were screaming as I limped to the bedroom to find a suitable uniform. Charley horses were already developing. I headed to the bathroom where a nice hot shower would rub some soreness away.

I stripped off the sweats with pleasure, and stepped into the steam, thankful for hot water. I washed and conditioned my hair. Once the soap was washed away, and I turned off the water, I dressed in black jeans, and a short sleeve white blouse. the charley horses already diminishing.

I stepped out of the bathroom, and glanced at the desk clock, realizing it's almost eight thirty, and I had to rush to brush and braid my hair before grabbing my purse. I ran out the door. I however congratulated myself when I pulled up, and it's still five minutes to nine.

Thank god for being on time. The kitchen is empty, and I loved it that way. Even though I loved my parents to death, I sometimes loved silence more. I walked straight to the refrigerator, and pulled out roast beef, and turkey. I spun at the door opening. Trey is by himself for once, and it would have been the perfect time to make peace.

However, when I glanced at him, he was concentrating on the wall. He fixed his gaze several inches above my head. He was leaning against the counter with two crates filled with eggs, and potatoes. So, it's to be all business, I thought. I got the check book. "Fifty-six even." He placed the notebook, and pencil back in his pocket without a word, and turned to leave.

He changed his mind at the doorway and turned half-way around "Did you get your answer?" I glanced up without a smile and shook my head. "I know you feel it's Greg who did the deed, but...." I interrupted. "It's him." I said, pointing a finger at his chest. "it is. I know it, but Ted said, his stupid ass is still in the joint. I don't feel, any better, and I know Greg did this."

Trey sighed wanting to say the right thing to make her feel better, but if Ted isn't convinced, there is no way it's Greg. "You've been with two different men...." I interrupted again, jumping off the stool, and shoved him. I shoved him away from me. I could tell it shocked him, and hurt, but it didn't stop the words from escaping my lips. "So that makes me a whore? Two men in my entire life doesn't make me the town slut. How dare you?" Tears started forming in my eyes, but damn if I would break down in front of him. Screw him. He isn't my friend if he thought that about me.

Trey looked like he is about to lose it himself. He didn't fight like this, and his face turned hard right before my eyes. I'd never since the day I met him saw it happen, and I had to admit it's scary, and arousing at the same time. "Don't interrupt me again," he stated. "Listen, and listen good, because right now you're on a one-track thinking mode, and you need to let that go. I never once thought you were loose. I said, you've been in two relationships, and didn't see either one prosper into more. I'm sorry you lost them, but if Ted doesn't believe it's Greg, and he'd be the first one to tell you if he did, then it has to be someone else."

I didn't respond. Tears started flowing against my will. I turned away from him. I wandered into the dining room and left him by himself. The fight left me as fast as it entered. I swung right back through the doors to find Trey still there, however he is about ready to leave. "Trey. I... I" I sighed and ran my fingers through my hair.

He could see the change. "It's okay." He whispered and smiled at me. Apparently, we were over our first fight, and I didn't deserve him. Bessie is right when she said, Trey is too good, years ago. I started prepping ingredients like I am supposed to be doing an hour ago. "So, what's new, and exciting?" he asked already forgetting the last two days. He leaned his back against the counter as he'd been doing for years and crossed his arms across his chest like he didn't have a care in the world. "You look out of breath." I said, lifting out the slicer from a cupboard under the counter.

He shrugged his shoulders. "I'm caught up now. I usually try to make it to your restaurant no later than seven, but I had three deliveries all scheduled before eight, so here I am. I have to be at Hankins at nine thirty." He glanced at his watch, but it's only nine ten, and Hankins is only two blocks down. He had plenty of time, and the owner never minded when he is running behind schedule. If only all his customers were that flexible. "For produce?" I asked placing the roast beef on the slicer and selected 1 for the thinnest slices.

"That, and pork. They picked up pork chops, and ribs from our farm a year ago, and they're packaged in the cooler out in the truck." He nodded towards the door. "They also placed a weekly order for blueberries, and corn on the cob. I guess sometimes blueberries are scarce." "Not at your place." I smiled getting out a pan to heat some Au jus sauce for French dip sandwiches. "I guess so," he smiled. "It took almost three years before our blueberries were good enough to sell. The first year is hard little lumps even at full season."

"What was the results the second year?" "More of the same. A few more productive berries, but still not good enough to sell. It wasn't until the third year we could. By that time, we were ready to rip out the plants, and heave them. They finally grew like they were supposed to." "Then I guess it's good you didn't give up. Those are my favorites even though the raspberries are mom's." I smiled, as I measured water, and Au jus mix. "Yeah. She told me that a few years ago. I take it you guys still offer the fruit, and berries cups?" "Yes, we do. I thought you still knew that. We haven't changed things that much."

"It's been a while. I haven't been able to come here for a meal since before you guys updated the menu. I thought she might be still using them for her pies. It's been good for our business, and we've had steady deliveries all summer, and fall so far." "Then it's understandable. How're Albert, and Luther doing?" "Still good. Luther's the same although he now has four girlfriends. I'm not sure if he even cares. Albert's pregnant again. She's due next month, and she's getting fat, and moody."

"Luther's a polygamist. I guess it's no different for them than it is for us. You have a veterinarian coming for the delivery?" I put the measuring cup in a drawer, replacing it with a plastic spoon, and started stirring the sauce with as we visited. He shook his head. "I tried the first time she delivered. She almost bit the poor guys arms off when he reached over to help her push the calf out. He ended up bouncing back on his butt in the mud and claimed she is too vicious to continue assisting. "

"He left without another word so, I ended up crawling on the ground, and delivered the calf myself." He looked proud at that. He had full intentions of helping her this time around too. I looked at him, smiling. I could hear the proudness in his voice. "Was she pregnant when I came to visit?" "Yes, she is close to seven months. She just didn't look it because she was laying down with you." "I didn't even notice. I was too busy thinking of other things." "I doubt she'll hold it against you."

"I think I just needed some one-on-one time with her." "She's good at that." He backed away and grabbed the crates off the counter. "Do you want to come, help with the delivery?" I smiled but didn't bother answering. He didn't need one. "I'll call you when she's close to delivering. That way you can be there for the whole thing?"

"I can't think of anything I'd rather do." I tore off a piece of paper and wrote down my phone number. "Yeah, I might want that," he smiled, and placed the note in his front pocket. Of all the things he normally lost, he didn't want this to be one of them.

"Don't forget to call me. Promise.?" I asked. "Promise. I should be going." he smiled as a goodbye, and I turned back to the lunch meats. I am giddy, happy, and excited all at the same time. It isn't even sex that made me that way. It's simply looking forward to seeing him again. I still felt horrible about yelling at him. Trey obviously isn't used to it, but he held his temper.

I finished slicing turkey, and placed both the roast beef, and turkey in containers. I snapped them shut and finished stirring the Au jus sauce. I grabbed a loaf of hoagie rolls and sliced them as mom poked her head in the kitchen. "Can you help here for a while?" She withdrew her head, and I grabbed an apron, and pad, and went to take some orders.

By noon, it had slowed down enough that I could escape back to the kitchen to finish making sandwiches and think about Albert. It might be fun to help deliver her calf. Surely, she wouldn't kick her legs at me. I put the sliced hoagie rolls on a sheet, and placed some sliced roast beef on them, with some sliced mozzarella cheese, and put them under the broiler.

The Way Life Used To Be

Once the cheese started bubbling, I withdrew the sheet from the oven. I folded the rolls and poured Au jus sauce in plastic bowls. There were five orders to fill, and this was the first-time mom was letting me fill them without her help. It's a test, and I'm determined to pass it.

I placed the sandwiches on plates and added potato salad to three of them. I added macaroni salad to the other two, and five bowls of fruit cups. I carried all five plates in both hands, and arms. I placed them on the serving counter and pounded the service bell. I shouted, "Orders up." I scooted back into the kitchen to make two barbeque chicken sandwiches, and a fried pork sandwich. The orders kept coming, but I held a steady pace. I was sweating rivers by the time there was a break in orders. I flopped myself on a stool and drank ice-water without gagging. I was that thirsty and didn't even want to grab a soda this time.

That is where I am with my arms folded, and my hands covering my face when Zeni walked in, all smiles at me. "Well done," she complimented, and joined me on a stool. She handed me a glass filled with Diet Pepsi. "I thought you could use this," she smiled, and scooted the glass towards me. I drew my hands away from my head and smiled at her.

"Thanks mama. I'm not used to this." "Takes time, you should have seen me the first month we opened. It's just myself, and Keith. He was in charge of the dining room, so the preparation fell on my shoulders most of the time. I had customers yelling their heads off when their orders were wrong. No amount of apologizing fixed it. There were times I wanted to fling their plates right in their faces. They were so mean, but I took it. I took it with a smile."

"They couldn't see my baring teeth with my mouth closed, but it still gave me small satisfaction." She took a deep breath and a drink of her iced tea. "I take it I had a much better first day?" "I'd say so. Look over here." She pointed to a pile of plates in the sink. "All empty." I leaned over to inspect and smiled. "I guess they liked my cooking." I drew back on the stool. "Or more accurately your cooking. Trey was here earlier. I wrote out the check for the produce."

"Thanks. I usually do that chore, but we were hopping out there." "Got to take over sometime. He invited me to the farm to help deliver a calf. His favorite cow Albert's about to give birth." "Sounds messy, tell me how it goes." Zeni said. She picked up the empty glasses to place them in the sink. "Will do." I jumped when we heard the bell ring. "Back to work." I smiled, slipping off the stool, and grabbed three orders off the rotating post.

We got right to work, and it was six thirty before we were done for the day. I threw my apron in a bin, to be washed. I washed the dishes, and had the floors swept when both Zeni, and Keith came into the kitchen to help finish. "All done." I smiled, and placed the broom, and a dustpan in the storage closet, and turned to face them. "Busy day today."

"It sure was." Keith answered grabbing the keys from the holder on the wall. "You coming to the house?" "Sure. I'll follow you there." Again, I was so thankful not to be going home alone. Plus, I wanted to talk with Bessie. It had been a while since we had a heart to heart. I wanted to see how it's going with Jim. I hadn't heard of any dramatic breakups from either parent, so I assumed all is still going okay.

I locked the dining room doors then the kitchen. I got in the car and headed towards their home. The living room is dark, but there were lights on in the kitchen when I opened the door. I didn't feel like talking to mom, and dad just yet. I ran up the stairs to Bessie's room where the door is opened. She sat at the rocker with her eyes closed and is rocking David. He had his eyes closed, so I whispered hello so I wouldn't startle her.

"Hey you," Bessie opened her eyes. She knew it was me before I said, anything. "What's going on?" I asked sitting on the bed. I decided not to tell her about my fight. As much as I loved her, she is a gossip, and this is sure to be spread. I didn't want to take that chance. "It's just about bed-time. Jim's downstairs talking with mom while she makes dinner. I wanted some quiet time before I headed down there. You hear about Sara's dinner plans for tomorrow?"

"No, I had dinner with her last night, and she said nothing. What is she planning?" "Some big barbeque. She phoned this morning to invite everyone, and it's at seven tomorrow night. You going to make it?" She turned her head, so she was looking at me face to face. "I'll wait until I talk to her myself." I said. "You don't need to. We're all going. Even Jim wants to, so it's all set." Bessie crossed her other leg and resumed rocking.

"I'll still wait. I ran the kitchen by myself today." I am still proud of that fact. "And how was it?" "No catastrophes. Everyone lives." "Well that's an accomplishment in itself." Bessie complimented and got out of the rocker to put him in his toddler bed. "It's hard, exciting, and I am very proud of myself. I even had time to clean the kitchen." "Want to continue your accomplishments by cleaning this room?" Bessie gestured around the room with her free hand.

"I'll leave that lovely task to you." I smiled and got up from the bed. "I'll see you downstairs." I pecked Bessie on the forehead. "I'll be there soon. He's almost asleep." I smiled as I headed downstairs, and into the kitchen where I found mom at the counter giving tips to Jim. They were bent over the counter talking, and oblivious to everyone else including Keith who is at the stove stirring. "Hey," I greeted coming into the kitchen.

Only Keith raised his head and turned it. "Bout time Baby. What took you so long?" "Visiting Bessie upstairs. She's putting David down for the night." I scooted further into the room, and grabbed a wooden spoon, and began stirring the spaghetti sauce. How my parents could put together a dinner in less than half an hour always amazed me, even though they did it for a living for the past twenty years.

"She thinks it's for the night. I swear that child still doesn't know the difference between day, and nighttime." Keith smiled even though he is exhausted every blessed night. He loved his grandson, but this is asking a lot of them. "It'll get better soon. Bessie thinking about getting her own place?" "She has said, nothing. First things first though. She needs a job, a good paying job then childcare before she can think about getting her own place. That's a lot to handle all at once." Keith turned down the burner and got a bag of spaghetti noodles out of the cupboard.

"I guess I didn't think of all that. I don't think she has either. Has she even been looking for a job?" I asked taking the meatballs that were placed on a paper towel and added them to the sauce. "A little from our computer in the office. Did you know that's where she, and Jim spent most of their time before you guys went to Big Al's? That dance isn't just the beginning of their relationship." Keith said.

Zeni, and Jim were still bent over another counter by the sink, and not paying the least bit of attention to what we were talking about, although we kept their voices normal. True to dad's word, David ended up joining us for dinner, and smeared spaghetti all over his face. Very little made it to his mouth, but he enjoyed himself anyway.

It's close to eight when I arrived home and was looking forward to a quiet evening. I was still so excited at what I did at Starlights earlier today, but the excitement is dimming already. I knew I could do it, and that is enough to make me want to do it again, and again. Working in the kitchen is a hell of a lot better than being stuck in the dining room taking order upon order, with a plastic smile on my face.

It's also nice to hear mom, and dad were retiring after the first of the year. I had six months to prove myself and am off to a good start. I'd be there at six thirty tomorrow, and mom would do nothing but oversee my breakfast preparations now that I nailed down a normal lunch rush.

The thing about breakfasts though is that they were unpredictable. You could never tell from one day to the next if it would be slow, semi busy, or wall to wall. I am almost hoping for a wall to wall tomorrow just so I'd know what it's like. On the slower mornings I'd have a chance to just breathe. I tossed the leftover spaghetti mom prepared for me in the refrigerator. I'd have it for dinner tomorrow night. Having nothing else to do, I checked the answering machine. No messages, I was scrubbing the counters in the kitchen.

The phone rang just as I turned away, so I grabbed it without thinking, and said, "Hello?" "Hello," It's Sara in her normal sing song greeting. "What's happening?" "Not much. I just wanted to call and catch up. Mark, and I had the best evening. I tried a new recipe we saw on some cooking show, and it turned out well. I'm just cleaning it up. Mark left to go to the store for tomorrow night." "What's for tomorrow?" I asked. "We made use of our backyard; we're having a barbeque.

It's only eight thirty, and early for once, but I didn't want to go to bed yet. I threw the couch blanket over my legs, and set the glass on the end table, so I could lay back, and continue talking

"Mom's making a potato salad which I'm very grateful for since that isn't on my list of recipes, I'm willing to try. Plus, she's so good at it. Dad's making some of his deviled eggs, and Bessie, and Jim are attempting to make strawberry shortcake for dessert. I'm not giving it too much hope on that though. So, there's not much left to bring, but don't let that stop you." She grabbed a bowl she had used to make the fettucine sauce and started rinsing it. "Sounds like a lot of fun. I'd feel bad though not bringing a damn thing. I'll make something." I offered.

"Baked beans. Is that too hard?" That is Sara's suggestion as she put the bowl in the cupboard. "Not at all. I even have a recipe. I'll get the ingredients tonight." I am getting excited about this. "You don't have to, this late. It might not be safe." Sara advised, and started drying the glasses, and putting them in the cupboards. "The suns still out." I said.

"Did you hear the latest gossip about Jim, and Bessie.?" I asked. "Nope, haven't talked to them other than to tell them about the dinner. Did they have a fight?"

"A big one. Right in the middle of tonight's dinner. We were all sitting at the table enjoying spaghetti, and Jim asks her in front of everyone for her to move in with him." "Already?" Sara interrupted. "How long have they been together?" "Less than two years, it's been a while, but she said it's too soon to move in together. She pissed him off. Drama at the dinner table."

"Did they kiss and make up before dinner ended?" Sara asked. "Not exactly, we were all just about done, and had lost our appetites by then, anyway. We took our plates to the sink and left the room. We heard every word while we gathered in the living room attempting to watch a movie. We ended up listening to them instead. It was very heated for a while, and I don't think I've ever seen Jim that mad before." "He did nothing wrong did he, like hit her or anything?" Sara sounded surprised she would even think it. For as long as she'd known Jim, and it went back to their elementary school days, he'd never shown even the slightest hint of anger problems.

I shook my head even though Sara couldn't see me. "No, he wouldn't dare. Dad would have his ass for sure if he did. Plus, I don't think he's that stupid. They just yelled for at least half an hour, and he ended up storming out of the house without a goodbye for any of us, and that wrapped up our evening." "Did she go tearing after him?"

"No, she did however ruin a plate by flinging it against the kitchen wall, and splattered spaghetti, and meatballs as she stormed upstairs herself, and slammed the bedroom door. We could hear the baby screaming all the way downstairs, and I hightailed it out of there after that." "Had enough?" Sara asked as she finished putting the dishes in the cupboards.

She ran a dishcloth on the counters and shut off the kitchen light. "More than, I headed home, and you called. I'm now enjoying a much quieter evening than I started with. I have no intentions of reliving another episode." I sighed as I picked up my glass and turned on the TV. I wasn't in the mood for a movie. I did want the background noise.

"You know Bessie. She never takes a night off from drama." I agreed, "I know, she's often very high maintenance, and we all deal with her the best we can." "I love Bessie to death, but It's tiresome listening to her whine, and drag people away from what they're doing. Bessie is hard to handle sometimes." Sara sighed. She didn't mean to sound so mean about it. "Bessie has on over one occasion, ruined an evening for me too Reesa." I responded, "I thought things were close to perfect between you, and Bessie. That she'd become your new best friend, besides Mark that is." "No, That's your job." Sara said.

"I don't even bother apologizing for Bessie's behavior when her crying bouts are on the rise. I just assume it's general bitchiness that caused her to be this way since childbirth didn't solve it." "I don't blame you there." "I just hope they'll be okay for your barbeque tomorrow. I'd hate to have two evenings in a row ruined." "I hope so too. Anyway, Mark just got back, and we have a very special evening planned." She giggled into the phone. "See you tomorrow."

"I laughed as I hung up, and just sat there sipping occasionally, and thinking about my sister. I felt so sorry for her even though she brought a lot on herself. I just could never come up with the words to express how I felt. I'd always be there for my sister, and hoped she knew that, but sometimes I'd rather not deal with her at all.

I crossed my fingers, that she, and Jim wouldn't ruin their dinner. Thinking about that reminded me, I'm supposed to make baked beans. I scrambled up for the recipe book I had tossed in a drawer, when I moved in. I thumbed through till I located it. Damn, I only had an onion, and the barbeque sauce. That meant another trip to the store, and it's close to nine now. I wanted to have it started first thing in the morning. I'd cook it in the crock pot before I left for work and let it simmer.

I grabbed my purse and made sure the credit card was inside. My keys were on the hanger, and I headed to a Safeway that is just down the street. I still didn't enjoy shopping there, but since Hankins closed at eight, there isn't much of a choice. I grabbed a cart, and grabbed two large cans of baked beans, bacon, and a green pepper.

I paid for them and was back in the apartment within ten minutes. I put the bacon, and green pepper in the refrigerator, and the beans on the counter. I grabbed the crock pot from a shelf above the stove. I put in on the counter, so I'd be ready to mix everything together in the morning. I walked back to the couch, intending to relax for a while before heading to bed, when the front door opened. Bessie came running into the room, pushing the stroller, and bawling.

The Way Life Used To Be

"Bess." I said. I opened my arms. Bessie came into them, and put her head on my shoulder, and cried. David was asleep and sucked his thumb. He wrapped the other hand around his favorite stuffed bear. "Why are you still upset?" I asked running my hand through her hair, which is matted, and wet, but I didn't care. This is what I did. Comfort her. "I think Jim, and I broke up already." She sobbed into my shoulder, soaking my t-shirt with her tears. "All because you didn't want to move in?" I asked, already thinking it's all Jim's fault.

"All because I had the nerve to turn him down. It's moving in together for god's sake. I'm not ready to do that. Men can be such babies." She sniffled and blew her nose with some Kleenex I had on the end table by a table lamp. "I think Jim could have handled that if you explained it that way." I advised. Putting a little distance between us. "Minus the baby part."

"I did." She whined. "No, you didn't. You told him, and I will quote your every word since we had no choice, but to hear them." I smiled to take the sting of my words away. "You told him to grow up and start acting like a man. You also called him a stupid moron for suggesting something so stupid, so soon in your relationship. How the hell did you expect him to react, and it's been almost two years. It's time to make changes." "Did I say all that?" "Word for word. Give it a night to calm both of you down. Talk to him in the morning without name calling, and yelling, and you'll get further." I advised.

"I'm a bitch." Bessie thumped the back of the couch with a fist. "Why does everyone put up with me?" "Because you leave us no choice." I smiled. "Because I'm a bitch." "We all love you including Jim. Talk to him in the morning." "I still think it's over." Bessie moaned and thumped her head on the back of the couch.

"You'll never know unless you talk. I heard you two are going to Sara's barbeque tomorrow. Talk before that, so you'll have it all worked out first. Then you can enjoy dinner." "I guess you're right. I take it you talked to Sara too." "About half an hour ago when I got home." "What are you bringing?" I pointed to the kitchen counter. "Baked beans. I'm making them first thing in the morning."

"Sounds good." Bessie pushed herself up and walked to the window that overlooked the pool. "Have you gone swimming yet?" "Few nights ago. It was nice, and nobody else was around." Bessie smiled pressing her forehead against the glass. "I'd love to live here." I didn't respond. I thought it was just a passing comment until Bessie turned her head. "I want to live with you." "You live with mom, and dad. Aren't you happy there?"

Bessie shrugged. "I guess so. I never thought once I moved out, that I'd be back within a year. I very much appreciate that they let me move back without a thought, but I'm lonely." "With a houseful of people?" "Most of the time I'm alone with David. I take care of him twenty-four hours a day, seven days a week, and I have virtually no breaks from him. I don't regret having him." She explained, seeing the look on my face.

Bessie thought it wouldn't be as hard as this. She needed more than just an hour break once in a while. "I just need some me time." "and that's where Jeremy is supposed to come in?" "Bingo, when we first got married, I stopped taking the pill. I actually stopped about two months before since he wanted kids right away. When I found out I was pregnant, I swear you've never seen someone so happy. His eyes bugged out to here."

She pressed four fingers to her eyes and made them wide. "For the first five months of the pregnancy, he was at my side so much, I wanted him gone. I've never had someone irritate me as much as he did. That may have been the reason he found someone else. I turned him away repeatedly thinking, it's the hormones talking. I've never depended on someone else ever."

"Doesn't mean you didn't need him there for you. I take it you will not go back to him?" Bessie shook her head. "I thought about it before Jim, and I got together. I even had dreams of him rushing through the front door of our old house, and falling on his knees, crying, and begging my forgiveness. He reaches for David and presses his lips to his forehead. Cradling him like he should have done when he was born."

I smiled. "That's a nice picture." "That's just it. It's a nice picture that will never come to life." Bessie pushed herself away from the window and wondered to the empty second bedroom that I so far haven't touched. I am planning on making something of that room soon. I lacked the willpower to do anything other than keeping the door shut.

She opened it, and stepped into the space, looking around at what she could do with this. The toddler bed would be perfect under the window facing the pool. It would be cool there, as there is a large apple blossom tree situated almost under the apartment. The closet is also a walk-in, and big enough for both of their dressers.

The Way Life Used To Be

"Are you picturing your stuff here already?" I asked leaning against the doorframe. I could almost hear Bessie's brain thinking out loud. Bessie whirled around, clapping her hands. "You've got to let me move here. It's so unbelievably perfect, and I want to get out from under mom, and dad's nose. Pretty please." She begged throwing her hands in front of her face and squeezed her cheeks.

"Just don't depend on me to babysit." "Is that a yes?" She squealed in anticipation. "Yes, need any help to move?" "No, yes, I don't know, yes." I finished, "let's get started tomorrow. You're ready to leave without telling mom, and dad?" "I had a talk before I came over here. Jim left hours ago, and I was crying when mom came up to my room."

"She suggested I need a change. She asked me to come see you. I think they're ready to be alone now." "You might be right about that. I'll help you move in the morning once my beans are started. Don't forget about Sara, and Mark's barbeque tomorrow." "I won't, I want to stay here tonight though."

"All I have is the couch to sleep on. Trust me, it's not that comfortable." "I don't care, I'll be fine." She smiled, and it's settled. I'm glad now that I absorbed it all, when I padded to my bedroom to get ready for bed. I only hoped I wouldn't turn out to be a pushover and end up being a babysitter.

I settled on the bed and stretched out. I listened with half an ear to Bessie settle David in next to her on the couch. It isn't near big enough for the two of them, but I wasn't about to give up my bed, selfish as that sounded.

It's close to nine the next morning before I woke up. I had to rush to get the beans started. I tore off my sweats, and dressed in red shorts, and a red, and white striped T-shirt. It's still hot outside with the temperatures in the low sixties, but steadily climbing. It would be sunny, and mid-eighties by afternoon so the barbeque would have perfect weather.

I left the room after flinging the comforter over the bed, headed straight to the kitchen, and pulled out the crock pot. Bessie is still asleep on the couch with David bundled next to her. He is covered with a blanket and sucked one thumb as he opened his eyes to take in his new surroundings.

I tried to be quiet as I sliced bacon. I gathered the strips and dumped them in a skillet where they started sizzling. The room filled with the aroma. "That smells so good." Bessie said, from the couch. She had raised her head at the smell and smiled. David turned his head and stuck the thumb in further as he studied his mom. He raised his other hand, and she scooped him up. She carried him with her as she walked to the kitchen and sat on a bar stool to watch.

David is perched on one leg, still trying to wake up. I had chopped up the onion, and it joined the bacon as I stirred them. "It's for the beans." I answered Bessie, and started on the green pepper "You haven't changed your mind about me moving, have you?" I looked up, "No I haven't. It might be nice to have some company around here. Especially lately, I've been so lonely." I admitted, and opened the two cans of baked beans, and dumped them in the crock pot.

"You have any plans on changing that?" I said, "not soon I don't. Want some coffee?" Bessie reminded me, "you don't drink coffee." I pointed to a pot that I never used. I kept it plugged in just in case someone did. "I bought that stupid machine when I first moved in. I have never used it, but now I have an excuse, so again want some coffee?" Bessie giggled. "I'd love it. I'll make it." She set David down. He began exploring the place. She headed back to the kitchen where I had set out the coffee, filters, and measuring spoon on the counter.

Once the coffee started brewing, I had added the green pepper, bacon, and onion to the beans, and poured barbeque sauce over the whole mixture, stirring. I then placed the lid over it and set to simmer on low. Bessie had finished her coffee and was ready to leave by ten. She didn't even bother with her hair, which is totally unlike her as we left the apartment together. We drove in separate cars, arriving at the house within twenty minutes.

Both Keith and Zeni were at Starlights. I wasn't scheduled until tomorrow morning, so I had the whole day to relax, and hoped that Bessie didn't have too much she wanted to move. We headed straight upstairs to a room full of mess, and Bessie laughed out loud. "Ready?" She clapped her hands together and started to sort clothes.

"This will take weeks. Why aren't you a better housekeeper?" I complained moving into the room and frowning at all there was to do. The bed is covered head to foot with clothes. Some dirty, and some clean, but all wrinkled, and looking worse for wear. I spread more clothes on the floor along with diapers, baby bottles, onesies, and the crib even had baby clothes hanging from the sides.

"You'd better do better at my apartment." Is my advice as I stepped through clothes. I wasn't sure what is lying beneath them, as the carpet

The Way Life Used To Be

is almost completely covered with clothes. "Scouts honor." Bessie mumbled and grabbed a box from the storage closet by the bathroom. She headed back into the room where she started throwing clothes inside. "Not like that, you need to wash them first, then fold them." I dumped the box and got the laundry basket from the closet. "Otherwise you're just wasting time."

I sorted clean clothes from dirty. I then tossed the ones that were ripped or stained into a pile to dump in the garbage, while Bessie worked on the beds. By the time I was a quarter way through the room, I had two loads of laundry ready, and started the wash. Then back upstairs to continue. It's close to noon before we realized how dirty we both were becoming. We are half-way done by that time. That is a major accomplishment all by itself.

"Want to take a break?" Bessie asked, pushing her hair away from her eyes. When she moved her hand away, the hair fell right back where it was. It covered her right eye in a very sexy way that is all Bessie. "and do what?" I asked jumping to my feet. My knees were in pain from being on the floor all morning, and I am ready to stop for a while. At the same time, I wanted to finish and be done already. "Get something to eat. Jim left me some money." She patted her jeans pocket.

"Before or after your fight?" "Few days ago. He's always giving me things, and said, he never wanted me to go without some pocket change." I smiled. "That's nice of him, and another reason you need to make your peace." "Yeah, yeah. I hear you. Let's go, I'm starving." We left the room as it was. The floor from the doorway to the bed is empty of everything except carpet, and the rest of the room still a mess. It's a definite improvement from this morning.

Bessie offered to drive. She placed David in the back seat and kissed his forehead. We headed to the mall. "What are you in the mood for?" She asked as she parked the car and grabbed the stroller from the trunk. She is a natural at this mothering thing. I envied her but had no intention of having one myself anytime in the near or far future.

"Chinese." I smiled as my stomach rumbled in agreement. We entered the mall through the doors leading to the food court, and the smells made my stomach rumble even harder. It reminded me I hadn't had a single bite to eat since last night. "There's a Panda Express over here." Bessie pointed to a restaurant in a chain near the bathrooms. "Sounds perfect, I just don't want too much as I need to save my appetite for dinner tonight. From what I hear, it will be a blast."

We sat down at one table that is empty, and Bessie set up David in a portable chair. She waited while I ordered then she placed her order. Ten minutes later I had a plate full of fried rice, sweet, and sour pork, and some kind of chicken in a peanut something sauce. I am feeling much better. Nothing like a plate of delicious Chinese food to fill the hole in my stomach.

"Did you, and Jim make up yet?" I asked taking a bite of that chicken in that peanut mystery sauce. "Nope. I called on my cell phone in the car on the way over to the house, but he didn't answer. Probably still mad at me." She got a sippy cup out of the tote bag and handed it to David. "Or most likely he isn't even home. Give it a chance to cool off." I stabbed another piece of chicken.

"Weren't you the one who was so insistent on talking to him as soon as I could?" "Yes, but you also might wait until you both cool off so you're not yelling. Not good for the baby." "He's only two, he wouldn't remember anything, anyway." "Your stressed, he's stressed." I remembered that from Jeff. That silenced Bessie as she opened her mouth and closed it saying nothing. True she is prone to severe mood swings, and always kind of enjoyed the attention, but not when it affected her child.

"I'll wait. I'm still a little upset." She concluded and finished her fried rice. David had eaten more than I thought he would, and there were just a few noodles left. I also ate the last bite of rice, and they threw our plastic plates in the garbage. "You want to walk around?" Bessie asked grabbing hold of the stroller. David is still drinking out of his cup and looking content. For a toddler, he is silent.

I shook my head. "Nah, I'm stuffed, and want to pack your stuff. It's already after one." We headed back to the car. We drove back to the house where both of us tackled the rest of the room. We packed both cars full to the roofs before heading to the apartment. Bessie had already decided where she wanted to arrange the furniture, so this trip is clothes, and one dresser.

We made three more trips, and by the time we were done, we were both soaking wet with sweat, and it's close to five. "Ready to call it a night?" I asked flipping my wet mop behind one ear. "I guess so. The barbeques soon, anyway. Want to finish tomorrow?" "After my shift. I need to be at Starlights at seven and should be off by four. I can meet you at the house again."

The Way Life Used To Be

"Sounds good. That'll give me a chance to get the rest of my things organized. I need Mark's truck for the beds, and my dresser, but he's already offered to get those things for me." "When did you talk to him. I've been with you all day?" I asked trying to figure her out. She had a knack for communicating with people behind my back, and it astounded me.

"When you were in the bathroom at the house. Believe it or not, I can talk on the phone, and get things done without you holding my hand." Bessie admonished, pointing her finger, and smiling. "I guess you can." I mumbled and went to check on my beans. I stirred them in the crock pot, and they were almost done. They smelled delicious. "We also need to go to the office to sign paperwork to add you to my lease. I'm on a month to month, but I'll get in trouble if you live here without being on it." I pointed the wooden spoon in Bessie's direction.

She is in the bedroom digging through clothes for a clean pair of shorts, and T-shirt. It's close to eighty degrees by then, and she wanted to be comfortable at dinner. She is hoping Jim would be there as he promised two days ago and not let their fight prevent him from being part of the family. "I hear you." She yelled from the room and smiled when she found a pair of tan shorts, and white t-shirt in one of the three laundry baskets, we lugged up the stairs.

She padded from the room to check on David who is sitting on the floor digging through a toy bin. Trucks, and cars were scattered all around him. Satisfied he is okay for the moment; she ducked inside the bathroom and started the shower. I smiled when I heard the water starting and thought there's no going back now. I just got myself a roommate, and hopefully this is the answer to my loneliness.

I added a little more barbeque sauce and mixed it one more time before replacing the cover. I had about an hour to get ready, and when Bessie emerged from the bathroom, hair wrapped in a towel. I hurried to my bedroom, and found a jean wrap-around skirt, and white short-sleeve t-shirt. It's a little dressy, but not too much so. This is just a barbeque, but I enjoyed dressing nicely, and had so few occasions especially lately to do it.

Once my own shower was done, and my hair hanging in ringlets. I brushed it, then pulled it in a French braid. I enjoyed wearing it loose, but with the constant humidity especially this time of year it frizzed out almost as soon as it dried. I slipped my feet into white flip flops and emerged from my room to find Bessie smiling by the front door, stroller in hand.

"Bout time," she laughed. We left together deciding to ride in the same car to help with the gas. I settled myself in the passenger seat while Bessie got David into the car seat. She flopped into the driver's seat and buckled her seatbelt. She started the car, and we were off. The sky is still deep blue with just a few clouds, and the weatherman proved to be right. It's eighty-two degrees, perfect weather for a barbeque.

Mark, and Sara's front door is propped open by a twelve pack of Coke, and the living room is empty when we arrived. We could hear voices from the backyard, and the smell of chicken, and ribs. I held both the bowl of baked beans, and Bessie's cake. We wondered through the living room, which was spotless, to the clean kitchen, and opened a screen door leading to the small deck, and yard. Mark is at the grill along with Keith who turned his head at the sound of the door slamming.

"Hey you two. Just in time," he smiled, and turned back to the meat. "Better late than never," I smiled, and placed the cake on one card table, and the beans on another. Bessie went off to look for Jim who had one hand draped on the fence talking with Trey. They are hidden from the deck and talking about Albert's pending birth.

"Are you getting excited yet?" Jim teased. "It's your third child you know." "Too bad I'm not a better dad. She's due soon, and she's already a pain in the butt." Trey smiled taking a drink of his Coke. He liked Mark's, and Sara's place. It's the first time he had been invited. "How so? Hey Bess." He turned at the sound of sandals in the grass making a soft squishing sound. No sign of their fight two days ago, and as much as she wanted to talk it out maybe it isn't needed. He looked at ease as he reached an arm around her shoulder and pulled her closer for a kiss.

"How ya doing Bess?" Trey greeted. "Good. David's getting bigger." She glanced back, and David found a car, and train set Mark had bought for him. He is sitting on the grass, trying to take apart the box cars. "Sure is. How's motherhood going?" He took another drink of his soda while talking to her. "It has its trials. I just moved in with Reesa, so I'm hoping to have a little more freedom now."

"When did that happen?" Jim asked. "What else have I missed?" "It happened earlier today. She was nice enough to help me pack, and before you ask, I've already gotten my blessings from mom, and dad. You don't have to worry." "Never said it worried me. Where does she live?"

The Way Life Used To Be

"Berkeley Luxury Apartments. I had to practically beg her to move in, but I eventually convinced her. I think she's happier for it., and I want to apologize for the other night. I'm just not ready to move in with another man right now, much as I love you." Bessie explained, leaning down into a cooler for a Pepsi. "No apology necessary. I think I spoke too soon too. You aren't addicted to Diet Pepsi's like Reecie Peecie?" Jim asked opening the top for her.

"Thanks, and No, I know what real soda is supposed to taste like." "Tastes like crap," I said, from behind. I had spent the last half an hour talking with Mark, and dad. I was envying the fact that they had houses, and I am stuck in a crowded apartment complex, but I chose to live there.

Dad is talking about their long-awaited retirement which they were still planning on sometime soon, after the first of the year. Less than two months to go, and he is already looking forward to it as much as Zeni is dreading it. She kept saying, what in the hell is she supposed to do with so much time on their hands. They hadn't been on a vacation in years, and he planned on taking her to Lake Tahoe for their first one. Not on the gambling side, but on the other where it's spacious, and quiet. At least a week of doing nothing, but maybe some fishing, and relaxing.

Zeni kept trying to find excuses to delay it, but he is standing firm. "That's how much you know," Bessie teased, and moved so I could be a part of the group. "Hey," Trey greeted still leaning against the fence with one tanned arm on the top, and the other holding his Pepsi. He declined wanting a beer as he hated the taste, to this day. A cold soda is enough to make him happy any day.

"Hey back. Did Albert give birth already?" I asked bending over to grab a soda. I popped the top and took a drink. Trey shook his head. I turned towards Bessie, and Jim who were hugging close, and she had her head on his chest. David is waddling around the yard in shorts, and no shirt. He had the two box cars clutched in his hands. "You tell him you moved yet?"

"I did. He wants to check it out later. Make sure we're living in a safe place." She did no more than toss her eyes in my direction before turning back towards Jim. "Why don't we make it a dinner tomorrow," Jim suggested. "I'll buy the stuff," I smiled. "Sounds good, I won't be off till about four or so. Want to meet me at Starlights or the apartment?" "Apartments fine, I'll get the shopping done in the morning, and we'll head over about three to get things started."

"Dinner's ready," Mark bellowed. The family swarmed to the tables, where Zeni's prized potato salad waited. Keith indeed made three dozen deviled eggs, and I made my beans. There is also corn on the cob, barbeque chicken, and ribs Mark had just taken off the grill.

All of us piled their plates high with everything spread on the table and found various places around the yard. Some of us sat in chairs, and some right on the ground to enjoy our dinner. Both Bessie, and Jim opted for the ground, and Trey joined them a few minutes later along with me. We seemed to have formed a group of our own, although no one would admit it. We talked together, ate together, and enjoyed the evening as the sun set.

"This is wonderful." Bessie smacked her lips after taking a bite of the beans. "I spent hours making it." I teased taking a bite of my beans. "Liar face, a crock pot's your new best friend." "Comes in handy sometimes. I did however put my heart into it. That ought to count for something." "Counts for everything Reecie. You're a very talented cook." Jim teased laughing and earning a punch on his leg.

Trey listened to them, sitting next to me, and he was so close. Our arms kept touching, but neither of us cared to move further away. I'm content, and happy, and I trusted him. He is turning into one of my best friends. "Your full of compliments tonight. I'm not sure how to handle them," I teased back. "You'll find a way. You always do," Jim kept teasing. I could handle my own though, always could.

"You guys been to any parties recently?" I asked taking another bite of my chicken. "Not since last week." Trey answered taking a bite of potato salad. "I will marry your mom for her cooking." He complimented and earned a punch in the leg himself. "At Bret's?" I asked rubbing the part of his leg I had just slapped for a few seconds.

"Yep. He, and Jan had their five-year anniversary last Saturday, and celebrated by having all of us over for pizza, and beer." "Was the beer good?" I finished my chicken and took a drink. "I wouldn't know. I had a Coke." He answered smiling. "Still not a drinker?" I asked, getting up to throw my empty can in the recycler. "I'll get you another," he offered. He was back a few minutes later with a fresh drink. "Thanks," I smiled at him. "No, I'm not a drinker. I still don't like the taste of it," he answered me.

The sun lowered, but we continued sitting together, plates thrown in the garbage, and just sitting. Our legs were spread in front of us, and

The Way Life Used To Be

hands behind. Mark, and Sara were holding hands, and sitting on matching lawn chairs, and Keith and Zeni were cleaning up the tables.

The rest of us joined in. We got all the food off, and leftovers doled out in minutes. Sometimes it paid off having a large family. None of us wanted Sara to be stuck doing all this herself, even if it was their idea to have dinner in the first place.

Once it hit nine, I stifled a yawn. It seemed a good time to end the evening. I am looking forward to an evening of quietness. I thought of inviting Trey to watch a movie with me. Then I thought better of it. Trey said good night with a gentle kiss on my cheek, another kiss for the hostess who thanked all of us for a wonderful evening. Bessie, and I headed back to the apartment.

Sandra Gutierrez

Chapter 17

David had fallen asleep in the car seat. Once we reached home, she placed him gently in his bed. She kissed his forehead, and smoothed his hair back, smiling as he snored gently, and flung his arms over his head. "That was such a nice evening," she smiled. She left the bedroom and joined me on the couch. "Sure was. I'm so glad Sara didn't forget about me. I don't think I've enjoyed myself so much for a while now." "Sara would never forget you, nor would anyone else., and you're in love with Trey." "Why beat around the bush?"

I whipped my head around. "Ouch, why do you make me do stupid things?" I rubbed at my neck. "I'm not in love. Do you not remember my resolve?" "Resolve is resolving, even as we speak." Bessie teased. "I watched you two tonight. Did you know you were touching him, and he was so enjoying it? I feel an oncoming love affair starting." "For heaven's sake, I only touched his leg for a second." I argued.

"So sure, he couldn't keep his eyes off you." Bessie said, turning so she could look at me. I said nothing at that. True there is a deep friendship between us, but that's where it ended. I got up to put the leftovers in the refrigerator while Bessie was in her room checking on David. He is asleep, so she smiled, and left the door opened so she could hear him if he woke up before she was ready for bed.

I strolled to the living room where Bessie sat, looking out the window, with a soft smile on her lips. "I take it you, and Jim kissed, and made up?" "Didn't have to, it was over, and done before I realized it. Mom told me what happened when he was just a toddler. That kind of abuse shouldn't happen to anyone, let alone a child. They're innocent, defenseless, and it should never ever happen." A murderous look came into her eyes, shocking me. I had never seen her look that way before.

The Way Life Used To Be

I studied her saying nothing for a while. She is no longer the local gossip, but had matured into a bright, caring, and sensitive adult. "When I told mom that Jim, and I were together, her first reaction was tears. She started crying in the kitchen, she grabbed me around the neck, and buried her face in my hair. I thought she'd yell at me for being with someone so soon after Jeremy. I thought maybe she'd call me a slut or something. She cried in my hair."

"That's what moms do. They may want to yell, and scream until we beg them to stop, and promise we'll do anything mommy says. When it comes down to it, they'll always have our backs." I said.

"Let me correct myself. Most do." I was referring to Jim without saying so. "When I heard dad kicked Jim's parents out, it kind of shocked me. I never would picture dad yelling at someone, much less kicking them out of the restaurant. I guess they didn't even pay for their food, not like they'd even want to."

"Mom said, it's the best decision they could have made when they made him the delivery guy. He seems to enjoy it." "Yes, he does. I have to say when mom told me all that, I came to respect him even more than I did before. Against all odds, he made it through." "That he did, well we got a lot accomplished today, and I'm officially beat, and off to bed." I smiled as I headed to my bedroom expecting to be up for hours, but my body knew more than my head. I was asleep as soon as I lay down and conveniently missed my alarm.

I cursed out loud as I grabbed a pair of black jeans. I pulled my hair into a ponytail and grabbed my purse on the way out the door without even bothering to say goodbye to Bessie. Her door is shut tight. I left the apartment yawning and hoping mom wouldn't catch me doing that. I am still on a test of manning the kitchen, and this time I am doing both breakfast and lunch. Zeni wanted to give me about a week of doing both before she would consider retiring. Less than two months to go. So far, I am more than proving myself.

It's almost seven when I pulled up at Starlights and rushed through the door. I threw my purse on a hook, and headed straight for the refrigerator for the eggs, and cheese. I dumped both on the counter, and ran to the pantry for the bagels, and English muffins praying I wouldn't be caught. The last thing I needed after so little sleep is to be yelled at for not being prepared. I am close to half an hour late. I hoped that it would be a slow morning, so I'd have time to prep.

Sandra Gutierrez

"Morning Honey," Zeni greeted. She came through the swinging doors with a smile, and a cup of Diet Pepsi. "Hey mama," I greeted. I was sitting on a stool smiling and slicing bagels. Zeni studied me from the doorframe. It's obvious what I am doing. If I pulled it off without messing up a single order, she would not reprimand me for it. God knew she herself had plenty of days where she rushed through, made corrections, and promised herself she never would again. Until the next time she made a mistake.

"How's it going today?" She asked handing me the cup and hopped on a stool next to me. "Okay, I guess. Got some decent sleep last night, everything's fine." I looked up from slicing, with a smile for her. "Thanks." I took the cup and drank from the straw. "Trouble already with your new roommate?" Zeni teased taking a drink of her iced tea and smiled.

She is already enjoying the quiet and hoped everything worked out with Bessie being in the apartment. Last thing she needed is for her to move back home, so soon after she just left again. I shook my head. "I'm starting to enjoy the company, believe it or not. After work tonight I have to take her to the office to add her to the lease." "David too?" "As a minor, I guess. I'll find out once we get there. I'm hoping Bessie can get a job soon, so she doesn't have to depend on Jeremy for support payments."

I smiled as I gathered up the unused bagels, English muffins, and tossed them back in the pantry. "Jeremy's been paying her through her account. He has a transfer set up for two hundred fifty a month right now and wants to make it more as soon as he gets his next raise." Zeni set down her coffee and sat on a stool. "That's better than nothing. I am sure it would be a fight to get anything more." I got out three frying pans, and set the burners to warm, then two cartons of eggs from the refrigerator.

"Your turning out to be a natural at this," Zeni observed. She took a drink of her coffee. "I guess I am," I smiled. The bell rang signaling orders were ready. "I'll be right back." I returned moments later with five orders. Three bagel sandwiches with ham, one with sausage, and a ham, and cheese English muffin minus the egg. Zeni fingered the orders. "Shouldn't be too hard. Need any help?" I shook my head. "Nope, I got it. How're you enjoying your quiet?" I cracked four eggs, and they started bubbling.

The Way Life Used To Be

"I have to admit, I was just getting used to having a young child around again, and now they're gone. I miss it except for the midnight screaming when he's hungry." "I guess I have that to look forward to. I heard nothing last night though. Am I in for a rude awakening?" I flipped the eggs, and spread the bagels on the plates, and then the cheese.

I followed with the English muffin and grabbed five fruit bowls. "I wouldn't think so, he's way over the waking up phase in the middle of the night." "Is Bessie, and Jeremy talking now?" I asked taking the hash browns from the oven. "A little, I guess. He called at the house four days ago to let Bessie know the money was transferred, and Jim answered the phone. It wasn't a pretty picture. Bessie got on the phone almost right away, once she had put David down. You could hear the shouting from outside. By the time Bessie was done, she had slammed down the phone, and come storming outside. She slammed the front door and yelled how unreasonable he was to have moved on without so much as two words to her. When she did the same, he got in a tizzy."

"I can't blame her for getting upset." I put the sandwiches together, and took out three plates, came back for the other two, and yelled "Orders up." There weren't any other orders ready, so I hopped on my stool, and took a drink of my soda. "Did she end up calling him back and apologizing?"

"No, but she ended up taking out her anger on her room. Ruined three pairs of shorts before she was done." Zeni smiled even though she was so angry at her daughter. It took everything she had just to remain cool. "I told her she could very well use her own money to replace them, damned if I would fork over the cash. She tried yelling at me for being insensitive. I came this close to slapping her face." She pinched a finger, and thumb together. "I wish you all the luck. You will need it."

"Your starting to scare me. Should I help her find her own place instead?" I didn't want any of my furniture ruined or clothes. True, I am doing better, but I didn't want to replace anything. Zeni shook her head. "I don't think that'll be necessary. You have a way with her, I seem to lack. More patience too I might add. I think with some time; she'll settle down now that she doesn't have an entire house to yell in." She finished her coffee. "You sure you need no more help?"

Rebecca, one of the waitresses, rang the bell. I hopped off the stool once again. "I'll handle it right now. If it picks up, I'll take you up on your offer." I smiled and pushed through the swinging doors. By that time the lunch rush was too busy for words. Against my will, I asked both Mark, and mom to help me. There is order after order, and I just wasn't fast enough by myself. Zeni understood, and dove right in.

If things kept up the way they were, she was thinking of hiring a part- time cook to help once she, and Keith retired. Just having me, and Mark run the place is fine, but this would ease the pressure some. I sighed once it was four. I tossed the apron on a hook and walked to the dining area to say goodbye. "All cleaned up in there?" Zeni asked smiling as she cleared two tables. "For now. All the dishes are done, and counters wiped clean. Should be good for the dinner rush." I opened my purse for the car keys.

"Good." She finished wiping down a table, and spread a linen tablecloth over it, and two sets of silverware wrapped in linen napkins. "Heading home?" "Soon. I need to run to the grocery store for some cereal, and milk. Then I'll head home. I want to get to the apartment office before she leaves at six." "Sounds good. Have fun, and we'll see you Thursday."

I smiled a goodbye and headed to Hankins to get my groceries. I ended up with more than I planned and didn't make it home until almost five. Bessie was waiting in the office with David in the stroller. I called her from my cell phone, once I had paid for my things, and was headed home. Bessie said she'd meet me in the manager's office to sign the papers.

Jim had called about three, he, and Trey would be there at five thirty to start dinner. Bessie had left the door open so they could just come in when they got everything together, so we did not have to worry about anything. "About time," she teased. I rushed in with my purse flying. I left my bags in the back seat hoping this wouldn't take too long.

"Sorry, I got here as soon as I could. Ready?" I asked Marlisa who was gathering the papers from my file. "Sure am." She smiled and handed over the papers. "And this is the new pet addendum if you have any new pets, the deposit for them is right here." She pointed to another paper. We signed our names, and once she placed them back in the files, she dropped the pens in her drawer, and smiled. "Well that does it. Not too harmful is it?"

"Not at all." I was relieved to be done. "All the other rules remain the same. Do you have any questions at all?" She directed that towards Bessie who just shook her head. "Well then, enjoy it here, and have a good night." She got up, and closed the door, and locked it after they left. It's close to six by then, and she could always reopen it if anyone had an emergency. "That wasn't too bad." Bessie smiled as she wheeled the stroller down the side-walk where I had parked my car. "I'll meet you at home."

She smiled, and headed down towards the apartment with David, while I got in my car. I'm happy for the first time today. I parked the car in my assigned slot, and I glanced over, and saw Bessie's car in the spare space next to mine. I got the bags out from the back seat and headed upstairs where the front door was propped open, and I could hear voices. I walked in, and found Jim, and Bessie in the kitchen together, plastered at the hip, and kissing, oblivious to anyone else around them.

"Should I get a room?" I announced as I made my way to the kitchen, bags in hand, and laughing at them. They drew apart. They weren't even surprised at being caught, and Jim looked over Bessie's shoulder, and grinned. "You jealous?" "Of that?" I pointed to Bessie and giggled. "I'm green with envy. Not sure how I will make it through the night." I placed the palm of my hand to my forehead after placing the bags on the counter.

"I'm not sure how either." Trey responded. "Hey," I smiled at him. I am pleased to see him, and he looked happy too. I scooted around them to leave the kitchen.

"Where are you going?" Trey asked putting his elbows on the counter, and folded his hands under his chin, smiling. It's the first time he saw where she lived. "I would excuse myself without further ado so Bessie, and Jimbo here could have the place to themselves for free groping."

"Sounds perfect for another night. However, tonight is out of the question." Jim stated slapping the counter. "We come bearing gifts." He used one hand to sweep over the stove. I strained my neck to smell the food, but the lids on the pans covered a lot. Still it's sweet.

They were making dinner for us. I had forgotten about Jim's offer last night. It made me smile, and I hopped on a stool. "You two get comfortable, Bessie, and I have this all organized." Jim advised, and so Trey, and I headed to the deck to enjoy the last of the sunshine before it lowered for the night.

Trey handed me a glass of Diet Pepsi. He poured it for me while I got a bag of potato chips to share while we sat on the patio. "Thanks," I smiled. I accepted the glass, and he took a drink of his own Coke. "I'm sorry for yelling the other day." I finally apologized and realized at the same time I am right about not telling anyone about it. Trey is no drama queen, and I didn't want to start a trend.

"No problem., and just for the record, I don't think you're the latest town whore. All I meant is there isn't enough time to have a healthy fight with either of them. So, how was your day?" He leaned back and crossed a foot over the other leg. "Busy." I took a drink. "I had the morning shift, and all went well, but the lunch rush is too rushy. I had to ask for help." "Rushy?" He laughed. "There's no other word to describe it. I am sure I am ready to handle the kitchen by myself. When I had to lower my head, walk through those swinging doors to ask for help, all it did is prove how much I can't."

"Don't be so hard on yourself. When my dad had his third heart attack, I convinced him not to go on any runs with me for at least a week so he could recuperate. I was also convinced I could do the deliveries by myself since I'd been doing them for so long. I knew those deliveries like the back of my hand. I was doing so well for the morning runs; I was getting a big head. By noon, I forgot one of my major clients. She was so upset at having to wait, she threatened to quit her business with us. That wasn't something we could afford. She was a long-time customer, who purchases a lot of our produce. I apologized over, and over, and she called my dad to complain."

"That sounds a little immature," I commented. I took another drink and ate a potato chip. "She could have just made it easier to forgive and forget." "Easier said, than done. I got home with my tail between my legs, and a lecture that lasted three fucking days." I giggled at the cursing. I had never seen his temper before. It somehow made him seem more normal.

Trey continued, not realizing what he just said. "I went on the damn deliveries three days without a hitch. The look on dad's face is enough to make me cry. I didn't, but I sure has hell wanted to. After that I asked Bret to be my assistant. I realized I couldn't do it by myself, and that it's okay to ask for help." I tilted my head looking at him completely differently than ever before. I understood what he was saying and agreed. It isn't beneath either of us to ask for help.

"Did you cry in private?" I asked turning my head to look at him. "Not about that. I lost it a few times when my dad had those attacks. The one right before Christmas last year is the worst. I wasn't even there when it happened. I was running late with two deliveries and didn't get home till almost seven. My dad was on the floor clutching his chest and my mom is on the floor with him, crying, and not knowing what to do."

"Did you know what to do?" I asked. He nodded. "Actually, I did. The year you enrolled in college, Bret, and I enrolled in a life safety course. It's required for my license, but I wanted to take it, anyway. We learned the basics of CPR for both children, and adults. I never had to use it until I saw my dad on the floor." "I bet he is glad you did." He nodded again. "Bet your ass he is. I didn't even think first. I ran into the living room with my heart in my throat, and I slid on the floor, and tore open his shirt. I busted every button in the process, and they were flying every which way, but I didn't care. Mom had stopped her crying by then. The paramedics were well on their way when I started the chest compressions." "Impressive." I smiled realizing how true that is. He saved his dad's life and never bragged about it.

"I wasn't thinking of the buttons flying, or my mom wondering what I was doing. All I saw was my dad." He closed his eyes then remembering every second of that night. It isn't as painful telling her about it, but his heart still beat wildly even to this day. "And what do you see now?" I asked He turned his head eyes locking. "The big picture," he teased making me laugh. "You still want to help with Albert's birth? She's getting ready to deliver soon. Should be any day." He asked putting his empty glass on the table.

I nodded in answer. "Want another?" I asked glancing towards his glass. He just shook his head. "I'll get another one in a minute, but thanks." "Is Albert in a lot of pain?" I asked taking a last drink of my soda. "So, so, I'd guess. Can't tell me what's going on with her, so I have to read her actions. She's been resting a lot, and when she's awake, keeps pacing."

"Will the birth be painful for her you think?" "Just like humans, which I still can't relate, but I try my best. The veterinarian I hired for the first birth, called to see if he could be of any help, but I said, I'd handle it. I'm not sure if he's still bitter about it or not, but Albert's not comfortable around anyone, but me." Bessie shouted from the kitchen. "Chow time."

We got up at the same time. This is the first time that I was opening up to him. He scooped up both glasses and followed me into the kitchen. Bessie, and Jim had set up a temporary dining room table, made of a folding table four metal chairs. Not the most comfortable, but the thoughts counted for something. David had his own combination chair table thing that snapped together.

Trey pulled out my chair while I refilled our glasses. I smiled at him as he seated me. "Why thank you," I said. Bessie, and Jim sat down after they placed the dishes on heat pads, and Bessie smiled at the group. "Well this is our first official dinner here, and I for one am glad we're all together. Jim, and I have an announcement." She glanced at Jim who is all smiles and nodded his agreement.

"What is it?" I asked a little too impatiently. "We're having a baby." Jim announced. He knew Bessie wanted to tell her sister, but he is bursting with happiness. His first child, and with the woman he loved more than anything. Bessie giggled out loud. She wanted to be the one to tell everyone, but she didn't care that Jim did. It would be his first and he is already excited and planning on setting up a nursery in his spare bedroom.

He wanted Bessie to move in soon, and she starting to feel more comfortable about the idea. "So, what do you think?" Bessie asked bouncing in her seat. David sat in his chair eating the hotdog Bessie cut up for him. He was looking at everyone and drinking out of his favorite sippy cup. "I'm still getting used to the idea. You sure you want two of these around?" I nodded towards David who is sitting back, swinging both legs under the table, and smiling. He looked at home. "Absolutely." Bessie said and reached over to kiss Jim on the lips. "I want so many kids, I can't keep count."

"Now you're scaring me." Jim teased and dug into his dinner. "And me." I said, trying to picture it. Bessie took a bite of her chicken. She, and Jim had decided on barbeque chicken wings, fried rice, and mixed vegetables. Jim drove to the store by himself as Trey was still on deliveries, but he didn't mind it. He even cooked most of the dinner at home to save time.

"Not me." Bessie stated. "I mean it. I'm the best parent in the world." She lifted her glass of water. "To me." She reached her glass towards the center of the table where three other glasses tinged with hers. "To you." We all said together and burst out laughing. When our plates were empty, I did the honor of taking them to the sink where I began rinsing. Trey joined me while Jim, and Bessie went to sit on the couch and talk. "You okay?" he asked handing her a glass.

I shrugged my shoulders. "I guess so. I'm feeling like that perpetual third wheel." "I know exactly what you're feeling. I'm pretty much in

The Way Life Used To Be

that same boat myself." He didn't feel that way now. This is a nice change. I leaned my head towards him, and he kissed my eye. "Thank you. We're a couple of loners," I told him. He smiled down at me and reached over for another plate.

Once the dishes were in the sink, and soaking, I wiped down the counters. I hung the wash-cloth on the handle of the stove to dry. I turned towards him, and he was leaning against the counter, arms crossed, and smiling. "All done?" He asked. "For now, anyway. I have my bedroom to contend with, but that will be for another time. Do you have to leave soon?"

"Yeah, I have a six o'clock delivery, and that means I'm up at three." "I had fun tonight. Don't forget to call me when Albert's ready. I don't want to miss it." He smiled, "you know what you said earlier about loners? I don't know anyone who would prefer an animal birth over a human. We're a couple of sick individuals." "You said, it," I laughed, and poked him in the chest.

Once Trey left, I smiled after he closed the door, and turned to head to my bedroom. I wanted to get started on my clothes. Since I had just reprimanded Bessie for being a complete slob, I would have to eat my own words. Jim said, a goodbye to Bessie which lasted five minutes before headed to his truck. Bessie headed back to her bedroom to put David down for the night. His eyes were already drooping, and he had a silly smile on his face as he was carried to his bed.

Three days passed, and Trey hadn't called. Carla, and I were enjoying a late lunch. I kept checking my cell phone on the off chance he tried to call. I worried that somehow, I just missed it. "Time will not go any faster by checking the phone."

Carla teased and nodded towards her lap. "He will not forget about you." I ate some of my chicken salad. I pouted and slammed the phone shut. "He might forget you know. Albert could go into labor any time. Trey could forget all about me. He cares so much about her, and then when it's all over, and she's delivered her calf, he remembers to tell me, and it's too late."

"You paint quite the pretty picture." Carla teased taking a bite of her cheeseburger. She had called me that morning to make plans to go shopping and have lunch together. We had lunch first at Bistros, and the food was every bit as good as everyone who ever ate there said, it was. "I speak a pretty picture." "I bet there'll be lots of steamy barn sex when Albert's done with the birthing thing."

"I don't think I'd ever want sex that badly as to resort to barn humping." "Maybe in Trey's bed than when you're all done. I can just see it now. You're in the shower together cleaning off all the mud, and nasty shit, and when you're done, he leads you to the bed buck ass naked, and flips you onto the bed. You resist only for a second when his physique, and charm win you over. You succumb to his charms. Am I getting close? Can you just imagine how perfect that would be?"

I did nothing but raise my eyebrow and shake my head. "You need help." "You need sex." "I will come to you when, and if that ever poses a problem." "I'll be here waiting. So, onto other gossip, how's the heat between Bessie, and Jim?" She ate another bite of her burger. "That I have to admit is out of this world. It is so freaking bizarre at the same time. I never thought Jim would settle down with someone, and that someone would be Bessie."

I ate more salad and took a drink. "I also have to admit I'd never picture the two of them together. However, since they are, and seem to be working out well together, do they have your blessing?" "Always did. I love Jim as a brother, and Bessie is my sister, literally so yes, they've always had my blessing. Did I tell you about the big fight between Bess, and Jeremy?" "No," Carla widened her eyes in anticipation of the latest gossip. She however could be fully trusted not to spread it. It's one of the many things I loved about her. I told her the complete story.

"That's stupid, they've been apart for years now. Speaking of Jeremy, I saw him last week with some brunette. She is on the chunky side, but he had his arm around her. She was squeezing his waist. I can't picture him getting his panties in a twist at the thought of his old flame hitting the sheets with someone else." Carla said, finishing her burger, and started on the fries.

"You would think he'd be okay with it, but apparently what's good for him is not good for her. Stupid male chauvinism." "Sounds like." Carla smiled and took a drink of her iced tea. "How's it working out having her as a roommate? You ready to pull your hair out yet?" She glanced at my head, but all hairs seemed in place. I left my hair down for once, and the low humidity in the air did wonders at keeping the curls soft. "So far so good. I just added her to the lease last night, and Jim, and Trey had dinner with us after that. It was a very nice evening." I finished my salad and pushed the empty plate towards the edge of the table for the waitress to grab. Carla had already moved her plate, since she had long finished her lunch.

The Way Life Used To Be

"When Bessie, and Jim were getting ready to put dinner on the table, Trey, and I had a nice talk on my balcony." "You seem to be getting closer." "You could be right." I agreed with her. The waitress returned. She took our plates and refilled our glasses. Both of us said no to dessert but didn't want to leave yet. There weren't many customers, and we were enjoying our talk. "Before Taylor, and I got together eons ago, I thought about going for Trey. He's a prime specimen, and I'm surprised he hasn't been scooped up yet."

"Scooped as in ice cream?" "Now there's a picture. A triple scoop of chocolate chunk on a tasty waffle cone. Let's get some." I laughed. "I thought you were talking about Trey, and the likelihood of his finding some hot young thing to spend the rest of these days with?" "That too, however, the hot young thing is sitting across from me." Carla stated, and I snorted.

"Snort all you want. All it'll do is make a booger escape your nose and embarrass you." I smiled and shook my head. "You ready to go?" Carla glanced at her watch. "Sure am. I still have a whole two hours before Taylor gets home, and I for one intend to make the most of it." I glanced down at my cell phone again, and frowned, wanting to throw the stupid thing away since Trey still hadn't called.

"Still think he will forget you?" Carla smirked taking some money out of her purse to pay for lunch. She disregarded my offer to help pay for it, since it was her idea. "He might." I grumbled snapping the phone shut again and shoved it in the pocket of my shorts. Once Carla paid, we were on our way to the mall where Carla had decided, I needed a bra, and-new outfit for helping Albert. We hit JC Penney's first, and I fingered a rack load of silk blouses, and skirts. They were a variety of colors, all bold, and shocking. They were tasteful at the same time.

"I don't know why I'm wearing a dress for getting down, and dirty in the mud." I grumbled, slamming the blouses on the rack where the hangers made a loud clanging sound. "Now, now, no need for dramatic violence." Carla pointed a finger in my direction, smiling. "Trust me on this. Jeans, and boots won't impress Trey." "I'm going to be knee deep in mud." I stated, drawing the attention of several shoppers. "I need some old ripped stupid jeans I would be happy frolicking in the mud with."

"Save the jeans. I know, I'm so fucking brilliant." Carla slapped my shoulder. "I don't know why I didn't think of this before. You wear the old sexy jeans that mold to your perfect ass for the birthing thing. Then

Trey, who can't help, but stare at your backside, decides in a moment of a pure sexual haze to ask you to dinner. Then you wear the dress that shows off the perfect ass to its perfection. When dinner ends, you end up in bed together for some sex."

"You decided that just now?" I laughed out loud and shook my head. "Have I mentioned how much I love you?" "I just knew you'd appreciate my honesty." Carla swiped a hand across her chest. "I appreciate your sexual fantasy. It's sick that you're picturing me with Trey. It should offend me in the highest order. Somehow, I can't get to that point in my life. I love you, and all your sexual perverseness." I kissed Carla on the cheek, and she put her hand around my neck. "However," I continued fingering some skirts, "I just bought out an outfit a few weeks ago."

"It was over four months ago, and that is a special occasion. You need new outfits for new events." Carla advised, pulling out a pink, and blue floral wrap-around skirt, and matching blouse. "Here it is." She flung the outfit to her chest to show me. I stopped to look at her. Carla proved she is right once again. It's only fourteen dollars and hardly made a dent on my card. I placed it back in my purse, grabbed the bag, and we headed out. Carla was in a much happier mood as she walked with one arm hooked through mine on our way to the car.

"I have more news." She whispered giggling. "Haven't you shared all your gossip yet?" I teased opening my side of the car door. "This will wait until we get to my house." She started the car. "It's good news." While she drove, with the company of the radio playing, I sat back relaxing. I fingered the cellphone, willing it to ring.

"Again, the phone won't ring any faster just by fondling it." Carla smiled teasing me. "You don't fondle phones. You fondle people," I advised. Realizing I sounded just like Carla. Carla laughed out loud. "Oh, you impress me sometimes." "Glad to entertain you. I'm willing Trey to call me by performing the magic touch with my phone here." I patted my pocket.

"You should try the magic touch on the man himself." "Ha, Ha." Carla turned into the driveway. "Shoot, Taylor's not home yet. I kind of wanted to give my news with him." "Can't you tell me over the phone?" I asked. "No, I want to tell you in person. I even picked up stuff for dinner for us to cook." It's close to six by then, and I am still full, from lunch, but I also didn't want to hurt her feelings. "I'll wait for both of you." I promised and flipped the phone shut just as Taylor came in.

The Way Life Used To Be

Carla jumped up, and kissed him hello, and clapped her hands together, saying "I'm so glad your home." "Miss me much? How are you doing Rees?" He asked reaching over Carla to give me a kiss on the cheek. He had just gotten off work, and was tired, and it showed. Even so he is still so handsome. His blond hair had darkened to more of a tarnished gold, and he now sported a full mustache. "I'm good. Carla's been keeping me entertained all day. So, what's the big news?"

Carla, and Taylor looked at each other before Carla lowered her gaze to her stomach giving her away. I smirked at her. "Am I the coach?" They both laughed. "No, You're the honorary Auntie." "Thank God for the simple things in life. How's work going?" I asked Taylor. "Good, just got a raise, and with the baby coming, it'll be good for us."

He smiled and headed towards the kitchen for a beer. "Come see the bedroom." Carla squealed and grabbed my hand before I could give an answer. We ran down the hall, and she flung open the door that used to be a guest room. Only company they ever had was his mom. She was up for a visit last month, but the full-size bed is now gone, and a crib stood in its place, covered in blue.

"Isn't it nice?" Carla asked running a hand down the comforter. It was homemade from her older sister and had a huge yellow bear in the middle. "Very, I think this is the only room that's clean right now." I teased looking around the rest of the room. By the window is a white dresser with blue bears on the front, and a stuffed matching bear on top. Baby clothes covered one corner yet to be put away, but it's neat in every other way.

"I'm giving you a baby shower," I announced. I had no idea how to give one, but that's where Bessie came in. Surely, she'd have tons of ideas. "Just make sure it's after you visit Trey. I know that's first on your agenda." "For sure, I should be going. Bessie has news too." She called earlier after I had already left to have lunch. I left after kissing them, and headed home, suddenly sad.

It isn't fair sometimes. Both Bessie, and Carla would be parents even though Bessie already is. Both were married, and I still had nothing. Life is cruel to me most of the time. I had very little to be happy about, except for helping Albert, and being able to run Starlights. Small accomplishments compared to what the rest of them were doing. I pulled into my normal parking stall and reached in the backseat for the bag. I'd put it in the closet until later.

By the time I opened the door, Bessie was sitting on the couch. She was all smiles while David was eating a sandwich. Jim is next to her, an arm casually draped over her shoulder. "Sit, sit, what's in the bag?" Bessie patted the seat next to her, and I plopped down, dumping the bag on the floor. I reached down, and took the skirt, and blouse out. "That's so pretty," Bessie gushed, fingering the material.

"Yes, it is." I put the clothes back in the bag and tossed it in my closet for the time being. I forgot about the outfit while we cleaned house. I vacuumed while she, and Jim organized her room, and got all the toys that were spread all over the living room back into a plastic bin.

We both knew that is a useless task as the toys would make their way back out in minutes. I eventually made my way to my room determined to do more than toss the comforter on the bed. I walked to my closet, pushed aside some clothes until I found the bag, I tossed in there hours ago, and took out the skirt, smoothing it, and then the blouse. They were not wrinkled as I selected a hanger to hang them up on the rack.

I stared at the closet for a while. I kneeled to clean up the mess. It's piling up, and nobody's offered to clean it for me. It's up to me to do it. I started out by sorting through the clean, and dirty ones. I found most were dirty. I needed to change my habits. By the time I could see carpet, I had piles enough for five loads of laundry, and only a handful of clean ones. I scooped up a pile of dirty ones and tossed them into a laundry basket. I was intending to start a load when the door burst open, and Bessie did a flying leap onto my bed.

"Why the smile?" I asked. "Just happy about the way things turned out. Jim's reaction is to set up the baby's room right away. Jeremy's was to let me do it." I smiled at her. "What is your news?" I asked grabbing some quarters off the dresser. Jim stayed in the living room while we talked. "I have a good chance on being a secretary for Jim's Aunt Tessa's office. She's a legal representative for some law firm downtown. I forgot the name, but she gave me an application which I already filled out, and turned in this morning, and she will call me once the board reviews it." Bessie clapped her hands in excitement.

"Sounds promising. How well do you know his aunt?" "So, so," Bessie made her hand into a seesaw. "We had dinner with her last week, and she's nice. I only know her a little." "Did she just up, and offer you a job?" I asked picking up the laundry basket. I left the room to grab some laundry soap from the bathroom. "Want to come?" "Sure." Bessie

The Way Life Used To Be

hopped off the bed with one bounce. "She didn't just offer me one. Bessie, and Jim are close, and I guess she's been the one who's been taking care of him since his mom, and dad split the scene. She made us burritos that were out of this world and is asking how Jim likes his job."

We walked out of the apartment after a quick explanation to Jim who just waved us by. He is busy playing with David anyway to pay us much attention. "Anyway," Bessie continued after we walked down the stairs. "He said, he still loved it, and she mentioned her secretary is going on maternity leave in a month and needed someone part-time to fill in. May even turn into full time work as busy as they've been. I thought at first, she was asking Jim to be her secretary, not that I could ever in a million years see him at a desk. It turns out she is asking me."

"What did you say?" We entered the laundry room and were thankful it's empty. I started a load. "I am dumbfounded at first since she didn't know me from Adam, but I guess something impressed her because she asked if I'd be interested. She had a pile of applications right there at home, and I filled one out after dinner was over. I'm excited at the same time."

"Well, it sounds good anyway. Just don't be too disappointed if it doesn't work out." I advised, grabbing my basket. I wanted to get back to the room to get the second load ready. The laundry room is open twenty-four hours which I am now thankful for. "I try not to be, but this is my first job opportunity. I don't want to blow it, and try as I don't want to, I know I'll be devastated if I don't get it."

We left the room and made our way back to the apartment. Once inside, I went straight for my room again, and started refilling the basket with clothes. "Why do you have so much laundry to do?" "Because I'm too lazy to care." I smiled as I filled the second basket, and started folding the clothes that were clean, and in another pile. Bessie studied me as I folded blouses, and skirts, making neat piles of them to place in the dresser instead of the closet floor. She glanced at the closet and could see most of the carpet now.

Jim is calling for her, so she jumped off the bed again, and went to put David down for the night. I went back to folding shorts, and Jim poked his head in to say a quick, hello. He sat down near the same spot Bessie was sitting only moments before. "Hey," he smiled. "David is getting fussy." "He does that, once dinners over, and it's time for bed. Usually takes a good hour to put him to sleep."

"So, how're things going with you?" "Pretty good." I smiled as I turned back to my closet to make sure there weren't any more clothes inside. I found it empty and backed out to grab a black t-shirt next to the door and shook it to get rid of any wrinkles before folding it.

A white piece of material fell from it, and I lowered my glance to find out what it was. It's my garter. I forgot about tossing it in the closet the day of the wedding. I caressed it before the tears started. "Oh. Oh God." I sobbed into the garter. Jim frowned as he realized what I am holding and slid off the bed to the floor where he kneeled next to me.

I buried my face in my hands still holding the garter. He pulled me close, so my head is on his chest and I let go. All those feelings I thought were gone came back to rear their ugly head. "Shh, it's okay." He whispered. "It's okay." Rocking, he said, nothing more as he held on tight while I sobbed into my hands. It's a full five minutes before I could lift my head. I had tears still falling as I sighed. "I'm supposed to be done."

"Sorry Rees. You'll never be done, and I don't say that to make things worse for you. I know what it feels like to be alone and have nobody to share your feelings with. It's a feeling that breaks your heart." "I thought I was over it by now. Are you talking about past girlfriends?" I asked gathering up the second load of clothes and tossed them in the basket.

He shook his head. "No, I was on a woman search for a long time now as you probably well know." I nodded in agreement but didn't interrupt. "I've never had a role model showing me what a good woman should be like. I had your mom for most of my advice, but an actual mom is not to be had. Despite it, I don't think I've done too bad. I have the best women in my life now." "What about Bessie?" I teased, and he threw an arm around my shoulder, and kissed my cheek.

"Don't tell her." He whispered. "Wouldn't dream of it." He smiled and left the room to see what Bessie was up to. I left too, to switch my laundry to the dryer, and started the second load before realizing this would be a very long night.

It really was a long night. I ended up doing three loads of laundry total. I folded every piece of clothing and put everything away neatly. I flopped onto my bed to relax for a minute. It's close to midnight, and I realized for the first time all day I am off tomorrow. I had no idea how to spend my day. I took a quick shower to wash off the grime, and changed into sweats, and climbed under my comforter.

The Way Life Used To Be

When morning dawned, it surprised me to find I am wide awake. I would crash hard later, but for now I would take advantage of it. I am still going strong when I arrived at Starlights for a drink, and it didn't occur to me, I am still in shock from last night. I still had no idea what I am doing. I felt like I am running on nerves. I grabbed a soda, and sat at the dining counter, staring at the counter tops. Three other people shared the bar, so I'm hidden from the front doors.

Mom noticed me sitting there. "How's everything?" She asked smiling. There weren't any customers needing anything at the moment. I shrugged my shoulders and sighed. I didn't respond which caused her to frown. She however said, nothing else. She just grabbed a wash-cloth and pretended to look busy by wiping down the counter. I continued to look down. She eventually walked into the kitchen. She didn't want to be around my negativity. I couldn't blame her.

Trey came in the front doors, intending to get a sandwich to take on the road. It's going to be an early day for once. Only one more stop, and that is it. This is such a rare occurrence that he honestly had no clue how to spend the rest of his day. It's early for lunch, barely eleven, but he could always use a sandwich. He'd take it on his last delivery, then eat it in the comfort of his house with the company of his TV, and an afternoon of quiet.

He ordered and sat at a bar stool waiting. It's quiet here with most of the tables still empty. Mark interrupted his thoughts. "Here you go man." "This'll hit the spot. How's it going?" "Not bad. It's been slow." Just then a couple entered. "Guess I lied," He smiled, and Trey waved a hand goodbye.

Once Mark had disappeared, he helped himself to a soda, and grabbed his wallet to pay for his lunch. Zeni was still in the kitchen. He paid for his meal and stuffed the change into his back pocket when he looked up to find me, looking down at my cup that is still full.

Another first for me. I had my hands in my lap. "Want to get out of here?" I opened my eyes and nodded as I followed him out the back door. He led me to his truck and opened the passenger door. I climbed inside and buckled my seatbelt wondering what I am doing. I just walked away without saying goodbye, and that just went to show how rude I am.

Trey got in the driver's seat, and we took off in silence. He made his delivery as promised, then headed home. I leaned against the door, growing more relaxed by the minute. We didn't say a word to each other until we reached the barn. I glanced out the window and smiled for the first time all day. "Is it time for Albert to give birth?"

Trey shook his head. "I want to show you something." I followed him past the stalls until we reached a section I hadn't seen before. "Meet Abbott, and Costello." Two brown, and white Appaloosas whinnied, and came trotting over to the fence where Trey, and I were standing. He held the bag with his sandwich in one hand and reached over the fence with his free hand to stroke the stud's mane. I laughed out loud. "You bought horses." "I bought horses. My best investment yet."

"They are such a majestic looking animal. How do you tell them apart?" "Abbott has a mark above his ear. It looks kind of like a birthmark in a way. Costello has more brown than white, especially on his left side, running down to the back hoof. I bought them six months ago. They're two years old." "Are they old enough to ride?"

Trey shook his head. "Not for another few years. Most thoroughbreds need to be at least four." "Then I guess you'll have something to look forward to." While I admired them up close, Trey left to go inside his new house. My eyes followed his backside as he disappeared. He came right back out seconds later with two apples he sliced in half. He handed me one to feed to the horses. Costello nibbled on my hand for a second trying to get at the apple and munched like he is enjoying his treat. I said a quick hello to Albert who looked miserable. I glanced up to look at his new house.

"You're full of surprises today." "Guess I am. Bret, and I built that a few months ago. I wanted my own place. Kind of like you." "It sucks sometimes being an adult." "It does indeed." That made me giggle as he sounded just like Jim, and I told him so. "Guess he's a bigger influence than I gave him credit for." "He's a truly awesome friend. He took care of me yesterday." "He cares all the time. Want to tell me what happened?"

As always, I opened up, and he leaned on the fence listening. "You can do one of two things in this particular situation. Let it eat you alive, or let it leave." I didn't deserve him, friend or anything else. I leaned closer, and he turned his head, and kissed my eye. No, I didn't deserve him. I looked around the barn and settled my gaze on Albert. She looked miserable, just lying there against the fence, head down, and she had her eyes closed.

"I'm surprised she hasn't popped that calf loose yet." "I am too, but it might be another day or so."

The Way Life Used To Be

He drove me back to Starlights, and it wasn't until he reached home again, he realized he forgot all about his lunch. I drove home, feeling empty. Only Jim is there. Bessie left with David to the store for some dinner. I sat next to him on the couch after putting my purse on the bed and changed clothes.

"How's it going?" He asked, and I frowned. "That good?" "Do you ever feel alone?" I asked. "Yes," he answered. "I feel hate inside." I admitted, referring to last night. I guess I wasn't ready to let it leave. "Do you know what it's like to hate someone?" "Sure, I do." "No, do you know what it's like?" He said.

When I remained silent, he continued. "I know first-hand how it feels. I used to feel hate towards my parents. Even after my dad, I couldn't let go of hate. I'm convinced it turned my heart black. I felt numb, and incapable of being a good person. That goal would always be just out of my reach. It's Bessie who turned me around." "I'm capable of many things. I've taken a life, and that, in itself should make her run in the other direction." I was surprised by his confession.

"I'd like to tell you that would never happen, but it might so I won't lie. I can tell you I've never seen her more content. As of now, she trusts you, and maybe that's enough." "For now, it is, and hopefully will always be." He said. I went on, "you would never hurt her. Physically or otherwise, I know you wouldn't. She knows that too." The door opened, and Bessie appeared, her arms full of bags. Even David carried a bag in both hands, smiling. "Hey," she greeted.

My cell phone rang just then. It's just going on four. This time I glanced at the caller id. "Hey Trey." "Albert's just about ready. If…" I interrupted "Be right there." I hung up, ran to my room, and changed into old jeans, and sneakers. That reminded me about Carla's fantasy, and made me giggle as I tied the laces, grabbed my purse, and ran out the door with a hasty bye, and jumped into my car. This is a better end to my day. I needed to apologize to mom, and dad, but there were more pressing issues at hand.

I had to watch my speed as I drove down the highway as it wouldn't do me a damn bit of good if I got a ticket. I turned off exit 282 east and drove a few miles before turning left where Hankins stood and entered his driveway minutes later. I am growing excited and got out of my car. I left the purse on the floorboard and rushed to where Albert is. Trey isn't out there. I walked around the entire length before I heard the music coming from his new house. I climbed the three cement steps, and made it as far as the open doorway intending to knock, before I found him there, leaning over his kitchen sink washing his hands, and singing along to Alabama's Down Home, when it hit me, and hit hard.

I love him. All the warnings left me as I let these new feelings take over. Trey turned off the water and dried his hands on a dish towel. He turned to head outside when he saw me standing there. He studied the change on my face. "Bout damn time don't you think?" "That it took a few years to realize what's been in front of my face the whole time?"

"More like half a lifetime. But it's okay. I'm a patient man you know. Albert unfortunately doesn't have any, so let's get this calf born." We walked to the barn and was greeted by a high squeak that sounded so similar to a pig. "That's Albert," Trey said. She is lying on her side, heaving loudly, and looking suddenly in severe pain.

"About time huh girl?" He whispered, and she opened her eyes, and lifted her head. "How can I help?" I asked. "I need to get blankets out of the barn to keep her warm, and comfortable. She'll do this on her own, but I need to be close to her just in case she has any difficulties." "I'll get them. Where are they?" He pointed to the barn doors. "On a rack right near the entrance. There's a bunch of army blankets that were donated to us years ago."

I rushed to the entrance, and pulled down three blankets, and ran back just as Trey had helped Albert on her feet to make it easier for her. Just as she made it to all four feet, I could see the bulge from her stomach. I could also see two tiny feet that emerged from her flesh, causing her to moan. "Baby's just about ready to come." Trey pointed to the feet. "I need to help with the head." He tossed on a pair of rubber gloves and reached in to help push the head through.

After about half an hour of pushing, and prodding, the feet were now dangling, and the head is just beginning to emerge, bloody, and tiny. Albert is pushing, and with Trey's help, the calf is born without incident. I sat there; mouth opened as I realized what I just witnessed. I felt like I didn't do a damn thing, but watch. Trey is smiling as he made his way back to me. The calf is on the ground, and Albert had lowered herself, licking the blood off.

"Well, what did you think?" he asked pulling off the gloves and left them on the ground. He'd throw them in the trash in the morning. It's getting late, and he had to be up early for deliveries. "It's incredible, and so similar how humans do it. You never blinked an eye either. Just shoved your hand in to help her." It still amazed me at what he just did.

The Way Life Used To Be

"I have to admit, it's easier this time. The first time she gave birth, and the veterinarian was here, I took notes so if she or any of my other cows gave birth, I'd be prepared for it. This time isn't as hard as I'd expected it. I still had to go to the clinic to get some medicine for her, but that'll wait till tomorrow. She'll be spending most of tonight cleaning the calf, anyway."

I smiled. "She's doing a good job so far." I nodded towards Albert who had cleaned the baby's head and is working on the neck. The baby still had its eyes closed, and from here, I couldn't tell what the sex is. The baby is cute no matter what it is. The baby made mewling sounds as it tried in vain to stand up already. She ended up plopping back on her butt.

Trey reached for my hand which I gave, and we made our way back to the house. He excused himself to wash his hands. While he was gone, it gave me a better chance to look at his house and admire his work. It took so much time, and patience to build something, and if the barn is any sign, he enjoyed it. "Sorry," Trey apologized coming back to the kitchen where I am waiting on a bar stool. My jeans were filthy, but I never looked happier.

"Perfectly okay." I smiled at him. "Want to go out for dinner tomorrow?" He asked joining on a stool next to me. "Love to. Are we celebrating?" "Of course. I'll call you as soon as I finish my last delivery. Just give me time to change first."

I had time to look at the inside, while he disappeared down a hall. My view is limited to the kitchen. The counters were marble topped with cherry wood cabinets. The cherry wood is extended to a kitchen table with 4 matching chairs. It was spotless and had a warm feeling. Something I'm surprised at, especially with his work-load.

He returned a few minutes later, dressed in clean blue jeans, and a red t-shirt. "Want a tour?" "Definitely." "This is my kitchen." Trey spread his arms. "You don't say." I teased. I followed him out of the kitchen to a rounded top open doorway to his living room. It's decorated in earth tone colors with a dark brown leather couch and matching recliner. A wooden coffee table separated them and had a single picture in a brass frame. The carpet is various shades of brown and looked pretty with the furniture.

"I like it so far." I complimented. "This is the first room I finished. I even slept on my couch for a month while I was working on the upstairs bathroom, and bedroom. There's only one finished. I have an office that could be a second bedroom if the need ever arises." "Why is it only an office?" "All that's in there is a desk, chair, and computer. I hardly ever use it, which is why it's only an office."

We walked up the spiral stairs, and he pointed out both the office, and bathroom. Trey is surprisingly neat, and that added points. "You hungry?" He asked as we made our way back downstairs. He kept his bedroom door shut, and I didn't have the nerve to ask to see it. That just seemed a tad too personal.

"A little, I guess." Really, I am starving, but didn't want him to feel obligated to fix dinner. "Have a seat and relax. Be just a minute." I'm sure it would be longer than a minute, but that's okay. I had nothing else to do, and I didn't want to go back home. I settled myself on a bar stool, and he placed a cup of lemonade before me on the counter. I sipped while I watched him work.

Trey took a chicken breast out of the refrigerator, and placed it in a pan, and started the marinade. "So, what did you think of the whole birth thing? Make you want to have one of your own?" He asked, smiling at me while he used a whisk. "Oh, yeah. I can't wait." I said, wanting to shiver. "I will be an aunt again, and an honorary aunt. I think that's all I can handle for quite a while."

He poured the mix over the chicken and slid the pan into the oven. "Honorary?" "As in Carla, and Taylor." I took a drink. "Cool," Trey said. That is so like him. He is most of the time a man of simple words. "Yes, it is. I'm so happy for them, but no it doesn't change things." "I think I might know where the problem lies." He said, while starting some Rice-A-Roni. "You haven't had the right person to steer you in that direction." That made me raise an eyebrow. "I hadn't thought of it that way." I admitted.

Trey smiled as he tested the chicken. "Almost done. Need a refill?" He nodded towards my glass while taking the rice off the stove. I waved aside his offer. I still had half of my lemonade. He got two plates out of a cupboard, and held them, as we went into the living room to eat by the company of a twenty-five-inch TV placed on a metal TV stand against the corner. I wasn't paying attention to what is on it. Trey is much more interesting to look at.

I glanced at the picture in the coffee table. He followed it. "That's my old high school girlfriend. I think that is sophomore prom." He said, taking a bite of his chicken. "She's pretty. Looking pretty sharp yourself." "You would think so." Trey laughed. "You done?" "Yes, thank you." I smiled back at him. He gathered my plate, and it seemed a good time to say good night. I am so tired I had a hard time staying focused.

"Be right back." Trey said, after putting the plates in the sink. He didn't have the same determination I had when it came to cleaning. He returned moments later. Once again, those feelings came over me, shocking my system. I approached him, and he kept his gaze on me. His mouth is slightly opened. I don't understand why I never saw him before. His hair, and neck, still wet when I reached him. I slid my arms around his neck and hugged him close. His arms wrapped around me, and he lowered his head as I buried my face in his neck, closing my eyes.

"Thank you for letting me be a part of this." I said, realizing it's my turn to support him. "I should go check on her." He sounded tired. "See you tomorrow." "Okay," I answered, and headed to my car. It's an exhausting day as I realized I had taken no time to relax at all. I drove to my parents' house. May as well get my apology over with even though it isn't warranted.

I sat in the kitchen with nothing on, but a light over the stove. Dad is already upstairs, so mom, and I sat at the kitchen table, drinking lemonade, and eating Doritos. That also reminded me of my dinner earlier. I didn't say a word about that though. I wanted to have that moment to myself. She waved aside my feeble attempt by waving one hand. "You're an adult, and it's not like you neglected your duties. If Trey got you to feel better, that's all that matters."

"It's weird when I am bawling into my stupid garter, and Jim of all people is there to catch me when I fell." "Jim has many qualities, one of which is caring." "That he does. I'd never seen that side of him before. Trey explained that he masks a lot of them." "We all mask our true feelings." "Yes, we do. Albert is gracious enough to wait until I got there before deciding to go into labor. I just watched, but it's amazing. Trey is amazing."

"I bet he is. What happened afterwards?" "When Albert is done, and cleaning the calf, I got to see his new house. It's beautiful." "I bet it is. I'm not upset you left, but I'm worried about your state of mind. I'm glad you weren't driving." "I am too, I'm still not sure why it affected me like it did. Jim has strengths I didn't know he is capable of. He admitted he took a life, and he said that gave Bessie the right to turn against him."

"Bessie is many moods." She began and stopped to take a drink. "Everyone whether we want to admit it is capable of violence. She could one day have enough of her baby screaming to the point she can't stop it, and snaps. I'm relatively sure she'd hate herself for it, but the tendency lives in all of us. Jim's not a murderer, but if Bessie decided one day to leave him, that would be her choice."

"I'd like to say she wouldn't walk away from the best thing that's ever happened, especially with a second baby on the way. I've already decided not to be a coach again if the opportunity presents itself." Zeni laughed. "Had enough the first time around?" "And then some. I should get going." I placed my cup in the sink and kissed the top of her head as she remained sitting. l left to get some dessert before going home.

I passed a McDonalds, and Burger King, before stopping at a Baskin Robins. I wanted a sundae. I placed my bag in the passenger seat. I couldn't wait until I reached home to eat. Suddenly, I wasn't that tired anymore. My cell phone rang before I parked, and it is Trey making me smile. "Hey, I forgot when I asked you to dinner tomorrow, I need to make a stop to the veterinary clinic to pick up some ointment for Albert."

"I can get it. I'm off at four so it's fine. I can do that much for her." "If you don't mind, that'll be a huge weight off my shoulders." He gave directions to the clinic. He is already feeling better. Tomorrow his day is completely booked. I made it home to an empty apartment, and that is fine with me. For once I'd be able to enjoy my treat by myself which lately is rare. I did however make it to bed at a reasonable time since

I had an early shift tomorrow. I didn't hear if Bessie, and Jim made it home, I am that tired, but the thought of Trey brought a smile to my face as I drifted off to sleep.

Chapter 18

By three the next day, I'm still happy as I headed out of Starlights. I decided not to tell anyone about this date yet. I wanted to see how it went before I got my hopes up again. I smiled as I left and headed to the grocery store. Might as well get the shopping done while I am out, and Hankins is right down the road. Thirty minutes later I am entering the store. Albert's medicine is totally forgotten as I wondered the aisles selecting food, I took almost an hour before I headed to the register.

I called once for Bessie but got her voice mail. I realized she must have heard from Jim's Aunt about the job. I crossed my fingers in hopes she'd get the job. It would do wonders for her self-esteem. I made it to the apartment with no problems. I put the groceries away and decided may as well continue with my domestic requirements and headed to my bedroom to grab yet another load of laundry. I doubt this chore would ever be completed.

It's close to five when I'm finished and sweat is pouring down my face. A shower is next in line. Trey still hadn't called, so I assumed he is making the last of his deliveries, and would give me ample time to bathe, and dress in my new outfit. The thought of him made me smile. I started some water, and the phone rang just as I am about to change. "Hey, you still up for tonight?" It's Trey and brought a bigger smile to my face. "Just about. I need about half an hour. That okay?"

"Perfect. I have one more delivery, then I'm done for the day. I'll be by in an hour. May as well make this official." He teased making me giggle. "That's the sound I know, and love. See you soon." He hung up with a smile and headed north. I sank in peach flavored bubbles and closed my eyes in anticipation of tonight. Maybe after dinner, I'd get to know him in that special intimate way I hadn't allowed myself to be in years. Hell, I'm already in love with him so this is naturally the next step. It made me moan thinking of him, and I had to bite my lip to stop it.

This is going beyond my control, and I'm exhilarated, excited, and scared me all at the same time. After all, we'd been nothing, but friends. Can you get past that and be more? The clock struck five thirty, making me realize I had less than half an hour before he is due. I climbed out of the tub and drained the water. I headed to the bedroom naked to change. Bessie still isn't home, so I didn't worry about getting caught in the buff.

I found a clean pair of underwear and dressed. I left the nylons I am planning on wearing in the drawer. Even though it's raining hard, and there is a clap of thunder, it's warm outside, and I didn't want to worry about sweating on top of everything else.

The clothes were a perfect fit still, and I caressed the silkiness imagining again Trey's hands on me. The doorbell rang just as I finished French braiding my hair, and Trey stood on the other side of the door. He had a pink rose in one hand, and the other arm against the doorframe. His legs are crossed giving him a casual look.

"Hey," He said. He handed me the flower. "Hey back." I accepted the rose, then lifted on my toes to give him a thank you kiss on his neck. I wrapped my arms around him, and he pulled me closer, burying his head in my neck. "That is better than any hello I had in mind." I said. I withdrew my arms so I could get my purse I had hanging near the doorway on a coat rack.

"You ready to go?" He asked, holding out his arm. I slipped mine through it. He drove past Bistros and turned right. Two miles down the road, he turned into Froggie's which is a Mexican restaurant, and I'm happy. "This place okay?" He asked. I smiled my answer. The inside smelled like garlic, spicy tomato, and all around delicious.

I breathed in the aromas, and we are seated with offers of alcoholic drinks. We both decided on sodas. Once the hostess is gone, I asked, "why don't you ever drink. Had a bad experience or something?" "Lots of reasons, the main one being I don't enjoy losing control. I've never had any bad experiences and never gave in to the peer pressure of drinking while I was in school. I just never liked the taste I guess." He explained shrugging his shoulders.

"I don't like alcohol either." I said, taking a drink of my soda. "You realize I have to make you drink water too." He tapped my water glass with the tip of one finger. He gulped half of his as soon as we set them on the table. "I should require you to submit a goodwill promise to me."

The Way Life Used To Be

"I already promised my dad. Why do you have to put a damper on my evening?" I pouted and took a small sip. He laughed "What is it about healthy drinks that makes you abolish them?" He asked.

"That they're healthy speaks for itself, but to make you happy, I will oblige." I lifted my water glass and took a bigger drink. "That's a good girl," he teased. I stuck my tongue out at him. "That's an immature girl." I threw a napkin at him. A waitress returned with our food, and we talked just as much as eating, and were both surprised at how natural this all felt. Like we'd been dating forever. "You get all your deliveries done?" I asked, taking a bite of my burrito.

"Sure did. We gained a new customer today too. Do you remember Tom Perkins?" Tom is a year ahead of me in school. He is a baseball player who got a scholarship to play professional with some University. "I remember him. I didn't know you were friends." "So, So. I guess. His dad just started up a grocery store. Seems excited about it." "Good news." I smiled at him. His cell phone rang causing him to groan. "I'd let this go to voice mail, but it's dad."

"Answer it." I said, without hesitation. "Hey pop, what's up?" He nodded to the waitress as she gathered up the plates. "Trey, Albert's having complications. Can you cut your evening short and come to the house?" "What's wrong with her?" His voice pitched several notes, and he remembered about the cream. He is about to ask me if I picked it up. He could tell from my face I had forgotten when I drove to the grocery store earlier. "She seems to be in a lot of pain. Keeps trying to lick herself, but she can't reach it. She's been ignoring the calf."

"He looks like he's doing okay from what I can see, but he needs his mom." Jacob explained, his voice starting to panic. He had no idea what to do with all Trey's animals. He had barely gotten started with the barn when he had those heart attacks. "You with her right now?"

"I am, mom, and I just got done with dinner. Want me to check on her again for you?" Jacob sounds more, and more panicked. "No, I'll do it. We're close to the house now. I can be there in ten minutes." He snapped the phone shut and turned back to me with an apologetic smile.

"I'm sorry." I reached a hand over his arm dismissing his apology and offered one of my own. "It's my fault. I forgot to get the medicine when I was out earlier. I'm sorry I forgot it. I'll get it now and meet you at your house." "Your car is at your apartment. I'll run by the house to check on her, if you don't mind. Can you run to the pharmacy?"

Sandra Gutierrez

I did nothing, but nod in agreement. Didn't even need one second to agree with him. "You okay with driving my truck? It's a stick shift?" Trey asked. "I'm fine. Mark taught me to drive a stick years ago. You go check on her, and I'll be just a minute." I am already grabbing my purse and scooted out of my seat.

He followed me and paid for our dinner on the way out. He kissed me goodbye as I climbed in the driver's seat, and he turned into the rain heading towards the barn. I turned the truck out of the parking lot and headed down the street. I turned left at the corner and headed towards the clinic. I am hoping they are still opened so Albert could get her medicine. I felt so bad that I forgot. I had every intention of making it up to Albert as soon as I reached the farm.

I reached the clinic, and the open sign still blinked so I smiled a thank you and climbed out of the truck. I am careful to lock it and headed towards the front door. I didn't know the area very well, and had to cross the dark street first, making me thankful I am inside where I already felt safer. I made my way right up to the counter as Trey reached home and went straight to the barn to check on Albert. He is soaking wet with rain drops. He didn't care in the least.

She is lying on her side, moaning. She tried licking herself, but only made it halfway before her body failed on her. Try as she might, she just didn't bend far enough. She lifted her head as footsteps approached, and Trey leaned down in the mud to check on her. "Hey girl." He whispered, stroking her wet head. "I'll make you better soon. I need to check on you okay?"

Of course, she didn't answer, but he crawled through two slats, and lifted one leg so he could see better. It's bright red and flamed. Damn, it looked infected. "Reesa will be here soon to help us." He ran a hand down her length, and she reached with her head to lick his face. She is soaked as well. He kneeled on both knees and petted her. She turned and lay her head on his lap making him cry.

I paid for the medicine with my credit card. I am not in the least worried that he'd pay me back. I didn't even care now since I am the one who forgot in the first place. This would be my gift.

I smiled as I left the clinic. My sandals clicked on the pavement as I reached for the hood and wrapped it around my head. I covered my hair, and only a little of my face showed as I pressed a hand to my throat to keep the hood together. I crossed the street, not seeing the black car come screeching around the corner. I barely had time to whip my head

The Way Life Used To Be

towards the sound when I am bumped on the right side spun a full ninety degrees and is flung face first into Trey's truck. I landed on my back as the car disappeared. Trey is getting worried when half an hour after she should have shown her beautiful face, she hadn't arrived. He said, a quick goodbye to Albert, and headed to his house so he could call her cell phone. No answer, but her voice mail. He left a hasty message and ran upstairs to change so when he is ready to apply the medication, he'd be properly dressed, and dry.

The phone rang as he flung his wet jeans in the hamper and is smiling as he reached for it. He frowned when the display read Bret, not Reesa. "Hey man, what are you doing?" He asked grabbing a clean pair of jeans from his dresser. "Not much happening right at the moment, but Jan's having another party in about an hour. You want to hang?" "I would, but I have kind of emergency here. Albert may have an infection, and Reesa's supposed to be here any minute with her medication. Sounds like it would have been fun though."

"Sorry to hear that. Want us to cancel. I can get over there to help you?"

"Nice offer, but no, you guys enjoy your evening. There's not much you could do, anyway. I'll see you tomorrow though." "Oh yeah, I forgot you wanted to take out the corn stalks. Be there as soon as I can in the morning." Bret smiled and hung up. Trey snapped the cell phone shut. He put on some galoshes and headed back outside. He was expecting Reesa to make an appearance.

It's quiet except for Albert's tail swishing, and no Reesa. He called her again. This time there is a little more desperation in his voice. Again, reached her voice mail. He headed over to his mom, and dad's house to borrow their car.

Reesa must have issues with getting the medicine he decided once he reached their house, and only Cynthia is there, smiling, and opened her arms to welcome him. She gave him a kiss on the cheek and asked about Albert. "She's fine for now. I think she has an infection. It's red, and she can't reach it. I think licking it would make it worse, but who knows with animals. They lick themselves any time they're awake." "Your right, at least about cats, and dogs is the extent of my knowledge with that subject." Cynthia smiled as she continued washing dishes.

"Where's dad?" "Still at the barn. He saw you check on Albert, and he wanted to fix a stall for her just in case she needed to get out of the wet, and cold for the night." "That's good, hey, did Reesa call here by chance. She went to get the ointment for Albert?" He felt bad that his dad is all alone in the barn and didn't even know he is out there when he checked on her. "Nope. Why did you ask her to call here?"

"I didn't. She's running so late, and I'm getting worried. I will call the clinic to make sure she made it there." He flipped his phone opened and frowned when he found out she made it there, purchased the lotion, and left over an hour ago. They were about to close for the night and had no more information than that.

Well that gave him a starting point. He would trace her steps best he could to find out what happened. She had never to his knowledge let anybody down and didn't think she'd be starting now. Cynthia handed over her keys, and he declined needing her to go with him. The door burst opened again, and Bret filled the doorway.

"Trey...." "What are you doing here. What happened to your shindig?" "Trey." Bret said, again more making him stop reaching for his mom's keys and turn to look. "Your truck is still at the clinic." Bret began. "Why? Where did Reesa go?" Trey's voice is getting high pitched with panic. Bret moved into the kitchen and started putting an arm around his shoulders. "Your truck is still there, but Reesa's been taken to the hospital." He said, as gently as he could.

"What the fuck happened?" Trey is yelling by this time and pulling his hair in frustration. "Please sit down. I'll take you to the hospital in a few minutes, but you need to sit." He forced him into a chair, while Cynthia sat next to him. She had one arm around his neck, and the other holding his arm. She started stroking. "When Reesa was done getting Albert's medicine it looks like, she was walking towards your truck when she was hit on her right side. She's in surgery right now as we speak, and her parents are in the waiting room."

"How did you know all this?" Trey started crying. He isn't in the least embarrassed in front of his friend. "I was on my way to Jan's, and the clinic is on the same street I had to drive down to get to her house. I recognized your truck, and the ambulance was already there, with Reesa on a stretcher. They couldn't tell me much, as I'm a stranger, and wouldn't even tell me her name. I got out of them what happened to her. They took off twenty minutes ago, and I headed to your house, but you weren't there. I'm glad I caught you."

"I need to go." He choked out the words and got up. "Right now." "Okay, let's go, I'm driving." Bret decided, and they left with a hasty goodbye to Cynthia. Trey sat stiff backed as he wished for the first time

The Way Life Used To Be

in his life that Bret would ignore the street laws and get him to her even faster than they were going. He was at a loss trying to figure out how the hell this could have happened. Reesa's predictions was for the guy to take a fall, not herself.

When Bret found a parking spot, Trey flew out of the car, and ran towards the emergency entrance. Zeni, and Keith were sitting side by side, when he ran inside, and went to them. "She's okay right?" He whispered, tears still falling. Zeni turned to him. She had tears falling and reached over to take one of his hands. They stood up together. "M...." Is all she could get out before falling to her knees.

Trey followed her. He had his arms around her shoulders. Keith is on one side of her, and Trey is on the other, supporting her. "I want..." She buried her face in her hands. "My baby." She choked. Keith understood as this is a repeat, but so different at the same time. She ran the other hand through her hair in frustration and ended up jumping up to pace.

"Do you know what's wrong?" Trey asked. "A broken leg for sure. She's bleeding internally, and they think she may have bruised some organs. Her head took the worst hit as she is flung face first into your window. The glass is shattered, and I think it's still scattered on the road." Keith answered his question this time as Zeni couldn't talk anymore.

Trey also ran a hand through his hair. He could not sit still waiting for news. Mark, and Sara hadn't shown up yet even though Keith called them. They would be there in the morning. They didn't want to crowd the waiting room. Mark was beside himself on the phone and wanted to know the instant there is any change. It's almost midnight when they heard she is out of surgery, and in the recovery unit.

They are all exhausted. They ran as fast as they could upstairs to the surgery unit and were directed to room 402. Zeni is the first one in the doorway and gasped. "Oh my god." She whispered, rushing forwards, and pressed her face to my chest. "Wake up." She rubbed at my arm, tears falling, but she didn't try to wipe them away. My head is covered in bandages, and my eyes were closed. I could hear faint voices, but it sounded like whispers.

Keith joined her. He pressed his head against his wife's as he closed his eyes and prayed. He hadn't been to church since he was a little boy. He prayed for his daughter to be okay. This couldn't be the end. She is only twenty-two, and not even a year out of college. This isn't over. Trey remained behind watching them, hover over her. He leaned against the door frame with his arms crossed as he studied them.

It brought back so many memories, most of them scary. He saw his dad in the bed with machines hooked up to him everywhere. He remembered how scared he was to lose his father. He was just as scared now at losing his best friend. A nurse came by about nine. Visiting hours were long over, but she found them a room nearby where they could grab some sleep. Trey opted to stay there in the room. He had small amounts of sleep in a chair that made every muscle scream in pain by the time the sun made its way over the horizon, saying hello.

Trey stood by the window, eyes closed, and leaned his face against the cool glass. The sky is cloudless. The storm from last night just a distant memory by now. It's only eight in the morning. Trey felt like he had been there for days waiting for her to wake up.

Cars streamed along the freeway with the drivers on their way to work, oblivious of the hell he is living. The window warmed from the sun's rays, but he remained where he was. He stared outside trying to make sense of all this. He was coming up with nothing. Surely, it's just a cruel trick of fate that brought her to this. His stomach is full of guilt that he let her do this.

Trey turned to the bed and eventually walked to the side of it. He pushed a chair against the bed rails and sat down. He lay his head on one arm, and the other stroked her cheek. Trey willed her to wake up. "Last night was so hard for you. I'm sorry you got hit." He whispered. His voice is hoarse, and eyes sad. Tears were falling still.

He couldn't seem to stop them from flowing. "Albert's doing better. I found the medicine early this morning when I left to change. There's no arrest yet from the person who hurt you, but this I promise you. I won't stop until he's put in the ground."

He moved his hand down to my chest and found I am breathing. That had to be a good sign, that I am breathing on my own. I am still unconscious, and my hair is matted against the pillow as my eyes remained closed. I could hear him more clearly now, but it felt like he is in a cave or something, and his voice sounded hollow.

He refused to leave the room feeling guilty again that he left. It didn't matter that it's very dark, and nobody noticed his absence. He knew it and made an internal promise to himself he wouldn't ever again. Eventually the nurses gave up asking if he wanted anything, thinking having him there may be what she needed to heal. Trey reached with one arm to brush my hair from my face, slowly, and repeatedly.

I felt his touch. "She's still infected, but with a few more doses, she'll be good as new. She's been asking for you. Wants to thank you for helping her. For being her friend." He took a drink of water to wash the lump that is growing in his throat away.

Trey swallowed, but the lump remained. He looked around, trying to get used to the machines that beeped every few seconds, and willed her to wake up. My head is still heavily bandaged and swelled. He ached to kiss it. He thought it might bring her more pain by doing so. Trey opted to ignore it the best he could, and held my hand, rubbing his thumb over my palm, bringing the fingers to his lips where he kissed. He closed his eyes while Keith watched from the doorway listening to him talk.

The love between them, unbelievably stirred him. Too bad Reesa is unaware of what is going on around her. There didn't seem to be much change, but the doctor would be there in a few minutes to give them an update. Zeni is getting them some coffee as they needed some caffeine. They only had snatches of sleep. They kept expecting to be roused from their sleep with bad news, so they kept one ear on the door, but it remained closed. Maybe no news is good news.

He leaned against the doorway similarly to what Trey was last night and watched as Trey closed his eyes. He dropped his head to the bed. Keith hated to ruin their moment, even if it's one sided right now. He lifted himself from the doorway by a shoulder, and moved further into the room, stopping at the foot of the bed, and to Treys right. Trey only glanced over, then lowered his head again. Keith reached over to squeeze his shoulder.

"She'll be okay you know." "Yeah?" Trey whispered. "How?" "Because she has you to wake up to."

"How do I even know she hears me?" Keith pointed to her fingers. "She's moving her hand." Trey glanced down and frowned. "I didn't even notice. Some boyfriend I turned out to be." He smiled. "Don't tell her." "I promise." "Do I need to do the pinkie swear thing?" Trey teased sitting up a little straighter.

"That's a well-known promise around these parts." Keith smiled wider. "I made her do that because that's how much I love her. This scene before you don't count." He nodded towards the IV that is feeding her the necessary nutrients. "I should hope so. I've been teasing her a lot lately about that." "Doing any good?"

Trey shrugged his shoulders. "A little, I think it is at least. We had our first official date last night, and I made her drink some water with her dinner. I thought for sure she'd hit me for it." "She'd regret it later, I'm sure. I'm sorry how your evening ended up turning out." "You seem to handle this better than Zeni. I can't help but keep thinking I caused all this. She offered to get something for me, and instead of getting it my damn self, I..." He couldn't finish.

"Need I remind you how headstrong our girl can be?" Keith asked not expecting an answer. Trey nodded. "Zeni doing any better than last night?" "No, she went down for some coffee, and should be here soon. I'm hoping she doesn't break down again."

"I imagine she will repeatedly. I know I've had my share of it." Trey said, glancing up. "There's no shame in that." Keith said, reaching the bed, and pressed a hand to Trey's shoulder. "I'm stronger on the outside than I'm truly feeling." He explained realizing how close he is to losing his resolve. Zeni couldn't stop crying even when they laid down last night to catch snatches of sleep. He spent most of the time with his arms folded in the back of his head and staring at the ceiling. His eyes were dry. It might have been because of shock or that he is so damn tired, it's too much work to cry.

Zeni had settled down and cuddled with her head on his chest and he found he was thankful when the sun came up, and they could leave that room. The lack of sleep is taking his toll, and when Zeni entered the room her eyes were red, and glistening. She carried three cups of coffee in her hands. He wanted to weep with joy. He accepted a cup and sat in a chair near the window so Zeni could have a moment with Reesa. Trey ended up joining him, and he didn't ask him for privacy. It wouldn't have done any good, anyway.

"Hi honey," She whispered. She rubbed a thumb over my soft cheek. "We're all here for you again."

I could hear her a little clearer. This bad luck thing would come to an end. Every time I had something to look forward to, it got snatched away from me somehow. How in heavens name could someone keep bouncing back from that time, and time again? I kept reminding her of that, and all she did is brush me off. Now look.

She closed her eyes, and sighed as Trey wondered over, and touched her hair. "I will find answers," he said, and touched my hand for a second before leaving the room. Enough is enough. Once he is out of the hospital, and took a deep breath of fresh air, he sighed as well, and climbed into his mom's car, and headed for home. A few phone calls were in order, starting with Bret.

Blissfully unaware of last night, Bessie is snuggled in with Jim when she turned to him beaming. "What's that all about?" He asked smiling back. He is lying on his back hands folded behind his head and enjoying the quiet. David is still fast asleep and made him thankful for it. He loved him almost as much as Bessie, but the sleep times were the best in his opinion. He is looking forward to when they would have their own baby.

He already had a new house in mind with three bedrooms so each child would have their own space. If he needed to, he'd get another part-time job to help with expenses, but his Aunt had good news for Bessie. Hopefully that wouldn't be necessary. "I'm so damn happy." Bessie gushed and brushed her hair away from her forehead where it fell back as soon as she moved her hand away. She then tucked it behind one ear where it belled out. "Because of me I take it." Jim stated and earned a pillow in his face.

"Because I get to move out soon. With the new baby coming, I think Reesa's place is way too small to fit all of us." She felt bad at the same time of wanting to move again so soon. "I wasn't planning to. I have another place in mind, I would like you to see with me." "Where? When?" As usual she asked multiple questions without waiting for an answer making him chuckle.

"Near your old high school about a block away. There's a house for rent that seems reasonable so I think..." "Let's see it now." She interrupted and earned a pillow in her face for it. He is gentle about it, and she started laughing. "You should get dressed first." He teased pulling at her silky nightshirt. "This might be inappropriate."

"Done." She flipped the shirt over her head, and stood up wearing nothing, but her underpants turning him on. She turned to her closet, tearing in looking for some jeans. "You see Reesa yet?" she asked finding a shirt and backed out of the closet. Jim shook his head and pulled on his own jeans he had dumped by the side of the bed the night before and put on some sneakers.

"I'll go see. I want to make sure she will not be mad at me for moving so soon." She headed out of the room and knocked on Reesa's door getting no response. "I think you'll be fine. If it upset her, you'd know it." "I guess she's okay then. She must still be with Trey." she shrugged her shoulders, and they headed out to see the house Jim is so excited about.

She didn't even bother checking her phone which she turned off the night before. It is full of messages. While they are gone, Trey had made it home, and Cynthia asked if there is any improvement. "No, but she's not any worse." He sighed and got a Coke joining her at the kitchen table. "You look like horseshit."

"I love you too." he laughed, and shook his head, running his fingers through his hair. "I feel so lost." "I know the feeling well." Cynthia is remembering when Jacob was on the floor suffering, and she was out shopping for groceries. The feelings of guilt dissipated somewhat. They are still there, no matter how much she tried to forgive herself, and told Trey so.

"I'd better check on Albert," he lifted himself from the chair. His muscles were screaming from last night, and he threw the can in the recycler. He got no further as he pressed his hands to his face. Cynthia is pressed against his back as he shook. "I'll check on her. Go back to check on Reesa. You'll feel better for it." He wiped his face with one hand and turned to take her into his arms.

"Thanks mama." He whispered as his cell phone rang. It's Carla of all people. "Hey sexy." She greeted laughing. "Have you seen my best friend?" She also had no idea what happened last night. After calling Reesa for hours, she assumed they spent the night together, and wanted details one way or the other. "Didn't you hear?" He asked and is greeted by instant silence. "Hear what?" She asked.

"About Reesa. Someone hit her last night." "I didn't. Oh, I heard nothing. I've been trying to call her for forever. Where is she?" "Sacred Glen. I'm about to head back there now." "On my way." The phone clicked in his ear, and he snapped his own phone shut with a quick goodbye to his mom who waved him off, and he headed out.

By the time he made it back to the hospital, he realized he never called Bret. That is the last thing on his mind as he entered room 312A and found me alone still sleeping. He rushed to the bed sorry for leaving this long, even though it had only been less than two hours.

"Oh, my goodness." Carla gushed from the doorway as she too rushed into the room, her coat flapping against her legs as she stroked my hand. "What the hell happened?" She sobbed. Trey told her the little he knew, and she stated, "we need answer, and I know just where to find them." She led Trey out of the room along with Bret who had just

The Way Life Used To Be

arrived and drove all three of them to Ted's office to get the answers she knew were there.

Instead of brushing them off, Ted did nothing, but lean back in his chair, arms folded across his chest and listened. "This is another hit-and-run." Carla explained. "This is the same person who killed Paul, and Jeff. The same person who tried to kill my best friend in the world. Reesa knew from day one who it was, and she got nowhere with it. We're not leaving until we do."

She had never spoken so firmly, and Ted smiled at her directness. "Okay. Let's work this out together. I've had my suspicions just like Reesa did, but last time I checked Greg was locked up safe, and sound as could be in a maximum-security prison. He was denied early parole. As much as I wish it was him, it has to be someone else. Let's brainstorm."

"There is no brainstorming here. It's Greg. He's found a way to escape or was helped by somebody. It's him, and no one else. I'd bet my life on it." Carla stated, tears of frustration starting to form. "I want you all to see what I'm seeing. What I've seen for the past nine years. It's right in front of me. Look at my screen." He pointed to his computer and turned it so all four of them could see the monitor.

There it is plain as day as Carla read from beginning to the end, and back again. "I'm wrong, how can we all be wrong when...." She glanced at the screen again, and pointed to the probation officer? "How the hell did his own cousin become in charge of his incarceration?" Ted flipped the monitor back to read it. "Carl Santana?"

"His cousin on his mother's side. He, and Taylor went to college together for a while. Didn't keep in touch or anything, but once when Taylor came to visit me, he made a passing comment about Greg. I didn't think much of it except I was thankful he was still locked up. What if he isn't? What if this is a coverup?"

It sounded so much like it was too good to be true, until Ted made two phone calls to the prison. His suspicions turned out correct. Carl released Greg, and doctored the papers without a second thought, five years ago. Greg spent just over four behind bars, so where the fuck is he now?

Apparently in plain sight, but just out of radar. "I'll get a team together, and we'll find him. He couldn't have gone far in so short a time. Far as we know, he doesn't have a clue that the mystery has finally been solved. Time to have a chat with Carl, and nobody breath a word of this. I don't want Greg to catch on and disappear for good this time." Ted stood up, and they all followed his lead. "I'll be in touch and hopefully sooner than later."

While he made more calls, Carla, Bret, and Trey headed outside where Trey gathered her close. "Thank you so much." Carla figured out what they had all wondered about, all by herself, and she kissed his neck. "Your welcome. Go make my best friend better." Trey took her advice without another word, and when he returned to the hospital, he found her entire family gathered at her bed, and crying, this time in joy. I am waking up, and my eyes were fluttering.

Ted did what he promised. He got no problems from Carl, who sat in Ted's office after being summoned to appear. He sat there with his head in his hands, and about ready to cry. Carl had changed a lot since high school. His jet-black hair is receding. He had gained a little weight too. "Honestly, I didn't mean to cause all this. Greg's been through intense counseling, and showed such improvement, they declared him rehabilitated. All that was left was the parole hearing, and that isn't scheduled until next year. I swear Greg cried every day begging me to let him free. All it took is my word, and he was out. They didn't even question me."

Ted sat there, tapping a pencil, "And how in the hell did you think it your right, or responsibility, or whatever the fuck you were thinking at the time to grant that wish?" His voice is rising by the second. He is so disgusted by what he just found out. It was right in front of him, and he didn't see it. Reesa could die and not have the closure she is so close to getting.

"I didn't think. That is the problem. I was trying to help my cousin. I swear that's all I was doing. I know they denied him early parole. I didn't tell him that. It would have devastated him. Am I going to get fired?" "That's the least of your worries. You still don't seem in the least bit contrite? Why is that? Are you, and Greg cut from the same cloth?"

"In a way, I guess we are." Carl swiped at his eyes. "Our moms are sisters, and Greg's dad, is a model citizen. Tried to steer Greg in the right track, but Greg had other plans. It goes beyond the stabbing at that store all those years ago. He felt like he is alone in the world and felt I was the only one who understood him."

"My dad is my best friend in the world so yes, we're cut from the same cloth. That's where the similarity ends. Greg went his own way,

The Way Life Used To Be

and I tried. Damn it I tried to help him. I would have never thought to falsify his records if it hadn't been for the fact, he's family."

"You do anything for family right?" Ted broke the pencil and threw it at the wall. "You don't do this." He slapped the computer. "You don't bend the rules to suit your own needs. Ever." "You're off the job as of this minute. I'll have Sargent Hook escort you to your new home."

"Wait." Carl cried. "Please, don't. Not yet. Greg doesn't know you have caught him. He might go over the edge if he knows. He'll run. I need to tell him." "No way in hell would I grant that. Give him an opportunity to run? You think I'm stupid?" "No, I just wanted to tell him it's done." "Damn right there, we'll both go."

He decided. Ten minutes later, they reached Carl's house where the black Camaro sat in the driveway. The garage door is down, and Ted had no idea what is behind it. "That your car?" He pointed. Carl nodded. "I've been letting Greg use it while I drive my newer Sedan. It's in the garage." They both got out, and Ted started looking closer at the Camaro. The driver's side looked painted recently, and when he ran his hand down the side, could pick out where the old paint ended, and the newer one started.

"Was this done in a shop?" "Was what done?" Carl asked looking in the window where the curtains swayed. He couldn't see Greg anywhere and didn't even know if he was in the house. "This is a recent paint job. If this was done professionally, I'd get a second opinion on it." "It isn't painted, far as I know. Then again, I haven't driven this thing for years. I thought about selling it, but I misplaced the title. When I released Greg, it didn't seem important to sell it. He needed transportation, and hates riding buses, so I let him drive it."

Ted squatted down to peer closer. "This has been painted, and I don't think Greg took it anywhere to have it done. Come here and look." Carl shrugged his shoulders, unsure where Ted is going with this, but squatted down as well, and lifted his sunglasses onto his head.

"See this?" Ted ran his hand down the side again. "Run your hand right here." Carl did what he asked and saw what he is implying. "This looks like spray paint." He dropped his hand and hung his head in shame. "Greg was the one who did this. He killed those two men with my car." He ran a hand through his hair. "I had no idea. I swear on anything I could..."

Ted interrupted. "I think for the first time today I believe what you're saying. Change of plans." He stood up and faced the house. "Is

Greg home?" "I don't know, I haven't been keeping tabs on him if that's what you're asking. What do you mean a change of plans?" "That's exactly what I mean. I am ready to come over here and lay into him. Drag him out in handcuffs screaming. I would have my satisfaction if I did so, but I have a change of plans, and you will help me."

"I'll do anything you ask. I mean it. Greg's changed. He's different now than he was before. He stammers a lot now and jumps from one conversation to the next. I think prison did that to him." "Don't do that! You're making excuses for him. Not at this late date. You have no choice, but to do what I say." "I'm not making excuses, but I need to right this situation. I'm the one who released him stating the parole board granted his freedom. I told him the first hearing was approved without him having to appear in person. All it took was a piece of paper I drew up to convince him he was free."

"Then you will go into your house and fix it. I promise you I'm not going anywhere, and if you're not out here in ten minutes with him in handcuffs, I'll do the honors myself, and with pleasure." "Give me fifteen. Please." "Not a minute more." Carl nodded his agreement, and entered his house with a heavy heart, and his hands shaking at the task ahead of him.

Greg was sitting in his room, listening to TV when Carl knocked once, then opened the door. "Hey." He greeted, turning down the volume. Greg too had changed. He no longer had the long greasy hair. They cut it military short, and he shaved his beard. Unlike Carl, he didn't look attractive. That is something never likely to happen. "We need to talk." No beating around the bush. Not anymore.

"Okay." Greg said. "I need to explain something, and you're not going to like it, but there's no going back. I made a mistake that will cost you." Greg jumped up pointing a finger and shaking. "I'm not going back there. You promised I'm done. I'm not going back." Carl sighed and nodded his head. "Yes, you are, I believed you when you said, you changed."

Greg interrupted still shaking. "I have. That slut got what she deserved." "That's the problem Greg, you haven't got what you deserved. Teresa did nothing to deserve what you've done to her. You are the one responsible for going to prison in the first place. That's your fault, not hers." "I didn't deserve four years taken from me." He started pacing the room, going from the dresser to the window, and back again.

The Way Life Used To Be

"Yes, you did. The courts have a procedure, and I committed a forgery by releasing you." Greg exploded. "Fuck their high and mighty procedure. It's not like I committed murder for gods' sake. Four fucking years wasted." "You did commit murder Greg, and the sooner you realize that, and man up the better," "You set me free. If you fucked up, you should pay the price." "Regardless of any mistakes I made, I need to re-arrest you. They never granted you early release. I made up the paperwork to get you out. That's my fault, and I'll pay the consequences for that, but you're going with me."

Carl turned around expecting Greg to be on his heels. He turned at the sound of a click. God damn it. He left his gun out in the open when he went to work that morning. Never forget your weapon. That is drilled into his head from the day he got his degree and was hired.

He turned back around to find his gun pointed at his chest. "I'm not going anywhere." Greg was still shaking, but still had the gun in both hands trying to control it. Carl had to remember his training. Shit, Shit. He forced a look of detachment on his face. That is another drill. Never show fear. "You think this is the answer? Shooting me and having the SWAT team take you down with force? That's what'll happen. You won't leave this house alive."

"Oh yeah?" Greg whispered and pulled the trigger. Five days later my right leg is set in a cast from foot to hip. I hobbled into the apartment trying to use crutches. Bessie is holding my purse and used her right hand to lead me to the couch. I flopped down already exhausted. The apartment is already a mess, but I didn't care. I closed my eyes and sighed so deeply; Bessie is sure I had fallen into a coma.

"Don't go to sleep yet." She said, in a rush. "I don't think I'll ever get a full night's sleep again." I said. I smiled in her direction. "Where is everybody?" "Mom, and dad will be here soon. They went to get some takeout food, and Trey said, he'd be here around eight."

Mark, and Sara rushed in just as Bessie is talking, and Sara went to the couch and fell to her knees. "Did you hear yet?" She asked. "Hear what?" Sara told me what Carla found. "Guess you were right all along." "I think this is one time I wanted to be wrong. I can only hope neither Paul nor Jeff knew what is happening. That they didn't suffer. Did Ted call yet?"

"No, we're still crossing our fingers on that one." Mark answered handing me a glass of water, and a pain pill. I took it without complaint and leaned back. Zeni, and Keith arrived laden with burgers, and fries, and all of them ate except for me. I just picked at the food. They left afterwards after sensing how tired, and sore I still am.

There is only Bessie who ended up tucking me into bed. This time there isn't a TV for company, but she crawled in beside me, and held my hand while she told me about the new job offer. "Does that mean you're moving soon?" I asked pulling the blanket closer to my chest. "Fairly, Jim, and I found a new house that we fell in love with and I start my new job in two days. Lots of new things so I hope you're not too disappointed. If you need me to stay though just say the word. I'll tell him to postpone it." Bessie offered.

"I couldn't do that to you." My cell phone rang, and it was Trey. I am half hoping it's Ted. "Hey you. What happened tonight?" "Ted called half an hour ago. Greg has been rearrested and is in booking as we speak." "I'm so glad. This was my prediction all along." It's finally over. I felt relieved. "I know that, and Ted does too. Want me to come over now?" "I'd love it, but it's late, and Bessie's been keeping me company. Can we see each other tomorrow?"

"Good old Bessie. Tell her thanks for taking care of you. I'll be there first thing. Hopefully with more good news." I said, goodbye, and hung up, dropping the phone on the floor. "Anybody else, but Ted calls, I'm not available." I stated and closed my eyes. Trey is good as his word and is there first thing at eight. "Ted will be here soon. Wants to tell you himself."

He helped me to the couch. I closed my eyes for a few minutes. Damn. I am still so tired. Ted arrived a few minutes later. He is all smiles. "Hey girl. You look a lot better." He complimented choosing to sit on an ottoman, rather than the couch. "How are you liking those crutches?" "Pain in the ass. You have good news I hope?" I asked.

"I do. Carl confessed to altering the records when he released his cousin. Been housing him ever since, and denied being involved with the hit, and runs. For some odd reason I believed him. Greg is solely responsible for both murders and is being booked as we speak. I wanted you to hear it from me, and nobody else. This is your private war, and you finally won."

I started crying. "It took two deaths to win. I feel like the loser in this situation." "No, I do. You've come to me multiple times, and I admit; I didn't take you as seriously as I should have. At least Jeff's death could have been prevented if I took any action at all." Ted looked so guilty I couldn't say anything else. I reached my arms up, and he hugged me so hard. That is my way of forgiving him. For the first time in ten years I felt relief.

When he left, both Trey, and Bessie rushed close, and enveloped me with their arms. "It's finally over." Trey whispered, and Bessie rushed to her room to call Jim to spread the news. While she was gone Trey took advantage of the privacy and held both of my hands while I sat on the couch still absorbing the news.

"I want to ask you something." He said. He reached for his back pocket. He came out with a box from Diamonds Galore, a jewelry store in the mall. I glanced down and started crying tears of pure happiness. "Yes." I said, before he could ask the question. I love making him laugh.

Sandra Gutierrez

Epilogue

It is strange sometimes how things work out. Greg for all his badass, you can't catch me attitude, ended not with a bang, but with a whimper. When he pulled the trigger on his cousin, the gun jammed, and he ended up throwing the gun to the floor in frustration. The gun went off hitting Greg in the thigh with a single bullet.

Talk about irony. I was hoping so much for him to resist arrest and have guns drawn, and the whole nine yards, but he went with hardly a struggle. He spent a day in the hospital getting the bullet removed. People when they risk talking about it, say he finally had enough. The guilt had caught up with him. I believe he knew at the end it was me he hit, and that's what ended his ride. He just wouldn't be able to live afterwards.

Now he gets to go back to the same prison he spent his first sentence at. This time though I'm spared having to testify. For that I will be eternally grateful. Bessie, and Jim had their baby girl, and named her Lisa. another shortened version of Elizabeth and something Bessie had insisted on. She moved out of the apartment, and into the house she, and Jim loved so much. They are planning their own wedding soon.

Speaking of weddings, I'm now a bride. Our wedding was the most beautiful, but I'm sure I'm not alone in thinking that. Doesn't matter though. Trey has been the most supportive husband I could ever hope for. He was there for me since the beginning. I guess I'm even more grateful for that. My cast came off last winter, and I will always walk with a slight limp, I don't care. Trey says that makes me the most beautiful unique person he has ever known.

Mom, and dad retired, and are looking forward to spending their first vacation as retirees in the Florida Keys. I have to admit, I'm

The Way Life Used To Be

enjoying owning Starlights along with Mark. Since I'm the one with the degree, Mark feels more comfortable handling the dining area. Just like dad did. I hired a part-time cook, and she's a very nice, hardworking person. I feel good about my second major decision.

I'm cut out for this after all. Sara got promoted again to assistant manager, and Mr. Hankins had a party to celebrate for her. They're hopeful to start a family soon. I moved out of the apartment myself, soon after Bessie did last spring. It's too lonely there without her, and much as thought I'd love my privacy again, I hated it.

After the wedding ceremony I moved into Trey's house even though he reminds me often, it's my house too. I've spent many months redecorating, and Trey so far loves my efforts. Keeps saying I should be an interior designer, but I think he's just blowing smoke.

Ted is right about one thing. Carl had nothing to do with either Paul or Jeff's deaths. He didn't know a thing about it, which is hard to believe. He is however sentenced to another section of the same prison where Greg is housed for falsifying paperwork. Carl only has to serve two years for that, compared to Greg's three consecutive life sentences.

Greg will never be allowed to set foot out of prison walls so now I don't have to look behind me or fear for Trey's life anymore.

I remembered Bessie's' prophetic statement nine years ago how simple our lives were back then before all this happened. I realized how right she is.

Life was good back then, and it would be again. I guess that's what it all comes down to. You need forgiveness to move forward. Hard as it is, I have forgiven Greg. I have peace now. I have closure.

Sandra Gutierrez